Enter the Bull's Burrow

J.P. Manning

Guardians of the East – Book 2

First published in Australia in 2021 by J.P. Manning
Website: www.lostbookproductions.com
Email: lostbookproductions@gmail.com

Cover design and map by Daniel Greenup

Cover image: iStock.com/Lutz Berlemont-Bernard

The moral right of the author has been asserted.

ISBN 9780648737612 (paperback)

A catalogue record for this book is available from the National Library of Australia

Disclaimer

For Peta

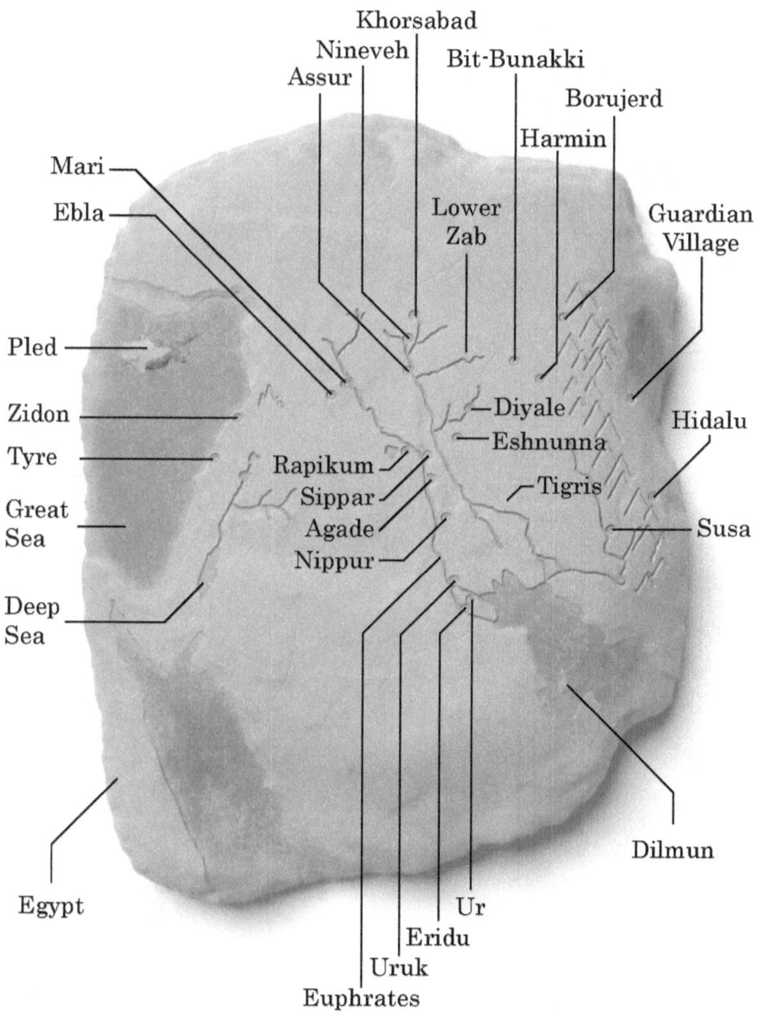

Khorsabad
Nineveh
Assur
Bit-Bunakki
Borujerd
Harmin
Mari
Ebla
Lower
Zab
Guardian
Village
Pled
Zidon
Diyale
Hidalu
Eshnunna
Tyre
Rapikum
Tigris
Great
Sea
Sippar
Agade
Susa
Nippur
Deep
Sea
Egypt
Dilmun
Ur
Eridu
Uruk
Euphrates

CONTENTS

1

Breakfast in Cairo

Cairo, Egypt 1850

The tree had a god-like presence. If I had ignored the knock at my guestroom door, I could be reading about it now. I could be learning how it affected Kar's brazen plan to seek out the God King, Sargon, fight him and prove his mortality. Instead, during a long breakfast, Victor told me about Austen Henry Layard and his discoveries in Nineveh—a giant winged-bull statue and stone tablet fragments. I feigned interest, more concerned with smiling at the right time than listening. A book with the allure of a treasure map beckoned me and I could not tell him. I did not intend to break my promise to the librarian, Babu, and his assistant, Lateef, that I would keep all talk concerning the ancient document secretive until our next meeting. Destroying that trust would be foolish and more deceitful than keeping Victor guessing. My greatest opportunity to be more than a sand scratcher could be compromised by a slip of the tongue. Sure, the librarian and his assistant would probably be keen to involve Victor, but that was their call to make.

'Friday?' he repeated.

'Some would say tomorrow is too late for what can be done today,' I replied.

'Don't you have a meeting tomorrow?'

'You're right. I also need to prepare for that meeting. You should attend. It is a private meeting but only because they do not know that you're back already.' I sipped my tea.

Victor leaned forwards, 'You are hiding something, Fred.'

'Why do you say that?'

His eyes darted between my face and the placement of my mug on its saucer.

'What are you seeing?' I asked, as I went to adjust my collar. *Had I been adjusting my collar frequently?*

Victor's eyes squinted and he smirked. 'You're not telling me something. I know you.'

'What gave me away?'

Victor's eyes widened. 'You delayed in opening your door this morning and you always adjust the handle of your mug after you place it. Normally you are talkative and try to humour me or act as the devil's advocate.'

I slumped in my chair. 'Gloria is marrying another man.'

Victor leaned backwards and ran his fingers through his unfastened, golden hair, trying to demonstrate concern.

A small whirly-wind grew in the empty street next to the teahouse and I covered my mug with my hand as dust was scattered on the outside tables.

The waiter simultaneously cursed in Egyptian and

smiled at me.

'I stayed too long. I understand her change of heart.'

Victor sat upright and wiped the table in front of him with his napkin. 'I'm going to offer you some advice, Fred. A good-looking man like you has no place in England. You would go home, lose your tan in weeks and end up working as a cashier, bookkeeper or librarian. Here you might end up digging empty holes but at least you'll maintain the look and dreams of an adventurer. You don't want what can be found in a library. You would explode if you were confined too long.'

I smiled half-heartedly. Was he setting me up to reveal what had been shared with me in the old library? 'Attend the meeting with me tomorrow, Victor. I can't imagine Babu denying you entry and we can make travel plans afterwards.'

He nodded, 'Tell me about your meeting with the young fellow.'

'Lateef's an interesting man. I could see myself working with him. The librarian, Babu, is whom I'm most interested in you meeting. He has an English wife as he studied there. Both men are very well spoken.'

'Interesting,' said Victor. 'What time tomorrow?'

'Noon, at his library.'

Victor checked his mug was empty before calling the waiter. He tipped him generously and received unnecessary assistance putting on his coat.

'New hat?' I asked, remembering the floppy felt hat Victor donned during our last expedition.

'It's a Coke, from Lock and Co. St James's Street, London. Spelt c, o, k, e but pronounced Cook, like the navigator.' He tapped its firm, narrow rim with his knuckle. 'It fits well with my hair untied.'

I stood to shake hands. 'Shall I meet you for breakfast tomorrow?'

'I suggest you get some sleep and then keep reading. It must be a good read that you hide it from a friend.'

'What?'

'Hu, your host,' he said with a cheeky grin. 'He told me why you were not to be disturbed. Blame for the intrusion rests with me.'

'I'm glad you enjoyed watching me squirm,' I said as we shook hands.

Victor raised his new hat to the waiter and nodded at me.

'The pillow,' I thought aloud.

'I was going to look under your bed next for the text.'

A tired gaze owned my face, 'You're staying at the same guest house?'

He winked back, 'I won't be a disruption. Read for me. I'll have a drink for you.'

***

A loud noise awoke me and I stared at the door to my room, waiting for a knock. Was it Victor and my host again, so soon? I'd only been reading for a few minutes before falling asleep. My dish of eggs and toast had sapped the last of my energy and only now, after a brief nap, was I feeling the reward. I was awake and heard shouting in the street. With the open-book in hand, I eased myself from my bed and walked to the window.

Below in the street, two hand-drawn carts had collided and a dislodged barrel had cracked. I smelt brine and assumed the barrels were filled with olives. One man pointed to a divot in the road, the other gestured urgently to his leaking barrel. Hovering at the window, a page of the book fluttering in a warm breeze, I looked not unlike the large woman across the street below, fanning her breasts at her windowsill. Trapped in time I was, as the cogs kept turning. Tomorrow was my meeting with Babu and Lateef, and I did not know enough to offer beneficial advice on a dig site. Maybe Victor's return was a sign; in the Fertile Crescent I could finish reading. I crossed the room to pour myself a cup of water. After relishing what the jug offered, I returned to my vantage point at the window. The men had exchanged carts in my absence. The leaking barrel was on its way to its destination and a courteous man remained to pick up the pieces.

I lay on my bed, propped upright with two pillows. Whilst I had already read the first few pages of this part, I decided to start again. Finishing part two of the book before my meeting at the library was my new plan. I had been introduced to a new voice before I fell asleep mid page and needed to gather my bearings. From the top drawer of my bedside table I eagerly collected my diary and fountain pen. My journal was also in this drawer and it looked at me for a moment. On its pages were my accounts of happenings and conversations I'd had since our unearthing of the tomb outside Cairo in May. I thought it best if I drew my map in my diary as I planned to share it with Babu and Lateef. My diary only contained meeting dates and times. There was nothing in its pages that could offend.

On the lower left side of a new page I placed a dot, signifying my location in Egypt. On the opposite side of the page I drew a line representing the Zagros Mountains. I then placed possible locations for the Guardian and Harmin Villages, and Bit-Bunakki, based on the site of Layard's Nineveh. This could all be corrected later. Right now, I had to keep reading so that new landmarks could be added to the map. At the meeting tomorrow, I would share my mud map with Babu. Hopefully, he would allow me to take the book with me if we travelled east into Persia—a land that seemed to find no peace. Like Victor, I wanted to begin the expedition while the discoveries in Nineveh were gaining attention.

My lost love, Gloria, never understood why we rushed to find something that had been buried for thousands of years. 'It could be a clue,' I would tell her. 'This could be the final clue that reveals the location of Troy or explains why the Egyptians built pyramids the size of mountains.' I wished I could tell her about my latest clue, an old book. This clue could reveal a lost people, the last god standing, or even the meaning of life. Gliding my finger across the red ribbon attached to the book's spine, I found where it parted the pages and opened the book to part two.

2

East and West

Tales of the King's triumphant victories in the East gathered flavour with each retelling. By the time the tales were retold in Hidalu, east of the Zagros Mountains, it was hard to know which parts were true. One thing was clear; Sargon's empire threatened more than just those in the East. Sargon, the King of Akkadia, now commonly referred to as Sharru-kin, the true king, had spread his empire to the borders of chartered Earth. Without an equal, he grew stronger and his rivals had no choice but to suffer beneath, or fight hopelessly against, his tyranny. His great feats were documented and preached from the city walls as a beguiled population gave thanks to their king for gaining the favour of the gods. Free from plague and no longer besieged by the supposed savage men of the mountains, Sargon's people were allowed to shape statues of honour and complete the construction of his capital, Agade. With the known earth conquered, the King set sail into the unknown and discovered new worlds and the precious rewards of foreign bounty. Never had the larger West felt so blessed.

The Akkadian stories that Arman and others shared at the Guardian table angered me to the point of sickness. I was frightened that the King now possessed Guardian maps and was using these to his advantage—setting his sights on previously unknown destinations. Salarn distracted me with new thought, explaining that the greatest threat to the empire was how quickly it was born. As Sargon's reign flourished, many a people were still recovering from the loss of what once was their world. In time, and under the facade of ultimate defeat by Sargon's armies, cities and once great villages were gathering hope in their quests to rebuild.

A spirit of rebellion was growing in the occupied city-states of Elam and Zidonia and the survivors' shared loss only hardened their resolve not to succumb to the new rule. With neither state controlling an army large enough to retaliate, it seemed all the rebellion leaders could do was talk and incite idle protest. Representatives of Sargon were posted on all corners of the earth and it was told that anyone who was caught instigating defiance would never be heard from again. Most of the early uprisings did not even deem mention in the courts of Agade. According to Arman, there was only one movement that elicited a response from the King himself. After his second secret mission to Hidalu, Arman told the Guardians that we had been identified as enemies of the throne. The King had heard that men from the Guardian tribe in the East had defied capture and had slain senior officers. In response, the King had promised the reward of land and vast wealth for our heads. With the Guardian village cast in ruin, it was assumed that anyone seeking this promised bounty would be looking for Guardians on the road. Any man bearing a tattoo of likeness was at risk. Senea's first journey was sure to be impacted and the Guardians' planned search for loved ones lost to the West was destined to become more than just a rescue mission.

Whilst Arman's news was alarming, it rallied the Guardians. It was the only news from the West that did not sing the King's song. Sargon, Sharru-Kin, The True King, The God-King, The Bull, whatever one wanted to call him, had been presented with his first threat. We were more a humiliation, a stain on the Akkadian's unblemished war record, but for a power-hungry king like Sargon, that was a threat. And as Samor, the Chief of the Harmins, explained in Bit-Bunakki, the Guardians were determined enough to keep digging. We were not defeated when the Akkadians destroyed our village and looted our maps and stories. Surviving Guardians were scribing new stories, and old tales and maps, hidden in Salarn's tower, were dusted off and read by many for the first time. The King would hear from the Guardians again soon.

3

Unions

Scribed by Fankisi, The Curious. Salarn's Tower. Balih Woods.

My husband, Tahnas, carried a stool out from inside and placed it next to his injured friend who stood near to the tower door. Tahnas had not been asked to do this and it hurt Unbetum to thank him for the gesture. Never had Unbetum asked for anything, for he prided himself on offering his services to others. Whether it was his wife serving him a meal, or a village chieftain offering him praise, he felt over exonerated. No matter what he had done already, if you thanked him or gave him homage, he would once more call himself servant to your needs. In the village days, I remember him rushing to help the women carry sheafs of grain from the fields. He had always been this way. Tahnas knew this when he picked up the stool, though he also knew that Unbetum would not be quick enough to do it for himself.

'You do not even need to say it. If you want to thank me, stay seated until we have arrived home from the scout ride and unbridled the horses. I will come to you,' said Tahnas as he walked away. Five paces later he looked back at his friend and pointed his finger, as if it were an order.

This made Unbetum laugh and, as he sat down, he continued the charade by pretending how uncomfortable the stool was.

It was uncomfortable for the brave man. If his body allowed, Unbetum would have already departed for Agade in search of his wife, Kinsufa. Tahnas had convinced the Guardians of a different plan. My husband's advice had been that we wait out the cold season and prepare for the planting of a crop before commencing the search for loved ones lost to the West. Even with this delayed departure, Unbetum would not be a part of the journey. His face, chest and arms were still bruised and covered in lacerations, which bled if he exerted himself. He was lucky he had not lost his sword arm. The Akkadian who cut his tattoo from his shoulder took more than just skin and the wound continued to weep through the bandages.

When the men rode out of sight through the trees, I turned to face Unbetum again. He stared upwards, though even from a distance I could tell he was fighting back tears. Watching the Guardian man sit alone intrigued my feminine side. When I was a girl, I would watch the boys train in the village circle rather than play with the other girls of similar age. I did not wish to join the men; I just wanted to watch. A Guardian by the name of Seeves conducted the mens' training and he was the only one who ever noticed my presence. Every so often, when he caught my eye, he would smile back and, from the cover of a stack of grain stems or the wall of a hut, I would pointlessly pretend I had not been looking. Seeves was not concerned for it was common for the young women to watch the young men when they were reaching the age of courtship.

Whilst it may have been a fascination with the young Guardian men that led me near to the village circle each day, I was not there solely to judge who would make my most suitable partner. In watching the newly declared men of the village learn, I felt that I could see them all for who they truly were. I was a curious girl and it wasn't my fault. My eyes, a gift from my mother, made me this way. Especially when my hair was tied back, I was told that my eyes were like deep wells begging to be filled. When I looked at someone, I often felt the person's return stare delve into me and I never resisted.

Now, as I watched Unbetum, again I felt that I was getting a rare glimpse of a Guardian's true character. I restrained myself from staring too long and resumed toiling the soil where we would sow as soon as the coldest day had passed. It had been a while since I had toiled the earth, but never had it been a burden, for I and the other women who shared the task that fed our loved ones were treated as queens. I had not received the same treatment when I had travelled north to Borujerd with Tahnas.

***

In Borujerd, Tahnas had found ongoing work protecting Lord Vanekebek's daily offerings at the city markets. His servitude had gained us accommodation in a large room that overlooked the palace gardens and, beyond the city walls, a majesetic view of the Zagros Mountains. He was highly respected by Vanekebek and eventually his allegiance to the lord had resulted in a new offering. Tahnas had agreed to be the Guardian for the city's harvest transfers. This meant travelling via Bit-Bunakki and onward to Agade to offload. Then, on the return, it was his duty to ensure the offering of gold and seeds returned in accordance with an agreed contract. If the first exchange proved successful, then future expeditions would only have him travel as far as Nineveh. Work on the road linking the cities had already begun.

On the night before his departure, we spoke of great dreams for our future. He told me that with Lord Vanekebek's favour, upon his return, control of trade from the city would become his governance. In this position he would be able to offer other Guardians a second home and ensure we were never parted again. He pulled me naked from bed and led me to the window overlooking the northern slopes of the Zagros Mountains.

'This, everything you see before you, could be declared our land and, whilst we may still have to call him Lord, you will always be my queen.'

'And, until you return, shall I join the other women in service?' I asked, safe in the cradle of his strong arms.

'No, you must do no arduous task. The life inside you requires all the strength you have. Walk the gardens. Look upon sights that will one day become more familiar than our huts in the village. Allow him to smell meals he has never tasted,' said Tahnas staring dreamily over my shoulder.

'Him?' I pulled myself from his arms. 'Do you know something I do not?'

'My love, I have spoken ill words. Please forgive me, for in the telling of my dreams for our future, I have recounted too many of the Lord's words.'

'I forgive you, Tahnas, but you now have to start at the beginning. What is true?'

'One more journey awaits me. I know Akkadia and I know the exchange is with the King of Agade himself. Upon my return, trade will be deemed my responsibility and the southern frontier of Borujerd my populace. You will still be my queen and we will send word to our friends in the east. They will be here in time for the birth of our first, whether a girl or a boy.'

'And until your return, I am free to walk the gardens and sleep at my leisure?' I asked, standing before him at the open window.

'Yes, Lord Vanekebek assures me that his own guards will be servant to you until my return.'

The words Tahnas spoke assured my safety and that of the new life I carried in my belly. On the day of his departure, I prayed to Enki for his safe return. I later wished that I had not been so quick to bequeath my other gods, for surely the protection of many gods betters the protection of one.

***

Awake in bed, the night before Tahnas's departure, we named our child. Whether a boy or girl it was the name we both wanted. Parbi was the name the old Guardian Seeves had given to his dog. We felt no misgivings in allowing our son or daughter to share the name, or carry on the name, considering that the dog had died a long time ago. He was a beautiful dog—large in stature with hanging upper lips and dark yellow eyes. We were both fond of the dog but it was my discovery in the village school that justified our choice. The stone tablet, entitled, *Parbi*, I assumed would be about Seeves's dog, but its crumbling face immediately identified it as an older work. Inscribed by Pardensai, the village founder, the tablet spoke of the language of the gods. Seeves told everyone that the name meant *happy one* and he may have been right. Pardensai had inscribed *Parbi* over and over again before finishing with, 'I hear this call and follow it into the woods. I take my time, for the voice is bouyant and boundless.' I told Tahnas of my discovery and we soon agreed that, no matter what the word truly meant, it was a good word and a suitable name.

***

Tahnas left for Agade at first light and I bid him farewell in the palace square. He sprung onto his horse's back and I climbed the stairs to the inner city wall to watch him ride away. The guards at their posts welcomed me and one guided me to the highest watchtower.

'Her man rides out,' the guard said to the archers posted to the high tower.

'Thank you,' I said, humbled to accept the shared respect for my husband. I watched Tahnas ride into the desert beyond the city's wall and I kept watching until the last camel in the caravan became one with the horizon.

A representative of the Lord of Borujerd visited me that night. He did not knock at the door or announce his arrival. Pale moonlight shone through the southern window in reach of my bed and all was quiet in the inner city. Maybe it was my unborn that signalled me to wake, for I was in deep sleep and the guard was deviously silent. When my eyes opened, my first sight was the unknown guard's silhouette, towering above me. I stiffened with fright where I lay.

'The Lord requires you.'

'Who are you? How dare you enter my room,' I screamed, pulling my bedding close for protection.

'I will escort you,' said the guard.

'I know my own way and I will leave when I am appropriately dressed.'

'Be quick or I will dress you,' said the devious guard, as he stepped back from breathing over me and hesitantly returned to the hall.

When I was clothed, I found him waiting outside my room. He was a short man and, in the light of a torch, hardly as threatening as he had first seemed. His eyes still bothered me—out near his ears they glared at me like different people. Fastened to his bronze breastplate was a blue cape that identified him as a head guard, a guard who liased directly with the Lord of Borujerd. He led me to the Lord's chambers without further exchange of words.

***

'Lady Tahnas, my Lord, as requested,' announced the guard as he walked away, leaving me alone at the door.

The door was slightly ajar and so I pushed it open and entered. 'Lord Vanekebek, I have been summoned from slumber to consult you,' I called out as I entered his silent chambers. The internal walls were lined with colourful tapestries depicting processions of people making offerings to a king and, on a table in the centre of the room, smoke was wafting from candles on an eight-armed, two-tiered candelabra. I received no reply and hence stayed close to the door. As I waited, a girl, no older than twelve, fled from one of the adjoining rooms and, upon seeing me, ran to my side. I did not know the girl but, just the same, I held my arms open and dropped to my knees to receive her. The young girl began to cry on my shoulder. 'Where is your mother?'

'In the kitchen,' said the frail, fair-haired girl, holding back her tears only long enough to say these few words.

'It is all right. I will look after you.' I cradled the young girl and, over her shoulder, watched the Lord of Borujerd fasten his robe as he entered the room.

'Fankisi. I was not told of your arrival,' said Vanekebek as he looked around for a guard to hold accountable. 'Guards,' cried the Lord. His hastened movement to the chamber door and having to raise his voice left the fat, slovenly man short of breath. Beads of sweat formed on his pronounced upper lip and threatened to fall as he lent over me, his bulging eyes hiding none of his impure thoughts.

I turned towards the door, but heard no reply to the Lord's cry. The girl was still crying and I pulled her close, smothering her tears on the soft cloth of my dress.

'Naten, it is time you returned to your mother,' the Lord spoke softly as his men finally entered the room.

Naten would not let go. 'It is all right, little one. Your mother wants to hold you even more than I do,'

I said with reassuring eye contact. Naten did not let go and the guards had to pull her from my embrace. 'She can walk on her own feet. Let her be,' I yelled as the guards dragged the girl, screaming, from the Lord's chambers. 'Are you not going to address them, my Lord?' I cried desperately.

The Lord of Borujerd stooped his bulbous head to my request. 'Fankisi, your husband is an honourable man. In respect of his name, I will forget that you just called me to your service.'

'But my Lord, I was called to your service. I was asleep until I awoke to an unannounced guard next to my bed.'

'Do the acts of that undisciplined guard give you the right to question the orders of a king in the presence of his subordinates?'

I looked behind and caught the devious guard smiling back at me as he exited the room. With clenched eyes and a bowed head, I replied, 'No, my Lord, I was out of place.'

'Yes, you were and, in view of your actions, I no longer wish your counsel tonight.'

Vanekebek, the self-proclaimed King of Borujerd, walked away from where I still knelt and I saw myself out.

That the entire southern frontier of Borujerd would be called Tahnas's populace now seemed to me a false promise. I was called on day and night to scribe for Vanekebek. It was usually a letter of confirmation for an action already scheduled for the next day. My tasks seemed pointless yet every day, and at the most unsuitable hour of the night, the wide-eyed guard would rap at my door. Each time, I would oblige with the hope that Tahnas would return soon. Each time, I grew more convinced that I should not wait for Tahnas to return. The strength of the Guardians flowed in my blood too and there was a young girl that needed one now.

***

It was not my eyes that lured so many men to my side as I strolled through the palace gardens each morning. I had learnt a way to carry myself from my favourite teacher and the nobles who hastened to meet with me in the gardens of Borujerd found a confidant they could talk to about things they would have never thought mentionable to a woman. As the days went on, I encountered more people eagerly waiting to seek my counsel. My words seemed to answer all of their problems, from how to treat an infected toe to mending a broken relationship. As I strolled slowly through the inner city of a morning, my walks grew less interrupted but, at the same time, I received more smiles and polite greetings. I also found time to reflect on my younger days. I gave thanks that the older Guardian, Seeves, had not pointed me out to the young Guardians he trained. I remembered the day I had thanked him personally for being indifferent. I remembered the young Guardians' awkward movements in their first days of training and how unapproachable they were after. Above all, I thought of the day Tahnas duelled Unbetum.

On that day, many young women huddled close to the village circle. I believed I knew these young men better than the other young women. Even so, I sat at a distance. These young women were my teachers. Whilst the young men continued to learn, the girls of the same age had already begun to teach. The timing of the harvest had crushed my plans. I may have been the oldest of the young girls, but I was still considered a girl. I wished I were older and, as I watched from one of the stools next to my father's hut, I tried to mount the courage to stand and walk closer to the duel in the village circle. I heard Seeves give some timely advice to Tahnas. If I were closer, I might have heard Tahnas's response that made the women laugh.

Seeves frowned. 'He is planning for your approach, Tahnas, be mindful.'

Tahnas saw an opportunity in his teacher's lingering words and attacked.

Unbetum smiled at his friend as he not only parried his blade, but also carried it on a haphazard journey that made Tahnas struggle to hold his grip.

'Now, Unbetum plays games. It could be his downfall,' commented Seeves as he circled the young men duelling.

Unbetum and Tahnas sidestepped each other several times before they engaged their wooden blades again. The young women watching waved to the young men waiting on the far side of the village circle and jaunted each time the duelling Guardians lunged, swung or taunted each other. In the near distance, I hugged myself in anticipation. Again, the young Guardians connected blades and, though made of wood, the sound echoed pain.

'He is predicting your–'

Seeves's words were cut short as Unbetum struck

Tahnas's sword to the side and stabbed his chest.

The applause of the young women was disrupted by my scream.

Unbetum turned defensively and Seeves smiled knowingly as he called the next pair of Guardians to duel.

Only one of the young women gathered at the edge of the village circle troubled themselves with more than a head turn or eye roll to my outburst.

Next to a hut close by, I stood upright with my arms crossed tightly at my chest. I met Unbetum's concerned stare and he followed my gaze to where Tahnas had dropped to the ground. I glanced to my right and saw Kinsufa approaching.

The next two young Guardian men circled ready to duel, yet, in the circle, Unbetum still looked down on his fallen friend. Seeves walked to Unbetum's side, ignoring the new fighters circling behind. Unbetum turned back again to face me.

My eyes swelled as if the last pail of water had been drawn.

'Men are strangers to such pain,' said Kinsufa as she neared me. 'If they were not, how could we ever call them men?'

I looked upon the young woman, now by my side. She was the only teacher who did not teach a particular lesson. Kinsufa would instead work with the girls as they farmed, sewed or wrote. This made her more like an older sister than an authority figure. Like Salarn's rare visits to the village, Kinsufa's words were like presents to those who waited to hear her long pondered explanations. When the girls asked Kinsufa why she was not one of their teachers, she replied, 'I am too scared of what I will say.'

Of course, this answer only intrigued the girls more and we asked, 'Why?'

'Why?' Kinsufa echoed the question.

'Why are you scared?' one of the girls had asked.

I remembered Kinsufa looking around to check that it was only girls listening before continuing the conversation. 'Because I would probably tell you things that may not be true.'

'Like what?' the girls had questioned her demandingly.

'I might tell you that there are many other worlds like ours, or that, long before we walked this earth, it was the playground of the gods. Then again, I might tell you that girls should learn to answer questions before they ask them.'

'Tell us more,' the girls had pleaded.

Kinsufa laughed playfully and ran from us as we reached out to grab her. 'You will have to catch me first,' Kinsufa challenged, as we gave chase.

On the day Unbetum duelled Tahnas, I had only to stand still to hear my favourite teacher reveal many an answer.

'The strength of the Guardians has to flow in your blood too, young one. If not, your fear will be a concern for your man.'

I remained silent as I stared in awe at the young woman before me. Bright sand coloured hair coiled to rest on Kinsufa's shoulders, covering the thin straps of her weightless, white dress. Before I could respond, more powerful words stole my attention. My own name was called from where the women gathered at the edge of the village circle. Tahnas parted the crowd and walked towards me, disappointing many other young admirers. 'What do I do?' I whispered to Kinsufa.

'You do not have to do anything but talk to the man you cried for.'

'How—'

'You feared for me,' said Tahnas as he brushed sweat from his brow through his short hair. 'My father did not attend for that very reason. How could a girl I do not know care for me so?'

'I know you,' I said.

Tahnas smiled back and I curled my finger and gathered the folds of my dress taut at my hip.

Unbetum cheered for Garforn, who had begun his duel, before following Tahnas out of the village circle.

Kinsufa stepped into his path. 'You fought well,' she said, losing herself in his eyes.

'We both did. I almost ...' Unbetum did not know how to respond when Kinsufa embraced him, closing her eyes and burying her face in his sweaty chest. Her affection for the Guardian was not reciprocated and she opened her eyes, but dared not let him go. 'He is bleeding,' said Unbetum, prying himself away from her warm hug.

'Wait,' said Kinsufa, making Unbetum turn back to face her. 'He is fine.'

When Unbetum looked again, Tahnas's father, Lan, was by his friend's side and I still idled next to them, my eyes absorbing and my body mimicking every subtle shift Kinsufa made.

'Let them be,' suggested Kinsufa as she delicately moved a thick coil of hair to the side of her face. She dipped her head but held eye contact. Her hand touched her breast as she adjusted her dress slightly.

Unbetum was no longer distracted and he realised what he had been ignoring. 'You are more beautiful than the sun that shares its face with a woman and deer drinking on opposite sides of a stream,' said the victorious man as he admired her reflective green eyes and full lips. 'I have wanted to say that for a long while.'

'Do you think of me as a deer-like woman?' asked Kinsufa.

'No. I think of the sun and deer, flowing water, everything I want for when I see you,' he said.

Kinsufa leaned backwards in his embrace. 'Many still think of us as brother and sister. There are many things we have not shared as a result.'

'Well, I must talk to you every chance I am given from now on,' said Unbetum.

She moved his arms so that they nursed her neck and they gazed deep into each other's eyes.

Behind them, Arcobon approached from the village circle. The next duel had begun with the clapping of wood and cheers from young women. Arcobon looked upon Unbetum and Kinsufa wrapped so firmly in embrace that the two were one. He dared not spoil the moment and walked on towards Tahnas. 'So, you were the one fortunate enough to duel with Unbetum.'

'You call this fortunate?' answered Tahnas, showing Arcobon blood on his fingers.

'Is the wound deep?' questioned Arcobon.

'No. He was too quick. He knocked the air out of my chest and I hit my head when I fell.'

'Did you see the fight?' asked Lan.

'I see everything,' said Arcobon, flashing a glance in the direction of Unbetum and Kinsufa.

Tahnas and Lan watched for a moment before Arcobon redirected their attention. 'And who is this?'

'This?' said Tahnas, turning the question on Arcobon. 'Her name is Fankisi and she shows me more concern than you old men.'

I dipped my head and held eye contact with Tahnas. My movement felt weird and I giggled. I cupped my mouth, fearing I had destroyed any chance at being recognised as a potential wife.

Lan turned from me to face Arcobon.

A smile broadened on Arcobon's face as he watched me try to hide my embarrassment.

Lan had to pull on his fur to get his attention.

When Arcobon turned back to face two smiling men he could not help but laugh. 'I am sorry, Fankisi,' Arcobon apologised, wiping joyful tears from his eyes.

Lan laughed with him and patted his shoulder as Tahnas also held back nervous laughter, seemingly at my expense.

My cheeks burned hot with blood.

'I laugh because your eyes make me both nervous and excited,' Arcobon told me. 'You are a beautiful and intriguing young woman. Tahnas will remain happy in defeat with you by his side.'

I smiled with the men.

'I take it that I have your blessing too,' Tahnas asked his father.

Lan nodded, 'You do.'

Tahnas hoisted me in his strong arms and twirled

me in a circle. He placed me back on my feet and delicately lifted my dipped chin. 'I will never grow tired of staring into your eyes.'

'I'm sure you won't,' said Arcobon. He patted Tahnas firmly on his back. 'Maybe you should take this moment to congratulate Unbetum.'

Unbetum and Kinsufa were still joined as if one. They stood close to us but their thoughts seemed to be lands away. Their eyes were closed and they did not move.

Lan watched them for a long while, as if transfixed, before nodding again in agreement.

'Can I confide in you, Lan?' asked Arcobon.

'You need not ask.'

'I fought Unbetum three days ago. He is to travel with me to Mari, though he does not know this yet.'

'He is ready,' said Lan.

'More than ready,' said Tahnas. 'He disarmed Garforn at training two days ago.'

'And me the eve before this duel,' revealed Arcobon.

'Then that is a lesson for you, Arcobon,' said Lan, 'you are lucky it was a wooden sword.'

'It was not. I dropped my long sword, for fear of losing my fingers, and took a step back to admire him. Unbetum asked me if I was all right and all I could say was ... yes.'

'What weapon did he brandish?'

'My old short sword.'

Lan shook his head. 'Knowing this, you let him fight my son today.'

Tahnas squeezed my hand before stepping forwards. 'I am fine father. It was wooden swords we duelled with today.'

Lan ignored Tahnas's defence of Arcobon. 'If Jamine hears of this, your sword will not protect you.'

'I had to know,' said Arcobon. 'Jamine will understand. I do not want to take him with me just because he is my sister's son.'

'Hmm. I understand. It all makes sense eventually. She was always destined for greatness.'

'She?' questioned Arcobon.

Lan tipped his chin in the direction of Unbetum and Kinsufa in shared embrace. 'Kinsufa has also found a worthy partner.'

'Yes,' said Arcobon. 'They share a bond.'

Tahnas was not as interested in what his friend was doing. He lifted my hand kissed it gently and then placed it on his cheek.

The older Guardians realised they were imposing on an intimate moment and decided to make their way to the village circle where Garforn was enjoying a duel with three young men and Seeves at the same time. The official duels had concluded and Garforn was just providing entertainment. Unbetum, Tahnas and Garforn were deemed ready for their first journey that day.

At some stage during the successive duels that continued until the last light of day, Unbetum and Kinsufa disappeared. Even in their absence, they were the greatest topic of conversation. Verian's adopted daughter and his daughter's son had demonstrated strong feelings for each other. For how long they had shared such feelings was of particular interest to the women. The men were more interested in impending travel arrangements. Verian's only son, Arcobon, announced that he was going to journey with his nephew, Unbetum, to Mari. On the far side of the Euphrates, they would spread word that no destination was too far and no risk too great with a Guardian by your side.

4

Judgement

Scribed by Jamine, The Dressmaker. The Village School.

I heard of Unbetum's duel with Arcobon before my husband, Lan. That was common in the Guardian Village. The men were more concerned with happenings outside the village, like the movement of deer, the location of Guardians on the road, or the construction of new cities. Knowing that my son was to duel Unbetum, I anticipated what was needed. A Guardian's final training duel was often followed by marriage and, for forty days, I had been weaving and stitching a new dress. It was rare for a man to leave the village before he was wed, and the next to leave was sure to be Unbetum.

***

I met with Kinsufa to measure her when the dress was almost completed. Kinsufa The Wise, we call her, for she knows things that were never scribed. Some would say that it is her time spent with Verian that makes her so knowledgeable. Yet even Verian is often astounded by her wisdom. After the passing of his wife, Hulan, Verian was comforted by the presence of Kinsufa, his adopted daughter. She cooked all his meals and often, as I was preparing a meal for my family a few huts away, I would hear her singing to him. She was singing to herself and cooking over the fire when I approached Verian's hut to take her measurements.

Kinsufa stopped stirring the contents of her pot and jumped to her feet to greet me. 'I was expecting you, Jamine,' she said.

'You were? I did not tell anyone of my visit.'

'I have been preparing for my marriage to Unbetum and need your help with a dress.'

'That is why I visit, Kinsufa. I have almost finished a dress and need to measure you.'

Kinsufa's excited expression suddenly saddened.

'What is wrong? Did you not predict my arrival?'

'I should have told you sooner that Verian has asked for me to wear Hulan's dress.'

'This news should not dishearten you. The dress I have made is not yet sewn to fit and, as you know, there is another marriage soon to follow yours. Tahnas and Fankisi are rarely apart. My boy loves the big-eyed girl.'

Kinsufa smiled and invited me to take a seat at the fire. 'Verian would like me to wear Hulan's dress and give it new life.'

'Can I see this dress?'

Kinsufa, half seated, sprung to her feet and signalled me to follow her inside.

I had not been inside Verian's hut since Kinsufa was a baby. I looked towards the back wall, where her crib once was. An empty bed filled this spot, reserved for visitors. It was clear which side of the hut was Verian's as it was as uncharacterised as the empty bed at the back of the hut. Where Kinsufa slept, colourful dresses hung on a railing and tall, clay vases were filled with painted dry flowers. Many of the flowers I had not seen before and their colours were that of the sky, trees and desert sand.

'The dress is already beautiful but I am too thin,' said Kinsufa, standing at a window so that a silhouette of her frame was seen through the dress.

'Hulan had a real mother's build,' I told Kinsufa. 'She mothered children through snow and seasons of drought.'

Kinsufa looked distant as she handed me the dress. 'I have few memories of her.'

'That is a shame because she could have told you many stories.'

'Mardias tells me some stories but I feel like she does not approve of my marriage to Unbetum. We do not talk much anymore.'

Mardias was Verian's true daughter, Arcobon's sister and the mother of Unbetum. 'Stand straight for me,' I said, avoiding a more difficult conversation. I measured the width of Kinsufa's shoulders and her height. 'Your breasts should grow if you have a child, but I will need to adjust the dress at the chest as well.' I kept talking as I measured her and hoped she would soon lead our conversation in a new direction.

'Jamine, do you remember the day my mother died?'

'Yes, it was a sad day. Hulan was a mother to us

all.'

'Salarn spoke to me that day.'

'He did? What did he say?' I asked, only remembering him standing at a distance when we buried Verian's wife where a crop would soon be sowed.

'He stopped my crying. I knew him to be my father's brother but I had never met him before. My body quivered in his presence even though I was not afraid of him.' Kinsufa knelt suddenly and looked up at me before continuing. 'He told me to look at the ground. I looked and could not see what he could. He knelt also and pointed again. I leant close and noticed the lush tips of new grass sprouting beneath dry grass. I have not cried since.'

I coiled my measuring string around my palm. 'Is that all he said?'

Kinsufa bounded upright. 'He also told me of a secret meeting spot.'

I gasped unintentionally.

'Do not be ashamed of me, Jamine. Verian knows that I visit the tree.'

'You meet Salarn there?'

'No, it is just a place where he leaves things for me. Salarn and Verian were also young when they lost their mother. I have only been to the tree twice. Verian visits for me.'

'Guardians do not like secrets, Kinsufa.'

'I know but it was Salarn who … and I tell you now because I want to show you something.' She rushed past me and signalled me to follow.

I followed Kinsufa outside and she explained that it was not a meal heating over the fire, even though it smelt delicious.

'They are stems from a flower that grows in the far west. It can be used to dye the white dress yellow.'

'That does not look yellow,' I said, watching parts of a flower bubble in the hot water.

'The dark colour will fade when mixed with white cloth. After the dress is yellow, like the sun, I would like to add the colour of the sky. Together these colours will create the green of new grass.'

'I will make your dress a perfect fit if you teach me this art.'

Kinsufa pointed north towards the woods and up at the sky. She then brought her fingertips together and smiled.

I smiled back and made awkward movements with my fingers that made her giggle.

***

Kinsufa, wearing a bright green dress that hugged her slim body, was wed to Unbetum. He wore the fur of a deer and together they stood before Verian as he placed his hands on their shoulders and recounted sacred words. The wedding was held the day before Unbetum left for the river city, Mari, with Arcobon. Unbetum and Arcobon were away from the village for many harvests and, in their absence, Kinsufa gave birth to Kar. Fellow Guardian women admired how attentive she was to the young boy. Often, she was noticed watching him sleep, so that she might be ready to smile at him, the moment he opened his eyes. Whenever she worked the fields, she would carry Kar on her back, and she would never stop talking to him, even though he was too young to respond. A few of the older women, who worked next to her, found themselves regretting how they had spoken of Kinsufa when she was a child.

Kinsufa's mother had died in childbirth, and Kinsufa's father, to most, remained unknown. Verian adopted Kinsufa and treated her like she was his own. He believed that both his mother and father had also been taken from the world whilst they still had so many purposes left unfulfilled. The Guardian women helped him raise her; however, just as the founding men had questioned their purpose before they became Guardians, some of the women questioned the part they played in raising a child with unknown origins. Despite Verian calling an end to the worship of gods, many still required them and believed that the baby, Kinsufa, was a bad omen that signed the death of childbearing mothers.

***

One day, whilst most of the men were absent on the scout ride, a group of expectant mothers stormed into Verian's hut and cruel words were soon voiced concerning the baby girl of unknown origins.

'Why do you look after her?' questioned a heavily pregnant mother.

'For the same reason we would look after your boy or girl should you not be so fortunate,' replied Verian's wife, Hulan. 'I love my tall boy who plays outside as much as I love this baby girl who rests peacefully under my watchful eye.'

'And I look after her because I am a mother,' said Verian's daughter, Mardias, nursing her own baby, next to the crib, opposite me. 'Unbetum is my life, but this young child has made me appreciate him, and life, more.'

'Please leave,' I pleaded. I was breastfeeding Tahnas at the time of the intrusion and knew that he would be crying all night if his feed was interrupted.

'Your children are not my concern,' argued the pregnant mother, looking for support from the other disgruntled women who had crammed into the hut.

'Your argument should be taken to the circle,' said Hulan. 'My husband has returned and until he leaves again I have the time to tend to this child. As you can see, this baby has enough women devoted to her upbringing.' Hulan smiled at Mardias and I, before facing the other women again. 'I suggest you return to your duties and allow us to raise the child without your advice.'

Another of the expectant mothers pointed her finger vigorously at Hulan at the end of the crib. 'We think you are ignoring your only son for a child ill conceived.'

Hulan took a deep breath. 'I am just doing what every mother should. Arcobon needs time by himself and time with his father. When he needs me, I will be a better mother.'

'A Guardian does not need a mother,' the woman continued to argue, repetitively pointing her finger and hoping its blunt tip, stabbing air, might somehow puncture Hulan's defence. 'Boys need their mothers and now is that time for you.'

'Get out,' yelled Hulan, getting to her feet. Her raised voice unsettled all three babies. 'Anyone who does not have all the children's interests at heart should leave.'

'Do you know the father?' questioned a woman stalking the crib behind Mardias. 'No one does.' She raised her voice so that it might be heard over the crying babies. 'A stranger that killed her mother has entered our village.'

Hulan stooped to cup the baby girl's ears from the cruel words.

'She killed her mother and her mother's only friend,' continued the woman as her stalk closed in on the crib. 'There is evil–'

'Be careful what you say,' bellowed Verian as he parted the skin hanging over the doorway and entered the hut. 'I have just returned from talking with my dead father and what do I hear?' he asked, daring an answer as he looked upon the faces of the many Guardian women filling his hut. 'The only evil alive in this village is women unable to appreciate new life. You do not need a name to be born.'

Salarn then entered behind Verian and all eyes shifted to his presence. Ignoring the women crib-side, Salarn signalled the rest to leave with a slight turn of his head.

For a long while all the women remained still.

'Leave now,' yelled Hulan.

The women closest to the entrance left the hut first and others quickly followed. Like startled deer escaping a hunt, they knocked into each other as they forced their way through the hut's door. Salarn and Verian waited until there was space to move freely. Hulan, Mardias and I remained crib-side, calming the unsettled babies. Kinsufa continued to cry and Salarn approached.

'You did not tell me,' he said.

'She is not mine,' replied Verian as he followed his brother to the crib.

'What is her name?' asked Salarn, allowing the baby to grab hold of his extended finger.

'Kinsufa,' answered Hulan as the baby stopped crying. 'It was the last word her mother spoke before she died.'

Salarn stilled his finger in the baby's playful arms and turned his face from all.

'What is wrong, brother?' asked Verian.

The women looked at each other and Verian raised his hand, signalling us to remain silent and give our elder time to ponder his thoughts.

'Where did you find her?' asked Salarn, with his head still turned and a slight tremble in his voice.

'Kinsufa's mother and another woman barely made it to Hidalu,' replied Verian, watching Salarn's face closely. 'She birthed the child there. All the Southerners could tell us is that the women were heading here.' Verian looked back at the women crib-side. 'Did I miss anything?'

'You did, father,' replied Mardias. 'Where the women came from is most concerning.'

'Tell me more, please,' requested Salarn, turning to face the women seated around the crib. The elder's face was grim as if sucked of life and he breathed heavily as he waited for a response. Slowly he lifted his hand from Kinsufa's gentle grasp and clasped it with his other, like he was treasuring her touch.

We looked at each other and silently decided it

was best if Hulan explained.

'They were on foot when they breached the mountains,' Hulan told Salarn. 'I cannot say how far their horses carried them, but they both wore necklaces from the Great Sea and no one can travel that far on foot. The woman who travelled with the mother refused to have her wounds treated and stayed with her friend until the baby's head showed itself. She did not ...' Hulan dipped her head and sucked back tears.

Salarn stared down upon the little girl who angled her swaying arms towards his long, dark beard—now old and grey.

'She did not know that the mother died with her,' continued Mardias, finishing the story. 'She acted like a Guardian would for the mother as long as she could.'

Salarn's deep-green eyes creased and filled with tears as he spoke the only public words he would on the matter. 'Kinsufa was her mother's name and the name should live on.' Salarn left the crib and walked out of Verian's hut to stare at the sky.

I followed Verian to the door where he told me to wait.

Mardias urged me to follow the men outside and, when I hesitated, Hulan rushed to my side and plucked Tahnas from my breast. 'Tell us what they say, Jamine.'

I quietly parted the flap at the entrance to the hut and listened in on the elders' conversation.

Verian spoke first. 'As I age, I find myself looking backwards more than ever. I was always quick to loose an arrow. I did not always make the right decisions, but I believe I made ones easy for you to make right. Can you uphold our father's name?' asked Verian of his older brother.

'I thought that this was a contract we sealed ceremoniously with blood twelve harvests ago.'

'It was, though since then I have partaken in many a journey. Recording what has already been discovered is the labour of my life now,' explained Verian. 'I am finished with travelling. I crave the contentment I could not find at the tower. Is there no peace for me?'

'I do not mean to speak harsh words, so hear me well brother,' said Salarn, bringing Verian's mournful moment to a quick end. 'Our father loved us both and all the people he led south to find a home. Since his death we have become something he would not care to imagine. He was a man of the gods. Every night, while you and mother slept, he would beg for an answer to his troubles and bow with humility. The gods answered his prayers and led him here to this heaven on earth, a place with water to well for and sheltered by a mountain range that climbs as high as it is wide. Regretfully, he believed all his gods travelled with him unnecessarily. He convinced himself that the gods were making too many a decision for him. Only in the darkness was he at peace. In the openness of day, he caught sight of his gods and this blurred his conviction. Unbeknownst to you and mother, he would walk into the woods at night to speak to his gods, shielded, he believed, from their control yet open to their silent whisperings.'

'How do you know this?'

'I followed him,' replied Salarn with no remorse. 'Do you want me to continue?'

'I will not interrupt again.'

'He could hear the gods talking and they did not

know he was listening. He discovered all his answers and, in doing so, was silent from that day forth. I am sure you remember the day he led the villagers to the clearing in the woods. The gods had planned for him to build there. Made purely from wood, the task would have been simple, but let me tell you that the tower was fashioned from stone as a sacrifice. The gods supplied us with water, wood and a warmer sun. Our father had nothing else to give back. Each night, I give thanks for his silent end of days and the rest his prayers and your leadership have provided. All spirits and gods that were denounced when you made the men Guardians are now alive once more in all's thought. What is silenced, finds new voice.'

'Did father talk to you that night? Why did he stop talking?'

'All was silent in the woods that night and his prevailing silence was ...'

'You will not say?' questioned Verian as he watched his brother struggle to respond. 'Is that why you left?'

Salarn's eyes were closed and they flickered like he was dreaming. It seemed like no response was forthcoming.

'Do you sleep well in the tower?' Verian asked, discontent without an answer.

'You should visit more often,' replied Salarn, his eyes opening and re-adjusting again to the light of day. He looked at his younger brother and would have seen an old man gazing back at him. 'The gods led our father to the woods. Do not ask me why, for I am still trying to understand. Our father found a home for us, but it was you who turned men into Guardians.

The rest is still to come. I understand your many sacrifices and let me of little understanding answer this way. You, my brother, have done everything you know as true and still you question your generous deeds. Let the Guardians find themselves, as you have before them. And know that when you turned your back on the gods, they stood waiting. We will know where to find each other as the village grows.'

'You knew the mother?'

'I knew Kinsufa like no other,' answered Salarn.

'I should have told you the day she arrived.'

'No, Verian, you did well. Please stay father to the child. I promise to uphold your name if I should happen to outlive you.'

'My name?' questioned Verian.

'Pointless are all the gifts that father shared without the purpose you gave his people.'

Salarn and Verian stood shoulder-to-shoulder and stared almost longingly at the sky. As I saw it, they were not looking to catch sight of a god. The size of the sky humbled them. The Guardian elders sought judgement from the highest authority and were not held prey to the pointless squabbling of man.

5

The Early Riser

Scribed by Fankisi, The Curious. Salarn's Tower. Balih Woods.

Every day, before the sun had risen, he woke silently from slumber, rolled his sleeping fur and slipped quietly out the only door from the tower. The men soon noticed that he was always the first to rise, yet was never present for the scout ride. It was not customary to ask why, at least not until his father had spoken to him first.

***

The long cold season delayed the sowing of a crop and the scout rides became regular hunting expeditions. Upon returning from the ride, the men would eat boiled oats that Salarn had stored from the previous harvest. Every other meal was stewed boar. There had not been a sighting of spotted deer since the attack on the village. Arman travelled regularly to Hidalu, the closest village to the south. Accompanied by others, he brought back grain and interesting stories concerning life in the West. Meanwhile the women, accompanied by the children, would search the woods for any wild berries, herbs and fruit they could find. These offerings throughout the season still kept the diet strict. The early riser was not present for every meal, though when he sat at the table, to which he had brought nothing, fellow Guardians glared at him and resisted voicing scornful words. It could not go on much longer without a confrontation.

At the Guardian table, Kar and Hemal were the only two who remained silent. Hemal was silent as his tongue had been cut out by the Akkadians and his entire family was likely dead. I helped bury his wife. The blue stone necklace she wore had fallen into her chest cavity by the time I found her rotting remains. It was impossible to recognise most of the other villagers who had died. All we could do was count the number of children, men and women that we buried. Only three women and four children were unaccounted for. When the men discussed plans to find those lost to the West, they tried to involve Kar. He listened to the various plans and tales of rebellion in occupied states without comment.

Prompted by Tahnas for his own opinion, Kar said, 'I'm still pondering a plan.'

'You're still pondering? Hopefully some of our plans help,' said Tahnas, raising his brow and looking about the table.

Jamine, sensing more would soon be said, ushered the children away early for storytime. Parbi was suckling my breast and I used this as an excuse to stand slowly and act inconvenienced. As we ascended the stairs, Kar rose from his seat, bowed his head to all at the table and followed our departure only as far as a new spot he had adopted on the giant fur on the ground floor. Nobody at the table said a word until they heard the top door of the tower close. Halfway up the steps I had stopped. I peered down from behind the railing. Parbi had never stopped suckling.

'Is nobody going to say anything,' commented Arman, scratching his fingers slowly through his thick, brown beard.

'He bowed,' laughed Tahnas, knowing that Kar would hear his remark.

Unbetum buried his head to the comment. As Senea's father, Gentuk, began to chuckle, Salarn deliberately knocked his cup of precious honey wine across the table and stood in his spot, shaking his head.

'Say what, Arman?'

Arman hung his head.

'My father burdened himself with a quest to find us a new home and a better way of life,' begun Salarn. 'My brother gave us a name and died protecting its importance. Now there is one tattooed with the same blood and you scorn him for not following a path already walked. We are allowed because we are not like the Akkadians. We almost died because we are not sided with them. Once again, there is one amongst us who does things differently and you shun him.'

'Salarn, with your respect, allow me to voice my side,' said Gentuk.

Salarn nodded in agreement but stayed standing, ready to object if necessary.

Gentuk stood in his spot at the table and reconsidered his words before voicing them. Unlike my husband, Gentuk was a man that could avoid notice. His beard was always cut short and his hair only partly covered his ears and neck. He would look no different to a merchant or traveller in the cities and villages he visited. 'We are the ones who feel shunned,' he said to Salarn. 'After meeting the Chief of the Harmins and experiencing life outside our borders, we felt that Kar would feel at one with us as his Guardian family. Yet, apart from the night of his return, he has chosen to avoid conversation. Even when we address him, he is found short of words that could explain his disposition.' Gentuk waited to receive the acknowledgement of the Guardians gathered, before continuing. 'We feel that maybe his time alone with you has influenced him.'

'Your words tell a heated story,' said Salarn from where he stood. 'Once again, do you see your chance alone on the hunt as time to confirm opinion you would not otherwise deem worthy of mention?'

Only Lan, the oldest man at the table, recollected the incident to which Salarn was referring. Lan's shameful reaction, alone, conveyed greater meaning to the rest of the men gathered.

'You have planned a journey that will be embarked upon at season's change. How many of you, I ask, took a moment to consider whether Kar shall travel with you?' questioned Salarn, leaving his words time to float over the silent table. 'He will not be by your side on this journey,' said Salarn, pointing beyond the table to where Kar now stood upright on the fur. 'Let all who are listening hear that I have only confirmed that decision tonight, for tonight I have heard once more a Guardian's name spoken of in vain disrepute. What angers me most is that, this time, it was by his own people.'

'I will talk to him tomorrow,' said Unbetum.

'If you need to,' said Salarn. 'If only the rest of you had given Kar, and time, a chance to make sense, you would know that his days are not wasted.'

The men at the table and Kar, who was standing nearby, heard the railing on the steps creak and looked up to see who was listening from above.

I made sure everyone in the tower heard my door close that night. I made Tahnas sleep next to the bed on the floor without a fur.

6

The Bull Is Close

Scribed by Kar, The Tree. Balih Woods.

Again, in the darkness of unlit morn, I woke silently from slumber, stowed my sleeping fur, and walked quietly outside. I walked across the clearing surrounding the tower before launching into a sprint. Through the still darkened woods I dashed with only my shoulder fur, hide shorts and sandals to protect me from the bitter coldness. I ran until the sun started to rise. I paused at the foot of a pine much larger than the others and bowed in front of the stone grave lifted from the ground by the pine's foot. Coloured horsehair was platted with my own light brown hair and hung longest from my bowed head. After a moment's silence, I ran on and did not stop until less-shielded light was penetrating the roof of the woods. I paused again in quiet reflection for a long moment before walking to a tree that, to any other, would have been as uncharacterised as its neighbour. There, I rested with my back against its cold trunk and looked back in the direction from which I had arrived. Standing in a laneway of trees before me were eleven stripped branches staked into the ground. My eyes wandered the woods nearby and, in every direction, more stripped branches were staked upright amongst the thick carpet of pine needles. The hum of crickets resumed and birds began to sing for the new day. I stood upright and looked behind the trunk of the tree I had been resting against. As I gazed upon a selection of sticks of differing thickness and length, I unsheathed my sword and laid it to rest amongst them as if it were no different. I then pondered for a long while before selecting the longest and thinnest stick.

With the stick held at my side, I paced deeper into the woods and began to twirl it faster and faster. Once I had re-mastered control of the weapon, my game began. I twirled the stick and paced forwards to encounter my imaginary foes. My weapon would slice the tip of the branches staked into the ground. This way they would fall, but never snap. Each stripped branch was spaced so that I would never have to stop swinging. When the last fell, I pointed my staff to the ground and looked up victoriously. I had won this time and pondered what game would challenge me further. Returning to my selection of weapons, I replaced the thin stick and sheathed my sword. The next game I was about to play was the most difficult. Again, my rule was that no branch could snap. This time, I had to cut the stakes and leave them standing. Never had I been successful at this challenge. The trick I had learnt was to keep my blade angled down and strike on the same side as the lean of the branch. Once I had re-staked all the branches, I took a moment to calm myself. I felt the cool breeze that was whisking through the woods and admired the delicate structure of pine needles about to fall to the ground amongst many others. Pine trees surrounded me and the paths between the pines in every direction were filled with straight branches, staked upright.

As I paused in quiet reflection, the silence bothered me. In the distance, I heard a bird singing yet the crickets nearby mimicked my silence. I closed my eyes and listened in on the real world. I heard the odd cricket croak but they were not in unison. They were used to my presence now and only when I ran or swung my weapon would they fall silent. With my eyes still shut, I turned my head in an effort to discover what had scared them. It was not long before they began to chatter once more. My eyes opened and I sliced the first stake. I had started well, with a clean cut. I stepped towards the second stake and cut it neatly as well. Against my rules I paused and listened along with the once more silent woods. I was not alone today. Something else was making the small animals cautious.

***

During my days spent alone, I reflected on my life before and after the Akkadian army had sacked the village. The story I could tell for now was complete, but writing the final verse had proved difficult. The Guardians were in search of loved ones lost to the West. I wanted to find the King responsible. When my thoughts grew deep and began to change my mood, I would become a boy again. I imagined a surprise attack by Sargon's army. They would approach the tower from the north and avoid detection from the men on the scout ride. It would be me alone to defend them all until help arrived. I could see clearly in the dim light of the woods and I dreamt of a gallant fight where an entire army would drop one-by-one to an unseen Guardian defender. Each stake was a representation of Otoug, the tall Akkadian that Salarn had assassinated in Bit-Bunakki. I was their lone adversary. Whilst these thoughts entertained me, I knew them to be childish make-believe. I knew I was avoiding the real world, but I felt I had good reason. I knew Salarn supported my time alone because he continued to leave wet clay tablets and dried food for me. Alone, I believed I could not hurt anyone or bring shame to a name. Some of my fellow Guardians thought the opposite.

Something had silenced the crickets and my playtime was over. Before me, in one line of sight, nine stakes still stood upright. I sheathed my sword and waited.

From a tree beyond the stakes, my father stepped into view. I remained silent. I was good at that.

'This is the only day I have watched,' he said. 'If I had not come, how long would you have played for?'

'Until I was ready.'

'I think you are still trying to control life by hiding from it.'

My emotions were now taking over and I chose not to speak.

'Do not distance yourself from me. I understand why you wish to be alone. Salarn also understands and, therefore, I ignore the opinion of the others. I followed you today not to talk, but to watch. Since your return, you have spoken in a different voice and I hear you clearly. You are a man before his time and I would like to offer you something new. Return with me to the tower and let me make you a weapon fit for a Guardian.'

I took a deep breath and pushed a hundred questions to the back of my mind before nodding in agreement.

My father drew his long sword and, after raising it once, it seemed to swing by its own momentum. He cut the tip off every stake he passed, successfully leaving the bottom halves planted in the ground. 'Do not fight alone if you do not have to,' he said as he sheathed his sword. 'Life presents us with enough challenges.'

I stepped to his side and helped him to the ground before he collapsed.

'Let us rest for a while before we head home. I rode most of the way here and I am more exhausted than you.'

His sword arm was still bandaged and lifting his sword in his other arm had expired all his strength.

I sat down next to him and, for a long while, we listened to the woods—the scratching of intertwined branches, the patter of falling pine needles and the singing of birds and crickets.

'I understand why I must stay,' I said. 'When I leave the East, I want to be ready to enter the Bull's Burrow.'

'Where is this place you speak of?' he asked.

'Pardensai wrote of the coming of the Bull. We cannot hide from King Sargon and we will not join him. We must enter his burrow and find his nesting place.'

He reached for my hand and held it with all the strength he had.

7

A Face in the Window

Scribed by Fankisi, The Curious. Salarn's Tower. Balih Woods.

'Good morning, Unbetum,' Jamine said to me as she exited the tower.

I startled and then placed my hand on my enlarged bosom and smiled.

Jamine walked towards the clearing, east of the tower, where she was planning the planting of a large crop. She did not seem bothered by Unbetum's absence or my seat in his place.

On Unbetum's stool, near the door to the tower, I sat watch over the children. The men would not return until they had made a kill and this sometimes saw them gone for the entire day. I watched my son, Parbi, lying on his back, staring up at the girls who danced around him singing. He was laughing at the funny faces they pulled as he rolled about, still too young to walk or talk. I smiled because the children were happy and I was interested in learning more about the game they were playing. I had never played it myself and I liked that they were discovering new ways to entertain themselves. With so few children remaining, I feared that they would grow old too quickly in a world I no longer knew. Only Jamine might have known that my mind was in two places.

***

I was haunted by memories of my final days in Borujerd. Once more, I had been summoned to the service of Lord Vanekebek. Whilst Tahnas travelled to Agade, I was learning the true nature of the man he spoke of highly before his departure. Often, the fair-skinned frail girl was present during my visits to the lord's chambers. She would sit on a cushion at the far end of the room, her head downcast and her skin growing paler each passing day. I had not spoken to her since the night she had cried on my shoulder but I felt like my visits were still to her benefit. If for no other reason, my time with Vanekebek was time he did not spend defiling her.

I sat down in my usual seat and waited for Lord Vanekebek to reveal his latest agenda. That night, he decided he would seat himself uncomfortably close to me at the table overlit by fat candles burning in an eight-armed monstrousity. He paused, as if a vision had come to him. I tried my hardest never to look at him and to concentrate on the tablet I scribed. Unfortunately, with him seated so close, my downcast eyes appeared to be wandering his lower regions. Vanekebek, as if he had forgotten the reason for our meeting, began talking of great feats for which he was responsible. I began scribing, trying my hardest to make note of everything he was saying. Void of the attention he was truly seeking, he reached across, took hold of my scribing hand and pulled it to his lap. He only tried this move twice and, on both occasions, I ran from his chambers with torn clothes. Despite my shrieks of alarm, the guards were always seated and noncholant as I fled through the doors. The Lord's vacated promises necessitated action that could not wait for Tahnas's return to Borujerd.

Though it was a long walk to my room, I felt like I lived in the same palace as Vanekebek. Guards manned every building in the inner confines of Borujerd and the few nobles I thought I could trust distanced themselves when I asked for their help. I questioned how a man like Vanekebek, if one could call him a man, rose to the seat of power. I felt stronger than him and, whilst his soldiers and guards obeyed his every command, so far he had proved too cowardly to make the orders necessary to fulfil his desires. Vanekebek tore my dress on two occasions yet he had not yet touched my skin. Following these incidents, I was still free to walk the city by day and the privileged treatment that was promised by Lord Vanekebek would have thus appeared to be upheld.

I thought of the fair-skinned girl locked in Vanekebek's palace as I strolled down a cobblestone path lined with bluebells beneath the taller palms. The sun was shining in Borujerd and the distant hum of ten thousand city folk, going about their daily business, could be heard beyond the palace walls. I liked it here, but not what it hid. How could such an ugly man rule in such a beautiful place? I diverted from my regular path through the gardens and headed towards the palace kitchen. My mauve dress rippled in the morning breeze and I checked that my hair was still fastened, as the garden path came to an end at a door shadowed by a chimney hugging the eastern wall. I glanced behind to see that I was alone before knocking with a wooden hammer. I thought again about what I should say. It could be a guard who answered the door and I already knew that they did not want to know of my concerns. The latch inside was lifted and the door opened. A grey-haired old woman wearing a white tunic looked up at me and then past me as if she was expecting more guests.

'I am looking for the mother of Naten,' I said, after deciding not to introduce myself first.

'What is her mother's name?'

'I do not know.'

'How do I know who she is then?'

'Naten's mother works in the kitchen and about twelve harvests ago she gave birth to a girl.'

'Oh my. What a beautiful dress you wear. How long before your child is due?'

'You do not understand my urgency,' I said, stepping forwards and holding the door ajar. 'Her daughter will be one with Vanekebek tonight.'

'No,' exclaimed the old woman, 'Lord Vanekebek chose a bride. It will never happen.'

'You are right. He will not wed the child. He will defile her again. Find her mother, please. I beg you.'

'Yes, lady, at once.' The old woman hitched her tunic that hung as thick as two-layered curtains and hurried from the supplies door towards the dining hall.

I stepped inside and closed the heavy door behind.

'It may be best if you keep your exit open,' said a voice from the darkness amongst piled plates and trays waiting to be cleaned.

'Who are you?' I asked.

'I am no one you know,' said a kitchen attendant as she stepped out in view. The woman's pale skin was flushed pink from a seemingly endless task of scrubbing plates in large, heated basins. 'She has not gone to look for the woman you spoke of.'

'Do you know the mother of Natan?'

'I can find her if she works here.'

I took a moment to study the woman's face and the way she held herself. I wanted to trust this woman and, despite whom I trusted, I knew that I had to leave quickly before guards reported on my whereabouts.

'Thank you, my name is Fankisi,' I revealed. 'Tell her I am a friend and want to help her daughter.'

The kitchen attendant smiled at me and gestured towards the door. 'You should go.'

I walked briskly through the courtyard back to my room on the southern side of the palace, in the inner confines of Boujerd. Checking first to see that the third-storey hallway was clear, I ran its length and slipped into my room, confident that no one, other than possibly a wall guard from a distance, had seen my return. I latched the door behind me and then bent to lift my dress over my head. My unborn now weighed heavy in my belly and I stood slowly, physically drained after exerting myself. I smelt mint and knew that it was from my own odour. Trickling perspiration coursed between my breasts and I wiped it with my hand before it gathered more momentum. Untucking the end of my bed, I stuffed the mauve dress beneath the sheets and walked to my wardrobe to find another. My fingers were trembling and I wished that Tahnas could be by my side. In his arms, all fear would be evaded. Alone, I questioned what I had done. Speaking ill of Vanekebek was a punishable offence and I had foolishly told the kitchen attendant my name. Changing clothes and untying my hair so that I could deny any involvement was all I could think of doing at this stage.

Wearing a green silk dress that hung weightlessly over my heavy breasts and draped my enlarged belly, I stood at my bedroom window looking upon the northern slopes of the Zagros Mountains. My unfastened hair lifted and patted my shoulders in the breeze. It was mid-morning and the snow-capped peaks softened the sheer cliffs in my view. I rubbed my bulging tummy and tried to see Tahnas's face in the reflective sky.

'What would you have done?' I asked the cloud-filled sky. At any moment, just like me, Naten could be called to Vanekebek's service and any idle time between weighed on my mind. In a moment of distracted longing, I saw Tahnas's smiling face and almost collapsed. Sucking in the strength he had given me, I straightened and stood confidently at the window. From the far side of the room, there was a knock at the door. I was expecting it.

'Who calls?' I asked, as I approached the door that I now kept latched at all times.

'We are here on order of the King.'

I did not like it when the guards referred to Vanekebek as the King. I knew the voice belonged to the short, wide-eyed one who took pleasure in calling me to the lord's service late at night.

Again, he rapped loudly before I opened the door.

Four guards waited in the narrow hall as the head guard entered once more without invitation.

'Does Vanekebek require my services?' I questioned him, looking across his face from one eye to the other.

The devious guard glared at me and then strode towards my wardrobe.

'Are you looking for something?'

He opened my wardrobe and ran his fingers across the hanging dresses.

'What is he doing?' I questioned, drawing the attention of the other guards.

They looked inside and saw their leader in the process of opening the bottom drawer.

'That is my undergarments drawer,' I complained. 'I will be reporting this to Vanekebek.'

He kicked the drawer closed—several times, as it did not close properly—and paced towards me at the door.

'Have you been outside today?' he asked.

'Yes, I walked the gardens as usual this morning.'

'In what you are wearing now?'

'Yes, and tomorrow I will wear one of the other dresses you felt the need to fondle.'

The head guard did not find humour in my insinuation and stepped towards me, forcing me into the doorway that was blocked by the other guards. 'There is an enemy of the King in the palace grounds.'

'Thank the Gods he was not in my wardrobe,' I said.

One of the guards chuckled for a moment before the short one exchanged a deathly stare. 'There are few pregnant women with brown hair. We will find her before nightfall.' He brushed past me trapped in the crowded doorway and I cringed at his touch.

The moment he was outside, I slammed the door closed and dropped the latch.

I returned to the window that faced south but I could not see beyond the tears in my eyes. The kitchen attendant was right. Vanekebek had been made aware of the accusations against him and, whilst I may have distanced myself, I felt like I had only made things worse for Naten. The guilt made me feel sick. It sickened me more than any loathing for Vanekebek or sorrow for Naten could have ever achieved. If only I had bid my time more wisely, I could have planned an escape for the young girl or even offered her refuge.

'Oh, Parbi, what have I done?' I cried. 'You are so young and I pray you are not burdened by my afflictions,' I said to my unborn, caressing my tummy as I strolled about the room. 'Oh, Parbi,' my voice croaked. 'Parbi,' I repeated and this time I felt a little stronger. 'It will be all right.' I lay on my bed and hitched my dress up beneath my shoulders, exposing my belly. 'You are sleeping now and will not know this happened. You look so peaceful. Sleep, my little Parbi.'

A shadow from the southern window caught my eye and I rolled my head to the side to sight the cause. There were no drapes or trees high enough to cast a shadow and the creeping vine was always cut wide of the windows. I was in a state of bemused relaxation and my only explanation for the shadow was that it was a reminder from Enki that I was still in his care. Lying still, quietly watching the window, I saw nothing and began to think that it could have been Enlil. Would the god of air and wind cast a shadow if he flew close? I had been thinking of him more in view of the events of recent days past. My thoughts of gods distracted me and, with their help, I wished to fall asleep but then I saw it again. There was something outside my window. I arched my back and flicked my dress over my exposed belly. I then lay still on my bed watching silently in hopes the presence would be revealed.

My room was on the third floor and the thin ledge that ran beneath the windows outside was not built to be walked on and could only be reached from one of the other windows on the same floor. That it was En-lil outside made more sense than a person clambering along a ledge barely wide enough or strong enough to support them. I thought of the others whose rooms were on the same level. I could imagine the wide-eyed, devious guard doing something stupid like this, but his short arms and legs would make it a near impossible task. If it were not for the noise, I would have settled on my first thoughts and walked to the window to say a prayer, but gods do not make clumsy noises. I almost laughed. The idea of someone clutching to the wall outside, only out of sight to those inside, seemed preposterous.

Whoever was outside had almost fallen. I heard crumbling stone patter on the ground and a controlled gasp as whoever it was steadied their balance. I walked to the southern window and peered outside. I could see no one, and my first thought was to look down. Crumbled stone lay on the pathway but the gardens were empty. I turned quickly to face the window on the western side of my room. It was closed. I crept to the window, knowing that whoever was outside could not move as fast and would still be on that side of the building when I surprised them. I reached the window and paused for a moment before opening it. I needed to be sure that there was not someone else waiting right outside. The wooden slats hindered my vision but, as I knelt, I could see the ledge that ran beneath the window was empty. I unlatched it quietly and then flung it open.

'By the Gods,' I gasped, withdrawing in shock. 'It is all right,' I then said, immediately correcting my initial response. Leaning back outside, I offered my hand. 'Reach out for me, Naten.'

'I did not know if it was your room,' she whispered.

'It is all right. We will talk when you are safely inside.' I beckoned the pale-skinned girl towards me.

Beneath us, three members of the court made their way along a path through the gardens. The slightest crumble of stone or glimpse of a shadow now and we would be seen.

I reached out to Naten, but she was braced against the wall and too scared to move. The three men passed below without looking up and Naten reached daringly for my hand, stepping towards me with her weight pressed against the wall.

'I have you,' I said reassuringly as she made her final step to the window. Our hands met and I pulled her quickly inside, stumbling and nursing my belly as I paced backwards two more steps than necessary. 'All thanks to the gods,' I said, trembling all over.

Naten looked up at me from where she had collapsed. Her dress looked ready to slip from her frail shoulders and her neck strained to hold her head upright.

Kneeling next to her, I tightened the knots on her dress and used my own dress to wipe dried spittle from the corners of her mouth. 'I am so thankful you found me.'

***

Parbi still rolled in the grass as the girls danced around him. It felt like I had been away for days but I must have only closed my eyes and departed for a moment. From the far side of the clearing, two men approached on horseback. Despite my mind lingering in the past, I was the first to notice their arrival. I watched from the stool at the tower door as Kar steadied his father's stallion and allowed him to dismount.

'Children, I need you,' yelled Jamine from the side of the tower.

'Go to Jamine,' I told the children, 'and Unbetum, you had better return to your stool before Tahnas returns.'

'Do not rush me young woman or I will hold you accountable for any injury I sustain.'

Naten lifted Parbi and hurried the other girls towards Jamine.

'You have exerted yourself, Unbetum. Let me fetch you some water and–'

'Stay, Fankisi,' he said as he sat down on the stool and watched Kar ride on to the stable. 'I need a woman's advice. It was Kinsufa who spent the most time raising Kar. Arcobon and Verian taught him to write and fight, but Kinsufa instilled something greater in him, something I see every time he chooses to speak his mind. I do not wish to change him anymore, for the men already believe that Salarn's influence has had a profound effect on his nature. Still, he is in need of more lessons. What is it that I can teach him?'

'I cannot advise you on the path of a man. Maybe you should talk to Jamine.'

'What does he not know that he should know by his age?' asked Unbetum, his distant stare signalling hope in any opinion that I might offer.

'Nothing, apart from maybe one thing,' I said, still unsure how honestly I should reply.

'Take your time. I am not going anywhere.'

I looked past Unbetum to where Kar was unbridling Unbetum's stallion. 'How to move on.'

He looked confused by this answer and so I explained.

'Not to forget or abandon hope in recovering what was lost but to keep living, with the past only serving as a reminder of what is most important.'

Unbetum shook his head. 'He has lived more of life in the last season than he has in every one before. He asks no questions and speaks for no one but himself. If anything, he has moved on too far.'

'Then maybe he needs to ask more questions.' Crouching next to Unbetum, I tried to gain the attention of his distant stare. 'Where does Kar go when he leaves the tower at dawn?'

'Where is not as important as why. Salarn's decision to take him on a journey was wise. It offered a distraction and, not only did Kar learn many things, but I feel that he also found himself in his travels. He has bold plans. I do not know if these ideas are his or Salarn's ...'

I placed my hand on Unbetum's shoulder, 'What do you think he needs to learn?'

'That just because Arcobon, Verian and his mother are gone, his training is not over. He is going to stay with us when the other men leave in search of those lost.'

'I know, I was listening last night too.'

'Of course you were.' Unbetum touched my shoulder and smiled.

We watched Kar as he walked towards us from the stable. Still at a distance, he stopped and looked across the clearing westward.

I looked at Unbetum, questioningly, and, a few moments later, one of the children let out a shriek. Motherly instinct told me not to be alarmed.

'Stay here, children,' yelled Jamine. She threw her arms to the sky as two of the girls ran to greet the men returning from the ride. The girls almost disappeared into the woods before the first horse breached the clearing.

Tahnas and Lan doubled on the same mount and the last horse carried the rewards of the hunt. The girls cheered and Salarn exited the tower behind me to welcome the men back.

Tahnas rode his mare to the tower door and he and his father looked down at me crouched next to Unbetum. Tahnas dismounted and Lan took the reins and rode the horse away to be unbridled.

I stood and greeted my husband with a hug.

'I am happy you are still seated,' said Tahnas over

my shoulder.

Unbetum looked at his friend disobligingly, 'Tell your father to hurry up and secure that horse. I need to pass water.'

Tahnas laughed and I poked him in the ribs.

'Why do you poke me?'

'He has been there all day,' I said.

'No,' said Tahnas, shaking my comment off as a joke, 'the man has lost use of his sword arm, not his mind.'

Unbetum cleared his throat. 'Your repeated order each morn is to remain seated until we unbridle the horses. I will come for you, is what you say.'

'That is what you say to him every day,' I confirmed.

'Your telling of this story signals that he did not do this today,' said Tahnas. He unwrapped himself from my arms and turned towards the stable.

Unbetum and I smiled at each other when his back was turned.

Tahnas had only taken a step when he noticed Kar standing idly nearby. 'We have been gone a while,' he said, glancing back at Unbetum and me.

'Did you sight any deer?' inquired Kar, breaking a long silence.

'Yes ... no, only boars. You know, we have never really spoken properly.'

Kar nodded.

'What brings you back before dusk this day?'

'Things have changed,' said Kar.

'Yes,' agreed Tahnas, 'Life will keep trying that

tired move.' My husband walked on but could not resist looking back at the young Guardian.

8

Move with the Night

Scribed by Arman, The Always Travelling Guardian, The Tower. Balih Woods

I was always travelling because I was sided with Delari. Without Delari, The Always Travelling Trader, I would be The Go Nowhere, Never Interested in Anything Guardian—the Guardian with a rugged face and a beard to match. Kar was thoughtful in his description of me. I knew, without use of a mirror, that I was not favoured with a beautiful face. A patchy beard eventually helped cover the blessing I received as a boy.

When I was young, nearing my ninth harvest, I was sick and locked in a hut far outside the village wall for twenty days. My skin broke out in painful, itchy sores that left my face and throat scarred. I was lucky. My mother and other entire families died and our huts inside the village wall were deliberately gutted with flame. Everything we had touched was burnt. When my mother and the other villagers died in huts built far from the village, they were also burnt. I was the only villager with the sickness that survived. After twenty days in the hut by myself, Arcobon and Verian moved me to a new hut, closer to the village but still outside the wall. They left me fresh clothes, water and food. I stayed in this new hut for another twenty days. Often, I would lie still, staring through a gap in the hut's wall at the grass stems outside. Sometimes they were still and sometimes they would sway back and forth in the changing breeze. The occasional distant sound of a villager's voice, carried in the wind, would repeat in my mind like a song.

The sound I remember most was my father's voice. When my father returned from a journey west, he came to visit me. He called my name and, at first, I thought it was a dream. When he called again, I stumbled to the doorway. I was not locked in this hut, but I knew to stay inside.

'What have the gods done to you, Arman?' asked my father, standing at a distance with Arcobon and Verian.

'They saved my life,' I called back.

Carrying a wrapped bundle, my father walked towards me, and Arcobon and Verian raised their hands in greeting before departing.

My father stayed with me at the isolated hut for another twenty days. At night he would tell me about his journey west to Bit-Bunakki and Nineveh. 'In the West, they name men with cures for sickness, Sunu. Only the Sunu can treat a god's poison. Even a Sunu could not have saved you, Arman. You should have died. A god must be vouching for you.'

During the day, we would use his throwing blades. At first, the hut was my target. Then it was an individual split log that made up the wall. After ten days, he was scratching marks onto the wood with a stone for me to aim towards. After twenty days, my father was still healthy. We burnt our hut and our clothes and returned naked to the east gate of the village. We washed ourselves in hot salty water that was prepared by the women and carried out to us by Arcobon, Verian and Gentuk, a young Guardian at the time. When Arcobon and Verian returned through the east gate, Gentuk lingered at a distance of ten paces.

'Verian does not think this is the work of the gods,' he said.

My father continued to wash himself vigourously and only shared a few glances with Gentuk. 'My boy and I think it is the work of the gods. Verian provided no cure, only food and water. Decide yourself, Gentuk.'

'My name is Arman,' I told Gentuk, my voice harsh and forever changed by the illness.

'We have all heard your name, Arman, son of Seeves. I leave the village tomorrow with a trader named Delari. He has only traded in Elam and wants to trade in the North and West before he returns to the East. When we return, you will probably be a Guardian.'

'He will be ready to take your place when you return,' said my father. 'Travel safe, Gentuk, and thank your father for our new hut.'

***

Like me, Kar probably thought his travelling days were over before they started. I read Kar's story after Salarn and, when Kar's absence was mentioned on the hunt, I tried to defend him. I told them of the ongoing journey he was writing about. It did no good. The men had formed an opinion of Kar. *Why would anyone write at such a time?* they thought. In response, I started scribing this tablet, my first tablet, and I planted a seed that would keep Kar from wandering for a while.

***

'Kar knows of a threat to our homeland that he has been unable to voice,' I said to the table of Guardians after I heard the top door of the tower close. 'This danger is not here nor knowingly there.' I had read a tablet scribed by Kar that spoke of a surprise attack on the village. Kar's response caught me and the other Guardians by surprise and I listened to him like it was Gentuk or one of the other experienced Guardians talking. His voice was clear and not loud or sharp.

'North of the Karun, where the mountains offer a passage east, the Akkadians have constructed a stronghold,' said Kar.

'Do you know this? How do you know this?' questioned Lan, exemplifying the sharp voice I just mentioned. As the oldest Guardian, excluding Salarn, he did not like that only the youngest knew such things. 'If you tell me some god-spelled script, the last of my hair will fall out and I will partake no more in this one-sided war.'

'There are no gods in this stronghold,' said Kar. 'I think we will find only scared men a long way from home.'

'You do not know this, Kar,' said Lan, shaking the thin hair at the base of his almost-bald head from side-to-side.

'He does know what we have ignored,' said Tahnas.

'We ride west to the mountains and often south into the plains to hunt. We have only travelled north as far as Verian's Pass. Another day's ride to our north is where they crossed the mountains. In Borujerd, they gather and it makes sense that they would send scouts ahead to a stronghold before an entire army ventured this way again.'

Lan shook his head, more slowly this time. 'If such a fort exists, our planned rescue mission is over. Kill them all and stalk the fort, I say.'

I noticed that I was scratching my fingers through my patchy beard. It was not itchy. I scratched it when I was thinking or nervous. At the head of the table, Salarn looked on. He only added his words when required. I thought it was time. 'What would you do, Salarn?' I asked.

Salarn shifted his gaze from me to Lan to Kar. 'I would keep listening to Kar before I added my own thoughts.'

Kar sat across from me, twisting the coloured braid in his hair as he looked around the table. 'You are right,' the young Guardian said to Lan and Tahnas, without making it clear which parts they were right about. 'The Akkadians attacked from the north. In Bit-Bunakki, they also have a massive encampment of soldiers. Salarn and I have seen them. They outnumber the ordinary folk. If the King has an eye on all corners of the earth, then surely there is a fort this side of the ranges, to our north. I believe that, near to where my father, Arman, and Hemal were rescued, the Akkadians have or are still building such a fort.'

'And how would you deal with this fort, Kar?' asked Lan, raising his palms and brow.

Kar pointed behind Lan, 'I would use that.'

'I will not look behind and be prey to your trap,' said Lan.

'You do not need to look.'

'You will all laugh if I look,' said Lan, clutching the strands of hair that surrounded his ears, to stop his head from turning. 'Do you mean the unknown, Kar, a surprise attack?'

'I do,' said Kar. 'But I do not know the woods or ranges that far north.'

'We do,' said Gentuk. He rested his head forwards in the rest of his bent arm and only raised his eyes to face us. 'We all know the lands north, but I don't think we want to go there.'

Tahnas sat upright and spread his muscular arms like he was about to embrace an old friend, 'I don't fear the Barbarians of the North.'

'I don't speak of the Barbarians, Tahnas,' continued Gentuk, raising his head. 'If the Akkadians do not think us defeated, then we hope they look for us in the west and on the roads between. We are cautious in our scout rides and hunts not to reveal our course home. If we are sighted this side of the mountains, we invite attack. If we attack this fort–'

'If we don't attack, do we forego two men on the hunt each day, leaving them to watch over the fort?' questioned Tahnas. 'Here's my plan. Tomorrow, before first light, we ride north to inspect the threat. Kar won't be travelling west with us, but I'd like him by my side on this journey. With your blessing of course, Unbetum.'

Unbetum nodded, 'If such a fort exists, you will

want him.'

'I'll ride with you too,' I told Tahnas. I liked that he always had a plan. He was not one for telling or scribing stories and preferred to live in the moment.

'I would not go without you, Arman.' He looked around the table and received an agreeable nod from Gentuk and a reluctant nod from his father. 'Salarn?'

Salarn stood and looked at each of the men seated at the table. 'I will join you also.' He pointed beyond the table to the tower's door. 'I sent word to the village when I originally detected movement in the north. I even suggested that the women and children move east into the desert and live in temporary huts until the threat was averted. The Guardians decided that they could reason with the Akkadians. We must learn from these mistakes. My mistake was staying at the tower and not doing more. Now we know our enemy, near and afar, and must not mistake our defeat of one or two, three hundred or four hundred, as anything more than a call to war.'

***

Everyone was awake when we left the tower in the darkness before dawn. Gentuk's youngest boy, Lagesh, did not take the news of our departure well. I could understand his tears but his shrieking, like a birthing mother, made me want to knock him over the head and put him back to sleep. Unbetum lowered his head as we rode away, and I wondered whether he was blessing our journey or thinking like me.

Kar led the way north through the woods to Pardensai's grave. The massive stone jutting from the ground was lifted on one side by the hefty, raised roots of the closest pine. Salarn placed his hand on the stone and said a silent prayer. He took over the lead, guiding us west though the woods to the mountains. It was important that we were never seen entering or leaving the woods, so, as we neared the grasslands that run the passage between the woods and the ranges, we regrouped and allowed our horses time to rest. We looked for movement or any activity nearby, usually suggested by light from a fire or torch. As it was still dark, it was safe to continue without a long delay.

'I would like to lead from here, Salarn,' requested Tahnas. 'It will be a slow ride until we have light.'

'I will ride last,' said Salarn.

***

The six Guardians, Tahnas, Lan, Gentuk, Kar, Salarn and myself, maintained a steady canter after first light. We rode north along the higher, sun-lit ground closer to the mountains. The shadow of the woods across the grass passage slowly withdrew as it neared high sun. Each of us placed our eyes to the ground and towards the Guardian who rode in front of us. The rider in front would signal any divots, rocks or logs to be avoided. I rode behind Kar and behind me rode Salarn. As well as watching the ground, Salarn and I scanned our surroundings, always looking for movement. To our east, Balih Woods formed a wall as tall as ten men, with the branches on the outer trees almost hanging in reach of the grass. To our west, steep rocky expanses, grass-lined rises and clusters of pines and low shrubbery formed the foothills of the Zagros Mountains.

As the sun removed the shadow cast by the woods to our east, Tahnas angled our ride towards the centre of the grass passage. This way, we avoided lurking danger in the woods on one side and the mountains on the other. Only an arrow aimed high from either side would reach us. Should this happen, we knew that we should keep riding. The worst thing you could do was to stop, or to take shelter on the far side of the pass. This ambush method was taught to all Guardians after Verian escorted travellers through the Northern Pass, Verian's Pass, and lived to tell the story.

Verian had arrived at the Guardian village with over a hundred men, women and children. His recount tells that most walked on foot and the horses looked just as tired. In the pass through the mountains, Verian and his party of travellers encountered the Barbarians of the North. He rode straight at them and ordered the strongest to follow. Verian then returned to the back of the travellers, shouting in his ride, 'Move faster.' He knew that the pass was where they would die. The barbarian threat ahead was designed to keep them trapped where they were. Verian wrote that his pull of the bow was not fast enough to stop the barbarians descending into the pass. They escaped because the barbarians' plan had failed. They were attacking in the pass and, when the travellers moved on, they stood still. It could have easily gone the other way.

***

Before the sun moved past the Zagros Mountains and cast a greater shadow, Tahnas slowed his stallion to a trot. He raised his arm and rotated it in a slow circle above his head.

'Ride south and circle back,' I told Kar. I trotted my mare west towards a dry waterhole, watching as the other Guardians quickly rode in different directions. The waterhole was shallow and would have quickly dried after the wet season. Since then, it had been used as a camp. Soil had been turned to extinguish a fire, and surrounding imprints in the soil suggested that a party of five or more had shared its warmth. I returned to the centre of the grass passage in time to meet Kar returning from the south.

Tahnas waved his arm forwards twice before he moved on.

'What does he mean, Arman?' asked Kar.

'Where Tahnas made the signal, we will enter the woods. Lan will enter where Gentuk does. Tahnas and Salarn will ride on.

Kar watched Salarn canter by without turning his head. 'Will they return tonight?'

'Where they camp depends on what they see ahead. We will rest in their absence. See you inside.' I rode ahead of Kar to the edge of the woods and ducked a low branch to enter the darkness. In every direction the trunks of the pines towered out of sight and inbetween the maze of trunks was a messy bed of pinecones, pine needles and dead branches. The pine needles knew how to destroy a fur and I was already looking for a spot that could be easily swept clear. This spot also needed to be close to a tree where my bedding could become one with its roots during the night rather than an obvious shadow in the moonlit gaps between trunks.

Kar entered the woods and, like me, took a moment to study his surrounds before climbing from his mount.

'Take your time in preparing a place to sleep. There

will be no fire tonight, or for the next few nights.'

He followed my lead in using a branch to clear the ground of pine needles before spreading his sleeping fur. 'Will Lan and Gentuk return tonight?' he asked.

'We will regroup in the morning.'

'How far is it to Verian's Pass?'

'Lan and Gentuk are probably only a short walk away,' I said, pointing north through the trees. 'If we hear them, or they hear us, terse words will be shared in the morning.' I looked deeper into the woods and pointed to a tree. 'Before I rest, I'll secure our horses to that tree with the low-slung branch. We sleep across the grass to Verian's Pass. Welcome to Barbarian Country, Kar.'

He smiled, 'Do you want me to stand watch.'

'No, it's safe to sleep. We have another long ride tomorrow. Stop enjoying yourself.'

Kar straightened his face for a moment, but the smile crept back. The young Guardian was experiencing the thrill of the ride and he had kept pace with the other Guardians from before dawn till dusk. He removed his shoulder fur and coiled it to create a pillow. Next to his fur he placed his sword and he sat down to take off his sandals. Before he lay down, he took a large sip from his water bladder. Staring up through the trees, wearing only his hide shorts, he seemed at peace and did not appear to feel the cold like me.

***

I awoke in darkness and tried to listen through the chorus of crickets and creaking branches. There was only enough light to see the trunks of the trees close by and a mound low to the ground where Kar lay. The horses were tied nearby, further inside the woods. If we did receive a surprise visit, then it was best if we escaped deeper into the woods. I could hear Kar's stallion and my mare moving about, their hooves crunching the dry pine needles. In the direction of the mountains, I heard softer steps approaching—two feet, not an animal. Reaching my arm slowly across next to my side, I placed my hand on a throwing blade and checked I still had all three. With my head slightly raised, I stared in the direction of the soft footsteps. *Clever.* They stopped behind the tree in front, not allowing me to sight their silhouette. I watched the trunk without blinking and soon a head peeked out from one side.

'I'd know that head anywhere,' I said, relaxing my hold of my throwing blade.

He pulled his baldhead, with whispy hair at the base, back behind the trunk.

Kar awoke to the sound of my voice and sat upright.

Nearby, another head peered out from behind the trunk of a pine. I did not recognise this head with long straight hair. The head moved out of sight for a moment before appearing on the other side of the trunk.

Don't say anything, Kar. The head grew legs as it stepped out from behind the tree. He took five steps and I only heard one. He was Salarn's height but his hair was straighter. Unless Salarn had stripped naked and gone for a swim before his walk in the woods, it was a stranger that approached.

Kar moved again, maybe reaching for his sword.

The longhaired figure raised one arm and signalled

the other, or others, to circle behind us. In his other arm he quietly raised a foot long blade. They could see where we lay and could hear our horses. Our horses had heard them first. I knew that now.

Silently, he stole another step closer to Kar and I kept my eyes on him as I listened for the movement of others. Behind the tree I rested against, I heard soft footsteps and saw Kar turn in my direction.

'Arman,' he whispered.

'Go back to sleep,' I replied.

The longhaired figure remained still for a moment, his blade adjusting slightly in his grip, his body readying for his next step. He charged forwards with heavy, crunching steps. His chest looked exposed and, as he took his third step, I thrust a blade towards his heart. It flew lower than I planned, embedding itself in his gut. I stood quickly with my two other throwing blades and, before I was fully on my feet, I met the man who I had thought was Lan. With one arm, I slashed defensively and used the other to stab him repetitively in the face and chest. I overstabbed. The scrape and crack of bone and the dull puncture of flesh told my ears and hands what my eyes could not see. Ribs, teeth, nose, neck—I did not know which jab would end him. When he fell, I turned towards Kar.

Kar was now standing and, in front of him, the longhaired barbarian plucked my throwing blade from his gut. With a blade in both hands, he lurched towards Kar. His laboured strike fell short as Kar bounded backwards. Before he could strike again, Kar's sword smashed down through the man's shoulder. He staggered about, bent over, somehow still holding his blade. With a full sweep of his sword, Kar almost removed his head. Barely held by stretched tendons, the barbarian's head dangled near his hands, like he was bending to fill a bucket at a stream. Blood pumped from his collapsing body in spurts and sprays, all aimed at Kar.

In the direction of the mountains, I heard more movement. 'Gather your goods, Kar, we have to move quickly.' I found the body of the longhaired barbarian and claimed my throwing blade and his blade. Leaving my fur where it was, I led Kar into the woods, towards our horses, anticipating another barbarian ambush.

The horses were agitated and, in the dark, it took us a moment to calm them. Kar secured his fur to his stallion and mounted. I handed him the reins to my mare and secured our surrounds by darting behind every tree nearby with a throwing blade in each hand. In the close quarters of the woods, I held them like daggers. I rushed ahead to a trunk of a pine closer to the edge of the woods and listened. Beyond the tree line, I could hear a horse. Closer, I heard gentle footsteps. 'Is that you, Lan?'

'It's Gentuk.'

I stepped out from behind the pine and saw my friend. 'We killed two.'

'There were three,' alerted Gentuk.

'Kar, there is another.' I raced towards him, stumbling but staying on my feet as I smashed through dead branches and across ankle-twisting pinecones.

Gentuk called out to Lan as he ran in the opposite direction, 'They only encountered two.'

Again, I prepared to attack as I approached every tree nearby and cautiously called Kar forwards.

Gentuk joined us in the still darkened woods. 'Move to the back, Arman.'

I retreated behind Kar and again tried to check every direction quickly enough. Every shadow was a possible foe and I begged for more light. As we approached the edge of the woods, I heard Lan call out.

'I have spotted the third. He is in my sights.'

Relieved, I stepped out into the grasslands between the woods and the mountains. Faint moonlight lit the grass passage for a moment before a cloud darkened the world once more. The cloud moved on and the slightest sheet of light spread across the stream of grass between the foothills and the woods.

'He is small,' said Lan, as he drew an arrow taught. 'He is younger than Kar. Do you see him? He's running for his horse.'

I took another step forwards and followed Lan's aim towards the small shadow bounding through the grass, fifty paces away. Ahead of him, I saw the horse he was trying to escape on.

Lan's arrow flew from his mounted position and pierced the fleeing child's neck. 'He shouldn't have gone for the horse,' he said, as he secured his bow.

'We killed the other two,' Gentuk told me, pointing out five riderless horses in the grass between the mountain steeps and us. 'Sorry we didn't arrive in time to stop them all.'

'I should apologise. I told Kar that it was safe to sleep.'

'As safe as it can be,' said Lan. 'I see they got close.'

I looked at Kar. Beneath the light of the crescent moon, I could see he was painted with blood. I wiped my face and flicked a splatter of gore on the ground. 'I want to collect my fur if you'll wait.'

'Hurry,' said Lan. 'We need to move fast and it's dangerous riding unfamiliar ground in the dark.'

'I could share your fur tonight.'

'Hurry,' repeated Lan.

***

We rode north from Verian's Pass, managing no more than a fast trot. With only the lightest shimmer of moonlight to guide our course, it was impossible to see through the grass and maintain a watch in all directions. The softly lit passage was narrow and we were prey to attack from all sides. An entire horde of barbarians could be ducking beneath the knee-high grass in front and we would not know until we were upon them. So, when Gentuk rode faster, or changed his course, so did we. When Lan called a halt, we all stopped and listened. When Kar, riding in front of me, pointed east and slowed, again we all stopped. He pointed towards the woods with his sword and, from that direction, we heard a horse approaching.

'Tahnas,' Lan called out, readying his bow.

'Good guess,' Salarn called back, arriving amongst us from the shadows as fast as a decending arrow.

We regrouped for a moment and I used the opportunity to pick pine needles from my fur.

Lan explained our encounter, sparing all the details. 'Five on horseback tried to follow Arman and Kar into the woods. They are dead.'

Salarn briefed us on his evening with Tahnas. 'We rode till dark before entering the woods. We counted ten fires along the range, between your camp and the plains ahead. No report of a fort.'

Salarn circled his mare next to Kar and reached out to touch his arm. 'Is any of this your blood?'

'No,' said Kar, 'all his.'

'Where were these fires?' I asked. 'Should we outride them?'

'Two more were burning further ahead,' said Salarn. 'Your ride this far has been too risky. Follow me into the woods.'

***

Salarn led us eight trees deep into the woods and we secured our horses near to Tahnas's mare.

'Now it's our turn to keep watch,' I told Kar, before he had a chance to settle with the other Guardians. 'Follow me and keep between the trees. Move when the trees move.'

Kar quickly tied his sandals and then followed me as instructed. When the wind picked up and the trees moved, so did we. I had to wait and watch after each movement to see that Kar was close behind. Hoping he was watching, I signalled to crawl the last few paces towards the edge of the woods. I began my crawl, uncertain whether he could even see me in front.

Tahnas turned to the sound of my encroachment. 'Always good to see or hear you, Arman. Did you bring Kar?'

'I thought I did.' I looked back at the pine where I had last seen him and around on the ground, trying to sight his shape.

Tahnas tapped me on the shoulder and pointed

across the grass to a divide in the mountain. 'A fire burned atop the second foothill until the sun slept. Further to the north, above the rise of pines, a torch was lit during the night. No movement since.'

'I'll watch the rises and the grassland carefully.'

'And watch out for Kar,' said Tahnas, looking over my head as he raised himself to a crouching position.

In line with us, only two paces away, Kar lay on his belly. 'Like a snake, Kar,' I praised him.

'Send word,' said Tahnas as he slunk back into the darkness of the woods.

When I turned, Kar was by my side. 'Who taught you how to move without sound? Was it Arcobon?'

'It was Tuley.'

'Garforn's boy?' I questioned, as I looked upon the ranges and the spread of swaying grass between. Turning to face Kar, I asked again, 'Tuley, the boy who was born into a man's body, taught you silence in movement?'

Kar glanced at me before directing his eyes back to the dark passage. 'We used to play a game in the village. Tuley called it Shadowing. We had to follow a Guardian without notice. He always won because he knew to only move when there was another sound.'

'Sound with sound, I like this,' I said, watching him lie still before I directed my eyes back to the dark foothills. 'I didn't have friends like you.'

'Everyone is your friend, Arman,' said Kar, his face never turning from his watch over the passage.

'No, Kar, I only have one friend. I have many Guardians that I call family.' I looked across at him and thought in the moment that we could be friends.

He knew what it was like to lose a mother and he knew how to smile at the strangest of times. His smile when he knew he was in Northern Barbarian lands was just like my smile when I evaded time at school, twelve harvests ago. Arcobon always caught me. Whether I was hiding in the woods or west of the village, where I was once locked in a hut, he would find me. Once, Arcobon even reached my side before I sensed his approach. He grabbed my throwing blade from behind as I was aiming and about to thrust it forwards. I learnt that the woods were a place to hide and a place where others can creep. I prefer the open plains, deserts and seas.

My time spent evading school resulted in me spending more nights with Verian. Arcobon would deliver me to the school and, if it were late in the day, I would be scribing tablets to candlelight long after the sun went down. I was tired, and so was Verian, when my lessons began. Then, walking through the village at night, back to my father's hut, I was always ready in case Arcobon surprised me again.

***

Kar pointed to a high cliff face, 'The sun is rising.'

'The sun is in their face if they look back upon us. Look for new movement. They have also seen the sun rise and will move if they are exposed.'

'I see movement,' said Kar.

'Where?'

'To my side of the divide.'

I looked to where a pass between foothills met the grasslands and watched. 'I see them, Kar. Count them

95

if you can.' They moved quickly to cover and the ones with horses led them to shelter. They did not ride.

'How many did you count, Arman?'

'Forty and eight horses.'

'I counted fifty-three and seven horses.'

'Fifty-three,' I repeated, making sense of the number. 'We are six.'

'Will we continue?'

'We will,' I said, and turned to see if he liked this idea.

He looked at me as if I was about to say more.

'I'm sure we will ride on. We must see if there is a fort this side of the mountains.'

'What if I was wrong? Will you and the other Guardian's hate me again?'

'We've always liked you, Kar, son of Unbetum and Kinsufa. And I believe your fort exists. It is too large a number to be a hunting party. Fifty-three barbarians have not been waiting for six Guardians.'

The sun slowly painted the mountains with light, first the peaks and then the crests of the foothills, as it rose in the east behind the woods. In front of us, in the grass passage, it was still dark. I asked Kar if he needed to rest. He was having too much fun. Every time I looked at him, he was facing a different direction. He was staring northwest when I noticed the colour of the blood on his hand. I rolled on my side and looked up through the trees. Light had reached the wood's canopy. The far side of the grass passage would now also be lit. By the time the other Guardians were prepared, we would have enough light to ride a safer path between the woods and the mountains. Kar maintained watch as I delivered the news.

***

Once more, Tahnas volunteered to ride first. Kar and I began with a dangerous course straight towards the divide in the mountains, where we had seen the barbarians return at sunrise. It was a fast trot through the grass, and we stilled ourselves before a gentle rise that led between two steep foothills. Kar had counted fifty-three barbarians disappear into this divide and, if they were watching, it looked like we were about to follow them. It was a gentle rise for two hundred paces between the steep banks until it reached a peak that prevented further sight.

From the south, we heard Salarn approaching. Salarn rode past us heading north and we followed him, building up to a steady canter through the low, well-lit grass at the bottom of the ranges. We passed Gentuk where the steep foothill ended and the next hill stretched north and rose gradually to sheer cliffs. Gentuk followed when Kar passed behind me. Ahead, wide fields of grass welcomed the light of new day and silently promised the reward of a safer ride, if we could make it that far. Across from me, concealed by the shadowed tree line, a horse was being ridden at similar pace. As we neared the wider plains, the rider closed the gap. From the west, Tahnas rode into my path and waved me forwards into the open fields. I looked back and saw Lan stroking his mare's neck as she rested and he watched us ride on.

***

The sun was hitting our faces on one side when we encountered a wide stream flowing east. Water had once gouged the earth a horse deep and five across in its determined flow. Now it could be stepped though by a horse and leapt, where it narrowed, by a man. Kar and I left our horses with the others and walked downstream to wash gore from our faces, furs and clothes.

'You should see your face, Kar.'

'Does it look like yours?'

I paused, not sure if he was referring to my scars. 'You look like you've gutted a pig and dumped the bucket on your head. Get it out of your hair or it will stick in clumps. I'm sure you don't want to cut off your lady braid.'

He knelt next to the stream and smiled at me before he submerged his whole head in knee-deep water. Ripping his fingers through his hair, he separated the dry blood. It coloured the water, as it washed loose.

I thought about washing my fur in his flow of water to get a reaction. Instead, I nudged him from behind with my knee as I walked further downstream.

Kar braced his fall with his arms and then flicked the blood trickling from his hair in my direction.

I felt the droplets land on the back of my legs as I walked on, smiling to myself. It was another twenty paces before the water ran clear again. I placed my sword and blades on a flat stone that surfaced where the stream had dried. I leant over and pulled my fur vest over my head, feeling it stick and grip to my arms and hair. Blood had dried on my face and neck and then, after mixing with my sweat, trickled on and coated my chest and stomach. When I removed my hide shorts, it looked like I was still wearing a red belt. I spread my sleeping fur and clothes and lay them to soak in the shallow water. The morning sun was warm. The water was still as cold as night. It numbed my knees and stung my flesh as I splashed it over myself. Bearing its chilly touch, I turned my fur, gave it a vigorous wriggle and retreated quickly to the flat stone. Closing my eyes, I stood and faced the morning sun, focusing on its warmth and ignoring the competing breeze. I almost fell asleep standing, but a noise startled me. It was one I had not heard since I had travelled between the northern cities—Borujerd to Assur.

In the direction of the mountains, the other Guardians stood watch while the horses quenched their thirst in the stream or grazed in the nearby grass. Closer to me, Kar was wringing his shoulder fur at the edge of the stream. I faced west, closed my eyes and tried to listen over the sound of the trickling water. Every so often, another sound was carried in the breeze. It was distant, almost not there. I raised my arm and looked towards the other Guardians. Tahnas noticed me first and, when I saw him walking in my direction, I lowered my arm and closed my eyes again to listen.

The sound was comforting. For me it was homely. I had spent almost half my life in or outside the northern cities and this sound, if it was what I thought, started at first light and did not cease till dusk. I stepped backwards from the stream and tried to listen again. Every time I heard it, I turned my head slightly, hoping it would sound clearly and remove my doubt.

'Put some clothes on, Arman.'

'No, quiet, listen,' I said, before following his advice. I bounded into the stream to fetch my shorts.

Tahnas waited patiently for me to stop splashing

about. He frowned at me when I returned and stood next to him, my dripping shorts distracting him more than my nakedness.

I stepped up from the dry bank of the stream and walked behind him into the grass.

When I was still, Tahnas turned his head slowly, training his ears to particular sounds and pausing when he was facing northeast. He raised his hand and then lowered it slowly until his bent arm angled his hand to his ear.

The other Guardians were watching from a distance and they all stopped moving. We all watched Tahnas.

He turned and looked at me before placing both his hands on the top of his head.

I placed my hands on the top of my head to ensure the signal was clear to the others.

Kar watched on, silently observing and not moving from where he sat on the bank upstream.

Good, Kar. If a signal is followed too quickly by action, the advantage is lost. Behind Kar, closer to the mountains, Gentuk moved first. He walked slowly towards his grazing mare. It was a long while before anyone else moved.

'Arman, are you clothed?'

'No. My clothes are wet and the breeze is as cold as the water.'

Tahnas sighed. 'I want this back.' He lifted his shoulder fur over his head and held it out to me, without turning.

'Grateful. I can't bear the cold like you and Kar.'

'That's all right.'

I took his shoulder fur and stepped forwards next to him. 'You heard it?'

'I did,' he said, staring northeast, contemplating a new plan.

'How far is that sound?'

'I think …' He looked at me with his mouth agape.

'You think?'

'No. No, Arman. That's a shoulder fur. Fankisi made that for me.'

'It's warm.'

'I don't care. It goes on your shoulders.'

I removed it from my groin and squeezed my head through the neck hole. 'Is that better?'

'I don't know anymore.'

'What about the sound?'

Tahnas took a deep breath and exhaled slowly. 'I hear metal workers, at least two. Kar was right.'

9

Stoking the Fire

Scribed by Kar. The Tree. Balih Woods

It looked like our village had been lifted by the mighty hand of a god and moved north before it was burnt. The trunks of more than nine hundred pines formed the wall. Even the gates looked the same. From our position at the edge of the woods, we could only see the gates on the southern and eastern sides of the fort. There was no way of viewing the other sides of the stronghold without leaving the shelter of the woods or riding further north. The woods continued further north but they snaked east and away from the mountains, creating an even greater grass divide. This was the best view we could hope for today. Tomorrow, it could be an even greater distance between the woods and the fort if the soldiers cut down more trees for construction and fires.

'What was our weakness?' asked Salarn, as he watched a group of soldiers use the strength of two horses to quickly close the eastern gate. Above them, archers clad in leather vests and bronze helmets looked on from battlements at the top of the wall.

'There was no weakness,' said Arman. 'They outnumbered us.'

Tahnas, Lan and Gentuk also shared our view of the fort but they remained silent.

Salarn slipped his hood from his head and turned to face me. 'Kar?'

'The wall,' I replied. 'Our village wall was a strength and a weakness.'

'Yes,' said Salarn. 'They hide behind the wall, always looking, like us, for a light in the night. And who is watching them?'

'Other than us, the barbarians are watching,' said Arman. He lay between Salarn and I, wearing Tahnas's shoulder fur and a pair of hide shorts that were tight on his thighs and baggy on his backside. 'The barbarians that Kar and I sighted were a war party.' Arman repositioned himself but it was his shorts, not the ground, that was making him uncomfortable. 'No telling if they have already attempted to sieze the fort. All I can tell is that the Akkadians are ready for an attack during the night.'

The ground surrounding the fort was lifeless. At one hundred paces from the wall, the Akkadians had completed a controlled burn of the grass that might have allowed anyone to sneak close. Freshly stacked fires were positioned towards the edges of this barren ground, ready to be lit again. To make it to the circle of fires we would have to cross fifty paces of ground that used to be part of the woods and another hundred paces of trampled grass.

'Arman,' said Lan, 'why would a barbarian war party ride south for half a day to encounter us? Surely this fort has their focus. Could they be mercenaries?'

Arman looked over my head to face Lan. 'They could be. They could be Akkadians dressed as barbarians,' he chuckled at his own joke. 'Are you wondering why they don't launch an attack during the day?'

Lan nodded. 'Why not attack the soldiers when they are cutting timber or building fires outside the safety of their fort? Why would fifty barbarians be camping south of here last night?' He flicked his chin up at the mountains that loomed behind the fort and then stretched forwards with one arm and splayed his fingers. 'Look at the cut stumps in front of us. Soldiers will probably cut down the tree between us tomorrow. Ponder this for a while. They ambushed you in the woods. Why would they not be waiting where we now lie?'

Before creeping to the edge of the woods, we had secured our horses and scouted in all directions from our camp. Lan's question still unsettled me and I looked behind and around at the other Guardians. Tahnas lay furthest from me and he was looking south, possibly still questioning our sighting of a war party.

'Why would we ride so far or not attack?' asked Salarn. He looked across at Lan and then turned back to face the fort. 'We are six of seven Guardians and we have ridden two days from home to be here. Before you think the barbarians' actions foolish, look at our own. Our new home, the tower, is safe. Out here, we are not, yet we had to make the ride and sight the threat.'

'You think the barbarians are threatened by us and not the fort?' asked Lan.

'I think they know and want this threat. They have

many camps through the hills and mountains. If fifty barbarians camp to our south, five hundred camp near this fort. They are always on the move. The land from south of Verian's Pass to the northern sea is their home and they won't abandon their reign in these lands. This fort might be their focus now, as you say, but they don't need to all gather here. They don't want to seize this fort like us. They want the fort. They want westerners to travel here in caravans carrying food and other riches.'

I thought of the valley bandits I had encountered on my last journey, starved and desperate, camped in hideouts overlooking the mountain pass, waiting, just watching as the moon changed face. The Akkadian's war with the world did not treat them as kindly. They were not rewarded with a promising bounty of future travellers.

'What do you suggest, Salarn?' asked Lan. 'We will be without light soon.'

Salarn pointed towards the fort. The mountains behind made the log wall look like a twig building in comparison. 'The Akkadians are the Northern Barbarian's next harvest and, so long as the Akkadians are threatened by the barbarians, they will continue to call for more arms and more soldiers. They will feed off each other, both growing stronger.'

Arman groaned and adjusted his position again. 'It would be a shame if we rode all this way just so Kar could cut off a head.'

I smiled and then buried my face in the ground to muffle my laughter.

'Is he all right?' I heard Lan ask.

'He's enjoying this,' replied Arman.

This made me laugh again. I did not know why I was laughing. I was scared. We didn't have a plan and soon it would be dark.

'Tahnas?' said Lan to his son. 'What are you thinking? You're too quiet.'

Tahnas raised himself on one elbow. 'An ongoing fight could be fuelled and the stars will serve us well tonight.'

'Tell us more, son,' said Lan. 'We're not getting any warmer.'

'Do you still have that blade, Arman? The barbarian one you gathered?'

'I do.'

'Do you think you could throw it precisely?'

Arman rocked his head back and looked at Salarn to one side and then back at Tahnas. 'It's a foot long and as heavy as ten throwing blades.'

'Do you think–'

'Yes, I can throw it precisely.'

'Good because if you can't–'

'I can.'

'Even in those shorts?'

The other Guardians, including myself, took a moment to look at his shorts that had extra room at the back and owned his thighs like a layer of callused skin.

Arman rolled on his side and I thought I saw Salarn smile for a moment before he turned back to face the fort. 'They have room at the front too,' said Arman. 'If I hid behind a tree, you could only hurt my pants.'

'You had a plan, Tahnas?' prompted Salarn.

The smile disappeared from Tahnas's face and his eyes tightened. 'We can't hope to take this fort and we need to be returning to the tower. Before we go, I think we should remind the Akkadians that they settle in Northern Barbarian lands.' Tahnas looked at each of us and saw the smile in our eyes. 'Take your last look at this fort, Guardians. You won't see it in the light of day again. Hopefully, you won't see it again after to-night. We'll leave them to settle the dispute.'

***

Salarn and Lan rode north and Gentuk headed south through the woods as the last stroke of red sky darkened like drying blood behind the mountains. Arman retreated to the camp to prepare himself for the night and Tahnas and I maintained watch.

'Are you liking this, Kar?' he asked.

I looked at Tahnas and his heavy leather skirt. Only his sword strap covered his chest. The wind howled through the woods, shaking the branches and stirring the mess of pine needles on the ground. His expression did not change. 'I'd like it more if I didn't feel the cold.'

'The cold keeps you awake. Welcome the cold, Kar. It will only hurt you if you sleep.'

'What if I get lost tonight?'

Tahnas leant forwards and looked me in the eye. 'One of us will find you.'

Arman appeared from the darkness of the woods. It was dark but not too dark to see that he was naked again. He had removed his clothes and blackened his skin with mud.

'I'll see you on the ride, Kar,' he said, as he stepped past me towards the edge of the woods, carrying the long barbarian blade that he had claimed when we were ambushed. Across the burnt space, trampled grass and fifty paces of stumps wafted the voices and commotion of soldiers in the fort.

'Wait,' said Tahnas, 'I'll need to take your blade. It will be seen in the night.'

Arman sighed as he handed over his own throwing blade that he'd tried to smuggle in his grip. 'You're right. I just feel naked without it.'

'You are but I'm sure you'll be wrapped in your sleeping fur and riding home before the moon owns the night.'

Arman turned to face the edge of the woods and Tahnas placed a hand on my shoulder, guiding me away.

'I'm not sure I understand my role,' I told Tahnas as we walked back to our camp.

'I'll direct you again when we are in position. We all need to work together if Arman is to be successful. You were picked to be the rider because you have good eyes in the night.'

Tahnas stopped walking and I looked about, trying to make sense of his stillness. I could hardly see a step in front and could not see behind. 'Tahnas?'

'You agree with my plan, don't you?'

'Yes,' I replied without pause. 'It may not change anything but it feels good.'

Tahnas started walking again, 'I want you to tell me what it felt like after.'

I untethered my stallion and Tahnas gathered the reins for both his mare and Arman's. We led them quietly back through the woods, north of where Arman was to begin his creep.

***

The circle fires were burning when we approached the edge of the woods, directly east of the fort. Thankfully, the sky was clear. Our plan relied on the rising moon. Its crescent face would rise above the mountains, shedding just enough light to see our path without revealing our movement. Higher in the sky, a bright star pointed north.

Tahnas slid a sheaf of wet grass stems from his saddle and nursed it under his arm. 'Wait until you lose sight of me and then look north. When Salarn lights the first fire, prepare to ride. You need to ride as soon as the second fire sparks. Ride due north and trust that we know the range of their bows. When the smoke thickens near the fort, head east for home. Don't wait for us.'

'I understand.'

Tahnas crouched low and disappeared towards the fort. I was on my own with the three horses, only hidden by a row of trees.

It was cold wearing just a shoulder fur and standing motionless. I wiggled my toes to make sure they were still there and kept my hands tucked in my armpits. The moon had moved since Tahnas left and, in the north, all was quiet and dark. Only the lower peaks of the mountains were illuminated as the moon rose and headed south through the sky. I never saw it move, I just remembered where it was last. Remembering where it last was became harder as it got colder. *Remember Arman. He doesn't have a shoulder fur. You have the warmth of the horses.* My eyes closed for just a moment and, when I opened them again, I could see a fire sparking in the north, near the edge of the woods.

I brushed Har Man's neck with my hand and then climbed onto my saddle. He stepped forwards. I restrained him by squeezing my thighs in my mount. 'We have to wait for the second ...' Before I could finish, a second fire was ignited close to the mountains. I released the tension of my thighs and tapped my heel gently. Har Man trotted forwards. The higher I sat in my mount, the faster we rode. I watched the ground in front, only sharing quick glances south to judge my distance from the fort. Ahead of me, a third fire was lit in the foothills. I was riding towards it and I was now as close to the fort as my planned ride would take me if I were allowed to continue north and slowly further away. That was the plan. Only for a moment would I be in range of their arrows and after that I would become one with the night.

The third fire was not part of our plan. The shadow in the grass ahead was also unmentioned in the plan. Maybe it was a bush or a log. I steered my stallion to its northern side and an arrow flew behind my shoulder, parting my flailing hair. Five more arrows whisked in front me. I looked south. In the haze of the circle fires, I saw the archers on the fort's wall bend in unison to reload their bows. Ahead of me, the third fire spread as individual torches were lit and carried towards me and up and across the foothills. 'Ten, twenty, thirty.' I was just counting the torches held aloft by horsemen riding my way.

From the south, a strange sound caught my attention and, when I turned, I saw a plume of smoke erupt from one of the fires. I kept riding at the same pace as I turned my stallion in a gradual arch back toward the woods in the east. Behind me, now, I heard their voices and the trample of their horses in pursuit. I cantered towards the woods north of the fort. Halfway across the grass plain, those giving chase slowed and regrouped. *Did they fear an ambush or know that I was already riding into one?* At the edge of the woods, my stallion reared back and stomped in a circle. I turned Har Man south and he preferred this course. We both wanted to ride home.

Closer to the fort, north of where I had begun my ride, I could see a wider entrance to the woods. Heading towards the opening, I watched the soldiers moving about on the log wall and tried to sight any shadows of movement in the flattened grass outside the circle of fires. The foothills to the north and south were awake with at least ten massive fires and the first fire that prompted my ride could no longer be seen through the wafting smoke.

I drew my sword as Har Man cantered towards the large opening to the woods and, just as we were about to enter, I steered him further south. The cave like entrance, created by higher branched pines, looked too welcoming. Once we were beyond it, I slowed Har Man and quickly dismounted. I entered the woods first and, in complete darkness, tried to listen above the noise rushing across the empty fields from the fort. When I thought I was alone, I led Har Man forwards, deeper into the darkness. We travelled east between the pines. Each step took us further from barbarian lands and further from home. I was happy to travel this way until morning. Without the stars or horizon in sight, all I could do was keep moving, relying on my last sighting of the North Star and a feeling in my gut that called me east.

10

One Weapon

Scribed by Arman, The Always Travelling Guardian, The Tower. Balih Woods

My fleshy parts took the brunt of my naked crawl. It felt as if every grass stem, especially the hardened, burnt ones, were determined to snag me. My arms and legs could tolerate the pain but I was asking too much of my most sensitive region. If I was fishing and caught a snag like this, I would snap the line. Snapping the line was not an option. A wriggle of the line would gain too much attention. Unfortunately, my bait had to stay stuck. I needed to wait for Tahnas and then rush the wall from here.

Slower than a drifting cloud, I turned my head to one side, my beard never losing touch with ground. Despite its mistreatment, the ground was my only friend. Removed from the ground's vicious embrace, my body would be sighted in an instant. At this distance from the fort, I could hear the guards conversing. I couldn't hear actual words, just the sounds of their individual voices. If I had my throwing blades, I could connect from here. I didn't have my blades. I had one blade, as heavy as a short sword, and one chance.

***

When I saw Tahnas move towards a circle fire north of the fort, I rolled only my eyes to watch the wall guards. I kept my eyes partly closed so they did not reflect the firelight and I had to rethink what I saw of the world, standing on its side in my contorted view. Most of the guards were seated out of sight. It would only take one to rouse the rise of all the guards. Glancing north, I saw Tahnas move again. Almost in time with his movement, the seated guards stood and orders sounded around the wall.

'Draw arrows.'

'Watch the woods.'

'South is clear.'

'There is movement in the west. Fires in the west.'

'Loose,' came the call from the northern side of the wall, followed by the combined *thwish* of fifty or more bows releasing their arrows. 'Watch, we have more lights in the north. Draw arrows.'

As the guards facing north bent to draw, dense smoke billowed from one of the circle fires north of the wall. The Akkadians manning the eastern side, closest to me, shuffled in that direction and I watched closely, my eyes now wide open. The guards I could see were distracted. I rolled my head to face the fort and noticed a group of archers maintaining their watch east. I only had one chance. Kar had made his ride and was probably returning. Tahnas had completed his task.

'Fire is moving south from the west,' shouted a soldier on the wall.

There was no need to turn to hear the alert. Be it their inexperience or fear, they did turn and I plucked myself from the ground and sprinted towards the wall. I did not know if I was sighted in my dash. The circle fires ripped in the wind and the movement of the guards pounded against my ears as I stood with my back to the wall, regathering my breath. Peering through a gap in the wall between two pine trunks, I sighted their leader. Alone with four others, maybe more, he stood near the gate on the southern side of the fort. From his shoulders hung a blue cape and he held his bronze helmet, the type with a nose guard and inward pointing flanks, by his side as his mouth widened and closed to each important word he shared with his small audience of soldiers. Torches lit the inner sanctuary of the fort but the thickness of the wall's posts, whole pine trunks, made it hard to see in all directions. I moved further south along the wall to get a better view. Inside, I saw ladders leading to the wall, barracks made from split wood and horses—one hundred or more— tied to posts on the western side. My greater enemy, the man telling these stupid men what to do, was so close. I wanted to call out to him. *Could there be a way to draw him close?* I lent out from the wall and looked up. Not even a single hand or spear tip was extended beyond the battlement. I turned my eye back to the gap between the logs and as I focused my attention again, my view was blocked. 'Yes,' I said. For a moment longer, I watched their leader, his mouth sounding orders or advice that I could not hear. My request was heard. A guard circling the wall retraced his steps and blocked my view. I drove the foot long, barbarian blade through the gap and it smashed through his nose and brain to the back of his skull. My work was done but I held onto the blade so that I could spike it upwards as his body slumped. Confident that he was pinned to the wall after his weight lowered the blade into a bite between two logs, I turned to face the woods.

It was one hundred paces to the closest gap between the eastern circle fires. It was another one hundred and fifty paces to the woods. I sprinted east, my hardened feet enjoying the challenge, my lower regions victimised by grass splinters that were driven and pressed with each stride. My pain did not slow my gait. Like unexpected rain, arrows pattered the ground in front and behind. In the south, I saw Gentuk fleeing and marveled at how close he was to me without my previous notice. I stepped between the cut stumps at the edge of the woods and tried to hold back my smile. The Akkadians had taken my wife and my home when they attacked the village. I had only taken the life of a soldier on patrol but he was close to his leader at the time. How I wish I could write that the Akkadian officer wearing the blue cape shut his mouth to his shouted words.

I found a gap between the pine branches and continued my sprint into the woods. Tahnas tackled me from the side and I was running so fast that he could not hold on. Off balance, I angled my shoulder to the ground and rolled into a pine with my other.

***

It took me a while to make sense of what happened next. I was on horseback but I did not hold the reins. My arm was clasped over the shoulder of the rider, to hold me upright, and we were wrapped in a shared fur. I touched the rider's side with my spare hand and tried to work out who he was in the darkness.

'Don't take advantage of me, Arman,' said Tahnas.

'Why did you halt my run?'

'Barbarians were moving into the woods behind us. You were going to escape one enemy by running into the attack of the next.'

'Have you found Kar?'

'Salarn and my father have gone after Kar. If not for Kar's ride we might have met more of the barbarians tonight.'

'Gentuk was running from the arrows with me.'

'I'm here, Arman,' said Gentuk from behind. 'I'm leading your mare.'

'I'm good to ride,' I told Tahnas.

He stopped riding to allow me to dismount. 'It's my fur but you need it more.'

'Do you want to tell us what happened at the wall?' said Gentuk.

I walked towards his voice with Tahnas's sleeping fur bundled high so that it did not drag in the thick, squishy floor of pine needles. 'I think I saw their leader. He wore a bronze breastplate, fastened with a blue cape.'

Gentuk handed me the lead to my mare. 'That's an officer's cape. A Borujerdian officer's cape.'

'Borujerdian or Akkadian, they are the same enemy now. He stood so close it hurt. As I contemplated my next move, a soldier patrolling the fort walked right in front of me. I felt that heavy barbarian blade break his face and hit the back of his skull.'

'Was it worth the risk?' asked Tahnas as we continued trotting through the darkness of the woods.

'I've never stripped my clothes for a better end.'

'That concerns me,' said Tahnas.

'You mean on this journey?' asked Gentuk.

I sighed, thinking of all my rides, this ride and our next. 'I was too long away from my wife. She was with me when I thrust that blade tonight. She is still with me.'

*****

I fell asleep many times during our ride through the night. At least, I think I did. Often, I would forget where I was or be surprised by a new noise in the woods. And I would be lost until I heard the sound of Gentuk and Tahnas riding in front. Whenever I became aware of the hardened lump of a dangling pine-cone, I would snap it from its branch. Then I would wait for Gentuk to pass under a branch and lob a cone from behind. I thought it might break the monotony of the sightless ride.

'Arr, right on my head.'

'Stay alert, Gentuk,' I told him, masking my smile from my voice.

'I'm trying. These big pine nuts don't like me.'

'Maybe I should not follow so close.'

'It's got nothing to do with you, Arman. If it didn't hit me, it would land as all the others do. Who knows, maybe a little memory of me stays with them as they grow into a tree.'

My smile faded. 'You believe in fate, Gentuk?'

'I do,' he said. 'Lateef is safe at the tower, my eldest is safe travelling with Delari and my wife is waiting for me to rescue her.'

'You still feel her?'

'Do you think I'd appreciate a nut hitting my head if I didn't. I know Belline's alive because I think of her each time I feel pain. Wherever she is, I hope my pain steals hers and she can find peace again.

My mare followed Gentuk and Tahnas east, even when I fell asleep. Through the night and into the early light of day we maintained our course. Eventually, the gaps between the pines widened and announced the eastern edge of the woods. We turned southward to avoid the blinding light of morning sun and the lower branches that prevented us from continuing on horseback. Our pace quickened. We wanted to be free of the woods and begin a homeward course. I knew I was not alone in my desire for unshielded light when Tahnas stopped riding and shook his head and groaned with frustration. We had to ride through the woods or risk encountering the barbarians on our return. They had served their purpose. Now we wanted out. Gentuk dismounted and held his reign for me to take. He walked ahead of us, lifting and tossing fallen branches to the side. Tahnas and I also dismounted to breach the final layer of pine bars that locked us inside the woods.

The short, prickly grass at my feet snaked like a river north and south along the edges of the woods and, in the east, the Kavir Desert tried to lure us out into its warm embrace. Like the Zagros Mountains in the West, the Kavir Desert was an imposing barrier that separated worlds. Life in the Middle East, between two worlds, had treated the Guardians well. We appreciated the West until they tried to take our lands.

And we respected the Far East like one does a stranger.

Tahnas pointed south, 'It's not the time to rest.'

I raised a hand to one side of my eyes and stared south. Slowly, I made out their shapes. They had not seen us leave the woods and were riding further away. It was our job to catch up.

****

Thirty days ago, I was one of six Guardians that left the safety of the tower to find an Akkadian stronghold east of the Zagros Mountains. It was Kar's scribed words that had prompted me to raise the matter at the Guardian table. I think we all knew of the threat. We all knew that, once discovered, our home east of the mountains would never be safe again. Faith, possibly ignorance, led us to believe that we could ride west and guide lost Guardians safely home. Bull-faced we remained, in spite of all we had seen. Our plans to ride west did not change. Again, we would leave the tower and risk more lives than we could possibly save. And this time, Kar would stay behind. It didn't seem right. Maybe, we should have all stayed at the tower.

11

A New Day

Scribed by Fankisi, The Curious. Salarn's Tower. Balih Woods.

Kar did not sleep soundly on the top floor of the tower. Maybe he did not sleep well on the ground floor either and only in the company of others was his wake from dream noticeable. Jamine told me that twice she had heard him call out during the night. She could not make out his words.

'He might have said, *anger*,' she suggested. She shook her head, as if her own suggestion was not accurate.

I adjusted my nurse of Parbi and clamped his playful hands. 'Kar probably doesn't remember. I hope he's not too tired.' I could say no more as I slept in the room below the others with Tahnas.

Naten wrapped her slender, white arms around my waist and jittered with anticipation.

*****

He was the last to rise and walked down from where he now slept again at the top of the tower. Past the open door to my room, he made his way down towards us. Near the door to Salarn's study, he leant over the step's railing. The torches were lit and Kar watched his father attempting to gracefully swing a long sword in one arm as he paced between the lower columns. He looked back into Salarn's study and pondered its lure momentarily from outside. It was a new day for the youngest Guardian man and he may have even entered Salarn's study once more had he not received a call.

'Kar,' bellowed Salarn. 'No one eats until you have trained and I awoke hungry at dawn.'

Kar bounded down the remaining steps and ran to the foot of the throne. Salarn, though seated, towered above Kar and smiled respectfully at the young man. Kar bowed his head to Salarn. His motion of respect seemed natural. Away on a hunt, the other Guardian men, my husband included, were not present to say why a simple lowering of the head was or was not a problem. This made me smile. There was a special connection between the youngest Guardian man and our elder. Most now knew that they were related by blood and I think, in that way, Salarn saw Kar as his replacement. Like Salarn, Kar did not tell everyone his every thought; he just did his own thing and gained a different type of respect, sometimes disapproval. The Guardians needed men like Salarn and Kar, just as they needed men like Arman, to tell a good story. They also needed Guardians like my husband, Tahnas, who always had a plan.

Salarn sat upright in his throne and pointed objectively over Kar's shoulder. Unbetum walked towards his son and, barely visible in the shadows, Kar made out our faces—the women and children. He looked anxiously at Salarn, surely questioning the reason for our assembly. Salarn did not move or speak.

'Concentrate on the greatest threat,' Unbetum warned Kar. 'Do not look for comfort or try to predict what this day has in store for you. For too many days, you have trained alone.'

Kar looked down at his feet and adjusted his stance on the bristled fur. 'Do you know what I have learnt whilst training alone? How can you say I have trained this way for too long?'

'Who taught you this wit, Kar?' said Unbetum. 'I will see if it is more than just game. Hold that stance, I need a weapon that will not vanquish you in a moment.'

When Unbetum disappeared into the shadows behind Salarn's throne, Kar made the unfortunate mistake of glancing at the women and children gathered. He saw me and we exchanged a smile. For a moment, Naten thought that the smile was directed at her and she stepped forwards from my side.

Kar jolted as he noticed Unbetum nearing his side and slashed downwards with his sword as he stepped away defensively.

'See this,' laughed his father, tossing the wooden spoon he had attacked with out of sight. 'If it were merely double the length, you would be on the floor.'

Kar frowned, adjusted his stance and stood ready.

His father stood still, his flickering gaze alluding to the presence of a different threat. 'Would you attack me without knowledge of the other weapon I hold?' questioned Unbetum.

'Not unless I saw any danger for myself or others.'

Unbetum looked towards Salarn, whose emotionless and calm face betrayed none of his feelings. 'A good answer,' praised Unbetum. With his weapon still concealed, he turned in our direction. Unbetum faced the women and children who were watching from the shadows at the edge of the torchlight.

Kar stepped between.

'What if I was holding a throwing blade?' asked Unbetum. 'I would let it fly and either you, or those you are protecting, would suffer as a result.'

'Throw it then,' challenged Kar. 'I know you will not.'

Unbetum hesitated and, in that moment, his shoulder fur was cut and fell to the ground in two pieces.

Naten shrieked and the sound was so startling that I don't even remember if I cried out also. The attack was not delicate enough to avoid contact with skin and Unbetum wiped blood from fresh wounds on the side of his neck and shoulder.

I stepped forwards to assist Unbetum. Jamine blocked my path and gestured that she should hold Parbi. I agreed and relayed my distress by pulling Naten close. My adopted daughter welcomed me with a grip that pushed air from my belly.

'You called him to duel,' said Salarn, as he watched Unbetum walk in a circle. 'I'm interested to see the point of this lesson.'

'If I had wanted, you would be on the floor,' said Kar.

Unbetum stooped his head as if he needed to consider the lesson's intention.

Kar bounded across the rug, closer to the throne

and away from the women and children. His smooth sandals slid on the fur when he tried to stop.

Unbetum turned, still concealing his hidden weapon. Behind his son he saw Salarn seated on the stone throne. 'What if I attacked now?' questioned Unbetum.

Salarn's contemplative smile disappeared.

Kar took one more step, so that Salarn was not behind him. 'I never read your account of what happened in the deadend pass,' he said to his father. 'I believe that you thought you could save the girl and survive yourself. You did. I will also believe in my blade and trust that I can defend myself and another.'

Unbetum cast a foot long throwing blade forwards in front of Kar's legs and, as it deflected upwards off the rug, it met Kar's blade.

Kar stepped over it and paced towards his father. 'I know where you keep your other throwing blade,' announced Kar. 'And I know that you only have one arm that could draw it and throw it in time. Yet you tell me not to predict life.' Viewing this as justification of his victory, Kar pointed his sword downwards to signal an end to the duel.

'I never named this a duel, Kar,' said Unbetum. He drew his other blade and rotated it between his fingers. 'In the real world, there is no practice. What you face will not be previously told in a story.' He continued rotating his blade.

Kar watched the blade and moved his sword slightly from side to side.

'Now I have your attention,' said Unbetum, looking beyond his son to Salarn seated on the throne.

Salarn also seemed spellbound to the motion of the throwing blade. If it was purposefully or accidently released, it could fly his way.

Unbetum rotated the blade one last time before pinching it to a stop.

Kar's sword, which had begun swaying side to side in time with the blade's hypnotic motion, steadied in his grip.

'Good,' said Unbetum. 'I was not with you on your first journey west and I don't think you needed me for your journey north. I hope to be with you on your next journey, if only in spirit.' Unbetum returned his throwing blade to the pouch that doubled on the side of his long sword sheath, strapped to his back and then knelt. Blood trickled down his chest from a new wound on his good shoulder.

I went to step forwards and was anchored by Naten's embrace. We had held each other back from the happenings on the far side of a flaming torch, reminding each other not to be tempted forwards beyond the arches. Above Unbetum's shoulder, the hilt of a long sword protruded, but it was not one the accomplished Guardian liked to call his own. He did not know where his sword was, only the face of the man who held it last. I'm certain the face of the tall Akkadian, Otoug, was etched in his mind. Salarn killed Otoug and brought back Unbetum's tattoo but who knew what happened to the Guardian's favourite sword? That knowledge could have made the loss even harder to bear. But Unbetum's weapon of choice no longer weighed on his mind. He told me what was most important to him now and that was what it had fought for whilst still in his hands—a new Guardian, a new weapon. Kar was his focus now. Unbetum had been absent for many seasons during Kar's upbringing and wanted to make up for his absence.

I don't think he planned to cause his son any embarrassment or use trickery. The morning's activities had led to this outcome. One cannot teach someone who is not ready to learn and there is no point in teaching a lesson already learnt. This is what the women told me when I was a girl. *Show me that you can skin a beast and the lesson is complete.* Both the father and son had gained a heightened understanding of each other and their own failings, and the training had only just begun.

Unbetum stood and carefully drew his long sword. He stepped closer to Kar. 'Now we will duel like Guardians.'

Salarn clapped his hands and the women ushered the children, who were reluctant to leave, outside to begin the day's work.

Cautiously, Kar pointed his blade to the floor and watched his father do the same.

I'm sure that everyone wanted to stay and watch, but that was not Guardian custom. We had our own work to complete. Naten and I were the last to leave and it took all my strength to resist telling the men to be careful. It was Naten that gave me that last heave out the door as I turned back, tempted to stay.

12

A Time and a Place

*Scribed by Jamine, The Dressmaker.
During the early harvest days. Salarn's
Tower. Balih Woods.*

Hemal spent his final days lying on bedding next to Salarn's throne, watching, when he was conscious, Kar and Unbetum duel and talk. I wet his head with a damp cloth, just as I would a child with fever. He could not swallow water or breathe unless I lifted his head and pounded his chest. Not even Salarn's special salt from the Deep Sea allowed for Hemal's cut tongue to mend. His skin changed colour and, even when he was resting, it looked like he had almost swallowed a fish, its tail fin wriggling inside his gaping mouth with each strained breath.

We buried him north of the tower, near Pardensai's grave. Everyone was present, apart from my son, Tahnas, and the Harmin, Boroe. They had volunteered to remain at the tower and stand watch over our new home.

Lan and Gentuk lowered Hemal's cloth-wrapped body into the grave and then Unbetum sprinkled water from a bladder.

Salarn dipped his head and shared a few words. 'Hemal died watching a duel. He will watch the real fight from heaven. His body lies near my father's and will also be gifted in new life.'

After a moment of silence, I led the women in a song for the fallen Guardian. It was a simple song, the same song we had sung at the beginning of the cold season when we buried the villagers where we had all lived at some stage of our lives.

> *'Born I was*
> *Lie I must*
> *For sure I strain*
> *To die is just.*
> *Beneath this stone*
> *Know now my home.*
> *Till my rebirth*
> *Earth be thy hearth'*

We repeated the words until Salarn raised his head from silent prayer and signalled Arman and Kar to step forwards. With short wooden spades, they began filling the grave as the rest of the Guardians followed Salarn back to the tower. He walked slowly, his dragging feet causing him to stumble. I called on Gentuk's young boy to walk by his side.

***

The sun had risen, though the clearing around the tower was still darkened by the shadow of the surrounding woods. A procession of men carried food, water and blankets from the tower to the horses tied near the door. It was unusually warm for this time of day and there was dampness in the air that suggested impending rain.

Fankisi sat in the grass next to a freshly sowed crop of barley with five children gathered in front of her. She wore her bravest face and the children probably thought that they were the only ones sad to see the men preparing to leave.

'Today the men will ride through the mountains to the desert on the other side,' explained Fankisi, pointing to a place most of the children could only imagine. 'They have many days' travel ahead of them and it will be a long time before we see them again. Only three of the men and Lagesh, who is soon to be a man, will remain to protect us.'

Lagesh turned back to face Fankisi but her attempt to make him feel better about the men's departure had failed. When his father, Gentuk, and brother, Senea, left before the village was attacked, Lagesh still had his mother, Belline. Soon he would be the only member of his family safe at home in the East.

'We will not fear for the departed or ourselves whilst they are gone,' Fankisi continued, 'because we know that we can look after ourselves and they can look after each other. It will be a long time though before they return and the men need to know before they leave that you will continue to grow. So, when you say goodbye, show them a face you want them to remember you by. Let them see you smile before they ride away and they will return,' she finished, smiling at the children kneeling or seated cross-legged before her.

'Can I go see my father now?' asked Lagesh. He bobbed up and down on his haunches, unable to sit still. One of his eyes was always more open than the other and, in his anxious state, he looked ready to soil himself if he was held back too long.

'Remember, you have to protect us now, Lagesh. We must wait for the men to be ready, or we might distract them into forgetting to take something that they may need.'

'I am not a child,' he told Fankisi. 'I can help them pack.' Lagesh ran back towards the tower and Fankisi paid little heed to his desertion.

The real reason for keeping the children at a distance was to protect their fathers from their own emotions. Normally, every child had something they wanted to question their father about before he left, just like every father had too many things he would like to share with his child. It could not be all said in a day but, in a moment, it was hoped that the most important words would be shared. For this parting, Lagesh was the only child, apart from Parbi, who still had a father to farewell.

Lan clasped my hand and led me back inside the tower and up the steps and ladder to the roof. My climb up the ladder was slow and a little awkward. My dress caught beneath my foot on one rung because I was too focused on my next step. I was getting old and so was my husband. His climb of the ladder was faster and more graceful but even he groaned as he stepped onto the roof.

From the roof of the tower, Salarn watched the sky. The high winds blew his scruffy grey beard sideways and reddened his nose. He prayed aloud to Enki, the Pattern Maker God, and saw good weather ahead. His men were in search of family, not war, and he felt that this endeavour would ensure Enki's protection until they reached the west. Once there, they would need to say their own prayers. He watched the men who would ride out after loading their horses. Many were already breasted with leather armour and had their sheaths loaded with weapons of choice. Salarn smiled at the sky. This was a smile to his favoured god, Enki. He gestured to those beneath. He was confident of the Guardian's success but not foolish enough to act overjoyous or voice his thoughts too loud. 'They will do what is right and complete your pattern with quiet guidance.' He looked down at Fankisi sitting with the children and across to where Unbetum sat with his son at the edge of the clearing. He held his stare for a long while before turning to face the sun's peaking face. Salarn closed his eyes and let the warmth race towards him from the Kavir Desert in the East. 'You have timed the planting of the seeds well, Jamine. The days will only get warmer now and the animals will return to the plains.'

Lan stayed by Salarn's side to discuss the planned journey as I descended the ladder through the trapdoor. As I trod slowly down the steps to the bottom floor, I felt weary. Lan and I were of the age to just watch. In our planned life, he would be at the school or training new Guardians in the Village Circle, both less than thirty paces from our hut. I would be close by and able to call him when a meal was ready.

I trod on down the stairs, out the door and across the clearing to where Unbetum was showing Kar something he had learnt as a boy. Unbetum held a small branch from a tree and dug his fingernail into it to peel away the bark. 'Now you try it here,' he instructed, smiling up at me.

Kar gripped the branch with one hand and dug his thumbnail in with the other but to no avail. The loose bark forced its way under his nail. Bearing the pain, Kar pushed harder.

'Stop,' Unbetum told him. 'Give me another try.' Unbetum took the branch and dug his own thumbnail into the same spot. His repeat effort had hardly made a dint in the stubborn old branch. He displayed this to his son and then turned away as a glimpse of daylight caught his attention.

Kar flicked the bark from under his nail and tried again towards the top of the branch, above his father's indentation. Without pain he striped the branch of its bark until he reached green flesh.

'You had better return. They will be leaving soon,' I advised Unbetum.

Kar held the branch out for his father to inspect.

Unbetum ran a finger from the successful end to the other and declared, 'Age will make you stronger, Kar. Your bark will grow thicker.'

Kar placed the branch next to the log they sat on and followed Unbetum to the tower. I walked towards the crop to assist Fankisi in the final moments before the men's departure.

'Remember what I said,' Fankisi reminded the children as she watched the last load being secured. 'Look at me,' she said to the anxious children already positioning themselves to move. 'Is everyone smiling?'

Two girls and her son, Parbi, were smiling, and

the only other child remaining, Naten, had fair reason to look sorrowful. Fankisi held them back no longer. The girls, followed by Parbi on his hands and knees, ran towards the men like raiding soldiers and voiced their demands. It was now up to the men to comfort the children's concerns.

Fankisi followed Parbi's determined amble through the grass with a saddened child by her side. 'Are you going to say goodbye?' Fankisi questioned the girl who walked with her.

'Yes, I just wish I had a father I could say goodbye to,' said Naten, staring down at her feet.

Fankisi stopped walking and crouched to hug the saddened girl. Naten's fair hair, parted in the middle, fell as straight as water each side of her face. Fankisi gripped her harder and more bindingly until she felt the girl collapse to tears in her embrace. 'You are the only child here who has reason to cry today. Let it out, little one. Let your father, wherever he may be, feel your sadness. Find comfort in my arms. I call my-self your mother now. One day you may even think of Tahnas as a father more deserving of your affection.'

Natan, with her face smothered by Fankisi's shoulder, sobbed and sucked for breath.

Tahnas stooped and lifted Parbi high in the air. The little boy laughed as Tahnas turned him upside-down and held him by his ankles.

'Kar,' I called out and pointed the young Guardian to Fankisi's side.

Naten lifted her reddened face from Fankisi's nurturing shoulder and tried to adopt a new disposition.

'Fankisi has to say goodbye to Tahnas,' I told Naten. 'I want you to stand with Kar, so that no one is alone.'

Fankisi looked for the first time that morn as if she were about to cry herself.

'Go to my son,' I told her.

Fankisi smiled at the young Guardian as she ran to Tahnas's outstretched arm.

Kar slowed his steps as he watched Fankisi run by.

Naten walked to Kar's side and, from a distance, they stood silently to watch the final preparations before depature.

Tahnas, with Parbi in shared nurse, held Fankisi close and spoke to her ear.

Salarn exited the tower door with my husband. Lan's ageing face was still my favourite. I remembered when it was framed by thick, brown hair and his body and arms were strong like our son's were now. He walked towards me with his arms spread by his side.

'I imagine my words will be very different to those shared by Salarn and Tahnas,' I told Lan as he approached me, speaking loud enough to gain my son's attention. 'I do not care what my men encounter out there. You are both to return home once your planned journey is complete. Return sooner if you don't find what you are looking for.'

'I only worry for those I leave behind,' said Lan. He smiled at Kar and Naten.

Arman spoke to Yisben's girls, hopefully explaining what their mother could not, or would not. Yisben, I think, still believed that she would return to Hidalu one day and resume life as usual. This was ignorance more than optimism. She idled near the door of the tower. She had been away too long and had not planned to return to the Guardian way of life. Her daughters were helpful in entertaining Parbi but soon they would be women and I would call on them more.

Next to the stable, Boroe of the Harmin village held two mares ready as Gentuk shared words with his youngest son. Lagesh had not reacted well when the men departed before dawn on their journey north. This time Gentuk had somehow managed to calm his son's emotions and make him smile.

Light slowly painted the top of the tower as important words continued to be shared between those who were leaving and those who would remain in the woods to protect our new home.

In front of me, Kar braved a glance at the girl wearing a faded blue Borujerdian gown. His eyes lingered on her face before coursing down her thin frame. The weave of the gown fastened on one shoulder with a simple knot was so delicate that fingers could tear it apart, and the colour of the dye was as gentle as morning sky. Her fair hair, brushed straight and free of knots, shone bright even in the low light and slid down to blossoming breasts. Her nose was thin, as if pinched closed, and her eyes also seemed reluctant to open. Kar looked back towards the other Guardians, still in the process of bidding farewell. He held a distant gaze that suggested he still pictured her face in his mind. I knew the look of an excited young man. It doesn't change with age. His eyes were wide, his hands useless by his side and his stance uncomfortable. Kar adjusted his shoulder fur. Maybe he compared Naten's appearance with the short-cut, dirty hair of the unlikely princess he had encountered in his first journey. Surely, he marvelled at how Anava, with her dark, dusted skin and bushy eyebrows, had stolen his heart. Naten's skin was fair like her hair, almost untouched by the sun. Is this not how men imagine a princess should look, for a real princess would not be allowed to walk unguarded outside like Guardian women but would spend most of their time with a private maid sheltered in a palace. Yet it was Anava who held regal facade for Kar. His account of his first journey made this clear and throughout the cold season he found many opportunities to raise her name and gather information on her character from the Guardian women. 'Will Badbe choose her husband?' he had asked one morning. 'Anava would like it here,' he had said when he returned from one of his early morning departures. I noticed his stance steady as Naten slipped a glance upwards.

Girls also betray their emotions. Naten's eyes searched for more than his eyes before she turned away. Unlike Kar, who had been lost in his own world since returning, Naten, out of place at the Guardian tower, had taken it upon herself to familiarise the new faces and customs. She knew the ways of the young Guardian who stood next to her and had witnessed many of his early departures during the cold season. She was the oldest of the children and he was the youngest of the warrior men. I think this made her feel close to him even if he did not spare it a thought. Fankisi had informed me of the rest of the girl's story. Naten's parents were poor folk who worked hard all day long—her mother in the lord's kitchen and her father in the fields. With the arrival of her younger brother, they saw it time to collect on her upbringing and Naten was taken to the marriage markets. A representative of

Vanekebek, the Lord of Borujerd, was the highest bidder. Her parents were paid handsomly for their daughter and not privy to the knowledge that she was to be passed on as a present for Lord Vanekebek's pleasure. The innocence of youth never allowed her to question their abandonment. When subjected to the Lord's perverse nature, she cried for them. They could not hear her cries. If not for Fankisi's unannounced arrival on one unforgettable evening, her parents would have never been any the wiser.

The men mounted their horses as those staying grouped near the door to the tower. Salarn stood still, his eyes closed and a crease of deep thought dividing his brow, as he said one last prayer.

'Enki,' he said, calling on the pattern maker and God of fresh water, 'lead my Guardians down the right path.'

Lan gave the call and the men followed him as he rode away across the clearing, not looking back. More than one child called out in earnest as the Guardians disappeared amongst the trees. It was the mothers' job once more to quell any perceived loss. In achieving this task, the women often felt like they were lying to themselves. We could not promise the safe return of any of the men. Countless times we had been rewarded for the optimism we shared with those too young to understand why the men must leave. Fankisi and I truly believed that if a man's last sight is his woman's smile, then he was destined to return safely. There was only one amongst those remaining who fully combated all sense of loss that morning. Naten, if I read her smile correctly, believed that her man now stood next to her. Maybe she would be old enough to understand his reason for leaving when the time came.

***

Life goes on. As always, there were men left to defend the women and children. Considering the number now completing the Guardian tribe, three men were deemed up to the task, four if one counted Lagesh. Salarn enjoyed sharing the tower and continued to break custom by allowing the women and children special invitation to the training sessions of his favourite new Guardian. Although he had strongly objected to the men's opinion of Kar, he understood why they did not like the young Guardian distancing himself. I did not have to part a tent flap this time to learn of my elder's secrets. My crop of barley had been successfully planted at turn of season and with my man away on a Guardian's journey, I was free to spend more time with Salarn. I could have sewn a dress anywhere. My humble stool next to Salarn's stone throne was my chosen placement.

Salarn often reflected on his younger days, recalling the many nights he spent alone. His travels had taken him further than most mortals would deem possible. He never feared the unknown path, for that was his calling. Kinsufa's mother, also called Kinsufa, he had met years later, and the well to which his father had led a lost people was nothing like the prosperous village it had since become. He strained his troubled mind to reflect upon thoughts long ago abandoned and I would still my sewing to offer him quiet. He worried that he had forgotten parts of his life and often asked me to confirm a tale he had told or a happening only witnessed by a few.

When still a young man, while Tahnas was still growing in my belly, Salarn had followed his father deep into the woods and learnt that gods were real and that they had voices. He had also learnt that it was only a matter of time before his own voice would be taken from him.

'This is my fate and one I avoid sharing,' he tried to explain. Salarn believed that he had only one life to live with the Guardians and it was nearing an end. Setting Kar on a path was one of the few things he did not regret. 'Kar needed a challenge. I gave him mine. For all the things we wish we could change, I am left with fewer each passing day. Hear me, Jamine. Despite my regrets, I would not change anything. New words and movement are now my only concern.'

It was Kar's well-timed questions and moments of prolonged silence that had awakened the oldest Guardian. Salarn saw himself in Kar, a part of his daughter, and that is why he was compelled to show Kar a glimpse of the real world. Like his best friend, Elkin, Salarn had grown old with something no longer attainable keeping him suspended in life. He had a deeper secret or calling that he needed to share before his time was over. I sat next to his throne but Salarn was often not in that throne when I looked up. All that remained was his body. He was likely in the Harmin Village, Elkin's Cave or Pled. I think he spent most of his time in Pled.

***

'Salarn?' said Kar in a soft voice from a distance of five paces.

Salarn blinked and opened his eyes to the young

man in front of him.

Once again, the young Guardian's timing was impeccable. Salarn had been woken from his thoughts just as they started to make sense and before he confused himself again.

'Love forgone, opportunities missed and favours undeserved; I do not want you to suffer this same plight.' Salarn said to Kar. 'I have discussed with Elkin a plan for you, and Samor, the chief of the Harmins, will help you make sense of this plan.'

Kar stared back at Salarn.

'A dedicated Guardian could halt the empire's spread if he found where the bull nested. When I found you black with soot in the decimated village, I wished the tears that had painted lines down your face were my own. They were your tears, Kar, and it will be you not me standing in the final confrontation. My father's last written words were, *The tower, now complete, is no longer yours.* Pardensai gave us the tower. I leave them you, Kar.'

I placed my hand on Salarn's and squeezed it gently. 'I should join the women,' I said, and I hitched my dress as I hurried from the side of the throne to where Fankisi and the others were gathered on the western side of the tower, opposite the stairs.

Salarn nodded approval over Kar's head to Unbetum.

Unbetum strode towards Kar with his long sword held ready to swing.

Kar was poised.

Unbetum swung fast and Kar avoided deflecting the weighted sword and instead stepped backwards and tapped the long blade from behind, seeing it on its way. Rolling nimbly across the thick rug, he was ready to meet the return blow and this time blades connected. The force made the younger warrior fall backwards and Unbetum pushed forwards. It was a one-sided fight. Kar was not only weaker and less skilled but his sword was only half the length and weight of his father's. The only advantage he had, considering his father's injuries, was speed. Unbetum's long sword counteracted this advantage. If Kar attempted to block a head-sweeping attack, he could end up wearing his own sword. Kar kept moving. He played on his father's only weakness. I saw it as a defensive measure and one that would hopefully see swords pointed to the ground before blood flowed.

Unbetum advanced, waving his sword from side to side.

Kar circled out of reach.

Unbetum's bad leg convulsed with each turn and he had to keep adjusting his grip, as he only had one good arm to wield his heavy weapon.

Every so often, Kar would step forwards and bunt his father's blade before retreating twice as quickly.

Salarn, from his high seat, no longer watched the duel. His attention was drawn to us—the women and children gathered in the shadows beyond the light of the flaming torches. I'm sure he wished he could see Kinsufa's face amongst us. Unlike Fankisi, his daughter would be wearing a content and knowing smile. Kinsufa would know that no matter how dangerous men fighting with sharp blades may seem, no harm would be allowed outside of real battle.

The children, except Naten, watched the duel like an invisible barrier held every part of them back, apart from their eyes. Naten watched like she was a part of the duel. Her eyes flickered and, with each near strike, she shuddered to one side or the other. She was as entertaining to watch as the young Guardian who bounded about on the thick fur, tempting his father to swing his weighted blade.

Unbetum had already challenged Kar's conviction and now he tested the youth's patience or was it the other way around? Could Kar persist with his defensive circling movements or would his mind tire and have him seek an end with a risky change of tactic?

At first fast and jolted, the fight now flowed with rhythmic grace. In and out and round and round, like a stallion being broken, Kar drew his father close before distancing himself. Nothing can last forever, I judged, as Kar parried another life-ending swipe. The pace quickened once more and an inevitable end bore close.

In the gloom beyond the torch-lit performance, Fankisi pulled Naten to her side and together they trembled.

Kar propped himself to retreat and instead turned on the spot. His blade sailed uninterrupted over his father's collapsing body. Kar pointed his sword to the floor and Unbetum laid his weapon to rest where he had fallen. Like the duel, the silence that followed the final swing seemed unending.

Salarn clasped the throne's armrests and eased himself onto his feet. He took two steps forwards and, from this vantage spot, he took a moment to admire his surrounds. It was like he had been away for a long while and was observing the changes. Maybe he pondered how many days he had walked the stairs to the sleeping quarters alone and lit only one torch to light his home. I wish I knew why Salarn had chosen to live alone. *What had he hoped to find in these woods?*

Kar offered his hand to Unbetum and helped him to his feet. The father and son, like Guardians of the same age, stood to attention, awaiting Salarn's direction. The whispered questions of children were met by commands of silence by the women. Salarn looked at Unbetum and Kar waiting patiently in front of him and, as if lost for words, bowed his head. He then turned to those watching from the shadows and looked for me. I was the only woman old enough to be there the day Lan, my future husband at the time, duelled his father in the village circle. I knew, without needing to be asked, what was called for. I cleared my throat and took a moment to remember words sung long ago. All the women knew the words, but I was the only one who had sung them for intended purpose and now, quite possibly, the only one who would ever sing for intended purpose twice.

'The seeds sown and life brings
Father and son and unthinkable things
Laugh or cry, sing or die,
Today we will see nothing lie
What we tell is though the father fell, all ends well.

Night will come and the song will end
To what was started the child will tend

Life with meaning
Time and reason
Stems slouch under the weight of seed
The younger steps in the elder's lead.'

My grandson, Parbi, who had only been born prior to the last harvest and was still finding his voice, listened in awe of the combined sound of the women's voices. When the song was over, he clapped his hands and bobbed on his haunches. I bent down to hug him like my daughter through marriage would have if not already caring for another. As Fankisi looked longingly at my embrace of Parbi, her arm was lifted. Naten walked from her side and out into the inner circle. Kar looked from Salarn's praising eyes in time to see Naten approach but he did not know how to react. She planted a wet kiss on his cheek and, pushing his hair aside, whispered something into his ear before returning quickly to the shadows.

Unbetum was shocked by her uncustomary advance and did not know whether to question his son or, for that matter, where even to look for consolation.

Salarn's laugh unsettled the awaiting Guardians even more. With his arms spread wide and welcoming, Salarn clutched at air until Unbetum and Kar were close. 'Everything is different now, my friends, my family,' Salarn said to the father and son in his brace. 'I no longer mourn the change.' Stepping back from Unbetum and Kar, Salarn addressed all. 'Too long has this tower been a sacred place. The woods can be our home so long as we respect its unspoken governance. As barley grows better in the unsheltered light of day, it is also so that a child will wake livelier to an open view of the horizon. Here in the woods, though, we can dig wells that will never dry and remain sheltered from the west until we are stronger. I want the tower and the trees that protect it to become a part of you all, and I want no question to go unanswered and no idea to be unvoiced. We are the Guardians of the East and time will not replace us.' Salarn walked back to his throne and adjusted his fur cloak as he sat down, satisfied that he had said all that was necessary. Everyone present was silent and so Salarn decided to expand upon his deliberation. He waved us forwards with both hands, 'Walk forwards into the light, with the confidence of the fair-haired girl, for the duel is over.'

The women and children stepped slowly forwards into the wavering torchlight and moved closer to his throne. Naten's approach was now the most cautious. She clutched to a fold in Fankisi's dress and shadowed her advance.

'Look upon this man before me,' Salarn proclaimed, eyeing out Kar. 'Today you watched him fight his own father. He looked like you last season,' said Salarn, allowing his words to echo as he now singled out Lagesh with a tilt of his beard. 'Yes, like you Lagesh, son of Gentuk, and as carefree as you, Cihnah, daughter of Janfas,' he continued. 'Kar was innocent and afraid of nothing that he had seen before. As far as I know little has changed. He still fears nothing he has seen, but he has been exposed now to many more of the evils we face in life. I wish to call an end to the days of walking into the unknown with lingering questions. Much was lost with the village but I believe something was gained. Change is a part of life and we live on because we also change. Let us always talk openly from this day forth. Right now, I feel like telling the children a story, though only if they want to hear one,' said Salarn, tapping his knee and calling the curious children forwards. 'It is a day to celebrate. Do you agree, Unbetum?'

'I agree,' replied Unbetum. He looked at Kar by his side and smiled.

Kar was almost as tall as his father but he had not yet filled out. Turn Kar sideways and he would fall between floorboards.

The children: Cihnah, Meera, Lagesh and Parbi, gathered at the foot of the throne on the thick, brown fur of an enormous animal that no longer walked the earth. The fur had travelled with the Guardians when Pardensai had led his people from the north. It felt coarse against exposed skin but its thickness made the centre of the gound floor as welcoming as a bed of grass. I noticed that parts of the fur had worn thin through a hundred seasons of footsteps and the occasional rapid movement of duelling Guardians. It saddened me that this sacred fur, the only reminder of the men and women who had led us to our home in the East, lay on the floor beneath our soiled feet instead of on the wall. Equally, it comforted me that Guardians slept and fought on this giant's back. Children now nestled at the neck of the beast and, where its head would have been, Salarn sat on a stone throne carved by my father and the men he called friends in his day.

'What story to tell?' Salarn pondered. He looked upon the faces of the children gathered and tapped his armrest. The children stared in awe as if already enthralled by the most entertaining story they had ever heard. 'Yes,' he finally exclaimed, 'the story of the spotted cat.'

For the first time since the children had gathered, there was movement on the floor. The children edged closer to the throne and got comfortable, ready for the beginning. Lagesh, who had relentlessly protested against being labelled a child amongst the surviving Guardians, discovered a benefit in his youth. Only four children would ever hear Salarn's story of the spotted cat, for he never told the same tale twice, at least not in the same way. I closed the arched doors to the tower and headed to where the women, Fankisi, Naten and Yisben, were seated outside on the grass.

The grass was almost waist high when we had arrived at the tower, but twelve horses had reduced it to ankle height. Four horses still grazed freely in the space between the tower and the circling woods, and only paces from where we sat the soil had been turned and barley seeds sowed. It was peaceful here. For a brief while, routine had returned to the Guardian way of life. The morning scout rides and the occasional short journey, several times to Hidalu and once north into Barbarian Lands, had been re-established. And now, once more, a long journey became the combined trial of Guardian men and women. The men encountered the unknown as the women tried their best to hold onto the known.

13

The Thin Branch

Scribed by Kar. The Tree. Balih Woods.

The sun was high above the woods in a clear sky. We sat on a dried log from a collapsed pine. Partly shadowed by the first layer of pines, it was a perfect position to sit and watch happenings at the stable, at the tower door, or east of the tower where the women now sat in a small circle. 'I am sorry for striking you in our first duel,' I said to my father.

He touched his neck where a wound I had inflicted had opened again, 'Do not say that, Kar. Today, you gave the people a chance to celebrate change.'

'Only because you were injured going into the duel.'

'True, only because I was injured,' he said with a forced grin. 'Still, a duel is a duel.'

'What we tell is that the father fell,' I sung.

'Stop,' he complained. 'Don't hear me wrong. I agree with the words of the song. The last time I heard it sung, I was not even as old as you and everyone enjoyed it apart from one man. Seeves, took it to heart.'

'Old man Seeves?'

'Yes, Arman's father did not like the words, even though, Raujime, Lan's father, did not feel shamed. Raujime was noble in defeat. It was only Seeves that heard the words of the verse as disrespectful to the elders. He told the tribal council, Verian, Hulan and Salarn, that only a song that celebrated both father and son was appropriate for such an occasion and that the words, as they were sung, incited an end.'

'I did not take the words to mean an end. I enjoy hearing the women sing.'

'So you should,' agreed Unbetum. 'I often thought of their songs when away from the village. I remembered your mother's voice and thought of you both. I imagined her singing to you.'

I dipped my head. 'She often sung to me.'

'If you were alone today, where would you go that would make you happy?'

I looked excitedly at my father. 'Maybe you have been there before,' I whispered.

He looked intrigued, 'Where?'

'To the tree.'

He looked in the direction of my distant stare. 'The tree where you hide your fighting sticks?'

'No, further, deeper in the woods,' I replied. 'Beyond my playground.'

His eyes widened. 'Will you show me?'

I looked at my father's injuries and worried that he would tire on the journey. 'We would have to ride fast to make it back before dark.'

'Then let us not delay.'

***

Deep in the woods, north of the tower, I unbridled my stallion so that it might graze freely in the lush grass.

My father walked past me with his eyes squinted as they adjusted to the light. 'This tree is long dead.'

'No, it is not dead,' I corrected him. 'If it were, the other trees would have filled this gap by now.'

He watched the horses graze beneath its leafless, ash-coloured branches. As lush as the pickings that surrounded the tower, grass circled the tree and ended neatly twenty paces from the trunk at the dense woods that shadowed further growth.

'Did Salarn show you this place?'

'I sighted it from the roof of the tower.'

'It's amazing,' he said, unable to close his mouth. 'What type of tree is it?'

'Can I show you something?' I asked, walking closer to the tree. I placed my palm on the tree's trunk and smiled. 'It is warm.'

'It gets full sun.'

'It's always warm and look at how the woods surround it in a perfect circle like they know not to encroach. This is a special tree.'

He placed his hand on the tree next to mine and shook his head in disbelief.

I watched with anticipation as my father's expression of disbelief morphed into a sense of contentment. I remembered what it felt like the first time I had touched the tree. It had taken me an entire morning to find it after spotting the clearing from the tower. I remembered how excited I was when I first noticed the light piercing through the branches of the trees ahead of me. When I saw what made the clearing possible, I had taken a step back. The tree was unlike any other. Its trunk was heavily gnarled and, unlike the pines, its barkless flesh was smooth to the touch. There was not a single leaf on any of its branches that spread outwards and upwards like the skeleton of a fire, yet I felt certain that it was alive.

My father withdrew his hand from the trunk and looked up, closing his eyes to the blinding light that found its way, unshielded, to this rare opening in the wood's canopy.

'What are you thinking, father?'

'I cannot make sense of it, Kar. What did Salarn say when he visited you?'

I had not told him that Salarn often visited the tree and delivered wet clay tablets. I assumed that my father must have been aware of arrivals and departures from the tower because of his regular position at the tower door. If he had read my tablet that detailed my first journey west, he would have known of the tree prior to this visit. 'I have never spoken to Salarn about the tree,' I answered. 'Salarn visited me often but we never spoke about the tree.'

'Maybe we should speak with him soon. I would like to know more.' He rested his hand on my shoulder and we walked away towards our grazing horses.

As I reached for my stallion, my father stopped walking and turned back to face the tree.

'Did you hear that?'

I took a moment to listen before placing the bridle back on my stallion's snout.

My father glanced up through the seemingly dead branches as he retraced his steps. 'It sounded like ...'

He stopped and looked down at his feet. 'Like a falling branch.' He smiled nervously as he lifted an unsual branch from the grass. It was almost perfectly straight and as long as he was tall. 'Was this here before?' he questioned himself. 'This could not have fallen from that tree.' He stopped talking. He looked at me waiting with the horses ready. Glancing upwards again, he studied the leafless branches that swayed gently and silently in a breeze sweeping across the wood's canopy. Tilting his head, he inspected the dark-red colour of the branch in his hands and admired its weight by balancing it on his palm. He tested its strength and flex by leaning on it like it were a walking stick. He decided to take it with him.

14

The Third Night

Scribed by Lan, The Desert Mapper.
Traders' camp, Nineveh.

Beneath a half moon and sea of stars the Guardians rode towards the Harmin village, led by the young Harmin, Boroe. Next to the charred remains of a watch shelter overlooking the oasis, the men steadied their horses on the rise. The last time I was here, this was the place where I was greeted and where I waited for a Harmin to run word to Samor, alerting him of my arrival. No one greeted us this eve. From a hut near the centre of the village, spears of light stretched out the door, roof and a small window from the only fire burning. One hundred huts surrounded this larger hut and sat quiet in the moonlight. Boroe handed his reins to Gentuk and I handed my reins to Tahnas. The Guardians rode the horses down to the water as Boroe and I walked towards the only fire burning.

Outside his hut, Samor stared east towards our approach from the darkness. 'I am not hallucinating this eve. I recognise the sound of your step.'

Boroe ran ahead and embraced his father. 'I am

sorry it took me so long to return. I feared the mountain bandits and making another desert crossing alone.'

'You returned. That is all that matters.'

'I have not returned alone.'

Samor looked over his son's shoulder and nodded at my approach.

'The rest of our small party will be here soon,' I told him.

'Welcome, Lan. It is good to see another old Guardian face.'

Tahnas, Gentuk and Arman would stay at the oasis until the horses filled their bellies. It had been a fast ride to the Harmin village. We did not glimpse even a single bandit in our passage through the mountains and emerged from the northern route in time to watch the sun setting in the west. I took the lead on the second morning and we rode northwest from the mountains to a secret desert shelter. There was room for the horses in the wide-mouthed cave that only a sandstorm from the south could breach. We rested during high sun and, determined to make good pace, set out again at dusk. The harvest moon lit the path to our next camp, a natural shelter formed in the bite of two sprawling plateaus. Although our route was not direct, the horses thanked us as we made the final leg to the Harmin Village, facing away from the rapidly waning sun and its trickery of light.

***

The horses filled the Harmin's stable that night. Side by side they would keep each other warm. Samor had almost finished repairing the roof and, as if expecting company, had kept all the troughs filled.

'Remember what I told you on our approach,' I said to my son as we left the stable.

Tahnas nodded and signalled me to walk ahead with Arman and Gentuk.

The Guardians entered the hut and found room to store our wrapped furs before finding rest near the fire.

Samor watched us settle. His eyes were wide as if he were still unable to fathom our presence. He spoke quickly about days wasted in the desert, long nights and suddenly finding Boroe walking in the darkness. '... I knew his step even in the night. You must know, Guardians, that Harmins walk differently. As people of the desert, we have learnt to move like sand. Our steps are not heard by the sleeping lizards or the–'

'How is Kardeen faring?' Tahnas interrupted, sooner than I had expected.

I'd made him aware of Samor's fondness for sharing the origin tales of the Harmins and his tendency to weave one tale into the next and talk all night and day if allowed. 'Kar's recount had me fearing the worst, though he still looks strong,' I said in support of my son's interruption, 'maybe ready to travel again.'

Kardeen raised his head slightly and Boroe shifted closer to his father so that Kardeen could see my face and the faces of other Guardians seated around his fire. 'I tried to tell them not to worry about me,' said Kardeen. 'If there are Harmins still out there, then they are the ones that need help.' His face was stern and, unlike Samor, he did not reveal any appreciation for the arrival of the Guardians or Boroe's return. 'You cannot tell that old man anything,' he said of Salarn.

'Do not concern yourself. We did not come back to see you,' laughed Arman, and he managed to get a brief smirk from the stone-faced man.

Gentuk got to his feet and walked to Kardeen's side. He gently placed his hand on the injured man's shoulder and knelt to inspect his wounds, the most severe being a gouge down his back between his shoulders. 'They cut you deep,' said Gentuk. 'What were you doing turning your back on a blade?'

'You are a strange breed,' said Kardeen. 'Salarn must be pressed to talk and you hold nothing back. I do not know which is worse.'

'Then tell us which is better?' said Arman.

The men laughed and Kardeen smiled, just for a moment.

Gentuk unwrapped his fur and searched his stores for some salt to boil before he re-found his place next to the fire.

'I can laugh now and it does not hurt as much,' explained Kardeen. 'I am feeling better. Give my thanks to Salarn for the smoking herb.'

'And mine,' said Samor, as he looked at the changed faces of men who had all, apart from Tahnas, visited his home on trading expeditions of the past.

'It will be a while before we see Salarn again,' I informed Samor and Kardeen, remembering, as I spoke, my wife's assertion that Tahnas and I must return as soon as possible. 'Do you plan to stay here?'

Samor had begun to relax in the men's company, but my question seemed to re-kindle uncertain thoughts. He looked at Kardeen, through the wafting smoke, and then at Boroe who once more sat next to him by the fire. Maybe they were the only Harmins left. Even if there were others out there, could the village once again be their home? Possibly due to his indecision, Samor turned the question back on me.

'Where do you go, Lan?' he asked. Turning to face the other Guardians, he continued, 'Why have you come here? Boroe could have travelled with the accompaniment of one Guardian.'

As I pondered Samor's questions, Arman sat up and chuckled at his own private joke. Aided by Gentuk's shoulder, he propped himself onto his feet and stretched like he was preparing to turn in for the night. He looked over the men's heads to the clutter of items stacked to the roof, filling the rest of the hut.

'Tell me, Harmins,' he said, 'where are you hiding that smoking herb of which you have been boasting.'

Tahnas rocked backwards and held his stomach as he laughed.

'He asks a fair question,' Boroe told his father.

***

Samor and Kardeen heard the news they had long waited for as a pipe was passed from hand to hand around the fire.

Gentuk stood when he had something to share. 'The Guardians are no longer welcome in Borujerd either. Tahnas was the last. All entrances to the city are now manned by Akkadian soldiers,' Gentuk told the Chief in a sombre voice, his eyes drawn to the low flames of the fire. 'They recruit any able-bodied man who presents himself at the gates, and no one enters without fit purpose. So, when the trader, Senea, and I arrived, I made a simple decision. Senea and the trader carried on the journey alone and I remained in Borujerd.'

'They saw you as able-bodied did they?' mocked Kardeen. 'Maybe I should go to Borujerd.'

'I made my decision to stay before a more compromising decision was even presented. Senea entered the city by guise as the trader's son. As ruthless and as stubborn as we may see the Akkadian's rule to be, trade is still a necessity, and they deemed the supposed father-and-son traders fit to enter. I returned to the farmers' camp on the outskirts.'

'Where do you think they are now?' Samor asked Gentuk.

'All going well, they should have reached Rapikum on the west bank of the Euphrates. But that is a contradiction in itself, for the longer you travel with Delari, the more worth you carry or seek to exchange elsewhere.'

'Indeed. He is a ruthless trader,' commented Arman. 'My wife, Gods bless her soul, never forgave me for being gone so long.'

'Have you had the pleasure of meeting him?' Gentuk asked the Chief as he sat again.

'Delari? No, I have not met this trader,' replied Samor. 'He must have realised how demanding I can be when the goods are laid out.'

'Or he does not like the desert,' said Arman. 'Twice I have tried to convince him to travel this way. He has the final say.'

The men's spirits were high in the moment but Senea was completing his first journey alone, and the last word Gentuk had heard of his wife's whereabouts were based on Unbetum's vague account of what he had witnessed before he was dragged north in shackles. Arman, Samor and Kardeen knew their wives were dead. Arman buried his wife's almost unidentifiable body along with many others where the village once stood, and the Harmins' wives burnt in a fire they built above the oasis. An uncomfortable silence filled the hut and, once again, Arman filled the void.

'Where are all the succulent details, Gentuk?' Arman questioned, slapping his friend's head playfully from behind. 'As informative as your account may be for our desert friends, if they fall asleep, it will be pointless. I will tell you about Borujerd,' he announced. 'The city did not change overnight. Trading is the whole point. Forget protecting what you already own. If what you trade does not gain the right offer, then you should have stayed at home. The cloth Delari carried had been paid for with three swords and ten silver shekels. Only in Borujerd or between the rivers could you fetch its true worth. Finely woven and fit for a king, Delari offloaded it for a more generous offer of twenty shekels and an afternoon of beer and chicken paid for by a happy buyer. Once cut and sewn, our host for the afternoon was sure to make the largest return ...'

Arman was known as The Always Travelling Guardian because he had only visited the Guardian village twice after he started travelling with the trader, Delari. The last time he returned, soon before the village was sacked, he shared many stories in the village circle. The story he shared tonight at the Harmin's fire was a story I needed to hear. We were only three days into the journey and already I felt weary. I was thinking that I should be back at the tower with my wife and Jamine would have agreed. Arman's tale reinvigorated our purpose. It began with unsettling, hot winds blowing through the streets of Borujerd. I knew the city well and could imagine the mudbrick construction of the square buildings that spread in all directions from the high walls of the inner city. Arman counted himself as a blessed man on this day, for he had been given the opportunity to retire early to the comforts of shade, good food and much appreciated beer. Arman was also confident that the quick trade ensured early rest that evening. Arman and Delari departed from the drinking hut, not needing dinner and talking freely. He led the horses with a trailing arm and, forgetting the seven potent mugs of beer he had consumed, tried to speak and act like a Guardian. 'Just look now,' he said wishfully, realising as the words left his mouth that, with the silver they carried, so many an offering was attainable.

It was late afternoon, and the unspoken promise of a bargain piqued Delari's interest. Who would it be today that had to leave tomorrow without the goods they owned? A trader looking to lighten their load might be prepared to offload it for half the usual asking price. It did not take Delari long to spot something of value. 'Arman,' he called out over the bustle of the inner-city markets.

The Guardian kept walking and hoped this would lure Delari away from the market stalls in an effort to keep up. The ploy did not work. Arman eventually stopped and backtracked to where the trader had entered the palace markets once more. By the time he had caught up, an exchange had already been made. Delari stood smiling next to an entire boar carcass, ready to be cooked. Arman stilled himself at a near distance, signaling that he did not want to play his part.

'Hope you still have an appetite,' said Delari, and Arman could only laugh. Delari stuck to his act until the Guardian's laughter died to a concerned sigh. 'For our friends in the camp,' the trader explained.

Delari and Arman walked towards their camp, leading their horses and watching the people prepare for dinner on the outskirts of the city. Everything was cast in an orange haze as the sun settled behind the desert ravines. Other traders with loaded horses also headed towards the outskirts, each admiring what the others carried. The only people out of place at this time of day were the Borujerdian soldiers and their leader. The leader's blue cape, attached to bronze armour, caught the remaining light and exaggerated their presence to all.

'They are a long way from the city,' commented Arman. 'Not a good time of day for them.'

'I am curious to know why?'

'When are you not curious, Delari? Let us keep moving.'

Arman and Delari kept walking as they observed the Borujerdian soldiers' behaviour. What was most concerning was that the five men were palace guards and not regular Borujerdian soldiers. Happenings beyond the inner city did not normally concern them, let alone require them to address it personally.

The head guard had cornered a lady carrying a pot of water, and friends of hers had gathered but held their distance under the watchful eye of the four guards still mounted. The frightened lady, who had been singled out, put down her pot of water and told the head guard what he wanted to hear. She pointed to a hut nearby and the head guard swished his blue cape to one side and offered her a piece of silver from a heavy pouch that weighed his belt down on one side. The lady shook her head to his offering. When she bent down to pick up her pot of water, the piece of silver landed in the dirt beside her.

The head guard climbed on to his waiting steed and led his comrades to the hut the woman had identified. Their confident advance was soon disrupted. In front of the hut, they saw Delari and Arman arrive and, behind the guards, followed a trail of irritated farming folk.

The boar required both of them to lift it to the ground. Once placed, Arman and Delari took a moment to admire it, ignoring the guards that flanked them. Delari walked inside the hut and Arman turned and looked up at the guards. The Guardian acted intrigued as he studied the men's faces and noted that the guards, who still held a view back towards the city, were growing anxious. The head guard glared at Arman, seeking acknowledgement. The Guardian did not give him the satisfaction but instead became transfixed by the snot bubbling in the nostrils of the closest steed. Delari walked out from inside the hut and broke the silence.

'No one home,' said the trader to Arman, glancing only briefly at the guards like they were ordinary bystanders.

The head guard could not handle being ignored

any longer. 'Maken the Farmer, father of Naten.'

Arman and Delari looked at each other questioningly. 'Yes,' they both replied.

'You, one of you, sold your daughter to a court official and she has abandoned his service and fled the palace.'

'Good for her,' mumbled Delari as he drew his attention back to the boar.

One of the horses shuffled forwards and the guard pointed his spear at the trader.

Taking a defensive stance, only short of drawing his sword, Delari questioned the guard with his eyes.

'You have misunderstood,' intervened Arman, talking to the head guard. 'Neither of us are the father of Naten. You mentioned his name and, when we said yes, we were simply acknowledging that we heard what you said, you being a guard of regal service and all.'

'Do not play games with me. I am ...'

'You are a long way from home and it is getting dark,' Arman promptly reminded him.

The guard closest to Delari withdrew his spear and looked back towards the palace that was a distant silhouette, almost unreal. The inhabitants of the city outskirts had abandoned their dinner preparations and they closed in on the guards like an innocent, though troubling, threat. Many were not long in from the fields and still carried hoes, sickles and shovels.

'Defstan,' shouted the head guard, and his four companions, though reluctant, turned and aimed their spears defensively at the encroaching crowd. 'We only want to take the girl home,' continued the guard in the blue cape. 'We have been told that her parents may know of her whereabouts. If you are not the father, then why do you settle at his hut?'

Delari pointed to the hut and screwed his face up as if the answer was obvious. 'Because here there is a fireplace and shelter, and when I am finished cooking this boar, I know I will be tired.'

'Then you know Maken and you put your life at risk for him,' spoke the head guard, nervously glancing at the people nearby holding tools not classed as weapons, but just as dangerous. 'Not even the girl will be hurt, for she is wanted back at the palace. Why do you not cooperate?'

'Because we cannot,' answered Arman, with a raised voice. 'We cannot help you, yet you are still here.'

The head guard grew infuriated. He was searching for words to express his purpose in a way that these seemingly ignorant men would understand when a new voice caught his attention.

'I am Maken,' announced a thin man—all muscle and bone—stepping forward from the crowd. He wore a sleeveless, faded yellow tunic that was stained from the waist down with dirt and dried blood. His hair and beard were almost the same colour as his soiled yellow tunic and his skin was dark from working in the sun.

Two guards turned their spears on him and he walked cautiously between them towards the head guard in front of his hut. He looked more concerned than fearful of their presence. Behind him, at the front of the crowd of farmers, a pale-faced woman hobbled closer, with a young boy wrapped to her leg and sobbing profusely. Women nearby tried to comfort her as she watched her husband stand before the mounted guards.

The head guard drew his sword, a slender bronze weapon with an elaborately crafted hilt that covered his knuckles at the front and turned on his steed to address the man. 'This has escalated out of control, Maken the Farmer. Why did you have these men do your bidding?'

Maken looked beyond the head guard to the Guardian and trader, also held at spear point. 'I do not know these men,' said Maken. 'I am told you are looking for my daughter. I have not seen her since last harvest when I sold her to you.'

'You have not seen her you say.' The head guard dug his heel into his steed and it turned abruptly, almost trampling Maken. 'What about your wife? Your boy?'

'They have not seen her either,' protested Maken, attempting to block the head guard's advance with his skinny, muscular arms held out wide.

'It is against the law to harbour criminals and until this matter is resolved you, your wife and your child shall accompany us back to the palace. 'Shackle them,' shouted the head guard, as he continued to advance past Maken towards the farmer's wife and child. It was not long before he realised that he was advancing alone.

'No one is going anywhere,' declared Arman.

The head guard was startled and turned to face the Guardian now standing at his side. 'You came for a girl who is not here. Your business is over. I suggest you look elsewhere.'

The head guard looked back at those he had arrived with—boys dressed as men in the uniforms of soldiers. They were still in front of Maken's hut where Delari had begun building a fire undisturbed. Their spears were pointed upwards.

'Defstan,' he shouted, and he watched his guards uneasily ignore his command. They looked at each other and back towards the city in silent agreement of where they wanted to be. As the crowd continued to edge closer, they held their spears close and upright.

'We are here on order of the King and you are all breaching the law and his governance of these lands,' bellowed the head guard as he danced his steed in a tight circle.

'Borujerd has no king,' shouted an unidentifiable man from the crowd.

'He talks of Vanekebek,' laughed another unknown man from the sea of faces.

Arman took hold of the reins to the head guard's steed and spoke into the tip of the bronze sword tickling his nose. 'Know that when you talk to the people, they listen for acknowledgement and turn a deaf ear to forced governance. Stand down. Talk to us on the same level and you will receive all the answers you seek.'

The head guard shifted his blade to the side of Arman's face and looked at him, though not into his eyes. 'Who are you?'

Arman followed the guard's queer gaze to his shoulder and answered, 'I am a friend, unless you see me as an enemy.'

'Do you know Fankisi?' the guard asked, spellbound by the mostly blue tattoo that adorned the

Guardian's shoulder.

Arman frowned. 'Fankisi? What has she to do with this?'

'That is what I want to know,' said the head guard, still brandishing his sword, though no longer using it to have his questions answered.

'Stand down,' Arman repeated to the head guard. Looking towards the farmer and his family he continued, 'Join us for dinner at your home, Maken. We can settle this dispute without violence.'

Seeing that the other guards had already dismounted, their leader resigned himself to Arman's offer and did as Arman had instructed.

A young man about Senea's age, seeing the danger removed, left the crowd and ran to Arman's side. He walked forwards next to the Guardian he admired, smiling up at him.

'Fitsbin, my young friend, can you do me a favour?'

'Anything, Arman,' he replied enthusiastically.

'Tell your father where we are. Let him know that dinner is on offer here later tonight, if he does not already have something prepared.'

Fitsbin's father was the friendly face Guardians sought when they arrived in Borujerd. Arman met him on his first journey, accompanied by Gentuk, and had stayed with him every other time a trader led him back to the city. On this trip alone, he had been in and out of Borujerd five times with Delari. Tahnas was absent the whole time. Even if he were present in the city, Tahnas's duties would have kept him occupied far too close to the palace to warrant any personal exchange with an independent trader like Delari. Tahnas was forging a larger relationship with the governor of Borujerd that he believed would create new trade opportunities. He imagined traders travelling with his escort, and them welcoming the protection and procured agreements of trade for their goods. In his dreams for a better life for future Guardians, like my grandson Parbi, Tahnas forgot for a while that men like to feel in control and that, for the simple folk, choice of when and where to travel is a treasured freedom. Even before Sargon's rule crossed mountains and sacked cities, a fear of authority and status amongst men was born. Man always had the choice to shelter beneath kingship, run away or remain indifferent or defiant. And many chose the more difficult life. Delari, influenced by the varied customs and governance of all the places he frequented, chose indifference, and Arman, who had now spent more time trading than in the company of his wife and the other Guardians, also accepted that one's boundaries are forever changing and called himself subject to none.

Delari welcomed the guards to take a seat on the logs surrounding his unlit fire. 'It is amazing how many men will fight for one girl,' he pondered aloud. 'Would you all agree?' he asked, catching the eye of one of the guards in particular.

'Yes,' replied the guard, nodding awkwardly and longer than was necessary.

Delari tipped his finger in the guard's direction, 'You were the one who pointed his spear at me,' he recalled. 'I like you. You should take off your helmet when a meal is being prepared.'

The guard looked around for his commander and,

seeing that he was distracted, he was quick to oblige. His fingers were trembling as he fumbled with the chinstrap. When he had removed his helmet, he did not know what to do next.

'Place it on the ground, friend, and take a seat at my fire,' instructed Delari.

'It is Borujerdian bronze. It will take half a morning to re-polish,' whined the guard, looking at the others for support.

Delari pointed at the other three guards and directed them with a wiggling finger to take a seat as well. 'They are going to do the same,' he told the first guard he had addressed.

The seasoned trader worked a fire lighting stick back and forth in a wooden gouge and watched patiently as the nervous guards fidgeted with their chinstraps and played with their breastplates in an effort to delay joining him by the fire. The first guard he had spoken to eventually sat down and placed his helmet on the log next to him. Delari found this amusing. 'How many harvests have you lived through, soldier?' he asked, with a smile. 'I would bet no more than twelve.'

'This will be my fourteenth harvest,' replied the young guard, thankful that the others were joining him.

'Fourteen,' exclaimed Delari as the fire began to spark. 'Your parents must worry for your safety when you dress each morn for duty.'

'My father was also a palace guard. When I am older, the "duty" you speak of will take me to the end of the earth and I will fight glorious battles for the true king, Sargon the Great.'

Delari frowned at the other young guards as they seated themselves by the fireplace. He could not think how to reply to the young guard's comment and so he just carried on with lighting the fire. First, fastening his long hair behind his neck with a thin strip of leather, Delari lent closer to the smouldering kindling and began arranging smaller cuts of wood around a growing flame.

Arman watched the circling crowd part as Fitsbin sprinted towards them. 'Right through the middle,' he rejoiced. 'There's so much life in that boy. You would never believe that he has been ploughing the fields since sunrise.' He turned to face the man walking by his side. Arman had forgotten for a moment that it was the lead palace guard and was surprised to meet a friendly face. He smiled back at the changed man and addressed him as a friend. 'Fitsbin knows he will get a piece of silver for a simple errand. It is his enthusiasm that entertains me. He would make a good Guardian.'

The head guard nodded like he knew what a Guardian was and looked more closely at Arman's tattoo as the Guardian walked next to him. Arman was a foot taller than him and this gave the guard a nice view of the shoulder tattoo that depicted a lone boat in a raging sea. The head palace guard was about to ask about its meaning when another voice distracted him to the point that he was about to draw his sword. Arman's hand beat him to the sheath and the guard immediately surrendered his grip.

'I want to thank you,' said Maken from behind the men. He had walked behind the head guard's steed up until now, after telling his wife and young boy to stay with the other farmers. Arman signalled that it was the palace guard who should be thanked and Maken dropped to his knees ready to kiss the guard's hand.

'That is not necessary,' declared the head guard, with his arms held back. 'My name is Izad, and this eve I have witnessed something not taught. The building of an unconquerable empire requires farmers and soldiers to meet like this. We have quarrelled but now we sit as friends.' He looked up at Arman like a boy wanting to hear praise.

'Let the man kiss your hand,' joked Arman as he sat down in front of Maken's hut, next to one of the other guards.

Izad kept his hands busy and tied his steed to a post. He smiled at an already distracted Arman and was still smiling when he caught Maken's eye as the farmer ushered his family home. It was not a derisive smile but a joyous one. The head guard, with eyes out near his ears, liked Arman, just like he had enjoyed Tahnas's company before he had left for Agade. He was envious of these men with tattoos on their shoulders. They went on adventures that scared him and came back smiling. And then there was Tahnas's wife—beautiful beyond words and she would never be his. Now, however, he had what he wanted, a reason for them to respect him. He could save Maken's life and protect Fankisi.

Izad's wide placed eyes moved towards his nose until I realised I was looking at Arman. Delari's fire in the farmers' camp became Samor's fire. I straightened my back and looked about, reconnecting with my placement in the Harmin Village.

'... And the rest is Tahnas's story,' finished Arman.

'It is not my story to tell,' objected Tahnas. 'I just stumbled in at the end.'

'And not a day too soon,' added Gentuk.

'It is Fankisi's story, and everything after is Boroe's to tell.' Tahnas humbly explained. 'All I can tell you about is my arrival and departure from Borujerd on the same day. That story alone would see us through till morning.'

'Then do not start. I return your favour and will interrupt you there,' said Samor, glancing around and smiling at some very tired looking men. 'Kardeen's already asleep. I have smoked too much. When do you plan to leave?'

'Never is too much,' said Arman, welcoming another pull of the pipe.

'With an offer to stay, we would like to leave by light of full moon tomorrow eve,' I replied.

Samor lowered his head as a sign of respect. 'I have rebuilt more of the huts. There is plenty of room for you all to sleep. I will go hunting tomorrow and we shall eat well.'

'Welcome news,' I said. 'I, like you, Chief, appreciate time by the fire.'

'In answer to your first question, Lan,' said Samor, 'I plan to stay. Alone until the end, if that be the way.'

Arman nodded at Samor's spot near the fire, 'I would too, Chief.'

15

The Family in the Sky

Scribed by Unbetum, Salarn's study,
The Tower.

On the night of my eleventh harvest, Verian led me back to the tower.

'We could make this journey blindfolded,' he told me as our mares trotted slowly through the darkness of the woods. 'They know the way better than me now. When I was living at the tower, I often visited the village at night. Any strange noise or light, or a bad dream, beckoned me to investigate. I did not like living so far from my people. Salarn is different. Unlike me, he has found a strange peace in the woods. He has found the peace that I could not find even with my wife, Mardias, your mother and Arcobon to keep me company.'

When we reached the clearing surrounding the tower, we were guided to the door by an unattended flaming torch. Verian took the torch from its holder and led me inside and up the winding stone steps to a solid wooden door that blocked further progress.

'Not many Guardians have been past this door,

Unbetum. Salarn has invited you to see what lies beyond. He was saddened that your father was not alive for your special day.' Verian handed me the torch and opened the door.

I followed him inside and moved the torch around in my arm to view the room. The wooden floor stretched to the tower's stone wall. It was empty apart from four support posts and a wooden ladder near the centre that led upwards to a trapdoor. I wondered if my father had been here before he died in his sleep during the previous harvest. He was not well after he returned from the south. It is told that he rescued four children from a burning hut and breathed too much smoke. That is the story now tattooed on my shoulder.

'Your mother once asked me if Salarn had a secret family living here,' said Verian. 'Many stories are told and retold. I like stories, but what you see tonight must remain a secret. Do you know what a secret is, Unbetum?'

I nodded and Verian observed me for a while before he climbed the ladder. After he opened the trapdoor, I reached upwards mid-climb and handed him the torch. He stepped through the trapdoor and the light disappeared. For a moment all was dark. Then I saw new light.

'Your father helped build this tower, Unbetum,' said Salarn as I stepped onto the wooden roof of the tower. 'Every villager alive at the time, apart from me, helped build this tower. I was away from the village on my first journey. It was a long journey.'

I had been told not to talk during the tattoo ceremony and had not received permission to talk again. This moment, I felt, was the time. 'I can see a deer in the stars.'

Salarn stepped to my side and I pointed out its face. 'I see the slender face of your deer tonight,' he said. 'I, the Guardians and those before us have always called it the Bull.'

'The Bull,' I repeated.

'It is good that you see faces in the stars,' said Salarn. 'You can call them anything you like until you write about them. If you write that you travelled in the direction of the deer's snout, you will confuse those who know this group of stars as the Bull.'

'I am not one for writing,' I told Salarn.

Salarn huffed. 'You speak as if you know who you are, Unbetum.' He signalled me to lie down on the roof next to Verian. Salarn then planted the face of the torch in a deep stone bowl, near the ladder. He lay down next to me. The sky was bright with stars and he pointed to the Bull and across to a group he called the family. 'All Guardian men must write of their travels,' Salarn told me. 'Maybe you'll write after you make a significant journey or have a child. What I don't understand is why you will be the last to write. That concerns me.'

Verian sat up abruptly and gripped his brother's shoulder with one hand.

'Rest, Verian, I just want Unbetum to know that no matter how fast or long his stride may be, there is no end in sight other than that conceived by the mind. I don't want him to endlessly search like me for something that is not offered to man.'

'Is that the secret?' I asked.

'No,' said Salarn, 'the secret is above us. Above

us is a map to the Guardian tower by the stars. The Guardians have drawn many maps of our homeland and none of these reveal the location of the tower. I want the map I share with you to never be etched to clay. We must never reveal the location of the tower. Just as the gods led my father, Pardensai, to our home in the plains, they also led him to this place in the woods.' Salarn took my hand in his and held it upright. 'Look at the family in the stars. They circle the tower with the sword arm of the mother or father always pointing to this rooftop.'

'She is pointing at me.'

'Yes, she is, Unbetum. It is her turn to point.'

***

Fourteen harvests later, the family of stars still circled the tower. Salarn, Kar and I lay down on the flat wooden roof and, like he had on the night of my eleventh harvest, Salarn used the stars to guide his storytelling. It became a regular evening event for Salarn, Kar and I. The sky was becoming familiar to Kar, and Salarn liked to test my son's knowledge. One night, after Salarn had shared his story of a journey to the Deep Sea to gather salt, Kar pointed to stars that would lead him south to the desert peninsula, beyond Uruk. Salarn then shared his journey across the Great Sea and explained how his life in the unknown far west ended with a call to return home.

Kar, like me, found Salarn's voice soothing and we would lie on the verge of sleep. Every word was remembered in this state of waking dream and Kar thought Salarn's tales to be strangely familiar, almost as if he had been present when the events took place. When

Salarn told him it was time to bring his latest story home, Kar agreed and vowed to finish it the next day.

'Find meaning in our travels north into barbarian lands,' said Salarn, 'and then open yourself whole of heart to an unknown world. Words will not answer your questions but they may inspire you to partake in a quest that will.'

Kar wished me quiet rest when I left the roof and descended the ladder to the top floor. He was surprised when I emerged again through the trapdoor a few moments later. I had to reach back down the ladder to re-gather something that I struggled to hold with my injured arm. When I stepped onto the roof, in view of Salarn and Kar, I revealed a new weapon.

Kar got to his knees and leaned forwards for a closer view.

A soft leather sheath was fastened neatly to the top end. I untied the knot that fastened the sheath and folded it down, tying it to a natural groove in the wood beneath the blade. 'This was my only addition,' I explained. 'The staff was heavier at one end but now it is balanced. The blade is bronze but the wood ...' I ran my finger down the staff, 'the strange wood is stronger.'

Salarn still lay with his head propped on a rolled-up fur. He watched as the staff exchanged hands and then diverted his gaze to the sky beyond.

There was something special about this weapon and one did not need to touch it to know. The wood was a dark red and as smooth as a stone shaped in a fast-flowing stream. 'Let it become familiar,' I said to Kar. 'It is a weapon fit for a god and I had little to do with that.'

Kar examined the staff thoroughly. He tried to flex it in his hands, but it had no give. He traced his finger along its smooth body and felt the sharpness of its pointed, double-sided blade. With it laid across his hand, he studied its balance. 'May I?' he asked, gesturing that he would like to swing the staff.

'Play freely. I regret not telling you sooner that it is yours. I made it for you.'

Kar wore the same look I did after touching the tree. It was like he weighed nothing and was only held to the roof by the weight of the staff.

'I wanted to make you a weapon fit for an accomplished Guardian, one that would be heavy in your hands at first but grow ever lighter until it becomes an extension of your arm. Then you showed me the tree and that,' I said, looking at the strange staff, 'that found me.'

I lay down where Kar had been and watched my son cross the roof to the other side of the trapdoor admiring his new weapon. Kar twirled the staff with elegance to the backdrop of a star making its way across the sky. He was not swinging it like a weapon. He was manoeuvring it like he could feel the wind on its face as it sliced the air. He brought it to rest and allowed it time to level. Every so often he would draw it to his chest and stand to unseen attention. When he looked back at Salarn and I, I think he thought we were watching him.

'Do you see it?' I questioned Salarn, breaking his perplexed gaze. 'A star does not fly.'

'I do not know where it came from or where it is

going,' Salarn replied. 'But it is not falling, and I have never seen one fly this long before.'

Salarn looked concerned. His eyes were tracking the star's southward movement. He sat up a little and propped himself on his elbows. He glanced sideways at me in the process and smiled. 'It is amazing,' he exclaimed, shaking his head like he could say nothing else but did anyway. 'It is a gift that we share.'

Kar stopped swinging the staff and looked upon the star trailing its light through the sky. He smiled and walked back towards us. 'Thank you, father. I am going to sleep now. If my new staff is next to me in the morning then I will know this was not a dream.'

'Sleep well, Kar,' I blessed.

'Do not hurry to wake,' Salarn called after him and Kar looked back up from the trapdoor. 'The staff will serve no purpose without you.'

Kar smiled at Salarn and me before climbing down the ladder and closing the trapdoor behind.

Salarn and I watched the star vanish into the southern skies. Even after it had disappeared, we continued to stare. 'I know the branch was not from the tree,' I said, still looking south.

Salarn turned to face me and I felt him studying my battered face.

'I do not know where it came from,' I continued. 'I know it is strong and I know he will fight with it.' I turned to face Salarn. 'Put my mind at rest. The tree, the staff and I, why do I feel like I am trapped in the dark? I feel that everything that has happened seems destined, yet I have discovered no reason.'

Salarn smiled at me and looked back to the stars. 'I

was hoping you were going to ask where the staff came from,' said Salarn, his voice tiring with each word. 'I would have preferred you asked a hundred questions rather than saving up for this one. Kar is also good at that.'

'I know much of the story,' I admitted. 'I know you are Kinsufa's father. Jamine writes that you met my wife's mother in a distant land, when you crossed the Great Sea to an island and wanted to stay. I know that you share my deep sorrow for her loss. I know that you visit the tree that Kar showed me. I know you did not bother me as I forged a blade for the staff. I know all this and ask, why me? What else can I do?'

Salarn pondered my difficult question. 'You also touched the tree, so I will speak openly. It is not an ordinary tree. Her roots grow as deep as the underworld. When she called my father, Pardensai, into the woods, it was all part of a larger plan. All will be different for you now, Unbetum,' said Salarn. 'If you knew too soon you would be gone too soon. Knowledge can give you power or be your greatest weakness. The desire of boundless knowledge can give you the courage to walk to the end of the earth or infest your mind with unanswerable questions. Kar needed you and you needed him and the tree needs you both,' answered Salarn and he knew immediately that I had not heard enough. He looked deep into my eyes in search of my true question of ponder. 'I found the staff first,' he continued, turning his gaze to the peaks of the Zagros Mountains, a faint resemblance of the massive barrier lit by the half moon. 'I pulled it from the Karun River. It had slept long enough and so have you, Unbetum. See your experience at the tree as a fitting reward, for you already had a deep understanding of life. The tree speaks to us and it is in a very old language.'

'A language of the gods,' I said, surprised and excited by my own words.

'Yes, the tree has ghostly white limbs yet she, the tree, is not a portal between life and death. She is that colour because she is dying. The tree is old and has lived through seasons of fire and ice. Now, on her deathbed, she is reaching out to us, hoping that one of us or all of us can act as a god in her place. She revealed this all to you in an instant and with time it may make more or less sense.'

'The tree did not speak to me,' I told Salarn, clenching my eyes to battle my confusion. 'You refer to the tree as a she, yet she bears no fruit or even leaves.'

'She did once. Before she spoke to Pardensai she was taller than the pines that protect her sanctuary. Her leaves were as large as a man's face and they glowed a miraculous green like the slippery slime that coats water coursed stones in the depths of the valley.'

'And her fruit?' I asked, 'did you ever see her fruit?'

'Her fruit ...' Salarn sighed and closed his eyes to the thought. 'Her fruit will never bring life because she stayed too long. She stayed when Anu left and now she is old and barren. Like you, she grows bitter, lamenting on loss.'

I smirked at his comparison. It hurt me to smile because it put pressure on the swelling around my eye and cheek. 'You saw her fruit?'

'I saw it rot faster than fish in the sun.' Salarn rested his head back and pushed his curly, long hair free of his face. He looked at me like he was about to share the most important detail of all but then paused, his face contorted, as if he had forgotten all thought.

I pointed to Salarn's tattoo and silently reminded him that he was the storyteller to a seated crowd.

Salarn inhaled a deep breath of the night's chilled air and cleared his throat before speaking. 'Kar is the one to see the tree's plan through to fruition. His tattoo shares with him your strength. He has eleven lives in battle, one for each of the arrows you wore when you risked your life to save one girl. The Guardians were almost cut from time by Sargon's assault. It was not our end because we have a purpose to fulfil. For greater reason than the protection of our home and people, our quest must be aligned with Mother Ki's. Before I left for Bit-Bunakki with Kar, I struggled to believe that you were still alive, somewhere. When I drove my blade into Otoug's heart, I thought of the tree. I also thought of Kinsufa, the mother of your wife by the same name, and realised that the strongest force that connects us all is our mortality. You have defied death many times, Unbetum, and I look at your scars the same way I look at the gnarled trunk of the tree of life. The tree is Mother Ki and she speaks with me. She is sharing the last of her life with us so that we might do what she cannot and rid this world of a god with foul purpose. Gods and man were not meant to live together, and it was only the Mother God that stayed with good intentions.'

'You told me on my eleventh harvest that I'd be the last to write.'

'I did, Unbetum, and I still know of things I don't understand. I still speak at great length and tell stories about everything except what I want to talk about.'

I stared at Salarn, replaying every word that left the old man's hair-covered lips. Salarn's voice was different but so was everything. Never before had I seen a star fly across the sky and never before had I witnessed anything like the presence of the strange tree. I still felt its warmth and it had been ten days since I had touched its trunk.

'Even with all knowledge there is a lesson to be learnt,' said Salarn.

'I hear what you are saying. That does not make it any easier. For the last few days, I have kept to myself, forging a blade and just looking at the staff. Everybody talks too quickly, apart from you and Kar, and things I do not want to know hauntingly seek my acknowledgement.' I stopped talking and sighed at the mother figure in the stars, pointing back at me. I breathed deeply and tried to still myself, but it was like a hundred voices kept talking. Turning to face Salarn, I shook my head. 'I am up and down, Salarn,' I continued. 'I think of bad things and good things like they are all rolled together. It keeps me awake and I do not feel that I need to sleep. And I keep seeing her face, like she has something to do with this, though it is not the Kinsufa I know.'

'She is the Kinsufa I knew long before you met your wife of the same name. She is Kar's grandmother,' said Salarn.

'Kinsufa is your daughter. Verian is your brother and Mardias, my mother, is his daughter. That means that I married my aunt. I married your daughter.'

'It happened for a reason I'm still trying to understand. Kinsufa was as beautiful as her daughter who shared her name. If I had done the correct thing and brought her home with me, everything may have been different. She might have been the only other who needed counsel with the tree. I hated my choice, yet I made it anyway.'

I stood and held my palm towards Salarn. I was afraid that one more word from him would confuse everything I had just learnt. 'You told me that there is no end to the world and that the location of the tower must be kept secret. Of all the great secrets you could have revealed to me on my eleventh harvest, you chose–'

'I was compelled to leave her in the middle of the night. The village called me through my father's silent voice and I left her in the far west without saying goodbye.' A single tear welled and spilled from Salarn's eye and he swatted it like it was a fly on his cheek. 'I still think I did the right thing. I questioned my decision for so long, waiting for a sign that it was right. To abandon the only woman I have truly loved to play my part in the Guardians' emergence was not a strong enough reason. How could it be that I felt compelled to leave her so suddenly and why was it that, when she later called for me, I heard nothing? All the knowledge in the world could not save us. If I had never touched that tree, I may have never met her, though if I had not touched that tree and had met her, then I would have surely married Kinsufa and brought her home with me to the village, despite her father's protest. When I abandoned her by returning to Zidon, I did not know that new life of us both was growing inside her. She never gave up hope of finding me again until she died in childbirth.' Salarn closed his eyes and shook his head slowly from side to side with discontent. 'Your stiff palm to my words is warranted.'

I lowered my raised palm to my side and gazed at the stars above. 'You found the staff because, in your continued search for understanding, you tested everything that you already knew. That is why you return time and time again to the Karun. My son also knew of the tree because of you and Kinsufa being his mother. Kar says that he saw the tree from here on the roof of the tower, yet I wonder what led his eyes to see it as anything more than just another clearing in the woods. He knew something already, just like you heard the call to return home.'

Salarn opened his eyes and watched me process the thousand thoughts clogging my once open mind. Since the night he had followed his father Pardensai into the woods, Salarn had tried to keep what had happened a secret. Our elder enjoyed nothing more than sharing a good tale, but this one was different. He had scribed it on a tablet as he mourned the loss of his beloved and then left it to dry like it was any other tale in the dark confines of his study in the tower. There was no precise lesson to be learnt from the retelling of this story, only opinion on something that would forever be judged. It was why he enjoyed solitude and quietly hoped that another would discover greater meaning in this ongoing quest before his last day, or be it last night, as the Guardian elder. I think he secretly liked that I was destined to be the last to write. 'I thank you Salarn for even attempting to answer my question. Your promise to the others, however, I still find concerning.'

Salarn opened his eyes. Though he did not turn to look at me, Salarn knew what I was saying and was unsure whether he needed to be defensive.

'Gone are the days of walking into the unknown. Let any question be heard. You said that to all the women and children. I have only told Jamine that Kar took me to a strange tree and I found a strange piece of wood. You speak of something greater. The tree, be it Mother Ki or not, is not advisable company for anyone not sure of mind.'

'What do you sense when in the company of the tree?' inquired Salarn.

'I am not sure.' I stared up at the stars again for comfort and, as I closed my eyes, everything grew brighter. I opened my eyes to avoid the brightness. 'Ever since Kar showed it to me, I have not thought in the same mind. My first thought was that the tree trapped a god.'

'Your first thought was right,' said Salarn. 'You know this.'

I looked at Salarn. His eyes were lit again like the stars above.

'The tree has trapped Mother Ki. She can knock on the door of the underworld with her roots, feel the earth through her trunk and talk with the world through her branches, yet she is defenceless against a god walking as a man. When I pray to Enki, her son, I feel like my words fall on deaf ears. Ki may very well be the last god standing.'

Still on my feet, I leant closer to Salarn, 'I am compelled to keep what we have spoken about secret, like you and Pardensai did before Kar discovered her. Part of me wishes I did not know.'

'Such knowledge is a burden that grows, Unbetum, and even though we both share it, it can never be easier to carry. It is why Kar does things differently. It is why you have cheated death so many times. It is why I abandoned Kinsufa against my will. I am not afraid of anything more than living a pre-destined life without understanding why. I may have an answer to your question, yet I feel selfish for even voicing personal opinion.'

'You must tell me, Salarn. My arms have been made weak yet a burden is something I could carry. I pointed at your shoulder before to remind you that you are a storyteller. If I could point at my tattoo, I would tell you that I am ready for my imposed duty. Just as my father risked his life to rescue children from a fire, I will do all I can to ensure the safety of the women and children who sleep beneath.'

Salarn began waving an outstretched arm in circular motion. 'When a god dies on Earth then their strength will remain and be shared with all. Could you administer such fate? I know I could not.'

I broke from staring at Salarn and sought refuge in the sky above. We were sharing the same thoughts now and it made me nervous.

Salarn sat up and bundled together the fur he had been lying on. He placed it next to my fur that was still spread. 'Whilst your thoughts are your own, make sense of them. The best way is to sleep where you are and avoid contact with others.'

I thanked him with a forced painful smile and asked one last question, 'Is it safe to visit the tree again?'

'Only if you want to know more,' Salarn replied and then descended the ladder, giving a delayed nod of assurance that he had answered correctly.

I stayed standing until Salarn had closed the trap-door behind. Then, faster than Salarn could have decended the ladder, I lay on my fur and stretched Salarn's fur over me for warmth. Where my arm and head were scarred, the chill penetrated to my bones. Of all my injuries, it was my heart that was the most broken. The loss of my wife, Kinsufa, had cut me deeper than any blade and it would never mend. I did not need it to, so long as it kept beating until my duty was complete. I had lived to complete what Salarn could not.

16

Return to Borujerd

*Scribed by Tahnas, Guardian of the West.
Traders' camp, Nineveh.*

By day I wandered the streets of Nineveh, visiting the many markets, drinking huts and trader camps. Of those I knew well, I would ask pointed questions about any sightings of Guardian women or children entering or leaving the city. I would ask strangers where I could find a slave who could scribe or weave cloth. My search for lost Guardians uncovered no new trails. I could not even confirm Delari's story of two women entering the King's Gate in Nineveh fourty days after our village was sacked. The King's Gate was ten times the height of a man, and both armoured soldiers and massive statues, shaped like bulls with wings and the head of a man, guarded the ramp that led to the gate. I recognised the head on the statues. The same head was stamped on the silver shekels crafted in Agade, the Akkadian capital.

When shadows in the city became long, I would return to the trader's camp where Delari and my fellow Guardians had chosen to stay for a while. Gentuk would often be waiting for my return, his face always hopeful, my face lowered until I had to share my regret. The only hope I could share was my belief that, if a slave survives to the next harvest, they are accustomed to living the new life. 'Belline is a survivor,' I would tell Gentuk. My repeated words soon felt pointless.

I changed my tactic for seeking information by gaining work at the Tigris River, offloading boats. Xemoth was the name of a boatman who travelled south as far as Agade and, each day I ventured to the wharves, I hoped I would encounter his boat ready for the offload. Gentuk continued to be the first Guardian I encountered upon my return to the traders' camp on the outskirts of Nineveh. We would walk back to Delari's tent near the centre of the camp and he would tell me of his day spent with Arman. They often met new traders arriving from the north and directed them to our camp if they had likeable offerings.

We would eat and share stories around our fire at night. Delari and Arman were not always present. They had begun a communal fire in the traders' camp. When they were away, my father would sleep and Gentuk would grind herbs or just stare at the fire. In the quiet, I thought of Fankisi. I pictured her combing her raven-coloured hair and turning to face me with her wanting eyes. My vision of her led me to write my first tablet and I knew it had to tell of the day I returned to Borujerd.

***

My journey from Borujerd to the King's capital, Agade, and back to Borujerd, had me gone for thirty-eight days. Knowing that Fankisi was heavily pregnant when

I departed, I felt a sense of guilt for thinking more about Lord Vanekebek and the future of Borujerdian trade. But if trade was to become my governance, then there was a lot to clarify before anyone less experienced set out for Agade, or even Nineveh, next harvest. The Akkadians had begun building a road north and I saw this as a caravan map that any bandit could follow. Then there was the matter of the grain from the south: twice as much seed from the same stem. These concerns weighed heavily on my mind, but what worried me more was the talk amongst the people of the west and the song the children sang. 'Goodbye to Elam,' was chorused like the motherland had already found its place in history.

The city folk spoke of Sargon's conquests in the East like he was a god and, no matter where the King was, he had a legion of disciples ready to sign any tablet or pay any amount of gold necessary for his kingdom to flourish. I anticipated that the exchange would be with the King himself and that I would be able to judge Sargon's motives personally, but the King was away visiting fellow gods according to his representatives in Agade. The exchange went ahead. I watched as the Borujerdian soldiers offloaded the bags of grain and I counted the Akkadian's gold before it was wrapped. The journey had been a success and my concerns were in earnest for, the moment I reached the first hut in the sprawl of small buildings surrounding the gates of Borujerd, everything changed. I saw my friend Gentuk and the matters of which I was about to be made aware required the most urgent attention.

The Guardian I had not seen since the day I departed the Guardian Village with my wife mounted his horse in the near distance and rode to my side.

'Fankisi has been in labour all afternoon,' informed Gentuk, seeing no time to say anything else first. 'She is at the palace birthing chamber. She seemed strong but she sent me away. She cries for you, Tahnas. She expected you home many days ago.'

'It will be a boy,' I yelled excitedly back at the men I led and those who heard my shout raised their fists in salute. 'I'm grateful, Gentuk. How long have you been waiting?'

'Too long to have this conversation now.'

I rode my stallion aside Gentuk's and we braced arms. Burdened by obligation, I made a difficult decision. 'We carry much gold. More than any Guardian has ever protected before. Can you see it safely to the inner-city gates?' I asked.

'I can do that. Find me after. We will be waiting on the road east.'

I circled my restless stallion to face my Guardian friend once more. 'We?' I questioned him.

'We will be waiting on the road home. Arman and Delari left for the village ten days ago and, yesterday, I found Fankisi with the help of a palace guard. You have a girl and there is another child on the way.'

'Twins?'

Gentuk shook his head. 'There is much to talk about. Sargon's army is here. A battalion arrived this morn from the Desert City. A larger force is heading east through the mountains as we speak. Sargon's soldiers even share the Borujerdian barracks. Go to Fankisi and then find me on the road home.'

My stallion kicked up dust as I tightened and loosened his reins, unsure whether I should ride on. This was not a decision to be made lightly. It was my duty to see that the cargo of gold and seeds arrived safely. It was against all custom to abandon my post so close to the gates, yet my wife was most important to me and to hear that she was crying my name made everything else subordinate. I had placed faith in Gentuk completing my mission until I had learnt of the Akkadian presence. 'Were they welcomed into the city?' I questioned him.

'They do not need to steal your gold, Tahnas. The Akkadians came prepared to stay and the army that headed east could already be approaching the village. We must talk later.'

'Do you know for sure that is where they were heading? Who ...'

A Borujerdian soldier approached from the caravan to see what the hold up was and I confirmed my decision.

'Esstire, this is Gentuk,' I said, introducing the soldier to my friend. 'He is a Guardian like me and will see you safely to the palace. I will ride on ahead and check the route. Thank you for sharing the journey with me. Move fast.' I nodded at Gentuk and waited for Esstire to relay the message to the caravan before riding ahead.

The Borujerdian farmers stopped working and stared in from the fields as I galloped wide of the huts towards the city gates. The guards in the watchtowers were alerted to my approach and a horn was sounded announcing that the caravan had returned. Past the city markets I rode as the populated laneway cleared in advance.

'Guards,' I called to an idle group of soldiers ahead. I slowed my stallion to a trot and waited for them to approach. The first soldiers I had spotted were Akkadian. Seemingly off duty, they milled near the magic shows at the city limits and watched the street theatre like the rich travellers of Tyre. Even the Borujerdian soldiers looked far from observant. One, however, seeing the blue crescent emblem pinned to my shoulder fur, realised that I was a representative of Vanekebek and suddenly became dutiful. He left the others and hurried to my side.

'The caravan from Agade has arrived. Keep the lane clear.'

'Clear the way,' yelled the soldier, waking his comrades to action.

I rode on. The palace gates were open and the guards assembled on both sides stood to attention as I stilled my stallion for a moment to notify them of the arrival of the caravan. They were already aware and so I made pace for the birthing hut that was adjacent the washroom in the far northern corner of the palace grounds. An old woman with wrinkles deep enough to hold a shekel saw me approach and, bent with age, she shuffled as fast as she could back inside. Birthing helpers accrue wisdom and experience each time they welcome a new life to the world. I was comforted that, from her apparent age, my wife was in reliable hands. I slid from my mount and rested my head against my stallion's side. Silently, I thanked him for the ride and asked him to wait. I unfastened my belt and used it to hang my sword on his saddle. Bare foot, wearing only a leather skirt and my shoulder fur, I removed and flicked Vanekebek's blue crescent brooch into the flowerbed that lined the path at the entrance to the room. I entered the birthing hut unarmed and as a servant to no man.

She reefed on her sheets until she was lying on the ground. With her bedding crumpled around her shoulders, she cried my name. 'Tahnas, hurry.' The birthing helpers told her to push harder. She pulled me close and I leaned over her, holding myself upright with my spare arm. Her clenched fingers dug into my back and side. She buried her screams in the nook of my neck. I bore her digging fingers like it was our sweetest embrace. I felt the hotness of her breath as she exhaled rapidly, and I waited as her hold on me tightened and then loosened.

Fankisi screamed and her scream was followed by the high-pitched scream of another.

17

The Gods' Truth

Scribed by Jamine, The Dressmaker,
The Tower. Balih Woods.

There was no routine to the scout rides. Unbetum and Kar rode in the morning, late in the day or, if the moon provided, the light of night. It depended upon their last discussion and Unbetum's health after their previous ride. Despite all their knowledge, they had forgotten that sound echos down and floorboards stop sight not sound. I heard many of the words shared on the tower's roof and I understood one thing for sure: change, greater than men not riding out at the same time, was coming.

Together, Unbetum and Kar explored the lands east of the mountains and always returned with a new story. There were too many stories to scribe. They spoke of places graced by hidden beauty and strange creatures, like the bird with wings spanning the length of a man and brown-furred animals with short snouts, twice the size of the deer that tracked the water. Salarn would tell his own stories whilst Unbetum and Kar were away, dwelling on happenings long before the West came to conquer the East. As I counted the days since the other Guardian men had departed for the West, Salarn spent increasingly more time seated on his stone chair. More time in the chair meant more time to share stories and it was not long before I chose to stop sewing a dress and put my hands to scribing a new tablet.

'Pardensai carved the words of the gods and the faces of forgotten creatures into this chair,' he told me. 'The voice of one god still repeats in my ear. Her voice silenced my father and she will silence me too one day.'

'What did she say to you,' I asked.

He chuckled and patted my head like I were a dutiful dog by his side.

I was not offended for I had chosen my seat and he welcomed my company like his brother Verian had in the village. 'Did she tell you a joke?'

'Do you know what seperates man from the gods?' he asked me. He looked across the fur towards the door.

'Our mortality.'

'I thought so once, Jamine.' He looked down at me, his eyes pained. 'Our difference is not so divine. The separation is our understanding. Understanding separates boys from men and men from gods. If you understand what a god does and are able to tell another this truth, then man becomes a god and a god must protect the truth.'

'I understand … I mean, say no more.' Salarn prided himself on telling a good story, but I did not want to push him to share this supposed truth. I was quite happy for nothing to change apart from the growth of my crop.

It looked as if he never left the throne but, every so

often, he was startled by the sound of a child's laughter or Fankisi reaching his side before he was aware of her approach, and our elder would speak of where he had been. A place on Earth where the sea is shallow and waves lap tirelessly on the shore. A place where daggers are worn like jewellery and men farm the fields for only half a day before returning to their loved ones. At home, their women paint beautiful pictures and shape delicate clay vases to hold the flowers their children pick. A land without a king and a people unburdened. Like the mysterious tree that Kar and Unbetum frequented, Salarn held these people sacred and prayed that they would never be discovered. Any stranger who set foot in that place would find what most men seek, but new men would turn what did not need turning, and fashion a new home. New men would ask questions like, 'Where is your King' and, when the people are distracted pointing to the sky, begin building city walls and place a man on the throne.

'It is the truth, even if it has not happened yet,' he told me.

I looked up at Salarn from my stool next to his throne. 'How can you know what has not yet happened?' I asked.

'Nothing can last forever without changing. Even Mother Ki and Father Anu will one day share my fate of silence before rebirth. Life is ongoing but men and gods are just vessels shaping its course towards the inevitable fate of change. All this being true, denying that the voice of a god has been deceiving me, there is something I must share. There are other lands out there that, in a comparable way to my sacred city of Pled, are not destined to be saved.'

I studied Salarn's face and followed his eyes to the tower door. Looking back at him, I noticed his head twitching like an unseen fly bothered him.

He looked at me. His eyes were now cold.

Looking about the room, I made eye contact with Fankisi, The Curious. Nearby, Yisbin sat on the giant's fur with her daughters in front. She plaited her eldest daughter's hair whilst Cihnah braided Meera's. 'Hurry to the throne,' I called out and the Guardian women and children stopped what they were doing and quickly gathered.

Salarn watched the women and children settle in front of him and for a while he did not move or speak.

Fankisi approached the throne, nursing Parbi, and placed a hand on his knee.

He gasped for air and his body convulsed.

Yisben and her daughters screamed.

Lagesh reefed open the tower's door and rushed inside.

With one hand gripping the armrest tightly, Salarn raised his other and brushed his tangled, white hair away from his face and stared at Fankisi. 'Take a seat, my child,' he told her. 'I need to talk to you all.'

'Can I get you some water?' she asked.

'Water,' he chuckled, and then coughed as he choked on his own saliva. 'I will have plenty of that where I am going. Before I go, I must tell you all where I have been. Like my father before me I have had the honour and ...' Salarn paused and took a moment to control his uneasy breathing. He looked at Fankisi and I, standing either side of his throne, and then at Yisbin and the children gathered on the giant's fur. 'I have had the honour and misfortune of meeting gods. Enki the Pattern Maker and Enlil the God of Air can still answer your prayers and this is because they have life in us all. Many of you seated before me will even outlive the Mother God, Ki. You, my Guardian children, are survivors and I need you to prepare for the reason you survived. The whole world, not just the East, needs Guardians more than ever.' Salarn's sword arm began twitching and he pressed it still in his lap with his other. 'My father was summoned to this land to fulfil a noble role in the game of gods. He wanted us to be a different kind of people and my brother, Verian, saw that happen. For a while, we lived as a godless people and I blame myself for letting them back into your lives. I strongly believed in Enki after returning from Pled. I believed in him because I saw his presence in the people I met. Please do not misunderstand me. I would dare not tell you that there are no gods. The message I want and need to share is simply that there is only one god on this earth who has not succumbed to the pleasures of man. Only Mother Ki kept her true form. There are, and always will be, many half-gods and gods born to new bodies and, whilst our Mother God, Ki, is still with us, we must do all we can to rid the world of those who would use their power to corrupt the balance required for life. Man-gods are mortal like Guardians. Guardians, thankfully, are also blessed with the strength of their fathers. Guardians can make a difference if they align their fight with Ki over a king. I have shared the word of ...' Salarn collapsed back in his throne and released the arm he had held still in his lap.

I leant close with my ear to his mouth.

'Regretfully,' he mumbled. His arm started twitching again and then his whole body contorted, stiffened and then slumped.

Fankisi pulled on his beard to wake him. Salarn's eyes were open but his body limp and unresponsive after his sudden convulsion.

'I know you see me,' she screamed. 'Talk to me or I will tell the end of your story.'

Salarn grabbed her wrist without shifting his gaze.

Fankisi kissed his cheeks gently and then held Parbi forwards like he might want to nurse him. 'I know you. I know you can talk,' she said as she tried to straighten Salarn's head. Fankisi allowed Salarn's head to rest. His eyes stared blankly at the floor. 'You had not finished,' she said, trying to look into his downcast eyes. 'Salarn, talk to me,' she screamed and reached once more for his head.

'Fankisi, let him be,' I said and tried to take Parbi from her grasp.

'He has always finished his stories.'

'He is just resting. Let him rest.' I went to lead her away but she resisted.

She stared mournfully at Salarn like he had died, but there was still life in the old man. He was just somewhere else and only he could tell us where.

18

A Princess of the East and West

*Scribed by Jamine, the Dressmaker.
The Tower. Balih Woods*

Life at the tower changed again after Salarn stopped talking. Unbetum resumed guard duty. He sat each morn on the stool my son had placed for him and he spent his nights alone in Salarn's study, with the door barely ajar. Kar embarked on scout rides alone and was often away from the tower until the moon lit the sky. I'm sure he visited the tree that Salarn had mentioned. The men, without Salarn, still sometimes conversed on the roof of the tower at night.

It had not rained since the other men left and so I had Gentuk's youngest, Lagesh, dig a new well on the eastern side of the tower, near the crop. Naten, the pale-skinned Borujerdian girl, volunteered her assistance. They seemed to work well together. I often heard laughter on my approach to check on their progress. I think they felt the reward of hard work with good company.

Naten's tunic, which she borrowed from Fankisi, grew more soiled each day. It hung past her knees and the neck hole was almost as wide as her shoulders. I'm not sure how she managed to get coated in so much dirt. Lagesh, who climbed into the well, would clean himself with the wipe of a dry cloth. Every part of Naten's exposed body was a different colour when she finished working each day. She looked like a white deer with brown legs when I asked her to kneel behind the stable. I had to help her bathe. She had either forgotten or never learnt how to clean herself without immersion in water.

Fankisi kept a close watch on Salarn whilst we ate at the table, looking for a smile or any other sign he was still listening.

'How was your scout ride this morn?' I asked Kar as I broke bread for Parbi.

'Interesting,' answered Kar, 'I set a boar trap, north of the mountain pass in the foothills. A bandit may end up fetching its reward and that was part of my reason.'

'You think they are that close?' I asked. 'Lan told me before he left that the bandits might have moved south to feed off the new Akkadian trade coming through Elam.'

'Some might have moved on. Others are still close. I keep seeing the same two. I think Salarn may have known them.'

'He does,' said Unbetum, answering for our elder. 'It is a shame he cannot tell us more.'

'Yes, it is, Salarn,' added Fankisi, prompting Salarn to talk.

'Where do you go after the ride?' I asked Kar and it seemed the answer to my question was of interest to all. Even Fankisi took a moment to ignore Salarn and focus her attention upon Kar.

'I visit a quiet place in the woods ...' Kar stopped talking and looked across at his father.

'You heard that?' asked Unbetum and Kar nodded. Reaching behind his stool, Unbetum lifted his long sword and strapped it to his back. He paced towards the tower door and Kar joined him, wielding his bladed staff.

The women and children sat silent at the table as I followed the men as far as Salarn's throne.

'They will be at the door soon,' Unbetum said to Kar. 'Make a run for the woods and divert their attention from the tower. I will guard the entrance.'

Kar agreed to his father's plan without question. They had heard movement outside and, if it was an enemy, we could be trapped in the tower. Unbetum reefed the door open and Kar disappeared into the darkness outside. He closed the door and slid the bolt.

At the table, Cihnah whispered something to her younger sister, Meera. When they looked up, they were met by a disapproving glare from the end of the table. Fankisi was eyeballing anyone who even swallowed too loudly and, when Yisbin leant down to admonish her children, she too broke the unspoken rule. Yisbin caught her children's eyes and gestured towards the door, conveying the importance of silence. Cihnah directed her mother to look at Fankisi and Yisbin also received a disapproving glare. Meera, the youngest girl, turned bright red before snorting accidentally and making her sister and Lagesh laugh. Fankisi turned back to face Salarn for comfort and was shocked to detect a slight smile creasing his face. She turned to face us in disbelief and, noticing what she had seen, I stared at our elder with bemused wonder.

There was a loud knock at the door. The sound echoed up the hollow tower and Yisbin screamed.

'Who is there?' demanded Unbetum.

'Kar.'

Unbetum unlatched the viewing window and looked out. 'Who is that with you?' he asked.

'You do not know her,' said a familiar voice outside.

Out of sight with no torches lit, Unbetum allowed the person to remain a mystery as he unbolted the door. 'A Guardian returns,' he announced.

The young Guardian's hair was cut short at his ears and around his neck, like his father's, and, for the first time in his life, he had grown a beard. His beard was patchy and not thick enough to hide his still boyish face and teeth-filled smile.

Lagesh knocked his stool over as he sprung from the table and ran to greet his brother.

Senea knelt to meet his brother's running hug front on. They collided and Senea lifted him in the air like he weighed nothing.

'You did it,' praised Lagesh. 'My brother is a true Guardian.'

'We are all true Guardians, Lagesh. I have just been on one more journey than you.' Senea turned back to face Unbetum and gestured at his bandaged arm.

Unbetum pointed at his face and showed Senea a

heartfelt, though contorted, smile.

'They still talk about you out there,' said Senea. 'In Ebla, farming men asked of the Guardian who fought three axe-wielding barbarians with a tiny sword. I told them it was your throwing blade and that you always carry two.'

The women and children were now standing each side of the table but, as if still captivated by Salarn's smile, they were silent and stayed close to him.

Senea introduced a young woman to his brother. She was tall with long sand-coloured hair. They hugged and she said something that made Lagesh slink away with shyness.

Kar stepped inside and closed the door behind. Unbetum whispered something to Senea and he looked past me, beyond the throne, before he found his companion's hand and led her further inside. Senea paused next to me and I shook my head whilst I smiled at the young woman he led. Salarn was waiting, I signalled, waving him on and stepping back. Walking wide of the table, Senea nodded at the women and children.

Jauntily, Salarn twisted his head to the side and looked at the boy he had met only once on the day he inscribed his tattoo.

Senea kissed his elder's forehead and then introduced Salarn to his companion. 'It is good to see you all,' he said, reaching down and taking his companion's hand in his. 'I bring good news from the West but, first, I would like to share with you hope in another form. This beautiful woman by my side is Yanereu. We met in Ebla, but she is from an island in the Great Sea. It was our fate to meet for she was in search of the

Guardians.' Senea stopped to listen to Yanereu as she spoke in foreign words that he seemed to understand as she repeated them. 'She believes we are gods,' he explained, 'Like the one her father's father used to speak of before–'

'Janke,' stammered Salarn, making Fankisi drop her cup as she turned to see his lips move.

'Yes, Janke,' responded Yanereu with heavy accent. She stepped from Senea's side and lifted Salarn's shoulder fur to see his tattoo. '*Un besquit,*' she announced to all.

'Janke is her grandfather,' explained Senea. 'She tells us that she knows Salarn. It is him.'

Grabbing Senea's arm, she shook it with excitement. She then raised Salarn's hand and kissed it gently. '*Un besquit vern sepp Taman.*'

'She is thankful to see this man she knows,' translated Senea.

Salarn's head was still locked where it had turned to face Senea, though now he smiled at Yanereu and she smiled back at him.

Kar carried some more stools to the table from beyond the stone arches. He placed them near Salarn at the head of the table and the others shuffled to create more space. Once all were seated, Unbetum cut meat for the new arrivals and Yisbin filled their plates with bread and boiled root.

As Senea and Yanereu ate they exchanged glances and smiles with the inquisitive young girls who were polite enough to ask questions about Senea's return through their mother. When Senea had finished eating, he turned to face Kar at the far end of the table, closest the door.

'You are almost my size now. I have heard of your journey north and I am not feeling confident in facing you in a duel with real weapons.'

'Your concerns are justified,' said Unbetum, who was seated opposite Senea. Unbetum showed Senea the wound Kar had inflicted on the side of his neck. 'Neither size nor age will govern a duel's outcome.'

'Tired hands will,' said Senea. He faced Salarn as he stood at the table. 'The men have made it safely to Nineveh. They have many friends there and they have been welcomed to stay in a traders' camp on the northern side of the city. I too felt it my duty to stay but, following the counsel of my fellow Guardians, I was instructed to return home. I was with them for two nights before the decision was made and it was not a Guardian who finally convinced me of this course. The trader, Delari, speaks like a Guardian. He has set up a stall in the traders' camp and my father and Arman guide traders arriving on the northern road to this camp. By day, Tahnas continues the search for those lost to the West.' Senea turned to face Unbetum. 'My father, Gentuk, wanted you to know that they heard word of two eastern princesses entering the King's Gate in Nineveh, in shackles, close to forty days after our village was sacked.'

Unbetum dipped his head as if the news had come too late. He was unable to look back up at Senea and did his best to leave the table unnoticed.

Yisbin pushed Cihnah's head straight and the young girl was about to complain when she realized Yanereu was watching her from across the table. Every day Cihnah would plait her hair differently and ask for different pictures to be painted on her cheek or brow. The young woman seated opposite her tonight wore her hair straight and untied. Cihnah's silver bracelets reflected light yet Yanereu's stringed shells looked fragile and unpolished. Cihnah stared in awe at the mysterious young woman seated opposite.

'I have asked Yanereu to be my wife,' announced Senea. 'She, above all else, gives my life meaning. In my travels, I have prayed to the gods and I believe they bid me well. In my time spent with Yanereu, I have been taught to think like a child and, in doing so, have remembered forgotten lessons. I have been humbled in my travels and rewarded in my return.' Senea stood and offered his hand to Yanereu. Speaking in a language that, apart from Yanereu, only Salarn could possibly understand, Senea proposed his vows. '*Yanereu, en tan mu sem veure lest, mu senene tu pout. Shun besquit vern sepp palege. Un tan sepp palege.*'

Yanereu stood and replied, '*Un vern sepp palage.*' She placed her fingers to Senea's lips as he tried to correct his mispronunciations.

Meera pulled on her sister's arm. 'What are they saying?'

'Listen,' said Cihnah, shaking her sister's arm loose and forcibly placing it on the table away from her as if it were an inanimate object. Her look of irritation quickly turned to one of admiration as she stared at Yanereu.

Meera resorted to pulling at her older sister's dress as Senea and Yanereu continued to speak in a foreign tongue. The young girl could not distract Cihnah or anyone else seated at the table. It had been a long time since any Guardian had been wed and, for Lagesh and

Cihnah and all those younger, it was to be the first marriage they had ever witnessed. If the Guardian women had had their way, we would have taken a few days to plan the ceremony and allowed time for me to finish the wedding gown I had been cutting and sewing at my own pace in anticipation of such a day. We were not given a chance and, in view of the beautiful, strange words now being shared and the confidence and unbridled happiness of the young couple, we accepted the simplistic beauty of the unceremonious union. We watched without objection. I passed Parbi to Fankisi and she nursed him on her lap.

Yanereu untied her laced, shell necklace and slid loose the stone ring it held. She placed the ring in Senea's palm and said more strange words.

Parbi laughed and so did I. His little body wriggled with glee in Fankisi's arms and she hugged him tight.

Yanereu cupped Senea's palm around the stone and rested her hand on top. Senea then offered his other hand to her and she removed a silver ring from his middle finger. She held it in her palm and he placed his hand on top.

'*Mehn sepp palage. Un Taman, tome vern sepp palage.*' he said and turned to face Salarn without moving his hands.

The old man's head was contorted but his eyes had nevertheless found a way to look at Senea. Salarn smiled with his eyes. His mouth did not move.

As the young couple faced the table, desperately needing someone to bless their union, Unbetum returned.

Stepping from the gloom of the arches, where he had retreated to gather himself, he placed his palms down on top of Senea's and Yanereu's and spoke in our tongue. 'Bless this man and woman with happiness, children and long lives. May you grow old together never wanting more. I speak for Salarn as no one has before me when I say that this union of a Guardian of the East and a Princess of Pled is of what the gods' dream and, even if our elder were still sharing words, he would find himself short of ways to express his delight tonight. We say prayers of thanks for your safe return Senea and we welcome Yanereu as a Princess of the West and now of the East. Be as one, my friends, forever.' Unbetum closed his hands around theirs and said a silent prayer with his head lowered before releasing. He kissed them both and then stepped back to stand next to Salarn.

The wed couple thanked Unbetum and they both approached Salarn at the end of the table and kissed his hand. Yanereu then slid the silver ring onto her necklace and I stood quickly to help her tie it in place around her neck.

Senea put on the stone ring and wriggled his finger until it was secure. He glanced at Unbetum for approval before he embraced his new wife.

As Unbetum watched on, Salarn reached out and fumbled to find his hand. Unbetum squeezed it tight and leant forwards to face his elder. They smiled at each other. When Unbetum looked up, his smile faded quickly, like it was not an honest smile he had shared.

Senea raised Yanereu's hand with his own and those at the table applauded. 'You have been most understanding despite our unannounced arrival. Please forgive us for wishing to retire early. We have been riding since first light and for many days.'

The woman and children did not delay in standing and approaching the mysterious woman with whom their fellow Guardian had returned. Fankisi kissed Yanereu and gently touched the silver ring now hanging in her bosom. Cihnah stood behind Yanereu, stroking the strange woman's long-hanging hair, and Fankisi's curious smile disturbed her not as she invited her sister to feel it as well. Yanereu turned and kissed Cihnah and then spoke gently to Meera in words the young girl understood.

'You are beautiful. I see the moon in your eyes,' she said, making the young girl giggle.

Senea spoke to his brother, Lagesh, as Yisbin introduced herself to Yanereu.

Behind them, Fankisi squeezed Salarn's hand as he squeezed Unbetum's and she asked, 'Why do you men hide so much? Do you mean to protect us?'

Neither man answered. Fankisi followed Unbetum's focused gaze to the far end of the table, where Kar sat.

Kar watched us greeting the new couple with his head tilted back and a content, almost dreamy smile owning his face. Next to him, Naten slouched with her head rested against his arm. Kar glanced down at her and, as if she sensed his eyes upon her, she looked up at him. Kar nudged her aside. Naten responded by sitting upright and pretending she was only interested in Senea and his new bride. Kar then placed his hand on hers and this time, when they looked at each other, something deeper than a smile was exchanged.

They looked at each other the same way they had on the morning the men departed the tower for the west. *Maybe I should complete sewing a wedding gown.*

Senea locked elbows with Yanereu and led her away from the children who continued to touch her like she was a tamed, exotic animal. The couple stopped next to Kar and Naten at the other end of the table and Yanereu stared at the young woman like she had found someone else she was looking for. Kar and Naten were the only two who had not rushed to greet the new couple, and now they stood to greet and congratulate them properly. The only two women who let their hair hang free of plait, tie or ribbon kissed and held eye contact as their lips parted.

'My name is Naten and this is my friend, Kar,' said Naten, unsure whether Yanereu would understand.

Glancing at Senea before he addressed Yanereu, Kar said, 'Salarn told me about the land of Pled. I would like to hear more.'

Senea looked between Kar and Yanereu and waited to see if she understood.

'Naten. Kar.' She bowed her head and spread her palms. 'Pled, like Guardian home is beautiful place. It is ...' Yanereu turned to Senea for his help in explaining.

'I think we should talk tomorrow,' he said. '*An gamahn toppe.* It is a long story.'

Yanereu kissed Kar and Naten once more before she reached for her man's hand.

Senea's hands reached for Kar's shoulders at the same time and drew him close, recklessly leaving Ya-nereu's hand a chance to hover idly. 'Tomorrow, when we duel,' said Senea, 'I will not fear for you but please go easy on me. I now know that I am not a fighter. You, by your namesake, are a warrior born and bred.'

'Tomorrow will simply be another lesson for me, Senea, and I will do only what I think is right.'

'You speak differently, Kar, as I imagined you would.'

'And you are still a little bigger than me because you have not been gone too long.'

Senea scruffed Kar's hair and shoved him away playfully. They were of similar height, but Senea had the width of a man.

'Are you ready to rest now,' I asked Senea.

He looked at me by his side and then past Kar at Yanereu and Naten standing together.

Yanereu nodded respectfully at the still intrigued Guardians as she and Naten stood before the gaze of all. Their pale skin and bright unfastened hair made them look like sisters. Both young women were adopting new lives with the Guardians and they shared a look that reminded me of Kinsufa. Unbetum's wife, Kinsufa, had a glow to her face that told all she was safe and in connection with that too often unattainable thing in life that so many unknowingly searched for every day of their existence. At peace with herself, awakened to things to come and safe in the company of friends, she always looked unburdened. Naten and Yanereu also looked unburdened and at peace in our home in the east.

19

A Broken Man

Scribed by Arman, The Always Travelling Guardian. Traders' camp, Nineveh

Twenty-four days after we departed from the tower in the east, we arrived in Nineveh. We had only stayed in Khorsabad for more than one night, always travelling fast towards the great rivers in the belief that the loved ones we sought would not have been sold as ordinary slaves in the outlying cities. In Nineveh, I was reunited with my trader friend, Delari. Gentuk rejoiced at the sight of his oldest boy. I think we all marvelled at the beauty of the woman Senea had met on his first journey. She looked timid but approached the Guardians without hesitation. I welcomed her embrace and remembered her soft touch for many days. Since my last night with my wife, I don't think I'd touched a woman.

On the night of our arrival, Delari introduced us to some of the permanent traders in the camp that overlooked the city and the river valley. When we returned to Delari's tent we discussed plans for the morrow. Senea wanted to stay with us and Gentuk supported this idea. Delari objected, explaining how long the young woman had waited for a Guardian in Ebla.

'She wants her people to be one with the Guardians,' said Senea. 'With your help, I can fulfil this quest.'

Delari looked at me and he didn't have to say anything.

'Senea,' I said, scratching my beard, 'we are in search of Guardians lost to the West. We are not here to rescue a people. After your departure, we discovered an Akkadian fort, east of the mountains. We need to find those we are looking for and return to the tower before there is movement from this fort.'

'Then I will make the journey alone,' said Senea.

'You will make the journey together,' said Delari. 'You will take Yanereu east with you and see her safely to the tower. Yanereu has waited too long to find rest.'

Senea turned to his father. 'I know the way to Ebla.'

Gentuk looked to Delari.

'You have the love of a princess, Senea,' said Delari. 'See to her safety before you risk your life, our lives and hers.'

Gentuk placed his hand on his son's shoulder. 'I agree with the trader. Escorting Yanereu safely to the fort is your task. We need you there.'

'Then I will travel east,' said Senea.

***

Despite our journey only just reaching the first of the big rivers, Lan seemed ready to give up the search. The delicate touch of Yanereu's welcome might have awakened his thoughts of Jamine and softened his committment. Tahnas tried to tell his father that he had been exerting himself too much, but Lan disagreed. I thought that some new company might change Lan's will and I took him to the communal fire in the camp. He spoke to no one and woke late the next morning, more disgruntled than a pig in a trap.

Lan lay on the floor with his head propped on a cushion. Gentuk and I sat down on separate logs near the smouldering coals of the morning's fire. We had been away for most of the morning before returning to find Lan in the same position.

'I cannot taste the food I eat, and I no longer have the strength to draw my sword.'

'Maybe you ate something that did not settle well,' suggested Gentuk.

'Maybe I should use the last of my strength to check your ears for you are not listening to me,' said Lan. 'Maybe, I would feel better if the two of you were not sitting in here sapping my air.'

I stood and left without comment.

Outside, cloth had been stretched in front of the five-post tent and Delari was trading olives. 'I don't understand why Lan is acting like a child,' I said to my trader friend.

'I can hear you, Arman,' yelled Lan, from inside.

'I can't hear you,' I yelled back.

'Are you here to help?' asked Delari. 'The people are beginning to queue.'

Delari had purchased two full barrels from a trader that Gentuk and I had escorted into the camp when we had spotted him arriving from the northwest. Olives were a delicacy in the western cities of Akkadia and Delari was determined to sell them all before nightfall. If Delari had not agreed to help the Guardians in our search for survivors, he would have acquired all eight barrels and travelled down river to Assur and exchanged them at the port. The return from two barrels alone would have covered all his costs.

I took the ladle from my friend and began filling the traders' pots. When someone arrived without a pot, I let Delari know and he asked such customers for an additional offer for our provision of a hardened clay pot and lid.

'A shekel, a fish, bread, make me an offer for a scoop,' Delari announced to those approaching.

Delari collected their varied offerings and I filled their pots with level scoops from the barrel.

'What is going on inside?' asked Delari, as we emptied the last barrel.

'Lan has lost his appetite and he grows weak.'

A pretty girl was next in line and she distracted Delari. 'A loaf of your father's fine bread is more than enough from you. Enjoy them, Silda.'

'He tells us that he cannot even taste an olive,' I added as I got to my feet and began scraping the bottom of the barrel. 'Only about five serves left,' I then said quietly to Delari.

Delari glanced at those gathered and saw two of his fellow traders at the back of the queue. 'We only have a few serves left,' announced Delari. 'No more fish unless it's dried and salted. Only generous offers accepted.'

The traders who knew Delari well, caught the

twinkle in his eye, and knew he would be fair with them. They stayed in the queue and so did a woman offering dark red dates in a grass basket.

Delari told me to give this woman a generous serve.

I delved deep into the barrel and swirled my scoop through the salty water until it was full with olives. It was the same amount I had given every other customer.

'Thank you, good man and I hope you can enjoy the dates while they are fresh,' she said to me.

I winked at her. I didn't feel guilty anymore when I played my part in Delari's trade games. The man Delari considered the most experienced trader in the camp approached next, along with the local brewer.

'There must be a hole in the barrel,' joked Delari.

'Witnessed it myself,' replied Isvah. 'I bought a barrel from the same load and sold each scoop for a half-shekel or equivalent in the inner-city markets. Ran dry soon after high sun. Now I want some for myself.'

'I like that,' admired Delari, 'Give me a half-shekel so it looks like a trade.'

'What about me?' asked Bessum the Brewer.

'It is a half-shekel for you too, Bessum,' said Delari.

'Why? I have seen you offer a scoop for a fish,' he questioned, as I filled his cup.

'I am only joking, friend,' said Delari. 'The olives are my present to you. How was your trade today?'

'I sold what I had,' replied Bessum. 'I have two empty barrels ready to fill when I get more barley.'

'Where do you source that?' asked Delari. 'Arman could travel with you.'

'Arman?' inquired Bessum. 'Does he feel like journeying south?'

I had my head in the barrel scraping the remnants together and did not like agreements made without my consent.

'Come if you like,' said Bessum, 'I have travelled alone ever since my father died and always returned safely.'

I hung the scoop on the side of the barrel and stood to address Delari's trader friend. 'Where do you go?'

'I suggested that you may like to travel with Bessum when he goes in search of barley,' relayed Delari.

'I would be happy to. When do you want to leave?' I asked Bessum.

'I was thinking tomorrow if–'

'Tomorrow is fine. Where do we go?'

'To Kalhu but I can go alone.'

'Do you want me to travel with you or not?' I asked. 'There will be nothing asked in return.'

'I'd appreciate your company, Arman. Though, as I was trying say, I know the route well and the traders there are honest men.' Bessum frowned, 'Are you all right? Your face looks tired.'

'It is Lan,' assumed Delari.

'He is not well,' I finished. I often finished the trader's words before anyone took advantage of them. Like the time Delari had offered all he carried to the first bidder, and then choked on a date seed before he had a chance to explain the starting price.

'Then maybe you should come and bring Lan along for the ride. It is only a day's travel and I know the shaman in Kalhu.'

'I do not think Lan would be interested,' I replied, turning to meet Delari's contemplative stare.

'Why not ask him?' advised Delari.

'To make all right, I will,' I said with delight, anticipating a defiant response from Lan. I parted the tent flap behind Delari's stall and stepped inside. 'Lan, would you like to visit a shaman in Kalhu?'

'Do you know him?' asked Gentuk.

'No, I have never been to Kalhu.'

'Yes,' said Lan, surprising me with his answer. 'I will go to him.'

'Maybe it is best if you just rest,' said Gentuk.

'I fear I will only grow weaker, a burden to you all if I stay. When do you leave?' asked Lan.

'Tomorrow morn,' I replied. 'We will be travelling with Bessum the Brewer.'

'That thought will give me rest tonight.' Lan looked at Gentuk and then at me. 'Have you seen Tahnas since he departed.'

'Tahnas is working at the river, Lan,' said Gentuk. 'He likes to see you resting when he returns. I'll walk out to meet him soon.'

***

It was a peaceful ride to Kalhu. Lan slept most of the ride with his head rested on heaped furs secured to the front of his mount. We followed the Tigris and welcomed the mottled shade of the date palm groves as we approached the city. Unlike the larger Akkadian cities, Kalhu was not walled and there was not a soldier in sight. The first men we encountered were two shepherds watching over their flock. They motioned at Bessum as if he were a friend and one even showed concern for Lan's tired appearance, clasping his hands and murmuring a prayer.

'Do you think it will rain?' Bessum asked the shepherds as he rode by.

'Before moon,' answered one and the other nodded in agreement.

Bessum thanked them with a raised arm and squinted as he faced a cloudless sky.

I looked back, admiring their tranquil resting place beneath the unfarmed date palms, closest to the river. 'They seemed quite certain.'

'They have much time to watch the sky,' said Bessum.

'Do you normally stay overnight?' I asked. 'It will be a full moon.'

'I can stay at the barley farmer's home. You may have to camp with Lan at the shaman's hut, if he does not have a quick cure.'

****

At the northern side of the city square, Bessum drew his mule to a stop and we waited for Lan's horse to arrive next to us.

'That is his home,' said Bessum, pointing to a large, thatched hut on our side of the square. 'Do you want me to go with you? Many fear to face him even in the light of day.'

'If they really feared him, he would not have a hut in the centre of the city,' I replied, noticing as I spoke that the city centre was almost empty of people. In the centre of the square was a well with a low, two-foot-high stone neck circling the bucket that dangled and swayed in a growing breeze from the south. Only one woman waited for the wind to blow the bucket her way this eve. Surrounding the well, at a distance of forty or more paces, were trader's huts spaced evenly between tall date palms. At the base of one of these palms, a group of three children watched as a boy scaled the trunk faster than I could climb a ladder. Behind the traders' huts were solid mud-brick buildings. The white paint on the bricks had been gradually washed away and now the buildings looked as if they were made of stone. 'An introduction is not necessary,' I told Bessum. 'We can meet you here in the morning.'

Lan woke up in time to watch Bessum continue south through the square.

'How are you feeling?'

'I am tired, Arman. Sleep does not seem to help me anymore.'

'Food, sleep and being locked in a hut are the only cures I know. Let us hope this shaman has another trick.'

'Do not call him that ungodly name. It makes me feel helpless.'

'Have you heard of a sunu?' I asked. 'That is what my father called these magical men. I remember because he told me that not even a sunu could have saved me when I was sick. There was no cure and I should have died.'

'Please stop talking, Arman.'

I obliged and led the way down the northern side of the square to the large thatched-roof hut that Bessum had identified.

'It seems too quiet,' said Lan.

I watched the long grey hair at the base of Lan's skull whip in the breeze and thought of the barbarian who I had almost mistook for him. 'It is quiet. I like it. I like it loud or quiet. In between is what bothers me.'

'That is why you are good to travel with, Arman,' said Lan as I dismounted and secured our horses to a post. 'You don't waste my time. I apologise for what I said to you and Gentuk.'

I nodded at Lan and stepped up to the hut's entrance. 'Greetings,' I said and then waited silently for a while before parting the door flap and peering inside. It was dark inside, apart from a few candles, and the smell of strange herbs made me feel unwell. I was about to lean back outside for a breath of fresh air when I heard a response.

'Do not let the light in,' said a gruff voice from the far side of the thatched hut.

'Wait here,' I told Lan, and I stepped inside, quickly sealing the flap behind.

'What brings you here traveller?' croaked the sunu.

I crouched below the trickery of the candles' dancing light and tried to sight the man who had addressed me. As my eyes adjusted to the gloom, I saw that he was kneeling at a small stone altar with his back to the door. 'My friend is not well. He is tired and cannot eat,' I explained, keeping my distance.

'I hear him crying. Bring him inside and keep the light out.'

I slipped back outside, trying my best not to part the door flap any wider than necessary. 'He will see you,' I told Lan. 'He heard you crying.'

'I'm not crying. My eyes are dry and the sand–'

'I know,' I said, 'I will wait outside with the horses.'

Lan spread the door flap and paused to thank me before he stepped inside.

'Keep the light out,' the sunu shouted.

I smirked and turned away from the door. I should have mentioned that request to Lan.

This was the part I missed most. Not waiting and hoping a friend could be cured but spending time in a new place and bearing silent witness to the lives of strangers, the buildings they called home and the work that fed them each night. The cities were growing more alike and, distracted by soldiers and forlorn faces, I no longer noticed the subtle differences. Kalhu, however, seemed untouched by the expansion of Sargon's empire. The people who traded in the square were quiet in their business. The shepherds did not feel the need to fence their flock and sat vigil in timeless bliss. The children who climbed the palms to cut dates had smiles on their faces and the holy men who sat in a circle near one corner of the square were dressed in sun-dulled cloth without a jewel to their name.

I looked around for a water bucket. Kalhu was different to other villages and cities I'd visited but I knew it was wrong to bring an animal to the well. The ash and coals from the sunu's previous fires were gathered in a perfectly sized water bucket. Even contained, the wind was picking at the contents and scattering the softer ash. My mare nuzzled my face and I stroked her nose as I turned my face to the sky. I was not thinking about whether it would rain. I had begun thinking about the village again. An unannounced tear welled in my eye and I woke up from my daydream. I wiped the tear clear and shook my head. Unbetum and Gentuk had reason to feel sorrow, for their wives could be in the hands of another, but I had already cried for my wife and laid her to rest. Maybe I had not mourned her long enough and being in a place that reminded me of the village had rekindled some old memories. 'You must think me a silly man,' I said to my mare, letting my mind drift back.

I remembered the first words I shared with Boroe when he split my shackles and freed me from a life of slavery. 'Find Unbetum,' I said to the young Harmin who came to my rescue that night. In Kalhu's afternoon light, I looked down at my wrists that were still scarred from being tightly bound for many days. I turned my hands and watched them rotate smoothly. Unlike Unbetum, I had escaped unharmed. It was Unbetum who stole the soldiers' attention. Unbetum, The Guardian Who Will Not Die, had enough noble conquests to tattoo a flock of children. Even in shackles, he proved hard to restrain. The Akkadian soldiers were challenged to find ways to humiliate him. Tahnas freed Unbetum and dismembered the guards standing watch but Unbetum had already lost more than his wife, sword and tattoo. He was the one who taught the other Guardians how to draw strength from their coloured shoulders. For this reason, Unbetum's father did not die in his sleep the harvest before Unbetum was made a man on his eleventh harvest. Unbetum lost his father the day the Akkadians cut his tattoo from his shoulder.

***

I will never forget that one afternoon we were all together and still young and uncompromised by the west. Unbetum, Tahnas and Garforn had completed their first journey and, even though I was approaching my fourteenth harvest, I was yet to leave the village and still completed weapons training on a daily basis. Sharing time with my older friends near the western gate, Unbetum spoke thoughtfully about his beliefs regarding the Guardian tattoo.

'All you have to do is touch your shoulder and think of your father, for Salarn has etched more than just his most noble moment. You carry your father's soul with you when you ride now and, together, the mounted courage and strength makes you unbreakable.'

'That is easy for you to say, Unbetum,' I argued, not understanding the significance of my tattoo. I was born many seasons after Unbetum, Tahnas and Garforn, who were all of similar age. Like Senea, I trained alone under the guidance of Arcobon. I was the young Guardian in those days. My father, Seeves, had trained all of my older friends and now spent more time with his dog than with me.

'Unbetum's words find meaning with me,' said Garforn. 'I touched my shoulder today whilst on the hunt. I did not say a prayer. I just thought of my father and remembered his skill and strength. He would have seen no reason for another arrow to be let loose.'

'And I saw your arrow drop the beast,' said Unbetum.

'The beast crumpled. From fifty paces, I knew my

aim could not fail.'

'That is what troubles me about your story,' I remember telling my friends. 'Your tattoo, Unbetum, depicts the day your father emerged from a burning hut carrying four children. He was not burnt. And your father, Garforn, took down six bandits with five arrows. I'm sure you also have good aim.'

'Nobody else saw the bandits until they were dead,' added Garforn.

'Why does this trouble you?' Tahnas asked me, 'And why did you not mention my father's greatest conquest?'

'Because my father's noblest conquest was bracing a ship's mast during a storm. Do you see any storms or water?' I pointed across the grass plains towards the mountains.

The older Guardians laughed.

'Are you trying to show us up?' questioned Garforn with mirth. 'I am sure my father would have preferred that to be named as his greatest feat.'

'Yes,' agreed Unbetum, 'what part of that story concerns you, Arman?'

'Has your father explained it?' asked Tahnas. 'Surely Arcobon has by now.'

I shook my head. 'Arcobon told me that he could not remember much of what happened that night because he had trouble holding on himself.'

'He needs to hear the story,' said Garforn, sweeping one of his thick arms forwards from his seated position on a log and knocking my legs from behind. He liked watching people fall.

I fell flat on my back and lifted my head, agreeing

with Garforn. 'I need to hear the full story,' I said. I needed to hear the full story for, when I thought about my tattoo, I just imagined a sea I had never seen and my father immersed in its depths hanging on with both arms out of fear more than bravery. Living in a land rarely frequented by rain, I thought that any strength I may acquire from my father's conquest was pointless. My father had spent more time in the village than any of the other Guardians. Since his return to the village during my ninth harvest, when I was sick and my mother died, he had only left once.

'It rained heavily for ten days and ten nights,' said Unbetum. 'Here in the village, the ground became sludge as streams flowing down the Zagros Ranges cut their banks and swept across the plains. We weaved toy boats during the downpour and raced them in the water that flowed through the western gate.'

'My boat was the fastest,' declared Garforn, pointing to the spot it had happened.

'No, your boat was the biggest, like you, and made mine bank itself,' defended Tahnas.

Unbetum waited for his friends to remember the point of the story before he continued. 'It was different in the west. Your father, Seeves, and Arcobon confirm that it rained for twenty days and twenty nights. And your father not only braced the splintering mast by wrapping it with hide and securing it with rope tied to all sides, he also hung on as the wind and waves dropped him deep into the blue. He was there when fastenings broke and used the little time he had to retie before his next plunging. Arcobon also held on and survived. We received the rain at home but not the furious winds. In the village, Verian prayed aloud to

Enlil for the first time. Tahnas, Garforn and I played games with toy boats as our elder screamed at the sky.'

'Enlil was the one who caused the Great Flood,' said Garforn. Garforn was just as quick to spot someone not sure of foot as he was to assure all of his opinion of the gods.

'No,' disagreed Unbetum. 'Prevailing evil intentions amongst man caused the Great Flood. The God, Enlil, decided that something had to be done. Either way, Garforn, we are not talking of the Great Flood that happened before our father's father's time. Seeves kept the mast aloft during that storm cut and painted on your shoulder, Arman. At home in the east, rain flooded some huts and fed our crops.'

'Only Salarn has travelled as far as Arcobon and your father,' Tahnas said in praise of my father. 'And their maps now show us how far they travelled.'

Unbetum stood in front of me and gripped my shouders. 'If not for your father's efforts to keep the mast erect during the night, all on board would have drowned. Instead, when the storm broke, they strung what remained of their tattered sail and eventually docked their waterlogged vessel west of Dilmun. Our maps stretch as far as that unknown island in the south because of your father.'

'Seeves and Arcobon then made one of the longest journeys ever undertaken and mapped their course along the way,' continued Tahnas. 'That is why they are happy to spend most of their time here in the village.'

'But when I touch my shoulder, what strength can I gain?' I asked. 'I might never make it to the water.'

Unbetum met my question with a joyous grin. 'The strength to do what is necessary one day and still have enough fight in you to do it again the next.'

I was still not convinced. 'Is that what you feel?' I asked, turning to Tahnas.

'You finally ask,' he said, standing from his seat on the log and walking to my side to show me his tattoo. 'For me, the mark of my father means safety. I do not fear death because I am the oasis my father found when lost in the desert. Like your father, my father mapped an unknown land. I need only remember to drink and all will be well. That makes me undefeatable like Unbetum.'

'You must think me a fool,' I said, hanging my head.

'I worry that you do not speak with your father. I thought you were close,' said Garforn. 'Look at my father's tattoo next time you see him,' he continued. 'It is so faded that one could not tell what it depicts, but he will tell you that the bright red circles are the barbarians' faces and the vibrant splash of blue is the Diyala River that blocked their retreat at the mountains.'

'As colour fades from the sight of others it sinks deeper into your skin,' explained Unbetum.

Garforn stood and grappled for my arms before lifting me from the ground.

I kicked him in his solid gut, and he threw me away like he was casting a fishing net.

'Look at your tattoo, all colour,' Garforn laughed, nursing his gut as I picked myself up off the ground. 'You would swear it was only cut yesterday.'

'More than three harvests ago,' I corrected him as

I got to my feet.

'Three harvests ago and you are still yet to leave the village, no wonder you are confused.'

'It will not be long,' predicted Unbetum. 'We will all be leaving again soon. I think your time is also coming, Arman. I pray we are not gone too long that we cannot all join again in this meeting place.'

'I will miss throwing you, Arman.'

Tahnas laughed. 'I will miss Garforn's face when he is kicked in the guts or between the legs. He grimaces and smiles at the same time.'

***

In quiet reflection, I placed my hand on my shoulder and watched the holy men retreat indoors and the children, who were gathering dates, rush home. Growing winds ripped at the long fronds of the palms towering above the huts in the square. Next to the well, I saw a woven basket turning and rolling with the wind. I walked over, leaning into the wind and taking pleasure in its fresh breath. A woman exited a stall on the southern side of the square, opposite me, and watched me for a moment before collapsing the supports to her shade cloth and rolling it tight. I picked up the woven bucket. It was made from date palm leaves and looked barely strong enough to carry berries. I knew immediately why it had been discarded but tried to make use of it all the same. My tunic could help hold water, at least until the horses wet their muzzles. I looked around the square and it seemed I was alone. Before there was time to question myself, I pulled my tunic over my head, folded it and layered it in the bucket.

I filled my bucket at the well and ran back to the

sunu's hut. When I arrived, the bucket was still half full, absorbing slowly into the cloth. I waited for my mare to drink half the water before offering it to Lan's stallion.

'That is all for today,' I said. 'I will fetch you more in the morning.'

My mare nuzzled me with a wet nose and I surrendered to her silent plea for more.

'One more bucket and then I will need to think about the issue of my nakedness.' I waited for the stallion to finish and then ran to the well again, wearing only a loincloth and my thin leather sandals. I could feel the wind slapping my almost naked body as I ran and knew that it was about to rain. As I drew more water, I noticed two returning fishermen had stopped to inspect what was happening. I stood proudly next to the well as I waved with one hand and wound the bucket with the other.

They exchanged a few words and laughed as they walked on.

'A fishing joke, is it?' I yelled out, my words lost to the strong winds sweeping through the square and carrying biting sand.

When my next bucket was filled, I returned and placed it at my mare's feet. I returned to the well for a third time and, this time, I offered Lan's horse first drink. Parting the tent's flap, I leaned inside, 'Permission to enter? Rain is coming.'

'Hurry up, Arman,' said Lan, 'Do not wait for the furs to get wet.'

I dashed back outside. 'Do not worry. I will find a proper bucket in the morning,' I told our horses as

I unloaded our wrapped furs. I carried the furs inside and then tied the tent's entrance flap closed as it began to flap in the wind.

The sunu stared at me over Lan who was lying on his back. 'Where are your clothes, man?'

'They got wet,' I answered. I unrolled my fur and covered myself.

Lan rocked his head back to look at me but the sunu drew it straight. He waved smoking herbs over Lan and chanted unknown words. The tent smelled even worse than before.

I lay back against Lan's wrapped fur and tried not to disturb them. Rain soon pattered softly on the thatched roof and fresh air vented through the tent flap. I felt healthy after travelling to Kalhu. Without intention, I had been cured of an unknown illness. I had only been pretending I was happy with my life. My smile was only there in the hope others would share it and give me real reason. Time alone to think was necessary and, in Kalhu, the memories that visited me from the past were fresh and abundant. In the same light, I saw hope for the Harmins and the Guardian village. I was planning for the future again.

***

When Lan woke me, it was dark. The rain still pattered softly.

'I have an appetite again, Arman.'

'That is welcome news. What was your sickness?'

'I was tired because I was not eating the right food.'

I sat up and looked to the other side of the hut,

where the sunu had returned to his stone altar. 'So, is he going to give you magical food, herbs and chants to replace meat and bread?'

'No,' said Lan. 'My body is still strong. It is my soul that is weak.'

'And he cured your soul?'

'He told me the cure.'

'Oh,' I sighed, 'we have to swim to the bottom of a bottomless lake and find an immortal snake.'

Lan's smile reached his eyes and he laughed briefly, looking behind nervously like he was ready to apologise to an awakened dragon. 'I will be returning to the village. I must return to Jamine. With her, I will be strong. Here I have no fight left.'

'You mean you will be returning to the tower?'

'The village is the tower now.'

'I understand,' I said, my deep frown hopefully suggesting my concern. 'I think I should stay with Delari.'

'I agree. You should all stay with Delari. Tahnas must continue his search and he will need you all if and when he learns of those we search for in the west.'

'You cannot return alone.'

'Sure, I can. The thought of returning has already made me feel young again. They will be happy to see me back at the tower and I will tell them that the search for lost Guardians continues.'

'Do you think Tahnas will understand?'

'I am sure you will be able to explain my reasons.'

'Will you return to Nineveh first?'

'And add a day to the journey? I can ferry across the river from here and head due east. Tahnas will be pleased to know that his wife, mother and boy will soon be in my care back at the tower.'

I shook my head, 'I believe this is a good decision.'

'You shake your head,' said Lan.

'I am imagining your son's response when I tell him why I arrive alone.'

'Tell Tahnas that it was my decision and I wait for him in the east.'

I was concerned about sharing this report with the other Guardians. Tahnas would surely question me for letting his father leave alone and without further consultation. I buried the thought. I had returned with worse news in the past. If Tahnas could see his father's face now, he would understand. Lan's path to happiness was a well-travelled road and one the others hoped to follow him down soon. I had learnt another cure for a broken man in my time in Kalhu. The sunu's herbs and scented candles were not required to remember the importance of loved ones, hope for the future and happy memories in keeping a man strong. All that was necessary was exposure to an old city and the old ways. In a changing world, filled with new people, I accepted that unwelcomed changes are frequent and long held ideals most vulnerable.

20

Breaking Custom

*Scribed by Fankisi, The Curious,
The Tower. Balih Woods.*

Senea and Kar carried Salarn from his seat at the table to his throne. Yanereu looked confused when we did not follow. I led her to the side of the tower and around the dimly lit arches to a spot where we must stand.

Senea walked out onto the giant's fur in front of us. He drew his sword and took a moment to swing it freely and make limber his muscles.

'Kar will duel with his small sword,' said Unbetum as he walked towards Senea. 'I will tell you only that it is light and made for his size.'

Kar placed his bladed staff behind the throne and then drew his sword in view of Salarn's distant, frozen gaze.

'The floor is yours, young Guardians,' announced Unbetum. 'Touch blades to commence and you know the rest.'

Senea looked for Yanereu beyond the torchlight. We could see him clearly, but he would not have been able to see our faces, maybe just the shapes of our bodies. Kar was now standing in front of him with his blade held close to his chest. Kar appeared relaxed as he looked closely at his own sword, seemingly waiting for Senea to move first. His brown hair hung past his shoulder fur and even longer where it was plaited with horsehair dyed green, blue and red. I had plaited two of these long locks when Kar was standing watch at the tower door. They made him look a little wild, part barbarian.

Unlike Kar, Senea had the appearance of a merchant. He wore a white tunic and his leather belt seemed more accustomed to carrying a hide pouch than a sword sheath. Whilst he was slightly taller and had started to grow a beard, his face looked younger. Maybe that is why he attempted to intimidate Kar with words.

'Beyond the mountains, in places you have only read about, I took many lives and all so quickly that I had to count later.'

'No lives will be taken today, nor pride.'

'Of that I am not so sure.'

'Then maybe I am wrong,' said Kar.

Senea and Kar stepped towards each other and tapped blades. They stepped away from each other and there was a moment of stillness before Senea lurched forwards. Kar blocked his downward slash and, at the same time, he leapt forwards, feet first. Too fast for Senea's slicing blade, Kar kicked the older Guardian's legs from beneath him and, as the older Guardian fell awkwardly, Kar flipped onto his knees and rotated his skinny bronze blade to Senea's throat.

Senea lifted his forearm so that he could point his sword to the ground.

Kar withdrew his blade, stood and pointed it to the ground. He then offered his hand to Senea and helped him to his feet.

Senea turned to face the women and children. He waved his hands by his side and in front to show Yanereu that he was not hurt.

He did not need to comfort her. Naten and Yanereu comforted each other. They followed me as I walked back to the next arch and closer to the throne.

'I can't believe the duel is over already,' said Senea, as he approached the throne with Kar. 'I did not expect my legs to be swept from me. I was too focused on my sword and yours.'

Unbetum braced arms with the younger Guardians. 'We have much to discuss while the day is still young. Senea, you spoke of urgency in your return, a people needing the Guardians' help. Are you ready to explain this? Where did Yanereu find you and why was she searching for the Guardians?'

Senea gestured towards Yanereu, his arm changing course when it was half raised and he realised that we had moved closer to the throne. 'In Ebla, she met a woman who told her to wait. I do not know how she waited so long for Delari and I to enter the city. According to the woman she lodged with, it was at least two seasons. Luck, destiny, call it what you like, but it was a spur of the moment decision for us to travel beyond Mari. If we had not, then I am sure she would still be waiting. Yanereu followed Delari and I all day whilst we traded and, when we set up camp, she stood in view at a distance.' Senea tried again to sight his woman's face in the shadows. 'The people of Pled want to travel to the East and be at one with their god.'

'Who is their god? Is she concerned that Salarn is not speaking,' asked Unbetum.

I held Yanereu's hand and led her into the torchlight. The other women and children hung back.

'Fankisi,' said Jamine, probably warning me against approaching without invitation.

Senea gazed at his wife. 'She hadn't met Salarn until we arrived here together. According to her father, a god by his name approached from the sea. He drew a map in the sand and showed them how he found them. He then camped on the beach for an entire season without saying a word. When he walked amongst the Pledians, they spoke aloud in the hope he would talk back to them.' Senea turned to face Salarn. 'You never said a word but smiled the whole time you were there. When the children approached ...' Senea paused and mused at Salarn's tired and mournful appearance. 'When the children approached you knelt and raised your shoulder fur to show them a picture of people celebrating water—your tattoo. Before you slept, you raised your arms to the sky and then bent to kiss the ground. 'Salarn,' proclaimed Senea, 'you are all I need in a god and I will fight for you. I will die for you. I will live until the day I know all your people are safe.'

With an awkward jolt of his wrist, Salarn beckoned the young Guardian closer.

Senea stepped closer and leant forwards.

Our elder's eyes were glazed and unfocused, and his muttered words were cryptic and harsh. 'Kar leaves.

Father and people stay. You die here.'

Senea's mouth gaped and he backed away from the throne. 'Tell me I heard wrong?'

Unbetum walked away from Senea, pulling his fingers down through his beard.

'Kar, what did Salarn mean?' Senea asked.

Kar also looked confused. He watched his father pace back and forth from the throne, lost to his own thoughts.

Behind me, I heard Parbi whining. I hoped Jamine knew how to settle him because I wanted to be a part of this discussion.

'Kar, Unbetum, what does he mean?' Senea's voice was shaky.

'He told you not to fight and die for him,' I released Yanereu's hand and stepped towards Senea. 'Salarn does not want you to leave. He wants Kar to leave. Unbetum and the rest of us will stay and live our lives here.'

'He said I would die here,' said Senea.

'Was there somewhere else you had in mind?' asked Kar.

Unbetum glared at me before he stepped past his son and clasped Senea's hands. 'Sometimes it is easier not to know but Salarn spoke to you for a reason. You have fulfilled your part in his eyes. Our elder travels alone now. He said you will die here but he never said that you would not leave and return first.'

'Then I will travel to Pled,' announced Senea. 'I see it my duty to–'

'Fankisi,' interrupted Unbetum, noticing me edging my way closer. 'We are in counsel. Why do you continue to approach?'

'Salarn spoke from the throne. We all deserve to hear his words.'

'I will tell you all once we understand,' said Unbetum. He clenched his jaw and this made a deep scar bulge to splitting point on his cheek.

'Do not make us wait,' I said. 'This is our home now and Salarn wanted to share it and all the things he had kept secret.'

'That is why he does not speak, Fankisi. He said more than he could.'

'I do not believe that. I am happy for him to rest and will understand if he never speaks again, but he has not been punished.'

'I did not–'

'I was not finished, Unbetum,' I continued, stepping between him and Senea. 'Salarn did not have to tell us more because now we have you. Do not wait for the other men to say what we women already know. Salarn has fulfilled his role and now you must act in his stead. Share your burden and let nothing be a secret. We hear everything eventually. Is it not best that it comes from you?'

Unbetum could not look me in the eye and manoeuvered past me towards Jamine's stool next to the throne. 'I need to sit down or this day will see me in bed before high sun.'

'You are only hiding from life, Unbetum,' said Jamine, from the darkness where the women and children waited. 'Life will not wait for you.' She handed Parbi to Cihnah and walked towards the throne to stand next to me. 'Your story will be told with or without you.'

I held her hand for support. 'Why must you go?' I asked Senea.

'It is my duty. Yanereu understands,' he answered and turned to face his princess.

Yanereu walked closer with Naten by her side and Yisben and the children followed. In the torchlight, the fair hair of both the young women glowed like dry fields at sunset.

'I know her language and I hope to have Kar by my side,' said Senea. 'If the men are still camped in Nineveh, we will visit them first. We cannot wait for them to return before leaving. The People of Pled need us now. Yanereu waited two seasons to tell a Guardian.'

'Do you think the same way, Kar?' asked Jamine.

Kar sighed and looked at Senea with downcast eyes. 'I want to help but I have seen the soldiers that camp to our north. We are not safe in our own lands. The Guardians also need Guardians. Even if we could rescue the Pledians from their home, where in this world is safe?'

'I agree with Kar,' said Jamine. 'You must listen to his reason, Senea.'

Senea did not seem ready to listen. His eyes clenched and he started breathing heavily through his nose.

'We should not go, yet we must,' said Kar. 'Senea and I should go for a ride. The best thinking happens on the ride and I have a boar trap to check. Would you like to come?'

I realised Kar was looking at me. Never before had any of the women ever gone on a scout ride. I knew for certain that Tahnas and Unbetum would disapprove but still I was finding it hard to say no. In Borujerd, the snow-capped peaks of the Zagros Mountains brought me comfort when Tahnas was away. I missed the open view of the mountains that lay beyond the shelter of the woods. The height of the mountains reminded me of the size of the world. They reminded me of Tahnas leaving me and returning.

'I will meet you at the stable,' said Senea. He walked towards Yanereu, and Naten stepped from her side as he hugged her.

'I know who would like to go,' I said to Kar.

'Can I?' asked Lagesh, rushing towards his brother.

Senea broke from his embrace of Yanereu, 'No, you have to stay and protect the tower, Lagesh.'

Lagesh looked confused.

I stared past Lagesh and waited until I caught Naten's eye. 'A scout ride, even if it be for one morning, might make up for some of your lost days,' I told her.

Naten walked past Lagesh towards Kar. 'I would like to ride with you.' Her sleepy eyes were wider than I had ever seen them before.

Jamine stood next to Unbetum and told him to rest and ignore what was happening. As the oldest woman, she too was struggling with the sudden changes of days past and needed Unbetum to be strong for her.

Kar gathered his staff from behind the throne and paused next to his father and Jamine.

Unbetum looked up at his son from his stool. 'I hope you know what you are doing?'

'I only know what I am doing now,' said Kar. He looked at Jamine and then at his father again. 'Jamine told you that life would not wait for you. I also received such advice. A friend of Salarn's told me to look for what lies beyond the horizon. In the foothills, I have a trap to check. We must keep venturing out or we are already defeated.'

***

Senea exchanged many strange words with Yanereu, as I bridled his mare and led her from the stables. Whilst he had learnt the Pledian's language well in their time spent together, there were still many things he could not explain. When he was unable to find the right words, Yanereu calmed him with a finger to her lips and a kiss.

Kar waited patiently with Naten sharing his stallion's mount. Her delicate pale arms were wrapped around his waist even though the horse stood still. She wore one of my tunics and it slipped past her shoulder on one side.

'Where are we going?' she asked Kar.

'We go west through the woods to the mountains. Have I given too much away?' Kar said jokingly as he stroked his stallion's mane.

Naten pulled on his shoulder fur to make him turn to face her. He turned and smiled.

Senea climbed onto his mare and thought of something else he wanted to say before he rode away. *'Yanereu un besquit.'*

The Pledian Princess touched her chest where Senea's silver ring hung beneath her thin white dress. *'Senea un vern semiteu mes fae.'*

Senea reluctantly pulled his gaze from his treasured wife and gave Kar a nod. They rode across the clearing and into the woods.

Yanereu approached me at the stable and stroked the noses of the horses that remained. They nuzzled close ready to be released for the day. One was the mare Senea had purchased for her before they departed Ebla en route to the fertile valley. A Guardian is not normally paid in silver, but ten shekels were requested in exchange for the mare and Delari agreed to offer Senea this amount for his services.

I opened the door to the stable and the horses stepped out and began picking at the lush grass.

Yanereu pointed to the grass and cupped her hands to her mouth.

'They are hungry,' I said.

She smiled at my response and pointed to where Senea had ridden into the woods.

'They will not be gone long.' I pointed at the sun and lowered my hand to the west before drawing it back to my chest.'

Yanereu smiled again.

I liked this. It was easier than talking to the men. 'Senea wants to help the Pledians.'

She opened her mouth and eyes wide and waved her hands around next to her head.

'Senea was angry,' I said and impersonated his tense face and nostril breaths.

'Yes,' she said.

I pointed west and cupped my hands in the shape of small breasts beneath my own. 'Naten will tell me everything,' I said, pointing west and raising a hand to my ear.

Yaneru pointed at my breasts.

'Naten,' I said, cupping my hands again.

'Naten with child?'

'No,' I said, 'Naten will tell me what happens on the ride.' I pretended I was Naten riding a horse back to the tower and then talking excitedly about what had happened.

Yanereu laughed.

She did not understand me.

21

Left Behind

Scribed by Senea. The Tower.

It was mid morning when we reached the boar trap in the foothills. Never before had a woman been present on a scout ride and it did not feel real. Kar leapt from his mount and helped Naten to the ground. I rode past them to view the gully between them and the next rise.

'What are you looking for?' asked Naten.

'Bandits,' I replied, distracted again by her presence.

Kar pointed to the trees on the far side of the trickling stream. 'They could be close.'

She gripped his wrist.

'You are stronger than you look. Hold this instead.' Kar handed her the reins. He walked through the long grass and used his staff to push aside dead branches that concealed the trap made from thick cuts of wood bound together with strips of leather. As soon as the trap was exposed, a large boar thrashed about and the wooden trap creaked with each jolt. Kar took a step closer and the boar charged at him, flexing the wooden bars until its head was caught. Stressed, the wild animal put its weight on its haunches and tried to pull its face free.

'Kar,' I said and, when I had his attention, I looked south.

Kar followed my eyes to the other side of the stream. Half an arrow shot away, two bandits stood together, partially hidden by the grass and bushes that thinned at the tree line. When they realised Kar was looking at them, they stepped out where they could be seen more clearly. One of them held a spear and the other had a bow and a quiver of arrows hanging from his shoulder. They stood at a distance, without raising their weapons or saying a word.

'Do they want your boar?' asked Naten.

I trotted my mare down the hill and closer to the trap. 'Let us kill it and keep moving before they call on more of their party.'

'They are not a threat,' said Kar. 'Those same two watched me ride west with Salarn and I have seen them on many scout rides since. Maybe they set their own traps or maybe they watch me and learn. The Guardians would rejoice if we returned with a fresh kill.' Kar looked at the bandits and then cast his stare down the foothills and south to where the woods and the mountains met the grass plains.

'It is your kill, Kar. What are you waiting for?' I dismounted and handed my reins to Naten. She now held both horses. A simple task as they stood still with their heads lowered to the grass.

'I am waiting for everyone involved to speak.'

'We all have,' I said. 'I do not even know if they

talk.'

'They do not have to speak to be heard. They remind me of the Pledians.'

'You do not know the Pledians, Kar.'

'I heard your story of Yanereu waiting at a distance. I know Salarn spent many silent seasons with the Pledians. Before Salarn travelled to Pled he stared upon the Great Sea and marvelled at the activity of the small fishing boats hugging the shore and larger trade vessels heading south for Mizir. Between him and a horizon set on water, he could always see something. Our view is not as endless at the foot of the Zagros' ranges, yet the pursuits of others are still observable. Like the people of Hidalu, those two bandits are our neighbours, not strangers. I wonder how many others they return to at night and whether they are part of the valley bandit tribe, the ones who paint themselves with mud and wear armour made from animal bones.' Kar stood next to the trap and the boar stared up at him through beady eyes, its dirty tusks locked with the wooden bars of the cage. 'One more night without fresh meat will not hurt us. We can hunt tomorrow.'

I grabbed Kar by his shoulder and turned him to face me. 'You are going to leave it for them? It is your trap, Kar. Leave it, not your kill.'

'I would have taken it if they were not here. They are here and they could have taken it first. For that reason alone, I want them to have it.'

'They are savages, Kar. They will not understand. If you leave it, they will think your actions are aimed at trapping them and the meat will be wasted.'

Kar strapped his staff to his back and drew a bronze

blade from his belt. He held the blade up in view of the two bandits and then placed it atop a large stone near the mountain stream. After placing it, Kar waved them closer. They did not approach and instead turned to each other.

'You are going to leave that too?' They will think you are crazier than I do.'

'Let them think,' said Kar. 'It is one boar and one blade.'

I sighed, 'You are different to how I remember you, Kar.'

'You do not like me anymore?'

'I feel I do not know you anymore. I have changed too, so I will not judge you like others might. Neither do I know these men who watch us from a distance. We should return tomorrow, cautious in our approach. If the boar is still here, we take it.'

'I agree,' said Kar.

'We are leaving the boar?' asked Naten.

I gestured to Kar and rolled my eyes. This made Naten smile.

'Would you like to ride?' Kar asked her.

'I never learnt how.'

Kar lifted Naten onto the mount like she was made of feathers and then climbed up and sat behind. He placed his hands on her hips and lifted her slightly to help her sit straight. Her thin, fair hair brushed against his face and he closed his eyes to the touch without moving his head from its stroke. 'Give the reins a jiggle and Har Man will know you are ready to ride,' instructed Kar.

I stopped my mare next to Kar and Naten. 'If our

fathers ever saw this, what would they think?'

'They may not agree, Senea, but even they could not tell us why.'

'Yes, they could. You left food that would have fed us, you carried a young girl to a dangerous place and now you let her ride for you.'

'We should not live governed by rules of the past. I have made decisions that I would not have had to for many seasons to come. And the girl has a name, Senea. Naten was not born a Guardian but she is one of us now.'

I looked at them sharing the same mount and noticed Kar's hand placed comfortably on her waist. 'Are you making decisions together?'

'No,' replied Kar. 'When I say we, I am referring to the Guardians. We cannot live by the old rules.'

My eyes tightened as I searched for trickery in Kar's words. 'My father has ridden west in the hope that things can once again be as they were. Are you saying his journey is pointless?'

'All I am saying is that things will not be the same. You should know that more than anyone else.'

'I do.' I confessed and slunk in my mount. 'Salarn, the teller of stories, only shares harsh words. Delari, once the greatest travelling trader, no longer wishes to move. Kar, my young friend, you speak like you have been to the end of the world. And Yanereu, the eldest daughter of Pled, beseeched me to save her people. Why now, Kar? Who is this Sargon that he can change the world in so many ways?'

'Some say, he is a god.'

'Who, the Akkadians, his disciples?' I dismissed

Kar's comment. 'He has taken life without reason; he has sacked cities and burnt villages to the ground. This is not the way of a god. Salarn, the quiet peacemaker, is a god. Sargon is a tyrant, a preacher of lies.'

Kar nodded in agreement. He watched loose strains of Naten's hair whisk in the breeze and flicker the light of the sun. 'If we can convince the others a mission to Pled is not to be delayed, I will join you. I accept that things have changed and hold hope that anything else that may change whilst we are gone is only for the better.'

'Where do you draw your hope from, Kar? The Pledians think we are gods and I am beginning to think that, only bound by love, I have accepted the duty imposed.'

'You have, Senea, though you do not have to be a god to accomplish their task. Understand what is required, believe you are ready and fight like there is no one else left.'

'Did Arcobon tell you that?'

'He and my father may have mentioned such words of encouragement, but it was Salarn and the tree that made me understand.'

'The tree?' I questioned him, glancing at Naten to see if she knew what Kar was speaking of.

'Would you like to see it?'

I looked back at the bandits still waiting at a distance. They had not moved and their patience made me look more favourably upon Kar's decision. 'All right,' I said, 'show me a tree that makes me understand and I will tell you more of a king who thinks he is a god.'

Kar feigned a smile, 'I do not want to hear any

more stories of Sargon. I want only one to be remembered.' He shifted his hand to Naten's exposed shoulder, already red from the sun, 'Hold on with your thighs. Not too tight.'

She jiggled the reins and the stallion cantered down the gradual slope towards the eastern plains. Twice she almost bounced from her mount. Kar corrected her balance with an arm around her hips and his other guiding her hold of the reins.

I caught up and smiled at them as I rode by. They rode north before entering the woods and I changed my course to catch up.

22

Acceptance

Scribed by Fankisi, The Curious.
The Tower. Balih Woods.

The trapdoor to the roof of the tower creaked closed and I sat up, trying to account for those present on the top floor. It was impossible to see in the dark of night and I needed to be certain it was not one of the children.

'It was Unbetum,' whispered Jamine.

I stepped towards her voice, trying to avoid standing on those sleeping nearby.

She found my hand and pulled me down next to her, spreading her fur over us both. 'They are above us.' She jiggled my hand and tittered.

'Kar?' I asked.

'He has been up there all night. Listen.'

The roof creaked as Unbetum lay down next to him. His limp had gotten worse and, though his arm was healing, his left eye was half sealed with swelling. Despite this, Unbetum still managed a rare smile and was always the last to bed, even if that meant sleeping and waking again around the time the women retired for the night.

'Do you know why Salarn stopped talking?' Unbetum asked Kar. In the quiet of night, we heard them clearly.

'He told his last story. He is complete now.'

'Will you continue to put your stories to clay?'

'I need stillness and I only find peace at the tree. Forgotten thoughts find me in her sanctuary. I want to stay by her side.'

'And yet, if we remain still for too long, all we hope to remember will be lost.'

'Are you siding with Senea? Do you think we should travel to Pled?'

'You must leave. That is all the tree and Salarn have made clear to me. I will take care of those left behind until your return.'

'I do not know how long that will be.'

'You do not have to,' said Unbetum.

'I see trouble ahead.'

'I know you will be ready.'

Unbetum and Kar slept under the stars and Jamine and I found it difficult to sleep beneath after hearing their shared words.

***

The days were getting warmer and the wet season teased the winds. Still, it had only rained once since the morning Tahnas and the men had begun the journey west. Our crop was starting to seed but we were unsure whether it was the lack of rain or the absence of full sun that slowed it. Under Tahnas's instructions, we waited for the seed to fatten and hoped for more rain before the stems dried. Jamine raised her concerns at waiting any longer before harvesting when all were gathered at the table for the evening meal. Unbetum and Kar mimicked Salarn's silence and Senea decided he would answer for them.

'Do not worry, Jamine. I think it will rain again soon and, if it does not, then the moon will sign a time.'

'Tahnas got the seeds from Akkadia,' I told the table, 'Maybe they prefer it there.'

'Maybe,' responded Senea. 'The crop is still healthy, as if it has found water beneath. Waiting a few more days cannot hurt.'

'It may,' added Jamine. 'If it rains like it did last harvest, the stems will sag and rot.'

At the end of the table, seated next to Salarn, Unbetum cleared his throat. He looked at Jamine before he addressed the table. 'Jamine is right,' he began, 'I see a delayed but long wet season ahead and there is nothing worse then cutting grain that has slouched. I propose that as soon as tomorrow we should begin thinning the crop.'

'I agree, Unbetum,' said Jamine.

'Does anyone disagree?' Unbetum asked all those gathered. All agreed and Unbetum took the opportunity in the prevailing silence to call to hearing a matter he judged of more importance. 'We have all heard of the plight of the Pledians. Senea's princess has asked for more than just his hand in marriage. If Senea and Kar are willing, I would like them to share their plans.'

'We have planned a route to the Great Sea,' explained Senea. 'One that will hopefully have us encounter the other Guardians before we proceed beyond Nineveh.'

My body quivered from my shoulders to my knees and Parbi woke from sleep in my nurse.

'Have you gone so far as to consider a path for your return,' inquired Unbetum. 'Safe passage through the mountains will be a challenge.'

'We are not as fearful of the route home as we are of leaving the tower under the protection of one Guardian. Forgive me in saying, you do not have the strength you once had, Unbetum, and Lagesh is too young to shoulder such a burden. In consideration of the time we will be gone, we feel that we cannot leave until the men return.'

'Finally, some sense,' sung Jamine, dropping the cloth she had begun weaving and standing with praise.

'Do you feel the same way, Kar?' asked Unbetum.

'It is not my decision, father, though understand when I say that the plight of the Pledians weighs more heavily on my mind than that of the Guardians. We are safe for now and we've heard they are not.'

Unbetum looked from Kar to Senea. 'Tell us Senea, how dire are the circumstances in Pled? You told me that Yanereu waited for two seasons prior to your arrival. Can they wait any longer?'

Senea shook his head. 'Mountain tribes, duteous to their peaceful neighbours, have settled in Pled. They saved the Pledians from the first fleet of Akkadian boats. The fear is, next time, there will be more boats and more soldiers.'

'It may already be too late,' deduced Unbetum. 'If what you know is based on Yanereu's account—'

'Her father made plans,' interrupted Senea. 'The Pledians moved inland beyond the hills the day Yanereu sailed towards Zidonia.'

'Then the only thing delaying your departure is your fear for us?'

'A worthy fear,' said Jamine, her raised voice echoing through the tower. 'They will not be welcomed in Nineveh, Unbetum. The men will scold them for deserting us.'

'Scold them? Do you think any Guardian would scold my son? How would you handle a scolding, Kar.'

Kar looked between Jamine and his father and then addressed the table, 'I would listen.'

'Your concerns are justified, Jamine, but they are not reason enough.'

'Why not?' asked Jamine and I worried that she was about to reveal all we had overheard and everything Unbetum had confided in us.

'It was Salarn's last instruction,' replied Unbetum. 'Kar will go.'

'And your decision has nothing to do with the tree?' asked Jamine, still standing, her eyebrows raised.

I closed my eyes and prayed for her to not say any more.

'What do you know of the tree?' asked Unbetum.

'Nothing,' spat Jamine. 'I am a woman. What would I know about the plans of men and gods?'

'You seem to know many things,' said Unbetum. He waited for Jamine to sit before he continued. 'Senea, does your fear for us mean you will stay if Kar departs?'

'With Kar by my side and comfort found in Salarn's words that I will die here, I am ready to depart.'

Unbetum stood next to Salarn and placed his hand on our elder's contorted shoulder. 'The Guardians are safe here in the woods and, when you return again, Senea, I will still be standing and it will not be Kar but your brother, Lagesh, I make you duel. It will be the first spectacle our new family from the far west will witness.'

Senea stood at the table. 'With your blessing, Kar and I will make the final arrangements.'

Kar stood at the far end of the table. 'Only in time will life be revealed and only with sacrifice will good things come to bear.'

Unbetum paused to consider Kar's words. He raised his cup with so much enthusiasm and pride that he spilt half of the water it held.

Jamine sat between Kar and Unbetum and opposite Senea. She picked up her cloth and needles and continued weaving.

***

The next morning Jamine woke the women and the children who were not already awake and ushered them outside to begin cutting grain. She, more than anyone else, was fearful of heavy rain in the days to follow. Unbetum had agreed with her the night before and that merely served to consolidate her concerns. She began showing the children, and Yisben, which stems to cut.

I stood back, watching Parbi rolling about in the grass nearby, content in his playful world.

'There is something about that boy.'

His voice startled me. I looked up and watched Unbetum walk closer. His stride was still strong, but I felt like the rest of him was falling apart, including his mind. 'I worry for us all, Unbetum. You must rest more; gods forbid you are silenced like Salarn. Senea and Kar are young and can sleep later.'

'See it as preparation for it will not be long before there is no scout ride and it is only myself to stand watch.'

'Maybe not,' I said. 'Once again, it seems Naten is one of the men. Will you scold her or your son when they return?'

'Naten?' exclaimed Unbetum. 'Is she not cutting grain?'

'They left before first light.'

'Why does he not tell me these things?'

I studied the brave man's face and watched him still his anger. 'You know as well as I do that Kar is older than his face signs. He is connected to Salarn by blood and I cannot question him. Only you can, Unbetum. We all look to you.'

'I understand Kar's intentions, Fankisi, and still I question him. Just as I am certain of rain this afternoon, I am certain that his path, like mine, ends with bereavement.'

'What life does not end with bereavement? Let him be a man and live with his decisions. We need an elder, Unbetum.'

'I should join in the cutting of seed.'

'No, you must rest. That's an order.' I pointed Unbetum towards his stool, still in place since the day Tahnas had carried it outside. 'Look after Parbi for me.'

***

As the sky grew dark and hid the high sun, Jamine called a short end to the day's work. What was cut was gathered and carried inside to be grinded another day. Carrying the last sheaf, I slowed as I approached Unbetum still seated on his stool at the door. I turned and scanned the sky above the circling woods. 'Looks like Jamine was right, though it may be no more than an overnight storm.' I knelt and Parbi toddled into my waiting grasp. His face and hands were filthy and I realised that he had been playing with horse dung.

Unbetum stood to assist me with the sheaf I held under one arm.

'I can carry it and Parbi. Why don't you go inside and rest properly? Lagesh would be more than happy to stand watch in your place.'

Unbetum returned to his stool. 'Kar is still out there and he knows his stallion prefers to be dry.'

I lifted Parbi and the sheaf and walked to Unbetum's side. 'What really concerns you?'

Unbetum, whether distracted or not, was always listening and these words gained his attention. 'I don't think I will see Kar again after he leaves.'

I rested my head sideways in front of Unbetum's stare. 'Without you, he would have hidden from his calling. Despite your injuries, you duelled him. You object to his leaving even though you support it. Everything you do and say makes him stronger.' I swayed my face in front of his until he was willing to look me in the eyes. 'I know you worry about him being distracted by a younger girl. Do you think Tahnas regrets his decision to wed me?' Parbi started pushing at my face and he managed to get a dung-coated finger in my mouth and another up my nose. 'Show Kar your love and he will return.'

Unbetum stood and took the sheaf from me. 'Forgive me, Fankisi. I have been thinking so much that I forgot my rule. I have been predicting life.'

I held his waist and stood on my toes to kiss his cheek.

***

Unbetum appointed Lagesh as sentry to the tower door. 'I arm you with a bow crafted by Elkin and strung by Samor.'

Lagesh, with confidence, investigated any possible threat. Often alarmed by the strange shadows cast by the trees, he would fasten an arrow, crouch and aim. He had never loosed one before, but no enemy would know this and, should he actually sight a foe, his plan was to holler first and then draw an arrow. Unbetum told him this would give any friendly visitor the chance to take shelter and scare away unwanted arrivals. Lagesh was only the second Guardian to receive a weapon before he was formally declared a man and he was honoured by the bestowed responsibility. The stool my husband had placed for Unbetum was now Lagesh's fortification and, though at times he ventured from it, intrigued by sounds from the other side of the tower, he was dutiful in never letting the door fall out of sight for too long. Above him on the roof, Unbetum took more time to rest and inspect the horizons for any distant warning signs of an approaching foe.

Lagesh seemed suited to his position except that it meant he had to stay at the tower when his brother and Kar rode away with Naten. Most often, he was already outside before the morning light, almost praying that something would happen that day to allow him to advance in favour ahead of time. The men thought he cried when they departed because he would miss them. Lagesh shrieked when the men left because he wanted to go with them. He had grown close to Naten in our time at the tower and now she too was venturing afar whilst he stayed behind. He had strong feelings for the beautiful, fair-haired girl I had adopted in Borujerd.

'One day I will be old enough to leave this post and pursue quests that are the source of women's admiration for men.'

I bent and cradled his head in my bosom. 'No, Lagesh. Women admire men for who they are before they leave and hope they will be the same when they return.'

He blinked his lazy eye open and shoved his hair back from his face. 'I do not care for Cihnah's obsession with dressing like a princess or Jamine's tales of love that can only be found once one has discovered their true self. I know what love is and that is what I feel for Naten. Not only is she beautiful, unlike any other girl I have seen, I know that she will only grow more beautiful.'

'That sounds like love,' I told him. 'Reveal your feelings to her slowly.'

'Slowly?'

'Be yourself. Listen to the woods. The trees don't rush like men.'

***

Lagesh misunderstood my advice. He ignored those who passed him via the tower door, seemingly intent on guard duty. He would try his best to force a smile when it was Jamine. He only looked forwards to seeing me. One day he called me proudly to his side.

I knelt next to him.

'I have avoided talking to or making eye contact with Naten for five days.'

'That was not what I advised,' I tried to tell him.

Lagesh pushed me aside.

'Lagesh, what–'

'Quiet, Fankisi,' he said. 'Do you hear it?'

I heard horses approaching.

Lagesh reefed open the door to the tower. 'They return with a kill. Get a fire burning,' he announced. A clap of thunder followed his announcement and rain began to patter.

'You have not seen them yet,' I said to Lagesh. 'How can you make such a call?'

Abandoning the grain that Jamine was instructing the girls to grind, Cihnah and Meera hopped with excitement and were let loose. They ran past Lagesh and me through the door and he smiled at them as they questioned him for answers they did not wait to hear.

From the woods to the south, Kar and Naten emerged, sharing the same mount. Senea rode into the clearing a few moments later with a boar secured to his mount.

'How did you know they had a kill?' I asked Lagesh.

'You told me to listen, Fankisi. I listen to them leave and to the sound of their return.'

I kissed his cheek. 'I am impressed, Lagesh.' I walked towards the stable with my arms spread to the cool touch of rain. The smell of pinewood and wet grass filled the air.

Cihnah and her younger sister, Meera, were the first to arrive at the stable, but they took a backwards step as Senea hoisted a large boar onto a hook and let it hang.

'Is it dead?' queried Cihnah.

Senea turned its lifeless head and roared, 'I want to eat you.'

The girls screamed and then giggled together as Senea allowed the heavy head to rest lifeless, void of manipulation.

Kar brushed his stallion and Naten walked towards the tower door carrying a wrapped parcel.

'What is that?' asked Cihnah as Naten ran ahead, sheltering it from drops of rain.

'Quickly, inside,' yelled Naten, nursing something heavy and wrapped in Kar's shoulder fur.

'Hurry, girls,' I said as the rain began to drop harder.

Naten glanced back at Kar and Senea as she was nearing the door. 'Forget them, Lagesh. It is raining,' she said as she ran inside, followed by Cihnah and Meera.

Lagesh was unsure how to respond to the girl who had gone on more adventures than he and had this day returned with something still held secret.

'I'll see you inside, Lagesh,' I told him. 'It must be

special if Kar wrapped it in his shoulder fur.'

A moment later, Senea rushed inside and Jamine handed him a cloth to dry himself with.

The door to the tower was closed from outside. I looked at Senea.

He only mused for a moment before smiling and joining Naten and, most importantly, Yanereu at the table.

I stood at the door a while longer and thought of asking Lagesh inside again. Then I thought of Naten and Parbi. She was at the table now and that is where I needed to be. I wanted to be holding Parbi and feel him squirm with excitement when she unwrapped Kar's shoulder fur.

23

Visions

Scribed by Lagesh. The Tower.

I was still thinking of an excuse for standing in the rain when my older brother reached the door.

'You have to see this,' said Senea as he ran inside to take shelter from the rain that had suddenly taken hold of the sky and dropped so heavy that the circling woods had disappeared from sight.

Kar stopped before entering and looked at me through a haze of water. 'Are you enjoying the rain?'

'I like the rain,' I replied with water masking my face.

'Really?' questioned Kar.

'Go inside and reveal your surprise. I will stand watch.'

The water sheeting down from heaven had almost become blinding. The only man-made shelter outside the tower was the stable and Kar noticed that I was not intent on heading that way either.

'Follow me,' he said, running in the opposite direction to the stable without looking back.

Left alone at the door, I took pride in closing it

and following Kar away from the tower.

I was finding it hard to keep up, despite the woods providing ample shelter from the rain. Kar set a fast pace and the woods grew so dark in spots that I, having never ventured so far, became worried about finding a return path should I become separated. Every time I slowed to listen, I would hear nothing for a long while before Kar backtracked and called my name from a distance. His voice echoed through the woods and was muffled by pattering rain and branches scraping together in the wind. When I fell too far behind, Kar took the time to walk all the way up to me and grab both my arms.

'Forget the gold they are unwrapping back at the tower,' he said, 'this is something you want to see.'

'Gold?' I questioned him.

'You had your chance to join in that conversation. No looking back, Lagesh.' Kar winked at me before wrapping his forearm around a trunk and thrusting himself into a sprint. Already, the slightly older Guardian had an unnecessary head start but I had plenty of energy after a morning spent seated. If Kar could set such a pace armed with a sword and staff, then I was determined to keep up with my lighter bow. I ran as fast as I could and only attempted Kar's propulsion manoeuvre once, before deciding I would practice it another day.

***

I began thinking that my time spent seated was actually a hindrance. My muscles had grown weak from sentry duty and we had run so far that we would not be able to return before dark. New fears were beginning to mount when unanticipated light began to appear in the path in front. I rounded the last few trees, jumped over a fallen branch and came to a stop next to Kar, out of breath. Kar smiled down at me, as I leant over and braced on my knees, panting for air.

I looked up at a seemingly vacant space in front. The rain was still so heavy that it was impossible to see more than a few paces in front. In the shelter of the woods, droplets dispersed into a mist as they breached the canopy. 'Have we run to the far northern side of the woods?' I asked, finding this explanation easy to believe.

'Not even close.'

I stood upright, still breathing heavily. 'We are a long way from the tower.'

'If we returned now, we would still not be able to make it back before dark.'

'I do not mind,' I said, 'I am with a Guardian.'

Kar's eyes brightened, 'When Senea places that same faith in me, I'm not sure if he is being honest or making fun.'

'You beat my brother in the duel,' I said. 'You defeated your own father. You could be the greatest Guardian of all one day.'

'To be the greatest, you have to stand the test of time, Lagesh. I won duels, not true fights, and the difference cannot be measured.' He pointed out into the rain and asked, 'Can you see it?'

I looked out into the clearing through the rain.

'I hope I have not made you run all this way in vain.'

'What am I looking for?'

'It is an echo. A relic to the day a god was revealed here.'

'What was here before?'

'I think the tree has always been here. Whichever god it was that chose to speak to Pardensai used it for a voice.'

'Enki?' I asked.

'I think it was Mother Ki,' replied Kar with a nod. 'I see it as a reminder that we are not alone. It was a reward for venturing this far. It is what you make of it.'

Like the rain was painting its shape, the branches began to form and they curved down and back to a thick trunk. 'It is beautiful,' I exclaimed.

'Most people, even when they can see it clearly, describe it as a dead tree.'

'No, it's not dead. I can see new leaves sprouting.'

Kar looked out through the rain that was beginning to slow.

'It swallows the rain faster than it falls,' I observed. 'Did you ever try to give it water, Kar?' I then asked, unable to shift my stare from the tree.

'I empty what water I have left before I leave,' said Kar. 'Now I think that I could have carried water and emptied it sooner.'

'Is it one of those trees that loses its leaves and drops seed before the cold season and grows again when it rains?' I asked, not waiting for an answer. 'How did it end up here amongst the pines?' Still intrigued, I continued with my questioning but did not venture closer, even as the rain settled to a slow patter. 'Did Pardensai plant the tree?'

'I think it was adorned in leaves and already held

a divide between the pines when Pardensai was drawn to its presence.' Kar shook his hair and dispersed a few droplets of water. He ran a finger either side of the plait in his hair that hung the longest. It was green at the tip.

We had stayed mostly dry beneath the wood's canopy. I took my first step forwards from the shelter with my palms spread, feeling the last drops of rain.

'This is my sacred place and, when I showed the tree to my father, it silenced him for a while.'

'Is that why he is angry now?' I asked, fearful of taking another step closer.

'He is not angry, Lagesh. He is just troubled by many thoughts and ideas.'

'What happened when he was here?'

'You will have to ask him that question.'

I looked back at Kar like it was a game and took a few more steps forwards.

'I have never seen life stemming from its branches. I thought this tree a skeleton, a relic. I believed it to be the tree that shook loose all its leaves when Pardensai ventured into the woods. The first Guardian tale, etched to clay by Salarn, told of his father's encounter with the tree. Pardensai never spoke after returning from the tree and now Salarn has also been silenced.'

'I have no need to go any closer,' I called out, as I collapsed to my knees. 'I now know what my brother was talking about when he said he prayed with his god.' I rolled in the wet grass beneath the outstretched branches adorned with delicate, new sprouts.

Kar walked closer and collapsed next to me.

'Can you feel it?' I asked.

Kar did not respond.

I rolled my head to look at him like this behaviour was appropriate and that any explanation forthcoming was unnecessary. Like Salarn, this was why Kar preferred to be alone, I thought, and I watched as Kar's eyes began to blink rapidly before his legs straightened and his body relaxed into the grass. I wanted to share the experience with Kar. I pushed Kar's side and my fingers dug into soft flesh as if Kar's muscles had turned to water. 'Kar, wake up. I want to tell you something,' I said, gaining no response. A moment later, I lay back in the grass, suddenly needing sleep myself.

***

We awoke at the same time. Kar leapt to his feet like he had fallen asleep during a battle and looked around anxiously. I awoke more peacefully, questioning my position in the wet grass. Above me a smooth white branch sprouted green stems.

'I had the strangest dreams,' I told Kar.

'Tell me,' said Kar, staggering about and clutching at his sides as if he was falling apart.

'It was as if the village was never burnt to the ground. The walls are no more and, in their place, there is a watchtower, almost as tall as the tower we now call home. That is where I am and, when I look down at the huts, the village is twice the size. There are crops growing in every direction apart from the south. In the south, there is a lake of water, one hundred paces wide, and horned beasts graze freely in the fields beyond as if they are no longer fearful of man. And ...' I stopped talking freely and looked at Kar. 'I do not know if I should tell you the rest.'

'Never be afraid to tell me anything,' said Kar. His eyes glowed green like the new sprouts on the tree and, as he was wearing only hide shorts, I noticed his muscles. They were not imposing like Tahnas's but they were all over his body. Like a skinny horse, he looked ready to run or leap. 'You are my best friend's brother,' he continued. 'That makes you a brother to me.'

'All right, I will tell you the rest of my dream,' I agreed. 'Naten is seated on the other side of the watchtower and her belly holds child. When I look up from the village at her, she is smiling and she says ... Well, I cannot remember what she said but it makes me happy and she points to the mountains and I know that she is talking about you. She tells me you will be home soon for the last time. I tell her that I will miss you and she tells me that she will not.' I paused again to see if Kar was still comfortable with my words before continuing. 'I cannot recall what happened next. It is another time and I am back in the watchtower and I am looking at one of the huts. It looks like a smaller version of the tower. I know that Naten is inside because I can see her face and a few women crowding around her, through the walls. The watchtower seems wider now and it takes me a while to reach the southern side. I climb outside and hang onto its railing. I look down and see that it is a long way down. I am not scared by the height. I let go and I do not fall. That is when I see you. You are talking to some farmers near the lake and you stop to look at me, only held aloft by the wind. Even though you are a long way away, I can see you are happy in your return. I climb back inside the watchtower and wake to tell you this story.'

Kar rocked his head back to look at the sky. The

low sun spread a warm light through the cloud cover above.

I stood and gazed around at the surrounding woods and then back at the tree. Like Kar, I now considered this a sacred place and did not care if night fell before we left. Nothing could hurt me whilst I was here, and my dream was like how Kar described the tree, 'an echo,' except that it was from the future. I walked closer to the tree, stopping a pace short of its trunk. I was thinking about touching it. Now that I was this close, I felt it was better if I did not. I did not question my apprehension, for just standing in the tree's presence made me feel complete.

'A splendid dream,' Kar finally spoke. 'When I first asked what it was about, I was curious to know if it was like mine. It was a completely different dream, though just as sweet. It is good to know that you will both be happy.'

'Do you believe it is real?' I quivered with excitement.

'Yes, and I am thankful that I keep doing things without asking why.'

I walked towards Kar with my arms raised to the sky. 'I am soaked through and feel warm all over.'

'I would like to confess something to you, Lagesh.'

'I will listen with open heart to anything you say.' I knelt in the wet grass.

'I planned to show the tree to Senea and Naten. Instead, I took them to Pardensai's grave. I believe that the older you are and the more you have gone through, the harder it is to accept something like this tree.'

'I am honoured that you chose to bring me here.

Maybe when the time is right, I can be the one to show it to my brother and Naten.'

'That may be why I changed my mind the other day. I leave that decision up to you, Lagesh, and only offer one piece of advice. Bring them here but let them experience it of their own accord. Do not tell them anything.'

'I will bring them here to the clearing and let the tree say the rest,' I said, as I stood in wet grass with my arms wide and fingers splayed. 'What do you think my dream means, Kar?' I asked, after spending a moment listening to the strange sounds in the woods after the passing rain.

Kar sat down next to me. 'It was a vision, a dream of the truth. If I told you mine, it may make more sense.'

'I would feel wrong in asking you to reveal any more.'

'For that reason alone, I tell you that I saw my mother again and she looked different. She wears her hair high and the shell bracelet that she always wore is now solid gold, heavy enough to weigh her arm down at her side. I do not know the place, only that King Sargon is there and so are many other kings. I walk down a road towards a gazebo overlooking a turbulent sea. The people around me stop what they are doing and begin talking about me as if I do not belong. There are many soldiers surrounding the gazebo, yet they do not confront me as I walk closer. The closer I get, the more content I feel. I have been waiting a long time to see her face again. When she steps in front of Sargon, she is not the same. It is not so much that she looks different; it is that she speaks differently too.

I am unable to say anything and she points me away, like I never should have come. I turn my back on her and leave Sargon without drawing my weapon. As I walk back down the road, the people applaud me like I now belong, and they ask me to stay at their homes. Their homes look like caves. I am smiling to myself and following my feet with my head downcast as I walk, avoiding their stares. When I look up, I see an unknown sea before me. I stop there at the edge of a steep cliff and everything goes white, like I have closed my eyes after facing the sun. That is my dream Lagesh and, like yours, I cannot make sense of it enough.'

'You called my dream a vision, Kar. If it is the future, then you will one day see the village as I have described and, maybe then, you will be able to tell me what happened that day in your dream when it all turned white. I will not forget what I have experienced this day and, when I hear Naten speak the words that I forgot, I will tell her, "This is the part I have been waiting to hear." And the future, as always, will be just a vision away, is that not so, Kar?'

'You must live the now, Lagesh. I long for things that make time itself a burden for me. I will try my best to smile when I can and remember what you have seen.'

'I do not like being happy whilst I sense sorrow in you.'

'The only sorrow I feel is in view of tasks that may never be achieved,' Kar replied, before standing with renewed vigour. 'I will be happy with my burdens as they are the path to my end, and I will not die until I have reached that view of an unknown sea. It will be there that I find my next path.'

24

Lost Souls

Scribed by Tahnas, The Guardian of the West.

On the twentieth day of our stay in Nineveh, when I was returning to our camp from the Tigris, I witnessed Akkadian soldiers dragging a man behind their horses. His only crime was a coloured shoulder, a tattoo that supposedly looked Guardian in origin. The tattoo, I was told, depicted a man riding a horse and I assumed that the spectacle of the man being dragged up and down the road by horses was meant to make a mockery of this. It reminded me of the need to keep mine covered. I hated the feel of clothing gripping my skin but forced myself to wear a short cut tunic that covered my arms to my elbows.

I stayed until the Akkadians' display of power was completed. Since arriving in Nineveh, this was the first time I had heard someone mention our name, even though this unfortunate man was not even a Guardian. It hurt to watch and not do anything but I thought, by staying, I might hear an announcement, some sort of explanation by the Akkadians. The man's clothes were eventually torn from his body as he was dragged across the hardened dirt. He kept screaming for another lap down the road. When he fell silent, two other soldiers approached with a hand-drawn cart, untied his hands and loaded his body. They wheeled him west towards the King's Gate.

As I walked on, I thought myself foolish for having stayed so long in Nineveh. If there were Guardians here, other than Gentuk, Arman and myself, they would be dead or used by the Akkadians to identify Guardians. The loved ones we sought were not here, I convinced myself, and I knew where I must look next. Mari, a farming city, west of Assur on the Euphrates River, was a likely exchange point for slave women. The men at the docks spoke of travelling there to find a wife. When I asked why, they explained that the city had a reputation for having the most beautiful women. I was told that slave traders keep their most desirable women away from display until they reach Mari.

Gentuk and I parted company with Arman and Delari in Nineveh and travelled south to Assur. There we met a trader who spoke of an Akkadian army making its way west to the Great Sea. We continued down the Tigris River via boat to the shores of a quiet fishing village. The trader travelled with us and exchanged his load of dried fish and grain for ten deer furs. We travelled west on horseback, between the rivers, to Mari. With Gentuk paying devoted attention to our new trader friend, I found the time throughout every leg of the journey to talk to the people and quietly gain more knowledge of Sargon's conquests. Our present journey would only take us as far as Mari. We would return to Assur to meet Arman before making our next move.

In Mari, we caught up with the army and watched them from a cleft in an overlooking plateau, trying to gauge their plans. Beyond the city, we admired the white mountains of Ebla, breaking the otherwise barren desert landscape. High above the sprawl of huts that surrounded the port, the white dome atop the steep steps of a ziggurat shimmered in the last light of day. Travelling via Sargon's new roads, the army would reach Ebla in just short of two days. Ten days later, they would reach the Great Sea and once more be able to establish Sargon's dominion amongst an already humbled population. Gentuk stayed with the trader as I headed towards the drinking hut to consort with the locals. I left my sword behind but had a throwing blade strapped to my thigh. If I did not return on the boat making the first river crossing, Gentuk knew to meet me in the markets.

Like many of the Guardians, I had always found it easy to make new friends, though sometimes it all started with a lie. I introduced myself to a group of innocent farming men as we boarded a boat across the river and escorted them to the local drinking hut, boasting of my generous return from trading the furs I had carried from Nineveh. I not only used this as a chance to pass as a trader, but also to ask questions about Sargon's accomplishments as we sailed between fields of grain on both sides of the river. It was a subject that each of the farmers felt ready to comment upon and I established immediate rapport with the men and engaged their company further by paying for the first round of drinks.

The drinking hut in Mari was more crowded than the city's markets and it was hard to hear conversation without turning your ear to focus. I liked this but our standing table, where we gathered, would have me seen by every man, and occasionally a woman, entering or leaving. Whilst I had convinced the farmers I was a trader, I had used my real name. Too often, the men shouted, 'Tahnas,' to gain my attention.

'They marched straight through the city like we were to be proud of them,' said Basim, the burly man in charge of channelling an even flow of water from the Euphrates River to feed the grain fields east of Assur. His tunic and hands looked as soiled as the other irrigators and his cheeks above his beard were blistered from the sun. 'I am told that Sargon's father was an irrigator like me. Does he give anything back to the people who work hardest?'

'He only gives to the high priests and they just spend it on their temples,' added Jemat, one of the men who dug for Basim. 'I plan to leave this nowhere life soon and head east with my family to seek the rewards for myself.'

'I agree,' said one of the other farmers, 'We work all day just to survive and surely we can do that anywhere.'

'I sympathise with your hard work, my friends,' I said, filling Basim's mug with brew before he continued. 'My home is Borujerd, far to the north and across the eastern desert to the Zagros Mountains. The farmers there, like you, work hard all day and their lord, Vanekebek, also calls himself king without favour.'

'That is what I tell them,' added Basim. 'We are irrigators and, so long as we turn the land for another, a supportive share is all we can expect.'

'You have the wealth to buy land now,' raised Jemat, addressing the man who gave him work. Jemat looked to be the strongest of Basim's workers. His shoulder muscles were like two small heads either side of his upset face.

Basim disagreed, 'The only land I am allowed to buy is too far to the south and new law states that irrigation is restricted to the portals to cities. We could work on digging the existing channels that far but if we were to do so then land prices would rise and I would no longer be able to afford it.'

'Then buy it now and let us help you dig water its way,' suggested Jemat. 'You have been good to us through godless seasons and we will return your generosity until it becomes good farming land.'

I put my hand on Basim's shoulder and silently asked him to delay with his response. I gave two silver shekels to the young farmer who had fetched our drinks upon arrival—intentionally too much—and asked him to buy another round. The young farmer had never held so much wealth intended to be spent all at once and looked at his employer, Basim, for confirmation.

Basim smiled at me and then nodded at the young farmer, encouraging him to proceed. 'As much as I would love to own the land I work, the Euphrates flows to Akkadia and thus I am subject to Sargon's law. You all deserve a night to drink and talk freely and I thank you stranger for asking us here.'

I embraced Basim and spoke to his ear. 'You do not have to thank me, Basim. I have travelled in search of women and children taken by your King and I follow his army.'

Basim broke from the embrace and studied me from head to toe. He leant close. 'You are a good man stranger, and I am not insulted by your deception. I must warn you against any further admissions.' Basim looked at the other farmers gathered around and said in a louder voice, 'A trader who does not horde his silver is hard to come by. We should all be thankful.'

I appreciated their tipped mugs as they throated their beverages in view of a new round to come. Only Jemat delayed in his toast and took the time to study me, noting my shaved head, leather skirt and possibly the tautness of my tunic against my muscular chest and arms. I knew his look to mean many things. Of most concern, Jemat could be one of Sargon's spies or he could see this as a chance to become one. He was surely entertaining ways to profit from my offerings. Jemat's arms were not as rounded with muscle as mine but they were still strong arms. As he lifted his clay mug to his lips, the bulge of his arm muscle grew and was on display in his sleeveless tunic.

'Is there enough for another round?' asked Basim and the young farmer nodded that there was. 'Keep it then and see if our friend pays again for the next.'

'Savage,' I shouted as I flicked another half-shekel to the young man.

The farmer dropped a shekel in his effort to catch the one thrown his way. He quickly found it on the floor, and I watched him hide the one he'd dropped in a pocket sewn into the side of his heavily soiled tunic.

I winked at the farmer and then smiled at the other men standing around our table. 'I enjoy my time drinking but I have been on my feet all day. Let us find a table with stools near to the music and I will further share my bounty.'

'If you do not mind being close to the soldiers, then I know the keeper of this establishment and he will have someone lead us to the most suitable table,' informed Basim, eager to provide a solution.

'Soldiers do not bother me. Show the way,' I replied, with my hand resting on the irrigator's shoulder.

As we approached the bar, I called the younger farmer close and asked him to warn of any danger.

'Will I keep the silver?' he asked.

'It is yours already,' I stooped to tell him, 'I just do not know the people here and I do not want to walk into a trap.'

'Who would want to trap you?'

'It is your job to tell me, young friend.'

He nodded excitedly, 'After the next round, every-one will be a friend.'

Basim caught the eye of a lady collecting empty mugs from one of the tables nearby and signalled her closer. We waited at the bar as she made her way slowly towards us, not deviating from filling her tray first.

'I know you are not a trader but I welcome you the same,' said Basim. 'Apart from humbled slaves, survivors of Sargon's war with the world, the only strangers we see in this city now are the pompous traders of Ebla, carting their stone south. Even traders like you,' he said with a raised brow, as Jemat stepped closer, 'do not visit as often.'

'We do not need the traders anymore, now that Sargon has unified the capitals,' explained Jemat, like he was personally responsible for this achievement. 'Akkadian grain is the purest and our army is the strongest. On the new roads we can transport our own.'

'I do not understand you sometimes, Jemat,' quarrelled Basim. 'You talk the King down all day whilst we work and now you bid him homage.'

'He is the strongest king to ever walk the earth and, for that reason, I respect him. I only wish he shared more with his people.'

I nodded thoughtfully. 'You are right, Jemat. He is a strong king but he does not share his power or wealth with men like you who might prove themselves stronger. Would you respect Basim if he treated you this way?'

'I suppose not but I hear that Sargon does share his wealth. His soldiers celebrate after every conquest and some return with the money to buy land here in the River Valley.' Jemat held his arm high and pointed at the soldiers gathered on the far side of the drinking hut. 'They all have silver for beer. Maybe what they do is what I am best off doing.'

'You did it again. You speak favour for the King that you insult when you lift a shovel.' Basim's tensed brow lifted as he turned to meet the woman he had signalled earlier. She was returning to the bar with a full tray. 'Good evening to you, sweet blossom.'

'I am busy, Basim. What do you want?' said the table servant.

'My friends and I are looking for a table close to the music. Can you lead us to one not reserved for soldiers?"

'What is in it for me?' she asked as she emptied her tray. The waitress appeared to be a lot older than me at first glance. Her hardened skin signed many days spent working in the sun before finding her job in the gloomy expanses of the drinking hut. She had adopted cold eyes to avoid the attention of patrons yet, despite her deceptive age and negative persona, one could tell that she had once been a beautiful young woman and, if a smile were to grace her face again, her ingrained beauty would still be revealed.

'Ubai,' yelled Basim, waving his arm high to gain the attention of the bar keeper, 'I steal her for a drink.'

The keeper looked back from the other side of the bar and frowned at Basim. He reluctantly raised one finger.

'We are down a table attendant this eve and it is expected that this will be the busiest night we have had since Sargon's last visit,' explained the woman as she took Basim's hand and led him between groups of farming men and merchants towards the soldiers occupying the side of the room closest the music. Two musicians were performing and they sat on stools against the far wall. The younger of the two musicians quickly strummed an oud and the other plucked a qanun that rested on his lap.

'Where is Bell? She sick?' asked Basim.

'She is always sick. Like me, she is sick of this work. At least I brave it.'

'At least she smiles when she does make it,' joked Basim to unlistening ears.

'What about this table,' I asked.

'If this is close enough,' said the woman as she turned to face me. 'I do not know you. Do you work for Basim?'

'How rude of me, Messim. This is Tahnas. He is a

trader from Borujerd.'

'Tahnas,' repeated Messim, 'that name sounds familiar.'

I pulled a stool back for her and she decided to sit.

'Thank you, Tahnas. I am not used to being treated with honest favour but all women enjoy it. I will let you provide me with drink any time.'

The table we had arrived at was in the middle of the room and the dispersed stools and drinks remaining on the table signalled that its previous occupants, probably soldiers, had abandoned it in a hurry and might return. The unwritten rule of control of a table resided on occupation and the irrigators sat down and got comfortable. The young irrigator, with two shekels tucked away at his chest, placed a jug in front of Basim before finding a seat for himself.

'As I was saying, look around, listen to the strum of the oud. These are the proceeds of conquest,' said Jemat, admiring the drunken soldiers dancing or talking so loudly that the music was muffled.

'Whilst his conquests continue, the city pays less for produce,' Basim told him. 'They are more interested in stone and timber. Only when all boundaries to Sargon's growing empire are secure will they pay what is owed.'

Jemat laughed. 'Then we should all be soldiers now and farmers later.'

'The King is not here himself, is he?' I asked.

'No, friend,' replied Basim. 'I have never seen him with my own eyes.'

'He has armies like this on every corner of the earth,' preached Jemat, like he knew the King personally. 'He never has to leave his palace in Agade.'

I knew this not to be true. Lord Vanekebek sent me to Agade to deal personally with the King and I made my exchange in his palace in his absence.

'Tahnas?' said Messim questioningly, drawing me away from the conversation and deeper thoughts.

I looked at her and once more saw her sheltered beauty.

'Your name, does it mean something?'

'It is an old name, Messim. I was told it means ageless.'

'I like that,' she reflected. 'It is a shame Bell is not working tonight, for she would run away with a man like you.'

'I am not looking to run away. Indeed, I cannot wait to return home to my loved ones.'

'As I am sure they are waiting eagerly for your return,' she said, leaning in front of me and hooking a lock of her hair behind her ear.

I tried to ignore her demeanour, 'Yes, it hurt to leave. It always does.'

'Bell came to us from the East as well.'

I was trying to listen to Jemat's rant at the same time. All my attention shifted to Messim. 'Is she from Borujerd?' I asked, keeping to my story.

'No, she is from a small village beyond Elam that was sacked by one of Sargon's armies. She was one of the only survivors. I think sometimes she wished she had died with the others. They offered her a job scribing but she did not write what they wanted, so they cut her face and sold her to the first bidder,' said Messim. 'She is beautiful, even with the deep scar across her cheek. Ubai is always looking for pretty women to work his tables. You know, I was once beautiful too.'

'She writes?' I questioned.

'Yes, and she has been teaching me. I do not think I will ever need to but, as Bell says, "If you can write, you can read." She says many things that I don't really understand.'

'Belline?' I asked, needing assurance.

'Yes. Belline. That is why I know your name,' said Messim, just as astonished. She reached out and touched my shoulder, covered by cloth. 'Her stories are true.'

In the corner of my eye, I saw Jemat watching on and placed her other hand on my thigh.

She smiled at me curiously and leant close, 'She never told me this part.'

'I have to find her,' I said.

'She is locked up in one of the rooms out back. Ubai has her under watch ever since her attempt to flee. If you are still here after close, you might be able to see her when I arrive home.'

'I do not want to put you in any danger.'

'I was thinking, that way, I could come with you.' Messim stood abruptly, making an emphasis on pushing my hand away. 'You cannot afford this trader and I have to get back to work.'

I stood as she departed and called after her, 'Then maybe when you finish work.'

She did not turn back and dismissed my call with a flick of her wrist. I sat back down and looked at the irrigators staring at me.

Basim laughed first and then the whole table of

men burst with laughter.

I laughed back at them half-heartedly. 'Is she always like this?' I asked.

'I try my luck every time I visit, my friend,' laughed Basim. 'I thought you actually had a chance for a while.'

'You do not have a wife?' I asked.

'Oh yes, I do. She is twice the woman Messim is.'

'He thought rats were getting to his food stores,' added Jemat, 'until he caught his woman in the act.'

Again, the farmers started laughing and Basim laughed loudest.

I smiled too without understanding how a man could speak this way of his loved one. Messim's abrupt departure also made me wary.

'Do not hear me wrong, Tahnas. She is the love of my life, only she is too large to make love to anymore,' Basim said of his wife, barely finishing his sentence before choking with laughter.

I appreciated the company of the jovial irrigators gathered at the table, all the while looking for a chance to move before Messim's shift was finished.

25

The Trader from the North

Scribed by Arman, The Always Travelling Guardian.

From the shade of a date palm grove, I watched the road north to Khorsabad and scratched my beard. The air was cool beneath the roof of long fronds and I could see north to the sand-swept horizon. There was always someone leaving or approaching the city. The traders leaving Nineveh had usually completed trade in the inner or outer city markets and I liked to wish them safe travels as they began their course on the new road north between the ravines. I would ride to meet the inbound travellers, hoping to secure new trade.

As the sun began to settle in the west, I moved behind the trunk of a palm and repadded my straw cushion by pushing it together from different sides. The straw inside had rotted and the smell reminded me of the wet season. It needed to be restuffed but I used the comfort of the smell as an excuse for putting the task off until another day. Before I was comfortable again, movement to the side of the road caught my eye. I readied my mare and rode to meet the lone trader arriving from an unusual direction with a cumbersome load.

I led the strange looking trader into the camp from the neighbouring plain and directed him to Delari's stall. Delari ignored the local farmer haggling over a price for a shovel when he saw me return with new business.

'Welcome to Nineveh,' Delari greeted the new arrival, no doubt noticing the matted coat and sunken flank of the trader's heavily loaded mare. 'What brings you our way?'

'He has travelled a long way, Delari,' I informed my friend, as I dismounted and helped the trader lift heavy, wrapped bundles from his duteous mare.

Delari finished his exchange with the local farmer quickly by agreeing to his first outrageous offer. He hurried to gather water and grain for the overridden horse.

***

Inside our hut, the northern trader unwrapped a small parcel and revealed a new invention. Delari asked him if he could demonstrate its capabilities and the trader was quick to oblige with a well-versed spiel. The northern trader's words fitted the display, though he had trouble speaking in this way. His voice was not commanding like Delari's or the merchants who shouted, 'fish,' or, 'bread,' to draw trade to their stalls. He spoke to the ground and his skin and hair was as filthy as a begger's. Delari was sceptical from the moment he opened his mouth.

'Behold, men of Nineveh, the future of warfare.' He displayed the weapon to himself and acted surprised with what he held. 'No longer will hunters or soldiers be impeded by lengthy bows with clumsy aim or arrows that deflect off armour.' He shook his head and almost looked up at us. 'Threefold the propulsion and easier to carry. I present to you, the fast bow.'

Delari reached out to gather the item, not realising that the northern trader was only just beginning. His hand was smacked away.

'This bolt was cast from bronze like that breastplate you have there,' he explained, his skinny arm pointed forwards like a spear from the cave of his hide vest. 'How, I hear you asking, could it penetrate its surface?'

I looked at Delari and shrugged my shoulders, my mouth clenched for fear of laughing.

'Allow me to demonstrate,' continued the stranger.

Delari jumped to his feet and sat next to me, away from the bronze breastplate that was nestled amongst his other random goods laid out for trade. Delari prided himself on carrying an assortment of goods and only sold out for a larger load of one item if he was sure he could offload it quickly. This was one of the techniques he had taught to the traders who shared the camp in Nineveh. Another trading secret he shared with our new friends in the camp was to remain unconvinced of the benefits of anything new presented to you until the final handshake.

The trader fastened the thin bronze bolt with his back to us. 'I carry twenty fast bows,' he said over his shoulder. 'This is what one can do.' Holding the weapon with only one arm the trader turned side-on to us and pulled a small lever with one finger. The bronze bolt sprung forwards across the hut and pierced the breastplate as promised.

I would have lurched to my feet if Delari were not quick to subdue me with a braced arm around my shoulder.

'That was Arman's breastplate,' said Delari, excusing my excitement. 'Continue your demonstration.'

'One of these fine pieces of work will only cost you five shekels and that, I am sure, for a trader of your eminence, is only a few day's work.'

Delari pinched his lips to hold back a smile.

The northern trader stepped over my sleeping fur to fetch his bolt.

'Do not be touching that,' said Delari jumping to his feet. 'I am intrigued as to how it works.'

'Do not take me for a fool, trader,' the stranger snapped, hastily fastening another bolt and glancing behind as he took a step closer to the tent's entrance. 'If we do not make a trade today, I will also be wanting my bolt back.'

I drew a throwing blade in the man's momentary distraction and kept it concealed.

He watched Delari approach the breastplate. 'You can admire its craftsmanship all you like once a deal has been made but this is a new invention and I plan to profit on that before more are crafted alike,' said the trader with another bolt now fastened and the strange bow held ready.

'My apologies friend, I did not mean to alarm you. I was only thinking that the bolt already stuck in the breastplate could save me a further demonstration. It was a fine piece of armour before you arrived.'

The northern trader nodded and unfastened the bolt he had loaded. 'Your friend told me you were the most revered trader in the land, and I begin to see why now. Inform me of your interest or I shall be on my way.'

'It is not that simple,' said Delari. 'I can also tell that this is not the first trade agreement for you either. How many of these have you sold on your journey thus far and how am I to know that another trader will not be here in a few days time with the same offering for half the price.'

'It will be more than a few days, but traders will arrive carrying the same. I have traded eight bows and had thirty when I left Catal Huyuk. Your King may have left our home to waste but we were a people of the land and, so long as we are free from shackles, we offer our gifts to the world at honest prices.'

Delari offered the trader a seat and immediately broke a loaf of bread to share with him. 'I offer you safe haven whilst I consider your offer,' said Delari, seating himself first and holding out his hands in offering. 'My friend,' he then continued, gesturing at me, 'is also a survivor and my interests are now greater than just wealth and success in bargaining. Let us take necessary time with our negotiations for I am sure my friend also wants to hear what happened to your homeland in the north.'

'I am a trader, not a hunter who brings meat to the fire. Unless you boast silver soon, not bread, I will be leaving to make trade elsewhere.'

'So, you are not native to Catal Huyuk?' Delari further questioned the man.

The northern trader re-fastened a bolt but stopped short of raising the bow's aim from the ground. His dark eyes flickered nervously between Delari and I as he spoke. 'Unlike the rest of my people, I was not content to sit idle and wait for our god to return. You told me you were not like the others,' rasped the northern trader, singling me out with a stabbing stare.

'We are not,' stated Delari, standing and stepping in front of me, slightly amused by the trader's unstable nature. 'If it is silver you want, a deal can be done but I would like to offer you some of my other goods as well. Maybe a healthy mare?'

The northern trader tilted his bow's aim towards Delari's chest and my usually wise friend covered his manhood with his hands as defence against a weapon that had just been shown to effortlessly pierce bronze armour.

'Avert your aim or you will die with regret,' I informed him. 'Everything you own apart from your feeble mare is in this hut. For your sake be reasonable.'

'I am protecting myself, Arman, if that is your name. The trader I do not fear but I saw you draw your blade and I tell you, I will not leave this city without proper return for my load.'

'He is one of the few you need not fear,' Delari tried to explain and once more offered the stranger some bread. He stepped closer to him and I imagined an accidental pull of the trigger sending a bolt straight through Delari's chest and onward into the next hut. The northern trader did not deviate his aim and so

Delari assisted him. He extended an arm with his offer of bread and attempted to push the bow's aim towards the ground with his other hand. The bolt was released. It streaked between Delari's thighs and deflected off a log near the fire, narrowly missing my head before disappearing through the thatched roof. Delari punched the stranger straight in the face and he fell backwards against his wrapped parcel.

I raised my palm, waiting for a moment to hear if the bolt hit anyone on its downward course.

When the moment had passed, Delari stepped towards the trader as he shuffled away defensively on his elbows and heels. Delari bent over and delivered another solid punch to the side of his head. The trader collapsed this time and did not move on the ground.

I stood and parted the door flap. After listening for a while with my head poked timidly outside, I returned to my seat near the unlit fire. 'That could have progressed better.'

Delari looked up from watching the lifeless, northern trader lying on the floor and was speechless for a moment. He patted his groin to see if the bolt between his thighs had taken anything with it.

I approached to see if the man was still breathing. His chest looked still and blood drained from his nose into clumps of already sticky hair on his upper lip. I put my palm close to his mouth. 'It's done,' I said.

Delari threw his head back and groaned. 'I only meant to give him pause.'

'I know you always wanted to be one, and now you are my Guardian. I wait to see now if I have taught you honesty as well.'

Delari stared at me. 'Is he dead?'

'He's breathing, Delari. You can still offer him bread.'

Delari exhaled. 'You scared me. I will give him more than a fair price for he has already paid for his ignorance.'

'It was not ignorance, Delari. It was appropriated fear, heightened by me drawing my blade. I am respectful of him for even noticing and I am even more respectful of you for taking control of the situation.'

'You told me at the beginning of the season that you respected me in the same way you viewed your Guardian brothers,' complained Delari. 'How can you say now that you are more respectful of me?'

'You aimed for a kill punch but did not use all your strength.'

'I might have used all my strength.'

'He threatened our lives but he did not deserve to die. You saved us and he still lives.'

'I understand now, wise Guardian,' said Delari with mirth. 'Did they ever teach you, in your many seasons spent learning how to best clobber a person, about the trade of obsidian? The people in the north, made everything from arrow tips to jewellery from the black stone, long before the use of bronze and long before there were cities between the rivers. That is what I knew when this man said he was from Catal Huyuk. What I also know is that Catal Huyuk has long been a wasteland. No man can say they are from Catal Huyuk.'

'I did not know this,' I said. 'He did arrive from the north.' I attempted to point north from inside the tent.

'Let me tell you more before he wakes up,' said Delari as he picked up the other half of the loaf, dusted it off and offered it to me.

I picked out some more dirt before taking a bite.

'You have told me stories about villages who live at peace without a King or Chieftain. This is one. Catal Huyuk, a thousand seasons ago, was the largest city in the world and no man was greater than the next. They mined their mountains until there was no more black stone. Some say the gods took vengeance on them for this and collapsed what remained of their hollowed-out surrounds. Others say they left because all the black stone had been mined. Whatever the true story may be, it happened long before the Akkadians came to rule. Maybe he was talking half-truth for I would not be able to distinguish a northern man from any other. At the same time, I find it hard to believe that he has only sold eight of these weapons or that he is the only one selling them.'

'His bargaining was quite impressive to begin with,' I admitted. 'Maybe he has only sold eight because of the way he concludes his deals.'

Delari looked up from studying the unusual bow and smiled at me. 'Yes, he was very protective. That is why I wanted to take my time with the negotiation. If his count is correct, I'd like to sell twenty and keep two.'

'It has all worked out well. Any other trader in our position would have finished him off. Wrapped him in his own cloth and dumped him in the desert, east of the road where he would not even be smelled.'

'I like the man for some reason,' mused Delari.

'Maybe he is a descendant of Catal Huyuk.'

'What about his price?' I inquired. 'Twenty-two at five shekels each is … More than one hundred shekels.'

'His price is fair. What he carries worries me most.' Delari stared at the larger unwrapped bundle and then back at the strange trader. 'Even if he spoke the truth and has only sold eight, it will only be a matter of time before this invention falls into the hands of those who will prosper adversely from its strength. I propose we keep one each and sell the rest for twice the price.' He handed me the unusual bow to examine personally. 'I think I have changed you, Guardian. Bury him in the desert, what talk is that?'

'Sargon changed me when he advanced upon the East. With my wife dead, you are my closest friend and the closest thing to home. I would move a body for you.'

'Thank you, Arman. This body can stay for now.'

'On the road or even settled here in Nineveh, I find a new reason to live each day. I would have withered and died if I had stayed too long at the tower.'

Delari watched as I examined the bow's construction, his eyes creased with deep thought.

'Do you remember the bow I strung in Eshnunna?' I asked, turning the new weapon over and looking at it from underneath.

'You used the sap from a pine to help you bind and tense thin lengths of tendon.'

'The tendon is strong and the way the bolt locks into its brace is incredible. I cannot understand how this would not affect aim. I want to try it over a longer distance.'

Delari's brow lifted and he pointed a finger to the sky. He stepped next to the trader's larger parcel and untied one of the leather straps. As he fumbled about, the northern trader roused. 'Do not worry. You are still in the same place,' said Delari as the trader convulsed and then sat upright without a plan as to what to do next. Delari handed me a bolt and then offered his hand to the trader.

The trader pushed his hand away and staggered to his feet.

'I see,' I exclaimed, as I sat down on my log and examined the bolt. 'You will have to ask how many he has of these as well and at what price. A bow is only as good as its arrow.'

Delari sat down opposite me and watched the trader re-gather his thoughts and look for his belongings.

'I trusted you,' he yelled at me with his back against his bundle.

'I know but when you yell it does not sound like a compliment,' I replied, distracted by the construction of the bow. I hushed the man's next predicted comment with a spread hand.

'That is good to hear. We are trustworthy men,' Delari told him. 'I did not mean to hurt you. I just wanted to talk. You made that difficult.'

'Do you want to trade or not?' he asked as he gently patted the swelling on the side of his head and wiped blood from his nose and lip with his forearm.

'I am interested,' said Delari, 'but I will not entertain a man who uses force as a means to an end. Sit down and rest or I will help you again.'

I had worked out how to lock a bolt in the crossbow and turned its aim on the trader.

'Arman, I do not think that is necessary.'

'What do you want?' pleaded the man.

'My friend and I are curious,' I began. 'You say these weapons come from Catal Huyuk. Did you play a part in their invention?'

'Yes, and my brother did not think that we should show anyone else. Sharing with the rest of the world was what led our god to leave us. Here I know this weapon will be used for war, but we made it for hunting. You have to creep up on the deer and rise from the grass to take aim. We found that the bow, even if tensed before we rose, spoilt our attack in movement,' explained the trader nervously and he was comforted to see me practise my aim on a polished-stone mirror rested on the other side of the hut. 'In the days before kings, we would have had hunters on opposing sides of the animals and they, not the first man to release an arrow, were usually the ones to land the kill.'

'Or be killed in the stampede. He speaks like a hunter. Do you agree, Arman?'

I turned my gaze to Delari and then on to the northern trader. 'You talk like you know the hunt. Can you tell me where to cut a deer to find its heart?'

'No, I will not tell. Kill one in my presence and I might teach you what must be done,' replied the trader.

I smiled and gave Delari a nod.

'Why have you travelled to Akkadia to sell these weapons?' he asked, still unconvinced of the man's motives.

'I have come to trade. Should I have walked in

circles in the desert?'

Delari stood and rolled the heavy log he was sitting on to the side. In view of the northern trader, he uncovered a secret compartment dug into the floor of the hut.

I placed the bow down and stared at the stranger.

The northern trader stared back at me and decided it was safe to tell us more. 'Everyone was sleeping the night our god abandoned us, allowing the mountains to bury his worshippers and make them dirt once more. Only those sleeping on the far eastern side of the mountains survived.'

'Did that make you angry with your god?' I asked.

'I was not angry for I was saved.'

I broke a new loaf of bread for the trader and offered him a seat once again. This time the trader accepted the offer and sat down.

'My name is, Arman. I did not lie to you. And the old man is Delari.'

Delari smiled and turned briefly to acknowledge the trader as he continued to search his hidden compartment. He was producing all manner of strange items and placing them nearby.

'My name is Uk-Ban Semberat, son of Sheptam, of Catal Huyuk.'

'You say your brother survived. Did your parents? I asked as I packed my pipe with herb.

'Many survived but they could not understand the abandonment. Lost without our god, we have walked in circles ever since. I watched those who chose to leave our homeland return to die. They are at peace now with our ancestors and will never know hunger or fight thirst again.'

Uk-Ban spoke like more of his tribe remained and I was one reliant on concise explanations. 'Where will you go when you are finished here?' I asked and waited a moment before pulling smoke from my pipe. Uk-Ban, distracted by Delari and the strange items he kept hidden and separate to his other goods for trade, fell silent and took a moment to drink from his water skin before he replied. I appreciated the trader's troubled nature for I always believed that a hasty man never had time to form his own opinion.

'You are a survivor?' asked Uk-Ban. 'What brings you here to the land of the new king?'

'Happiness for me is found in this herb I smoke and in helping others find a better reason to live.'

'What is that?' Uk-Ban asked.

'This?' I questioned, looking at my pipe. 'It is a distraction from the hopeless feelings that consume me between better times.'

'You are not happy you survived?' Uk-Ban continued with his questioning.

'What do you want to know?' I asked, my voice growing louder. 'I face life each day. I do not plan for the future because that failed me. My friend Delari helps me live this new life because his future is found in his next trade.'

'I do not understand,' confessed Uk-Ban, picking at his beard as if looking for something.

'You do not have to understand him,' said Delari as he leaned over and presented a palm-sized statue to the trader. 'We live our lives to make sense in our own way.'

'This is from Catal Huyuk,' said the trader with restrained concern as he polished the marble statue handed to him with his filthy fingers. 'These were never traded. How are you in possession of such a sacred object?'

Delari smiled at Uk-Ban and took a moment to calm himself before speaking. 'I knew you would be excited to see a relic crafted by one of your kinsman a thousand seasons ago.' Delari also looked excited and spoke defensively. 'I have carried it for all these years just to show someone who would understand. Now, with it presented and intended as a gift, I do not like being questioned for returning it to its rightful owner. I also want answers. How was it that a lowly merchant in the markets of Khorsabad happened to have this relic laid out on his rug like it were only as valuable as the replicas crafted in fired clay? I know the statues that depict a woman seated between large cats originated in Catal Huyuk. I attained a relic from amongst the imitations.' Delari looked across the dead fire at me for approval.

'You did well keeping it for this day,' I complimented Delari. 'All I know of Catal Huyuk, I have learnt this eve,' I told Uk-Ban. 'From what Delari tells me, it was the greatest place on Earth, long before I was even walking like a man. So, let me advise you not to question the man who believes in you or I will disclaim his stories as myth and remember your people as I have seen you.'

Uk-Ban stared at me past the marble statue in his hands and reluctantly handed it to me like it was the first time anyone had ever parted with the possession.

As I looked upon the smooth rock, shaped to resemble a fat woman seated between two cats, the northern trader began to explain his concerns.

'Every child was given one: the boys before their first hunt and the girls when they first bled. It was a reminder that our mothers cradle life and the animals that allow us to live trust us to only kill what we will eat that day. The cats, like the men of Catal Huyuk, were born to hunt and only reveal their true nature to their mothers. No one from Catal Huyuk would have ever willingly parted with their most sacred gift.'

'I understand,' sympathised Delari and handed the trader a strung pouch, filled with silver. 'That is forty shekels. All I have. You can count it if you feel it necessary. I would like to buy all your short bows and every bolt you carry as well. The statue that I purchased for a half-shekel is a gift and if you decide that you want more for your bounty then look around my stall and find other items that interest you. I leave the bargaining open to your discretion.'

'Where did you find the statue?' asked Uk-Ban. He looked at the statue longingly but did not reach for it when I tried to return it to his hands.

'I found the statue in the Khorsabad markets. All I can tell you otherwise is that the man who sold it to me did not know its worth even though he had shaped statues of similar face. I am honoured to have met you Uk-Ban and to have finally returned this item to a man who values its true worth. As a trader, that is what makes me happier than any other offering this world has yet to reveal to me.'

Uk-Ban lowered his head, humbled by the respect shown to him by a trader in Nineveh, a stranger. He turned to face me and I handed him the statue.

Uk-Ban received it graciously this time and bowed his head with respect to both of us. 'I feel ashamed of the way I acted in your presence. I never thought that traders could be so understanding.'

'We are not traders,' I corrected him. 'We are both Guardians. We stand steadfast in the face of unforgettable wrong so that we might learn one day how to sleep soundly.'

'You speak like my father would if he had lived to see these days and, if he were here, he would tell me to stand strong. I asked for five silver for each bow and I have another request as well.'

'Name it,' said Delari. 'I will consider.'

'I wish to lodge with you until I am sure of my next path. Too much has changed in my mind upon our meeting, and I no longer wish to travel alone.'

'Only with respect for your plight, I ask, how many of you survived when the mountains collapsed? Are there more men like you from Catal Huyuk?'

Uk-Ban bowed his head and then held his newly acquired statue aloft.

'You do not have to answer, Uk-Ban. I will secure more silver. Stay with us and together we might learn a better way to prosper in the west.'

I silently agreed with Delari by lighting another pipe of herb. Uk-Ban seated himself next to me and, as I was blowing smoke, he held the statue in front of me. I turned away to exhale the last of my smoke and coughed.

'She is at peace again,' said Uk-Ban, wiping blood from his nose on the statue and then removing his hide vest to wrap it securely. He placed the wrapped statue at his feet and hummed a song I had not heard before.

26

Arms Trading

Scribed by Arman, The Always Travelling Guardian.

I dressed the next morning in a fancy green tunic and adorned my fingers with sparkling silver rings like I had too much wealth. Uk-Ban, already comfortable in my company, suggested I wear a necklace as well. 'Stop telling me what to wear. Your hair is a sight a barbarian would wake to and scream if he had a mirror.'

'We have a mirror,' said Uk-Ban as he stepped to the side, picked it up and angled it at my face.

'What are you doing? I know I look like a fool. Your eyes were meant to save me from looking into that revealing thing.'

'You look like an ugly man who wants to be a woman,' critiqued Uk-Ban.

'Thanks for sharing. You look like you have not bathed for many seasons and I know this to be true. If you want to help, put on my sandals and hold your advice.'

'I do enjoy this, Arman. Never before have I played games with soldiers.' Uk-Ban was quivering with excitement as he slid his slimey sandals from his rotting feet. He may not have bathed for weeks but he had, that very morning, agonisingly combed thick knots from his hair with an eating fork and washed his face in a bowl that, as a result, became half-filled with sand and tiny, wriggly animals that had made a home in his infested beard.

'This is not a game, Uk-Ban. If they think of us any less than rich travellers, they will seize the weapons and tell all present that they were stolen, and we will fetch no return.'

'I understand,' he said as he strapped on my sandals. His own sandals were worn through at the soles and the leather straps only hung together by a tether. 'Maybe I should wear the necklace,' he said as the idea sounded in his head.

I glared at him.

'What about my hair?'

'Uk-Ban,' I blurted, 'please stop telling me your every thought. When Delari returns you should probably wash your face again. Do not worry about your hair or that stupid necklace.' It was not my intention to insult him. Even when I yelled at him, I could tell that Uk-Ban was not listening or taking me seriously. I paced back and forth, uncomfortable with my attire and eager to play my part and put this all behind me. 'Where is he?' I asked and held out a finger immediately to silence Uk-Ban before he spoke.

Delari approached the tent from outside. 'Are you dressed, Arman?' he asked, as he held the door flap open for a young woman to enter the stall first. Her eyes doubled in size and she turned her head quickly to avoid laughing in my face.

'No, that will not work,' judged Delari immediately, raising a hand to shield his eyes. 'It grabs at your ... at your waist.'

I sighed loudly and returned to my log to pack a pipe. 'Well, what do you want me to do because I am regretting the entire plan.'

'Help him would you, Silda,' requested Delari.

Delari thought her opinion on my costume was necessary and had gone to fetch her whilst Uk-Ban and I changed. Silda was the eldest daughter of one of the permanent traders in the camp, Ashipa the Bread Maker. She had become friends with Delari and I during our stay and enjoyed playing a part in our tactical trade games. Her dark hair was tied back in a single plait, accentuating her smooth face and delicate frame. Her fine cloth dress draped from her shoulders as she bent to inspect my ring-adorned hands and, as her exposed, small breasts pleasantly teased my eyes, I thought of a different plan. 'Delari, I think–'

'Quiet, Arman. Let Silda make her judgement.'

She placed her hand on my shoulder to ease her kneel. 'I do not think you need so many rings and, if you are going to wear this dress, I think we need to paint your face.'

'Delari said it was a rich-man's tunic.'

'It's a dress, Arman. It's tight at your waist because you're tall. How did you get into this?'

'Into the dress or listening to Delari?'

'Wash your face and hands,' Delari told Uk-Ban and he placed a bowl near the tent's door flap filled with water.

'I have washed,' said Uk-Ban.

'Wash again. I am returning to Isvah's hut to prepare the goods for trade. What we are about to do could change everything. We are going to bait the palace traders for every piece of silver they have and ensure the acquired wealth is put to better use.' Delari closed the door flap and opened it a moment later. 'I would like to call them side bows or maybe lever bows.' He bit his lip and sighed.

Uk-Ban looked at his hands not understanding why cleaning them again was necessary.

Near the centre of the trade camp, there was a small hut erected, intended mainly for the use of travelling, short-stay traders. Isvah would often request a small offering for its use but he shared it with his friends for no charge. He even used it himself from time to time when he had goods of a dubious nature that he sought to offload. Like Delari, he lived at the stall he traded from and some trade was best kept separate to personal life. Isvah had once acquired a barrel of honey beer and, whilst he tasted the brew himself and was assured it was fit for consumption, the price raised suspicion. If it were stolen, he did not want the true owner arriving at his home for retribution or a purchaser returning to complain of people falling ill after drinking too much. The small hut was well positioned, close to fellow permanent traders, and, once a deal was done, one could return home without fear of repercussions.

***

It was mid-morning when the palace traders entered the trading camp led by four soldiers with another four following close behind. Near to the saddle maker, another eight soldiers guarded a wagon and waited for the signal to come and collect the larger purchases. The palace traders made their first stop at the fishmonger's stall. They helped themselves to some smoked fillets on the counter as the monger un-wrapped some fresh fish for them to inspect. The accompanying soldiers mingled nearby and also felt it was their privilege to sample whatever they liked before bargaining had commenced.

The largest soldier in the trading party departed from his allies when he spotted Silda smiling at him from in front of the dressmaker's hanging works. It was not the first time he had seen this beautiful peasant girl, but it was the first time he had caught her looking at him. Just as he was getting close, she walked on and he followed her around the dressmaker's hut to where she disappeared inside her father's stall. Disappointed, he came to a stop and looked at Ashipa blocking the entrance.

'Blessed morn to you. Can I offer you some bread?' Ashipa asked the lured soldier.

Thankless, the bulky soldier extended his hand and snatched the offering. 'Is that your daughter?' he asked, only after his mouth was full with his first bite.

'She is.'

'Ask her to come outside to commune with me?'

'No. She has chores to do.'

'She can do them later,' insisted the large soldier, wiping crumbs from his mouth and brushing his hair back with spittle.

'Morning blessings,' I sang, as I approached Ashipa and the soldier. I bent to sniff the still warm bread stacked on Ashipa's table. 'As fresh as new day,' I praised, fanning the scent to my nose with limp wrists.

'Cooked this morning, friend. Can I wrap you some loaves?'

'I will take four,' I said, rummaging through my pouch and placing an un-negotiated amount of silver on the table.

'Two shekels, very generous of you,' thanked Ashipa.

I turned and smiled politely at the large soldier only to be met with a very concerned glare. 'How are you this morning, Soldier?' I asked, with my ring-adorned hand outstretched in greeting.

The soldier took a backwards step and hid his hand. 'What is wrong with you, man?' he questioned and pointed at my face. 'Do you see this?' he continued, requesting Ashipa's judgement.

'I see my favourite customer this season,' Ashipa replied. 'I have wrapped four loaves and some flatbread.'

'Thank you,' I said, tilting my chin to the soldier as I left the stall.

'Master, you must come quickly,' cried Uk-Ban, as he ran to my side and pulled on my dress.

I wiped Uk-Ban's clutching hands away like I did not like being touched and handed what the soldier hopefully saw as my servant the bread to carry. 'All right, be calm. I am sure it is not going to run away like I wish you would sometimes,' I replied, smiling at Ashipa.

The soldier shook his head at me with disgust as I

followed Uk-Ban. I looked back a few steps later and the soldier was gesturing to his face, referring to my pink cheeks and black-lined eyes. 'Blessings this morning,' I sang to the next stall owner, worried that the soldier was not following.

Uk-Ban rushed back to my side. 'People are gathering. Come quick.'

'Hurry on then,' I said, hitching my dress to lengthen my gait.

Giving up on a chance to talk to the trader's daughter, the soldier followed me with renewed interest, all the time chewing on a large stump of bread. He looked back towards his comrades and signalled one of the others to follow him.

When the palace traders reached Delari's temporary trading hut, led by the large soldier, a small crowd had already gathered. Delari stood at five paces from a bale of hay that he had fitted with leather armour. On top of the bale was a round clay pot painted with a smile and two blobs of paint for eyes.

'Please do not stand there,' Delari called out to a group of children gathering behind. 'This is dangerous,' he alerted all, holding one of Uk-Ban's bows aloft. 'It is the most dangerous weapon ever invented. I call it the Side Bow.'

The palace traders parted the crowd to acquire the most unobstructed view. The locals who had gathered first did not like this but they did not have a say. The soldier's rule and the penalty for opposing were non-negotiable. Delari delayed his speech until the crowd had reshuffled.

'Not only will this heavy bronze bolt pierce the

leather with precise aim but, at such short range, it may even pass straight through the thick bale of hay as well.'

The palace guards sniggered amongst each other and pointed at Delari and his target.

'I see we have doubters,' scoffed Delari, 'Doubt is understandable. I once shared this scepticism. I now know that the doubters will be impressed by this weapon's capabilities.'

'Delay not then,' encouraged the lead palace trader. His appearance was remarkably similar to the Borujerdian commander I had sighted north of the tower, only this man's cape was red and his beard shaped like a perfect spear tip.

'The Side Bow, everyone. Pray one is never aimed at you.' Delari fastened a bolt and took aim.

'Wait,' I called out from the back of the crowd.

The palace traders looked around, angered by the delay.

I stepped out in view opposite them and pointed at the leather armour. 'This will not do,' I began. 'The armour ...' and that was all I could say before the laughter drowned my voice.

'That is the ugliest woman I have ever seen,' said one of the soldiers.

I opened my arms wide and accepted their jaunts like I could listen all day and not be offended. 'You would not know what real beauty is after spending your whole life in your heavy war suit,' I yelled at the soldier who made the first joke at my expense. This just made them laugh louder. Almost everyone in the camp had gathered by the time I got a chance to finish what

I wanted to say. As the palace traders wiped tears from their eyes and hung off each other for support from their aching sides, I spoke again in my unique, rich trader's voice. 'I think that if we want to see this new bow's true capabilities then it needs to be demonstrated on solid, bronze armour. I think it will be deflected and that is why this trader chooses not to use it.'

Delari shook his head at me and singled me out as he looked around the crowd. 'Maybe this man,' he said, delaying for a moment, 'if that is how he likes to be referred to, has the silver to waste on destroying fine armour. If so, I will allow the request. I am a mere trader and inventor by chance and, whilst I have tested the weapon's strength on bronze, I do not have the wealth to spoil another breastplate.'

'That is a splendid excuse,' I said, 'though I for one am not convinced.'

A few of the soldiers were still restraining their laughter and were silenced by the palace traders who validated my opinion, despite my strange dress. They made room for the large soldier who had followed Silda earlier, and he walked out into the display area and started to remove his bronze breastplate.

Delari disappeared inside the small hut and returned a moment later with the breastplate Uk-Ban had used in his demonstration. He lifted the breastplate and peered at the crowd through the hole. 'It is your choice,' he told the palace traders. 'I will not offer return for the damage.' Delari held the breastplate aloft for all to see and then handed it to me.

I displayed it to Uk-Ban like it was the first time we had seen it and we acted surprised. Uk-Ban's reaction would have convinced me. He grabbed me like he was frightened, and I pushed him away before stroking his matted hair. 'My apologies,' I said and returned it to Delari before stepping back amongst the crowd.

The large soldier looked at his comrades and they signalled for him to continue. He walked toward the bale of hay and rested his breastplate in front of the leather armour.

'Damaged or not, I will be getting that back,' he told Delari, making sure the palace traders overheard his demand.

Both parties agreed and the large man found a spot at the front of the crowd, making everyone nearby shuffle for an unhindered view.

'The Side Bow, dangerous even in a child's hands,' announced Delari. He took aim and pulled the small release lever.

His arm rose when the pressure on the tendons was released and I turned towards the target, hearing it connect with something but unsure of the result. 'Out of my way,' I shouted at those crowding in front and blocking my view.

'Stand back,' shouted the lead palace guard and I stood my ground as others rushed from my side.

The large soldier returned to his breastplate and, when he tried to pick it up, he discovered that the bolt had stuck it to the leather armour. He reefed at it and, when it gave way, found himself holding it high in the air for even those at the back of the crowd to see. The bolt emerged from both sides.

I began the applause and the rest of the crowd, apart from the palace traders, clapped loudly in appreciation of the demonstration. Clapping my hands above my head with exuberance, I approached Delari. I whispered something to Uk-Ban in view of the palace traders and the man from Catal Huyuk rushed away to fulfil my orders.

Delari bowed to the applause and then began trade negotiations with me.

The palace traders still conversed amongst themselves in disbelief.

'Twenty Akkadian silver shekels?' I exclaimed, as the first of the palace traders approached, 'That would mean a total of four-hundred.'

'I do not ask that you buy them all,' said Delari and he ignored me briefly to welcome the palace traders.

'Do not worry about them. I am interested. Could you sway on the price if I took them all?'

Delari now ignored the traders and turned back to face me. 'It takes me ten days to craft one and I am not about to sell my life's work and the time it has taken me to travel here for any less,' he confirmed with conviction. 'Twenty silver per side bow, non-negotiable.' Directing my attention to the presence of the palace traders, Delari continued, 'I would not expect a trader, even one with acquired wealth, to buy everything I carry. These men I am sure know the price of invention and the strength it will have in their hands. If I were you, I would make an even more generous offer for just one or two.'

'We will take every one you have,' said the lead palace guard.

'And you witness,' said Delari, smiling boastfully at me. 'Would you like the bolts I carry as well?'

'Everything,' confirmed the lead palace trader.

'I expected your appreciation,' rejoiced Delari. 'I carry twenty bolts as well, counting that one,' he said referring to the bolt in the large soldier's hand. 'The bronze bolts I will let go for five silver each. That is a total of five-hundred silver shekels for everything I carry.'

The palace guards began conversing quietly amongst themselves and I watched them through my black-lined eyelids, only half pretending to be anxious.

As their secret conversation continued, Uk-Ban returned dragging a large, wooden chest and, struggling with the weight, placed it awkwardly at my feet.

'We will give you five silver per bow and meet your five for each bolt,' announced the lead trader.

'I offer you the requested four-hundred and only ask that the bolts be included as good faith,' I bid and signalled Uk-Ban to open the chest.

This time Delari ignored the palace traders and bent to inspect the chest. He delved his hands into the silver inside and let it trickle out between his fingers. 'You know how to secure a deal, trader. I was wrong to judge you on appearance. Maybe when this silver is mine, I too will find myself painting my face and dressing as I please.'

'We will make another ...' began the lead palace trader.

I silenced him with my splayed fingers, each adorned in at least one silver ring.

The palace traders were offended, yet also transfixed by the reflective light display from the eight rings that adorned my fat fingers. Delari was also taken by surprise because Silda's last words, as he left that morning, were that I wore too many.

'Let me assure you,' I said, lowering my hand but making sure I kept it angled at the sun as I did so, 'whether I am a man or not, I dress this way with good purpose. In the North, even those who are not traders know my name, and when I walk into the markets, anyone with something special to trade will recognise me and seek me out.'

'You are a long way from home, trader. This is Nineveh,' said the large soldier, standing up for his smaller, speechless comrades. 'Things happen differently around here.'

'Do they?' I asked, looking around at the crowd that was yet to disperse. 'My offer still stands.' In my loudest voice I announced, 'Four-hundred silver, ready for your counting, friend.'

The crowd in the external camp cheered. 'Take his offer,' and 'sell to the pretty man,' I heard people yell. The lead palace trader did not blink as he studied my face.

'Why do you not voice your acceptance, trader?' I asked Delari, never averting my eyes from a locked stare with the palace trader. I swiped away a hand touching my dress, thinking it was Uk-Ban still playing his role. As a girl started crying, I shrugged my shoulders.

Delari stepped between us. 'I swore I would not sell unless my asking price was met. Four-hundred silver already in front of me is too tempting.' He turned to me. 'You have ...' As Delari extended his hand to seal the deal the lead palace trader requested he hold off.

'We would like you to consider our final offer.'

I encouraged Delari to shake on the deal without delay, but my friend put his hands behind his back and turned his attention back to the palace traders.

Nearby, the large soldier smirked at my attempt to secure the deal. I turned his attempted belittlement on him. I tapped Uk-Ban on the side of the head to gain his attention and signalled for him to open his hands. From the pouch attached to the belt at my waist, I counted more silver into his cupped palms and, as the palace traders were about to make their final offer, I raised the bid. 'Four-hundred and twenty.'

The lead palace guard waited for Delari to turn his way. 'Four-hundred and twenty-one.'

'I can offer you other goods as well,' I said, once again gaining my friends attention.

The lead palace guard signalled the tall soldier and he put his hand on his sword and took a defining step forward.

'I see now,' I mused. 'This is what you were referring to when you said things are different here. I will not be intimidated. My offer is now only four-hundred if they cannot provide what they offer.'

The lead palace guard laughed at me and stepped back as two soldiers walked forwards carrying a chest similar in size to the one Uk-Ban had placed but twice as heavy.

'Stay if you like as he counts it, you foolish looking man. I think you should return to the markets where you are welcome, for we will not be as forgiving if we make your acquaintance again.'

'Then I shall make the most of this meet and travel with honest tales to tell.'

'Let us go inside,' suggested the lead palace trader, stepping forwards and guiding Delari towards the shelter of the small hut.

Delari shook his head. 'You signalled your soldier to draw a sword on an innocent trader. I cannot trust you to treat me any differently.'

Offended, and to the amusement of all the local traders who watched on, the soldiers who placed the chest counted out the four-hundred and twenty-one silver, one shekel at a time, into an empty chest Delari provided.

27

A Night in Nineveh

Scribed by Arman, The Always Travelling Guardian.

Delari had received his first asking price of twenty shekels per bow, making this his largest return from a single trade agreement. The festivities of the day, and that is how the people referred to them, had severely hindered, if not halted, trade elsewhere in the camp. Utum, more commonly known as Glum when he was not listening, complained about five of his toy animals being pilfered whilst he was observing Delari's display.

'It was probably one of the children,' said Ashipa.

'Well, who else would steal toys?' Utum questioned Ashipa, raising his voice when the others started laughing. 'It is all humerous until the soldiers decide not to visit again. They are my best customers.'

'Do not worry about the soldiers,' assured Ashipa. 'The city markets only sell what is often found and traded here first. Your customers are not going anywhere. Who knows, the next soldier to buy a toy from you may actually give you what you ask.'

'I doubt that,' replied Utum.

'Oh, Glum,' grumbled Ashipa, forgetting for a moment to refer to him by his proper name, 'we all lost something today. Try to concentrate on what we have gained.'

'What did I gain? I lost five toys and sold none.'

'I only sold six loaves and, thus, was able to provide the whole camp with bread tonight,' announced Ashipa.

'How about you, Delari?' asked Utum, his beady eyes glaring at the trader through the flames of the fire. 'Anything you want to share with the camp tonight?'

Delari looked up from staring at his feet and met flame-whipped eyes with Glum. He turned his head from the fire and, nearby, he saw Ashipa smiling in quiet reflection. Ashipa, like other select permanent traders or farmers in other cities he had frequented in his travelling days, made him feel at home. He received a warm smile from his friend. Watching from a distance, I saw how respected Delari was. No one spoke, apart from children and their mothers asking them to be quiet. I questioned my part in his life. I delayed my approach.

Delari stood and looked around the fire. Beyond the fire, the high walls and square heights of the temples of Nineveh slept in comparative darkness. 'I want to thank you all for being away from your trade for me today. It was a trade I did not want to make, for we all know the hands in which these weapons are now, and yes, they are real weapons. I want you all to know that I did consider the options and it was not silver that swayed my judgement. The weapons that I sold today are already out there somewhere. It was only a matter of time before they were replicated and produced for the purpose of warfare by Akkadians. Maybe I helped Nineveh be the cornerstone of production. I am not proud of that accomplishment.' Delari paused and took a moment to admire the faces staring back at him though the campfire and appreciated a soft pat on the back from Bessum the brewer, who was sitting closest. He cleared his throat and looked away from the communal fire in the direction of our tent and I knew he was looking for me. 'I bought what would be sold and traded it for the highest price anyone could think to ask. You, traders of Nineveh, helped me do this and, Utum,' he said, acknowledging the glum man slouched on a log across the fire, 'you followed the crowds to see it happen. I saw you smile today when you saw Arman.'

Utum smiled again and the children nearby cringed at the sight of his rotten teeth protruding from his pronounced gum.

Delari looked around for me again. 'I am responsible for the halt in trade today, but I offer Isvah a fair share of my profit and the responsibility of its fair distribution.' Delari hung his head for a moment and then looked up and cast his eyes across those gathered, 'In view of the deal I have made, I will not be safe as a trader in this camp any longer.'

'No,' objected Bessum. 'You do not have to leave. Return to your tent. That is why you traded from Isvah's hut.'

'Bessum is right,' stated Isvah. 'You can move on but, if what happened today does affect the camp, you will be blamed and not able to defend yourself in your absence.'

'I would have no defence if I remained,' replied Delari. 'In the event of inquiry after my leave, you can say I headed south again to Agade. Tell them I was a stranger to you. I feel at home here even though I have seen and heard what Sargon has done to other villages I also like to call home. Like the spotted deer in the east, home for me is where I stop walking to drink. I settled here and got comfortable, but I cannot stay.'

'Why not?' I called out, and signalled Uk-Ban, the old man from Catal Huyuk to walk forwards. 'Never before have you let another choose your path.' I watched from behind clothes hanging on a rope between two huts as faces gathered by the fire turned to the sound of my voice.

Ashipa stood and, beyond the light of fire, he would have only made out the slender silhouette of Uk-Ban standing still at a distance. The men and women remained seated. I hoped that they waited for me to seat myself next to Delari as I normally did, ever since we had started the communal fire. The traders waited patiently but they could not control their bored children. Uk-Ban welcomed the children's fast approach until he saw that he was just in the way. He emerged from the flock and announced to all a call that we had agreed upon.

'You have waited long to see him and here she is, the master of disguise, the man with painted eyes, he is the woman with man thighs.'

I almost choked with surprise when Uk-Ban completed the announcement without stumble or pause. A young girl hugging my neck also added to my choking sensation. With at least five children dangling from my arms and more pulling at my notorious tunic, a dress as I learned it to be, I was reintroduced to the crowd that once thought they were getting to know me. 'Blessings this night,' I sang, with the same pompous flavour I had added earlier.

There were several traders amongst us who knew of Delari's plan for maximum return. The fishmonger closest to the entry to the markets, the dressmaker, Ashipa the Bread Maker and Isvah the man who traded anything that came his way, all welcomed me with applause. Ashipa's daughter, Silda, clapped the loudest and shook her father's arm with delight. The entire gathering joined in and cheered for me as I approached, but once again broke into laughter when they realised I was still dressed in the same ridiculous fashion.

'I am welcoming of the laughter now,' I said, as I sat down at the fire, still nursing one of the children. I placed the young girl back on her feet and turned to face Delari. 'What do you think? If I headed north, dressed this way, could I make a name for myself as a trader?'

'You have made a name for yourself. Of that, I am sure. As a trader, however, well, a trader spends his wealth on new items, not face paint and dresses, and besides, without Silda's help you would just look scary.'

'You know what troubles me?' asked Ashipa, addressing me from the end of the fire.

'How I came into possession of the dress?' guessed Delari, referring to my outfit.

'No, I quite like the dress. How is it that you had enough silver to fill a chest?'

'Good question,' supported Isvah. 'That negates one of your most important lessons: silver has no value until it is used in trade.'

Delari nodded his agreement and smiled at Uk-Ban who was seated on the far side of Bessum next to the dressmaker. 'Would you like to answer for me, Uk-Ban?'

The man from Catal Huyuk dipped his head and averted his eyes.

'Our new friend is the true inventor of the side bow and, though I only had forty silver, I offered him more,' continued Delari. 'I promised him the rest when I made the deal that he helped be successful today. That is all that was in the chest he carried. Uk-Ban carried forty silver and dressing cloth layered beneath made it look five fold the amount.'

The dressmaker congratulated Uk-Ban for not only being the true inventor but for the part he played so well during the trade negotiations. 'I think I could learn some tricks from you, Uk-Ban,' he said, loud enough for all to hear, and then did not waste a moment in drawing his cord to measure him up for some new clothes.

'Do not be taking advantage of him,' I warned. 'He already has plans for how he will spend his silver and I am the one most in need of a new wardrobe.'

Uk-Ban's head spun to the sound of laughter from all sides of the fire. He looked like he had never enjoyed life so much. 'I want to dress like Arman,' he yelled.

'I want to dress my way again too,' I said.

'I am joking,' he told all.

Silda left her father's side and approached Delari. She did not want us to leave and explained to the trader that if he were to do so, so many of the changes we had made would be forgotten.

'I must keep trading and I will not be looked on favourably by the soldiers anymore. They do not like it when they do not control the trade. If they discover that there are already more side bows out there, they may even return to collect their silver. They can do that. They can do what they like.' Delari explained.

'You sold them at my father's hut. They will not know to find you at your stall and they will never recognise Arman without the dress.'

'You don't believe what you say, Silda. I will only be safe until I have to trade with the same men again.'

'I think you always planned to leave.'

'You are right. I have kept moving my whole life and here is where I have felt most at home. The strangeness is I do not need a home. Discovering new things and taking them to new homes is my purpose and allows me to sleep fulfilled wherever I am.'

'I understand, Delari.' She looked at me and stretched her legs before the fire and hitched her dress to her knees. 'I think I feel sad because, unlike you, I will never leave Nineveh. I will never know the type of happiness you feel or share with others in the next place.' She pulled two clips from her hair and shook it loose over her shoulders. It hid her eyes from the firelight and Delari could no longer tell if she was happy or sad.

'Do not sell yourself to a helpless fate,' said Delari, gently touching the young woman's dark hair. 'You are still so young and many a mysterious face will enter these markets before you have time to bother yourself with the departure of an old man like me or Arman. I plan to return again one day and, when I do, I know then that you will understand what I am saying. Chances are you will not even be here.'

'Will Arman return with you?'

'I hope so,' I said,

'I think so too,' said Delari. 'I cannot seem to get rid of him.'

It no longer mattered to anyone gathered around the communal fire that only one trader had secured more than adequate returns for the day's work. Fish, bread and fruit that was not sold were shared, and the dressmaker convinced Uk-Ban that, if he did not get new clothes soon, then one day he would find himself naked and paying too high a price out of necessity. I passed my pipe around the fire and had another puff of smoke every time it was returned. Bessum the Brewer uncorked a full barrel and filled the people's mugs. Isvah, who was handed the responsibility of distributing the wealth, shared it evenly. This excited Utum and was understood by men like Ashipa, who had already attained wealth to see themselves through slow days of trade. The people were also celebrating our presence. Delari and I had entered the traders' camp as strangers. In twenty-five days, we had made it more like a small village.

'My largest mug for you,' said Bessum.

'Thank you, friend,' I said, exchanging my pipe for the beer. 'Pull it slow for I have packed the herb tight.'

One of Bessum's eyes twitched. 'More than the other night?'

'Twice as much,' I informed him, already knowing that the brewer would accept the challenge and almost certainly be thankful later for the experience. Next to me, Delari and Silda watched on, waiting to see if he could pull the smoke through in one breath. Nearby, Ashipa was approached by five of the young boys.

'Men ride our way from the north on horseback without light,' said the boy's speaker.

'How many?' he asked.

'We can only make out two.'

'Two does not sound threatening. Watch them boys and let me know if things change.'

The boys ran off, excited with their responsibility, and I turned back in time to see the brewer gasping for air and coughing loudly. 'He likes it,' I chuckled, retrieving my pipe and packing it for Delari. 'You know, if I ever return to the tower, this will be the first thing I share with the Guardians.'

'Maybe it is best you stay with me,' said Delari as he accepted the pipe.

I pondered his response. 'You know what else I have been thinking?'

'I am listening,' said Delari before he started to pull smoke.

'I would like to visit the Harmins again. They would be thankful for anything we carried their way and I ... I worry if it is just the chief and son who remain.'

Delari exhaled a large plume of smoke before responding, 'If we must return to the East, I will accept that course.'

'Who are these people?' asked Uk-Ban.

'The three surviving Harmins,' I answered. 'They were once the largest desert village in the East, comparable even in size to the city of Bit-Bunakki to their north. Like your people, Uk-Ban, they were hunters. They had nothing to trade but what was given to them by travellers who paid generously for a place to rest.'

'No one will travel that way anymore,' added Delari, 'not with Susa in ruin and new roads leading away.'

'I would like to go there,' said Uk-Ban. He leaned forwards to see me and the wrinkles around his eyes looked twice as deep in the light of the fire.

'Yes, I could see you there,' I told him.

'What about your brother in the North?' Delari asked him.

'He is at peace with the others now. I am not ready to join them yet.'

I packed another pipe, noticing that I only had a few days supply of herb left. 'Do you plan to return one day like the others?'

'This is as far as I have ever travelled. My return journey will be my last.'

'I like this man,' praised Bessum, rousing to life next to Delari.

'So do we,' said Delari.

My attention was drawn to the far side of the fire as the boys returned from their scout mission.

'Two men approach on lightly packed horses,' the boy's spokesman announced. 'Should we go meet them,' he then asked, eager for action.

'No, stay with us by the fire,' said Isvah, who was seated closest to the boys.

'What if they are soldiers? What if they are thieves or if they vanish in the dark?' stammered the boy, not content to just wait and pressured by his friends as the spokesman to gain approval to leave again.

'I let them go earlier,' said Ashipa. 'I'm happy for them to watch the approach.'

Isvah looked through the fire at Ashipa and nodded. 'Do not leave the camp. I do not want to be blamed if anything were to happen to you.'

'Approaching from the north at night, it will not be soldiers,' Delari called out to Isvah.

'Someone should go with them,' requested Ashipa's wife from our side of the fire.

'It is not the first time they have welcomed travellers,' Ashipa reassured her.

'Maybe Arman should go, just to be safe,' she suggested.

I reminded her that I was still wearing the green dress and laughed at the request. I laughed alone. 'You are serious. Sometimes I do not understand people. Well, fear not,' I said, getting to my feet. 'Save your laughter for when I return.'

'Take this,' said Delari, offering me his dagger.

I shook my head. 'You think I'm not armed because I'm wearing a dress? I'm disappointed, Delari.'

'He does not like his dress,' commented Uk-Ban.

'No, I do not like it anymore either,' said Delari.

The dress is not the problem I thought as I walked away. For a night, we had had twenty-two powerful weapons in our possession. We should have left in the night and taken Uk-Ban, the inventor, with us. I could tell he was not searching for wealth. We could have taken Uk-Ban to Elam and changed the force of power. To the people living in the cities between the rivers, the highlanders were known as savages, but to the northerners who did not care for speculation, the Elamites had always been welcomed and respected. The people of Elam sung songs to announce their arrival in cities like Nineveh and brought with them exotic plants stilled in their homeland soil. When Sargon became king, he named them barbaric. When he sent diplomats north to Kalhu and Nineveh, he learnt of their reach. An alliance, therefore, or the conquering of Elam were Sargon's best options in view of world domination, and he chose the latter. I wasn't proud of my involvement in the distribution of arms to the Akkadians. It was too late to quarrel that decision. The new arrivals, who I met as they entered the camp, were in the wrong place at the wrong time. My next decision would not be made easier with fancy costume or any amount of silver.

Those gathered by the communal fire fell silent and listened to the sound of someone approaching on foot.

The youngest of the boys ran to Isvah and told him loud enough for all to hear that the new arrivals were my friends and planned to stay overnight.

'Silda,' yelled Delari and she turned and looked back. 'You told me earlier that you would miss me if I left. I warn you not to make the same mistake with these men. They will leave before you even know them.'

'Then I have nothing to fear,' said Silda. She looked at me leading the horses towards the light of the fire and then ran past me to greet their owners.

Delari found himself alone on the far side of the fire and I think I could make more sense of his sorrow than he could. He wanted to hold Silda back so that he might warn her that the young man arriving did not concern himself with others and, like Salarn, with whom he believed Kar would be travelling, was defiant to a purpose not shared. He stayed seated at the fire as I introduced Kar to Isvah and the others crowding around us.

Delari placed his hands next to his sides and was about to stand when hands gripped him by the shoulders and kept him planted. 'You would have already killed me if you did not want something,' shouted Delari, begging for more attention than the frown I shared with him from a distance. 'Arman watches over me. Do you wait for him to look away before slicing my throat?' Delari lunged forwards and freed himself from the grip. He turned and saw the young Guardian who had travelled with him to his present destination.

Senea extended an arm to greet Delari and the trader lowered his arms.

'I thought you enjoyed surprises,' said Senea.

'You are lucky I knew it was you,' informed Delari, displaying his palm and revealing the sharp blade attached to the ring on his middle finger. When men brace arms, this weapon, concealed in the wearer's palm, could easily slice a wrist.

'I thought I told you to destroy that horrible weapon.'

'And I thought we both told you to return to the tower,' I said as I approached. 'What are you doing here, Senea? Why are you not with Yanereu? It is pointless rescuing anyone if our home in the east is not safe.'

'She is safe back at the tower with the other women.'

'You rescued a princess, Senea,' said Delari, 'is that not enough? Return home and take care of her.'

'You know how much I love her, Delari. I cannot stand still whilst her people are wiped from the earth. By accepting her hand, I accepted this duty.'

'Where is Salarn? Why did he allow this, having seen the Akkadian fort east of the mountains?' I asked.

'I travel with Kar and no one else. It is only Unbetum and my younger brother, Lagesh, protecting the tower.'

'Lan should have arrived by now,' I told them. 'It has been twelve days since he departed Kalhu.'

Senea smiled at Delari, 'I thought you were going to ask how we planned to make it there safely. I am not able to answer these questions. All I know is that the Pledians are in danger and they wish to live at one with their Guardian family.'

'I understand their plight,' said Delari, shaking his head. 'Speaking as a man who has never found the love of a woman, I cannot understand how one could risk their life after already being blessed by the company of their own princess.'

'It was not easy to leave her but just try to fathom what it would require to stop me from returning.'

Delari sighed. 'Unbetum, what did he have to say?'

'He is confident of our safe return.'

Delari stared at Senea for a long while before dismissing his concerns by rocking his head back and groaning. He had released discontent groans like this during our days in Nineveh more than he had in all our shared time in the north and west. 'What would I know,' he admitted, 'I never understood a word Ya-nereu spoke. Did you find our tent?'

'They are staying at Isvah's hut,' I added.

'Do you think that wise, Arman?'

'Guardians elsewhere in the camp tonight is welcomed. Take a seat, Senea.' I told the young Guardian. 'I will bring Kar.' I jerked my chin when he motioned to follow me and waited until he sat on the log next to Delari.

The boys, who had spotted the new arrivals from a distance, were helping Kar unload the horses at Isvah's small hut near the communal fire. They left to fetch water from the well for the horses. Silda stood nearby. I only noticed her when she moved. Light from the communal fire was dimming and the crescent moon created strange shadows as it fell upon the huts and tents of the camp. 'Kar, let me re-introduce you to Delari,' I called out as I walked his way. 'You would have only been a boy when he last saw you.'

Bessum interrupted our path and offered us filled mugs of beer. Kar nodded his thanks and I offered to drink Senea's.

Silda poked me in the side as we walked back to the fire. 'What?' I asked, looking down at her by my side.

She looked up at me with a scrunched face.

Kar, I mouthed, tipping my head his way.

Silda nodded quickly with brow raised.

'Wait, Kar,' I said, pausing for a moment and holding my arms out to stop the young man and woman who walked either side of me. 'Kar, this is Silda. Her father, Ashipa, is the bread maker.'

'Silda,' repeated Kar. He smiled at her and then looked at me before walking on.

Silda slumped against me. 'Did he even see me?'

I wrapped my arm around her shoulders, feeling the frailty of her body beneath the thin cloth of her dress. 'He saw you. If he looked at you a moment longer, he might have abandoned his journey,' I said, hoping to comfort her and believing my own words. 'I have to consult him now. You should talk to him in the morning.'

'You have grown,' said Delari as he stood to greet Kar. 'Tall and a little wider like a horse that has found its legs.'

'It is good to see you again, Delari,' said Kar. 'You look no older. Not even your hair has grown.'

'That is because I cut my hair. Sit by the fire,' he said, pointing to the log. 'We have much to talk about before we retire.'

'Tell me again why you are dressed this way, Arman?' said Senea, who was already seated next to Delari.

'Important matters first,' I requested.

Silda left my side and sat next to Senea. Kar was soon seated next to her.

'Silda, I have serious matters to discuss with these men,' I explained.

Senea looked at her and around at the many other eyes watching from all sides of the fire. 'Are we all friends here?' Senea questioned Arman.

'Yes, though not all plans need to be shared.'

'What plans,' said Kar, smiling courteously at Silda and disrespectfully at me at the same time. 'We are on a quest to save the Pledians. If one beautiful, young woman puts us at risk then we are doomed already.'

Delari and I exchanged frowns of disapproval.

Senea supported Kar's argument. 'No one even knows who they are. They risked Yanereu's life in sending her to the western shores and, likewise, we now risk our lives by returning to save the rest. She trusted the Guardians and I have learnt to trust others.'

'You talk like nothing can stop you, Senea. Blind faith will not save your life or theirs,' I said sternly and waited for Senea to object.

Senea looked around the fire at all those gathered and knew that it was Delari and I who had made such a large-scale gathering possible.

'We have been on the road since dawn,' said Kar, breaking the momentary silence. 'I cannot finish this,' he then explained and offered his mug to Silda.

She accepted it but then felt embarrassed for imposing and stood to leave. Kar stood at the same time and Senea followed his lead.

If I had been more welcoming, Kar might have stayed by the fire and told us more. He might have complimented Silda further. They might have even become fond of each other. 'Where are you going?' I asked. 'I have much to share.'

'We need rest,' answered Senea.

'Do you still plan to leave tomorrow?' I asked.

'At dawn was the plan. Enjoy the celebrations, we

will talk to you before we depart.'

I looked at Delari, unsure of what I should say. Delari prompted me to say more with a jerk of his arm. 'We will talk in the morning, young Guardians,' I called after them.

'Friends?' inquired Uk-Ban, as he sat next to Delari.

I watched them walk away. Their leaving the tower troubled me as much as the news that Lan had not yet returned. At any moment, there could be movement from the Akkadian fort, north of the tower, and we were far. I sighed. 'They are family, Uk-Ban. Young and invincible they see themselves.' I leapt to my feet and hurried to catch up.

Silda led them back to Isvah's small hut where Delari had traded that day. No words were exchanged on the walk, even though her suggestive glances gave Kar many opportunities. When they arrived, they thanked her and apologised for not joining in the celebrations.

'We are not celebrating anything really,' she explained. 'Delari announced tonight that he plans to leave and we have only gathered around one fire since he settled. I remember you, Senea. I did not think I would see you again so soon.'

'Sleep well,' said Kar, excusing himself from the pleasantries as he parted the skin at the entrance.

'Can I fetch you some water,' she asked before he disappeared.

'I helped myself to your well.' said Kar, displaying the water bladder strung around his shoulder before stepping inside.

'Please thank your father again for us, Silda,' said Senea.

'This is Isvah's hut. My father makes bread.'

Senea nodded. 'Thank you for seeing us to rest.'

'That is what I do,' she said as Senea entered the tent. She raised her arms and screamed silently at the sky. 'What I do?' she repeated as she paced back towards the fire.

'What concerns you, Silda?' I said.

She startled and tried to compose herself before realising she had nothing to hide from me. 'Delari was right. There's no point getting to know these men.'

'A man on a quest is hard to please,' I told her.

'I share a prayer with you then,' she said. The bridge of her nose was angled to the moon and her arms straight by her side. She prayed that Delari's second promise would be fulfilled and held hope that before she was too old another pleasant yet mysterious face would enter the camp. Hopefully, this man would stay or take her away with him when he left. She could not stand to grow old in the same place she was born with tales of happenings beyond the horizon seeming like they were a world away.

'I know how you feel, Silda.' I said, and I told her about my days spent away from the village and many harvests spent training and writing as my Guardian friends arrived and left on new expeditions. At some point during the telling of my tale, I realised that I was speaking to all those at the communal fire. I felt Silda's fingers gripping my arm and smelt the wood that crackled and churned before me. Like Kar, I had found my heaven. The traders' camp was like a village on the outskirts of a city. It offered me all the peace and excitement I needed. It was a shame that I had to leave it behind.

28

The Rescue

Scribed by Tahnas, The Guardian of the West.

Inside the Mari drinking hut, it still seemed to be night. Shortened candles told otherwise. Jemat, the irrigator with large shoulder muscles and a strange respect for the king, had joined a table of soldiers and they boasted about their lifestyle, encouraging him to enlist. Sargon always needed fresh blood and the soldiers who sold Jemat on the rewards kept hidden their rank. It was not the duteous but the poor or newly recruited soldiers who protected the camp whilst the others caroused, and the higher-ranked disciples of Sargon wanted more obliging men at their disposal. They would ride the next leg of their journey to Ebla only carrying their personal supplies. On our way to the drinking hut, we had passed the camp of soldiers who would make this journey on foot. They did not seem as optimistic about today's travel plans.

At the neighbouring table, I sat with Basim, the head irrigator, and watched his youngest worker court a slightly older lady. His other men had left a while ago but even they had drunk too much and stayed up too late. It was going to be a long day of work without shelter from the hot sun for the irrigators. Basim decided there was no point in stopping now.

'I will head straight for the fields when the sun rises and, until then, I will appreciate my friend playing his luck with a lady.'

I acted drunken, turning my head slowly when Basim spoke to me or laughed at the antics of his young worker. I was more interested in the talk from the officers seated at the table behind me. They spoke like they were already returning triumphantly from the Great Sea. The drinking hut was where they planned to call assembly. According to the most outspoken officer at this table, Sargon's orders were that the obliging high class of the city be paid an offering and offered sanctuary and a new life further south between the rivers. The officers without women were also encouraged to choose a bride here, for the women of Mari were renowned for their beauty and submissive demeanour. Mari had served its purpose, according to their victorious talk. Stone and timber would now be transported through Ebla. In Ebla, Sargon's army would garrison a stronghold on the West, and trade north of Rapikum on the Euphrates River was to be no more. The Zidonians would dare no longer encroach on his boundaries and Sargon could concentrate on improving trade routes to the East. With both regions under manageable control and the prospect of creating a new settlement on an Island off the Zidonian Coast, Egypt would submit to his influence and allow him rule over sea trade.

'Show her how you dance,' encouraged Basim, clapping his hands out of time with the young musician's slow pluck of an oud.

The woman being entertained by the young irrigator realised as she looked around that she was the spectacle for many stray eyes and saw it as time to leave. The young irrigator began a quick step dance and, before he had time to take his eyes off his feet, his admirer was pulling him away to a less congested part of the hut. He waved with a trailing arm and Basim applauded the young man's success.

'You should be at work,' said Messim, as she began clearing empty mugs from our table.

Basim looked towards the high windows and saw the first light of dawn filtering through the slats. 'Already? This will not be a good day,' he groaned, turning back to face Messim. 'Unless I may offer to escort you home, then it could at least start well,' he suggested.

'Go home to your wife,' she instructed.

He shrugged her comment off and gulped down the last of his beer, including the barley that had settled. It dropped into his mouth like sludge.

'It is fine to blame me for all your worries,' she said, 'but you may want your wife on side when you explain how you lost your strongest worker.'

Basim was belching in appreciation of his thick gulp when her words reached his ears. At the neighbouring table, he watched Jemat salute cups with his new soldier friends.

She added his mug to her tray. 'Down a worker, this will only be the first of many long days for you.'

He faced Messim with a tired face. 'I never thought he really would.'

'You knew what he was like, Basim. Is it not true

that he sold his first daughter before she could even sew? Did you really expect him to be more loyal to you?'

Basim knocked his stool over as he stood. 'Make him a soldier,' I say. 'He'll probably kill a sleeping officer to advance his rank.'

She attempted to take the mug from my hand. I cradled it close.

'You taking him with you?' asked Messim, gesturing at me.

He snuffed at her question. 'I hardly know him,' he eventually answered as he staggered away. 'See you soon. Save me a table.'

Messim watched him leave and then bent down next to me. 'Do you remember me, Tahnas?' she asked.

I remained hunched over at the table. 'Have you finished work?'

'Almost. The dawn parade will arrive soon and there will be nobody at home until Ubai chests his returns for the night.'

'If I find my way to the back, will you signal me when it is safe?'

'Yes, from the higher window, but you will have more than one guard to deal with as the door has to be unbolted from both sides.'

'Do not worry about that. Show yourself at the window and tell Belline to be ready to leave.' I swilled the contents of my mug and handed it to Messim.

She added it to her tray and ignored my departure as she finished her work.

***

I watched from the cover of empty barrels stacked in the corner of a small courtyard behind the drinking hut. The split timber buildings on all sides were two levels high and flaming torches lit the entrance to each. Hidden in the long shadows of early morn, I saw the table attendants return home. When they knocked at a door, a viewing window was opened and a guard inspected the new arrivals before unbolting the door and allowing them entry. They were not uniformed guards but, still, their presence troubled me. I did not expect it to be an easy rescue but what concerned me most about the guards' presence was their necessity. A door bolted from the inside could keep a woman safe. Messim had told me that Belline had tried to escape and I realised that the guards were there to keep the women locked inside. The empty barrels I had lifted and stacked on the other side of the locked gateway so that I could climb over and venture this close were also a sign of my presence. I needed to get in and out as quickly as possible and not just to avoid detection. We had arranged to meet Arman at the Port of Assur, twelve days after our departure from Nineveh. That left us five days. If we did not make it to the meeting place in time, Arman would suspect we had encountered trouble on the road.

Three other women arrived before Messim finally crossed the courtyard. Two women walked to the door at the far end and the other knocked at the door closest to where I was hiding near the gated lane. The light of day was beginning to reach the shadowed courtyard and I troubled my mind with another of Messim's comments. '*The dawn parade.*' Was she referring to new women taking over from those who had worked through the night or did she mean that the guards would also be replaced? I looked through the gate I had scaled to the lane next to the drinking hut. The building on the other side of the lane was a granary and its walls were even higher. It was my only escape route. I turned back to the courtyard as Messim walked past me at a distance and entered a building on the far side. Again, a guard checked who it was before unbolting the door from inside and allowing her entry. I could not see if this door guard was armed.

I sat down for a moment behind the barrels. Since arriving in Mari, I had not eaten and I had consumed ten mugs of rich barley beer. From a pocket in my skirt, I pulled out my strength potion, a slice of dried, heavily salted deer. I chewed slowly on the tough meat and hoped it would give me new strength before the false strength of fermented barley wore off. At the far end of the courtyard, I heard a door open and I peered out from behind the barrels. I was careful not to let any light reflect off my shaved scalp. A guard held the door open for four scantily dressed young women to exit and then closed it behind. The guard then extinguished the torches braced either side of the door before following them to the drinking hut. They spoke freely and happily as they made their way through the courtyard. One of the women paused and held her arms to the sky so that the rising sun might reach her fingertips. The others turned and joined in the search for sunlight and the guard did not seem to mind their delay. They jumped about and raised their arms high until one declared, 'It touched my face.'

'You lie,' said one of the other women, pushing her and starting a playful scuffle.

'Enough play. Ubai made it very clear that you start on time today.'

'Oh Imrah, work, work, work. Is that all you care about?' said a dark-skinned woman flirtatiously as she grabbed the guard's arm and nursed it on the walk. Her transparent white dress boasted her curvaceous hips and large, sagging breasts. The other women followed, whispering to each other and laughing at the guard's displayed embarrassment when he turned. No sooner had they entered the drinking hut, another door opened in the courtyard behind. Again, a guard ushered the way for the women. Only three women left this building and they were less vocal than the others. They walked ahead as the guard closed the door behind and extinguished the torches.

Warm sunlight streamed across the high roof of the drinking hut and reached the door at the far end of the courtyard. The first of the dawn parade seemed fully aware of the blessings of sunlight that they were missing when they scrubbed spilt beer, spittle and blood from the floors or cut hanging wax from candelabra inside the gloomy expanses of the scarcely occupied drinking hut. When they finished work, the sun would already be setting. I tensed my jaw and vowed I would not allow Gentuk's wife to share this fate any longer.

A guard had allowed Messim entry to the building opposite me. No women had left this building. *Was a guard about to lead more women from this door or was that the last of the dawn parade?* Messim was yet to signal me from the second-floor window and light was quickly stealing the opportunity for a shadowed approach. The torches at the entrance to the building Messim had entered still burned. They were no longer necessary. All the others had been extinguished and time had lapsed. I had to make my move before Ubai returned.

I tilted an empty wooden barrel and hoisted it onto my shoulders. Even empty, it was an effort to lift. I planned to place it in front of the door that Messim had entered and when the guard checked to see who had knocked, he might think he had been rewarded for his night's work. Whatever he thought, it would hopefully draw him outside to investigate. I crossed the courtyard and placed the barrel. I drew a dagger and tucked my tunic into my leather skirt so that my throwing blade was ready to draw. I did not have the advantage of my long sword or the promise of a fast escape on my stallion. Both were in Gentuk's care. It was morning now and that meant I only had to make it to the markets to meet him. After relishing a moment of stilled thought and the time to centre my balance, I raised my hand to knock.

'You must be joking,' yelled a guard as he stepped out the backdoor of the drinking hut.

I transferred my dagger to my other hand and drew my throwing blade. Luckily, the talk was not directed at me and I had a moment to reconsider my plan.

The guard closed the backdoor to the drinking hut and entered the courtyard, chuckling to himself. 'What's happening here?' he questioned aloud in a drunken slur. He slowed his step and looked about as he approached the barrel sitting next to the first door. Either side of the door a torch burned and further illuminated the scene.

I heard him draw a short sword from a leather sheath.

The guard walked wide of the door and knelt. 'Pud,' he yelled, taking cautious steps closer to the door. 'Pud, open up,' he yelled again. He rapped on the door and then retreated defensively.

The boarded window on the second floor opened. 'Out of the way,' yelled a guard as he pushed past someone to see below.

'What kind of sick-hearted, man-labour have you been divulging in Pud?' questioned the guard standing below in the courtyard. 'Get your ugly face down here now and clean this up. If Ubai sees this, he'll throw you out with the slop.'

Pud released a guttural groan from the window above. I heard him stomp across the floor and slam a door shut.

The guard in the courtyard leant a little closer, possibly to check if I was still breathing. 'No, not me,' he quarrelled with himself, stepping back as if unimpressed by the sight of my exposed rear end.

The door was unbolted from inside and Pud's shadow was cast over me as he leaned out for a closer look, without venturing from the threshold.

'This is unacceptable,' lectured the other guard.

Pud stepped from the doorway and past the empty barrel I had placed.

'Do you remember what happened now?' asked the guard, maintaining his distance from where I lay face down with my leather skirt also pulled down.

'Did you do this?' Pud questioned him.

'Ask me that again?' The guard challenged, stepping forwards. His sword flickered light as he raised it.

In front of my face, against the wall, I saw Pud's

shadow. He pointed his finger and shook his head. He was standing directly behind my bare backside, angled upwards at the door's landing.

'This is Imrah's doing,' said Pud. 'He lets his girls get away with anything. They must have dragged him out of the drinking hut.' Pud stepped towards the guard.

As soon as Pud had walked clear of the door, I sprung to my feet.

'Look behind,' yelled the guard.

I lunged and stuck Pud in his chest with my dagger and then quickly advanced on the other guard.

'You want to take me with that short blade?' he challenged. He swung his sword wildly as he stepped towards me.

'Not with this short blade,' I told him as I quickly drew and thrust my throwing blade.

The guard deflected the blade with his sword though not in the desired direction. If he had let it fly its course it might have stuck on his leather breastplate, instead the blade was coursed upwards. The guard dipped his head and the blade shattered teeth as it lodged in his cheek. Dropping his sword, the guard clasped his hands to the gore spurting from his face. The hardened sand beneath his feat changed colour as he stumbled, blood splattering and pooling around his feet.

I finished with Pud by driving my dagger sideways into his skull at his ear. I then paced up to the stumbling guard and withdrew my throwing blade from his cheek. With little resistance, I lifted the guard's arm and stuck him with the same blade beneath his armpit. From this angle, the tip of the blade reached his heart and I did not have to wait for him to die before I draped his lifeless arm over my shoulder and hauled him towards the door.

'I can help,' said Messim, stepping past the barrel towards Pud.

'Where is Belline?' I dumped the guard inside the door and looked down a narrow corridor leading into the lower part of the building. On both sides of the doorway, there were steps leading to a second floor. I leaned outside to check the course was clear. 'Messim, where is she?' I asked again.

Messim was struggling to drag Pud's dead body to the door. 'Upstairs,' she answered, pointing out which of the flight of stairs I should climb. 'I am sorry, Tahnas,' she apologised as I stepped back inside.

I ignored her last comment as I bounded up the stairs and unbolted the door at the top. The floor was messed with straw from a torn bed and trickles of wet blood were tracked from one end of the room to the other. 'Belline,' I called out, 'are you here?' I reefed open wardrobes and peeled back curtains in a hastened search before stilling myself to listen. From the furthest corner of the room, I heard suppressed air forcing its way to her nostrils. 'Belline, it is Tahnas.' I walked towards the breathing sound.

'Leave, Tahnas, before more guards arrive.'

'Have they made you crazy? I am not leaving without you. Gentuk waits for us in the markets and your eldest, Senea, has met a princess. You would have to give me an unheard-of reason to leave.' I found her crouched behind bunched blankets with her arms wrapped tightly around her legs. I stepped towards her and hoisted her up in my arms. She was like dead weight, so I held her like a baby, close to my chest. On the way down the stairs, light from an open window allowed us to see each other's faces clearly. It was the first time we had seen each other since I had left for the Desert City long before the village was sacked. I saw the deep scar that Messim told me about and a fresher wound on her other cheek. I also felt warm blood on my arms that nursed her and noticed that her dress was coated with blood below the waist.

'I tried to escape,' cried Belline.

'This time you will.'

Messim stood in wait with a small, wrapped bundle of stores.

'How do you leave here?' I asked.

'Through the drinking hut.'

I stepped sideways through the doorway and then hoisted Belline higher in my arms as I crossed the courtyard.

Messim extinguished the torches and closed the door before following.

I had stacked barrels that would allow the women to climb over the locked gate but Belline did not even seem ready to walk. I placed her down and removed my short-cut tunic, folding it neat and tight. Spreading her legs, I blindly placed my tunic between her thighs. 'Press it to the wound, Belline. I know it will hurt but you must stop the bleeding,' I told her before diverting my attention to the gate impeding our escape.

She rocked her head back and let her arms rest limp next to her side. Messim arrived and immediately sought to help her friend by applying the cloth more precisely to Belline's wound.

The heavily braced gateway was locked and twice the height of a man. The Belline I remembered would have easily leapt from the barrel I had placed and then climbed onto my stack on the other side. I contemplated whether it would be easier to wedge the gate open than try to carry her over.

'Wait, Ubai,' screamed Messim.

I turned to see the barkeeper returning to the back door of the drinking hut as fast as he could, while carrying a heavy chest. A guard stepped out into the courtyard and saw what was happening at the gated lane. He drew his short sword and charged at me. I drew my dagger in time to parry his blade as I stepped to the side. Before the guard could swing again, I stuck him twice in his side. The sword loosened in his grip and I pushed it aside effortlessly as I slit the guard's throat and shoved him away. I did not stop moving as I hoisted Messim to her feet and lifted her by her thin waist onto the barrel next to the gate. 'Climb over and help me lift Belline to the other side,' I instructed Messim.

Belline moaned with pain. I knocked a barrel onto its side and stepped from it onto the upright barrel next to the gate. I then lifted Belline over the tips of the gate and into Messim's arms.

Messim struggled to hold Belline's weight on the other side and the barrel she stood on rocked. Leaning against the gate, the barrel found new footing.

'Her husband, Gentuk, will meet us in the markets,' I told Messim, 'Wait for us there if you were honest of your intentions and still want to join us.'

'I can help,' said Messim.

'You can help by seeing yourself safely to the markets,' I said as I climbed over the gate. I lowered myself onto the next barrel in my stack and lifted Belline down a level. Looking towards the end of the narrow lane that bordered one side of the drinking hut, I saw Messim pause and look back before heading in the direction of the markets.

I carried Belline high in my arms and took long, quick strides towards the end of the lane. In front of me, a trader stopped his cart upon seeing Messim flee. I continued towards him, thankful when I heard the guards call out from the gate behind instead of sealing off my exit. I reached the front, northeast corner of the drinking hut and walked towards the markets, glancing at those still drinking on the front porch in the morning light.

Basim, the irrigator, had only made it to the front porch before finding another drink. When he saw me, he looked down at his mug. He upturned it and stumbled down the steps and across the road to catch me. 'What happened to her?' he called out, his clumsy steps leaving him further behind.

'She's losing a child,' I replied without turning and risking the display of my uncovered shoulder.

A group of Akkadian soldiers, also slowed by brew, advanced on the scene from the southern door to the drinking hut.

'Do you know the man?' one of the soldiers asked Basim as they watched me walk away.

'He is a fur trader from the north,' answered Basim.

I entered the wide lane that led to the market square and offered an old beggar woman a shekel for her blanket. The blanket smelt like urine and dark stains hinted at the source of the smell. I wrapped it around my shoulders and draped it over Belline's legs. 'Open your eyes, Belline,' I told her.

'What is that smell?'

I was glad she noticed. 'We'll be with Gentuk soon.' I nursed her like a child in my arms as I ran the length of the lane towards the market square.

The rising sun stung my eyes as I entered the markets. Traders were erecting their stalls and barrowing their goods from the road to the port. Only Gentuk noticed my hasty arrival. He abandoned our horses and approached slowly with his sword raised. His eyes were raging and his jaw was clenched. Belline looked pale and lifeless in my arms. He seemed intent on marching straight past me and onwards into the city to exact revenge. Belline turned her head to the sound of his step and with that slight movement he dropped his sword. He fell to his knees in front of me and held his wavering arms wide.

'Oh god be true. Let me hold her,' he cried.

I lowered her into his arms.

29

Down River

Scribed by Kar.

'Is that you, Kar?' said Senea, still half-asleep. Moonlight slid through the slightly parted door flap, reaching his exposed foot. Senea kicked his fur down until his foot was covered and protected from the chill of night air. The flap was pulled further apart and, like a shadow, someone silently slid into Isvah's hut. Silhouetted by the moonlight outside, I was not even sure if this someone was a woman or a man. The flap fell back into position, leaving the hut in complete darkness once more.

Senea's belly grumbled and I heard him roll onto his side. Another noise coincided with his roll. It was the sound of bronze scraping leather—the unmistakable sound of a blade being drawn.

The hut's door flap was reefed open and moonlight exposed a hooded man standing still against the opposite wall with a dagger drawn.

I stepped over Senea and swung my sword at the assassin's dagger. It knocked the bronze blade from his grip, cutting through cloth and flesh to bone at his wrist.

Arman rushed into the hut with his sword pointed like a spear. Before the flap closed behind him, and before the assassin's unsettling whine peaked, Arman drove his blade into his neck.

Senea lurched beneath me and wrestled with my legs in the dark.

I fell backwards onto my fur.

'Be still,' said Arman. He waited and listened for any sound outside. 'The Akkadians have returned for their silver. Gather your goods and meet me outside.' He slid through the entrance flap.

I rolled my fur and slung my staff and water bladder over my shoulders.

'What happened?' asked Senea, as he rolled his fur.

'Ask Arman later. We have to move on.' I sheathed my sword at my waist and exited the hut.

Isvah's hut was in the centre of the camp and over the thatched rooves of twenty huts I could see fresh blood-coloured light reflecting off low clouds in the east. In the camp, it was still dark and there was no movement. I lifted my fur onto Har Man's mount and a hand gripped my shoulder from behind. 'Not the time for a lesson,' I said. The tip of a blade pressed against my exposed back. It was cold and my back arched to its touch.

'Where's the trader who sold weapons at this hut today?' questioned the man who had caught me off guard. His voice was coarse but it was not Arman. It was an Akkadian accent and his attempt to speak softly that made his voice sound different.

'He told me we could stay here,' I replied. My

spread hands rested against Har Man's hind leg and chest.

'I don't care for you. Where is the trader?'

From beneath Har Man's flank I felt something stiff prodding my thigh. I hesitated to look down. Stallions sometimes react in surprising ways to added commotion. Behind me I heard Senea kick the hut's door flap aside. He kicked again when the heavy skin did not move the way he wanted it to. The blade to my back moved slightly as I sensed the man behind me turn.

I glanced down and beneath Har Man's flank I saw a throwing blade being offered to me from the other side.

I heard Senea drop his fur and draw his sword. 'Fight me,' he said.

The blade was pressed more firmly against my back and it pierced my skin. It's cold touch now felt warm.

'Drop your sword or your friend will die,' said the Akkadian.

I drove Arman's throwing blade under my arm and into the man's gut.

He stabbed at me as I turned. If not for the staff slung between my shoulders he would have stuck me deep.

Senea swung his sword at the man's hooded neck.

My assailant's short-bearded face was unveiled as it dangled loose in front of his hood and blood spurted in his final turn. The blood looked black in the light of early morn and the Akkadian's face was like all the others I had seen. He looked like Otoug to me. All Akkadians looked like the tall one Salarn had confronted on my first journey. This Akkadian was shorter than me and I wished I could have brought him down without help from my friends.

Arman caught the Akkadian's slumping body and dragged him inside Isvah's hut.

Several traders appeared outside their huts, roused by the commotion.

'Return to your homes,' I told them. They followed my advice.

'He cut you, Kar,' alerted Senea.

I touched my back and looked at blood on my fingertips. 'It's not deep. It will dry soon.'

Arman returned from Isvah's hut and helped Senea fasten his fur to his mount. 'Trot your horses softly north out of the camp. Ride wide of the city and enter the port from the north, like new arrivals.' He took a breath. 'Delari and Uk-Ban are waiting for you on the road north, near the palm grove.'

'Will you follow?' Senea asked Arman.

'I will catch you before you reach the port.'

***

The wharf in Nineveh was filled with fishing boats and barges heaped with grain that was loaded the day before. The fishermen, wearing only loose-fitting cloth shorts or draped in sun-dulled coveralls, spoke joyfully of netting easy catches with the river running low after a season of sparse rain. There were only thin clouds in the sky, yet the wet air suggested that a storm could build over the course of the day. Arman pointed to the only docked vessel capable of transporting horses and not already loaded with grain. Delari approached the boatman ahead of us to acquire his services.

'Good day,' Delari said in greeting.

The boatman did not reply and looked past the trader at Senea and I standing close, Arman holding our horses and Uk-Ban leading his mangey mare by a rope. He stood from where he rested near the reeds at the end of the dock and walked towards his vessel. Like a snake, his thin tongue kept whipping in and out of his mouth, coating his cracked lips with spittle.

'We are looking to go down river as far as Assur.'

'Wrong boat.'

Delari was surprised by the man's bluntness. 'Wrong boat or wrong boatman?' The boatman did not reply and Delari followed him to the boarding plank. 'I will pay you well with Akkadian silver. I propose a shekel per horse. We also carry dry food and seed.'

The boatman leant on a mooring post and looked back to the end of the dock, 'Horses are no good on my boat. I wait for grain.'

'Do not play me for a fool, boatman. Horses will not tip this vessel. I offer a generous sum of silver and other goods. You can make use of the morning and return for your load of grain.'

'It's easy to go down stream but, in Assur, soldiers wait. If I arrive with bandits, then I will be considered a bandit.'

'Bandits?' questioned Delari. 'Is that why you are defiant?' He looked at my long hair and the staff and sword I carried. Standing next to Senea, he in his white tunic that was neatly fastened at his waist, I must have looked the part. 'We carry goods for Sargon himself and these men are the only reason I have returned safely from the East,' Delari lied, pointing to us. 'They will ensure our cargo reaches him and you have a part to play.'

'I am not interested,' declared the boatman, patting his fringe forwards as it lifted in the wind. 'Wait for Xemoth. He can read and has an interest in Sargon's stolen items. He will arrive soon. Offer him your silver and leave me be.'

'When does he arrive?'

Again, the boatman ignored Delari and so the trader turned and gave us a signal to board.

'I did not agree,' objected the boatman, his hand ready to signal the guards in the watchtowers.

At the height of five men, the nests of the watchtowers allowed the archers extended reach with their bows. If we took the boat with force, their arrows would reach to the far side of the river.

'Name your price,' said Delari, boarding the vessel and prompting the boatman to his feet again.

'One hundred.'

'I will give you a shekel for each horse and for each man.'

'Eighty and I only take you as far as Kalhu.'

'Eighty is an absurd price. I offer ten shekels. Let the man you spoke of, Xemoth, transport your load.'

'Xemoth's boat only carries ...' began the boatman before stopping himself short.

Delari smiled at the man, amused by the truth that he had let slip. 'You do not wait for grain. You wait for the palace traders. Your boat is the only one capable of transporting horses. You lie and call my companions bandits.'

'I must wait for them. They have already requested that I stay docked.'

'Let me show you something,' said Delari and he led him to his mare that Arman was walking onto the boat first.

'I have told you already that I am not interested in tablets. I cannot read and I want this horse off my boat.'

'Tablets? Who said anything about tablets? You do not have to read this,' said Delari, as he removed one of the side bows he had kept easily accessible.

Senea and I led our horses across the boarding plank and distracted the boatman. Uk-Ban followed us cautiously. Like me, it was his first time on the water.

Arman reassured him and helped him with his old mare by taking hold of the reins and calming the horse with soft words. He secured her between the other horses behind the shelter of the mast where the boat was widest.

'This is what the palace traders will carry,' continued Delari, as he fastened a bolt and displayed the weapon to the boatman.

The disgruntled boatman looked at the strange weapon closely, 'What is this?'

Delari turned it over for display and, when he saw that the boatman was distracted, gave Arman the signal to cast off.

'A bow that can be released with one arm.'

'They will kill me when I return and they will hunt you down,' complained the boatman, still intrigued, if not wary of the loaded weapon. His body began trembling and I knew for certain at this point that the boatman had made an arrangement with the palace guards.

'Take us downstream and across river at the bend. Ten silver and you will be back before they arrive,' promised Delari, growing impatient with the man's stubbornness.

'Twenty silver and that weapon,' said the boatman, before losing his footing as the boat was released from its mooring post and lurched into the downriver flow.

Uk-Ban took fright and grabbed hold of the mast.

'Twenty silver,' declared Delari, steady on his feet. 'Not my weapon.'

Arman corrected the rudder and coursed the boat into the deeper midstream current.

'This is my boat. You do not know what you are doing,' yelled the boatman, as he lurched across the deck arriving short of Uk-Ban at the mast.

'Thirty silver,' announced Delari, once more gaining the boatman's attention.

Back at the port, I watched an Akkadian descend the ladder of the southern watchtower, probably intent on sending word that their planned transport vessel had already left. Above him the archers watched on, never drawing an arrow.

The boatman stood beneath the hung sail and shook his head at Uk-Ban's smiling face. 'I want that weapon,' said the boatman, turning back to face Delari.

Senea did not like the way we had occupied the boat and walked to the stern end to rest. Uk-Ban stayed close to the mast and watched as I stalked the boatman's shadow and stood behind him as he challenged Delari. I held my staff upright in one hand, with its blunt heavier end resting against the deck and the bladed end concealed in the soft leather sheath my father had crafted.

'You drive a hard bargain, boatman, for such a small offering on your part.'

'I am no fool either. I know you do not trade with Sargon. You may pass as a trader, but your mercenaries would not be allowed entry to any city,' he explained, turning to point us out and startling when he realised I was so close.

'Forget yourself, boatman, for your stance has put your life in jeopardy,' warned Delari.

'We have to kill him,' I said.

'Be reasonable,' objected the boatman. 'You have seized my vessel. You have ignored my requests. Pay me what I am owed and let us go separate ways at the first bend in the river.'

Delari shook his head, 'Your way is whence we came, to meet soldiers.'

'We cannot allow that,' I said, with my staff gripped by both hands. 'The Akkadians know the boat has left. We can gain a day on them.'

'Stay out of it, boy,' objected the boatman without turning from facing Delari. 'Show me silver trader or I will drop anchor.'

Delari cringed as he witnessed me collapse the man with a stiff downward strike of my staff. 'I did not want to do that,' I quickly explained. 'He was about to do something stupid.'

'I hope I am never about to do something stupid,' said Delari, believing he could have talked the stubborn man into an agreement.

I lowered my staff and used it to lever the boatman onto his side. Delari knelt and took a small dagger from the man's limp hand.

'What happened?' questioned Arman from the stern of the boat. The horses had blocked his view.

'Sail on, Arman,' Delari called back, 'Kar just saved me from tiresome negotiations.'

Uk-Ban held on tightly to the mast even though the river flowed smoothly and the vessel cruised at a steady pace. 'Faster, Arman, cut the water and let it spray,' he said.

Arman shared a smile with Senea, but the younger Guardian's mind was elsewhere. 'Something troubling you?'

'We could have ridden south. We did not have to seize this boat.'

'You should be talking to Kar about those concerns. Delari told me the boatman agreed with us boarding.'

Senea stared at Arman.

Arman returned his stare before shifting his attention to the coursing banks and keeping the vessel midstream.

'I close my mouth to my thoughts. Wake me when we arrive.'

Arman smiled at me and pointed to an eagle rising from the water with a fish clasped in its talons.

Senea and I had retired early the previous night and, despite almost being assassinated, we had not sought greater counsel on our journey to Pled. We raced against time, travelled without a plan and now Senea was opposed to what happened as a result.

I sat on the edge of the vessel, near Uk-Ban at the mast. If I fell off, I would probably drown. Even so, I did not fear the water. I had heard stories about the Tigris and now we cruised in its current, hot desert winds cooling as they crossed its divide.

Delari knelt next to the unconscious boatman and started rifling through his clothes. He found another small dagger concealed in his sleeve and a pouch of silver.

'How did you do that?' Delari questioned me. 'He fell fast yet he does not bleed.'

'My friend, Tuley, showed me a gentle spot where the neck meets the shoulders,' I said, my legs dangling over the east side of the boat, appreciating the wispy touch of fresh water that leapt each time we hit another boat's wake.

'Do we drift by?' yelled Arman. He pointed out the date palms announcing our approach to Kalhu and Uk-Ban pointed as well, like an excited child.

'Stay midstream, Arman,' Delari called back. He faced me again. 'You hit him on the shoulder and he sleeps like a baby. Did you mean to kill him?'

I twisted my legs to the deck and walked closer. 'I thought he would be rousing by now.'

'Do not show concern for him, Kar. He would not waste a thought on you.'

'Was he right when he said that we would not be allowed entry to any city?'

Delari pointed at my hair, my shoulder fur and the sword at my hip. He ignored my staff because, when the blade was covered with a leather hood, it looked more like a walking stick that older travellers often carry. 'Help me carry him beneath and then search his stores for suitable clothes. One would only have to lift your fur to see your tattoo.'

I took hold of the man's ankles and Delari gripped him under his arms. Uk-Ban braved a step from the mast as he leant forwards and opened the trapdoor leading below deck.

The girth and strong structure of the vessel made it perfect for transporting people and animals along the Tigris. The boat was also large enough to be called a home by one comfortable with the sound of slurring water close beneath. Only separated by the pitch covered reed hull of the boat, I would surely sleep on guard. The only light below deck came from small gaps between the deck's planks. At only half the height of a man, it was cramped and felt damp. As I searched for clothes, Delari found a coil of rope and began tying the boatman's hands and feet. He immediately found a use for one of his newly acquired daggers that not only had a dangerously sharp tip but also bladed sides. The blade cut the thick rope with ease. It was an Akkadian soldier's dagger, only the boatman had wrapped the handle in cloth so that it was more manageable with wet hands and suited to his type of work.

'If Tahnas and Gentuk do not meet us in Assur, then we will have to change our plans,' I told Delari, holding up some of the clothes I had found.

'They will be there,' replied Delari, 'and those clothes will do fine. Tie your hair back with cloth.'

I removed my shoulder fur and slipped my arms through the sleeves of a tight-fitting coverall. It was common attire for peasants, man and woman alike, and would have been a perfect fit on my last journey. Leading up to the Guardian's delayed harvest, my shoulders had widened and I could see and feel my muscles growing. Salarn's meals were not just filling my bones.

Delari glanced up at me and smiled, 'You are wearing it backwards.'

I was not used to such clothing and took the trader's advice. Amongst the trader's goods, I found more clothes and headed topside with shorts and a tunic for Uk-Ban.

'Kar?' Delari called after me.

I looked back down through the trapdoor.

'The boatman spoke an interesting tale before you put him to sleep. You may want to hear what he has to say when he wakes up.'

'I will return soon.'

***

Uk-Ban hid behind the mast when he saw me climb back onto the deck. He did not recognise me with my hair tied back at my neck and my skin covered to my knees. When I offered him clothes, he placed his hand on his heart and knelt before me. I secured my shoulder fur, staff and sword to my stallion's mount before joining Arman and Senea at the stern of the vessel. Uk-Ban still held on tight to the mast as he awkwardly removed his old clothes.

'Wise move,' said Arman, referring to my change of appearance. 'Sargon has a keen dislike for the Guardians. I am not sure what story it was that made it to his ears. Maybe he heard about Tahnas and Gentuk slaying our captors and freeing so many or maybe he heard your story about what Salarn did to the tall soldier in the Desert City.'

'Both good reasons to fear us,' I said, 'and he should fear us.'

'Do not forget that we are in enemy lands now. The people here will even recognise the boat we arrive on and soon learn it is not ours to control without the boatman on side. Is he on side?'

I shook my head.

Senea opened his eyes and sat up. He addressed Arman abruptly. 'We should have just paid him what he asked.'

'You could have offered some of your silver, Senea.'

'We need it to cross the sea,' he argued.

'That is right,' agreed Arman. 'Things like this happen when you rush and do not have a plan. You must stop telling me what should have been done. I have been in worse predicaments than this.' Arman concentrated again on the river's flow.

We were fast approaching the docks of Kalhu and cruised past fishing huts on the eastern banks at the city limits. Uk-Ban waved at the men casting their nets for the first catch of the day and they returned his greeting.

'He is awake,' announced Delari, returning to the deck.

I headed towards the bow, only stopping to re-gather my staff.

'Kar,' said Arman, giving me pause. 'Keep us midstream, Senea.' He handed control of the vessel to Senea and followed me to the bow. When he passed Uk-

Ban wrapped to the mast, he asked, 'Are you keeping watch for mud banks?'

Uk-Ban, wearing his new tunic with his old hide vest atop, looked like he was just admiring the river's banks as the boat streamed down river. He returned Arman's smile and pointed to the places we quickly passed.

***

The boatman struggled against his restraints but it was pointless. His wrists were bound tightly behind his back and tied to his ankles. He flipped himself about on the floor. I thought of a fish pulled from water as he breathed heavily and groaned with each tensed and pointless flip. He tried to kick me and just hurt himself more. 'I told you to wait for him,' he yelled. 'You ask me questions I cannot answer. Xemoth could have shown you the answers.'

'What is he talking about?' asked Arman, joining in the conversation late.

'Untie me and I will save you.'

'Be quiet,' Arman ordered the boatman, his voice ten-fold louder in the submerged confines of the vessel's hull. In a calmer voice Arman then asked, 'What is he talking about, Delari?'

'In Nineveh, he tried to offload our river carriage to another, a man by the name of Xemoth, who has an interest in the prizes of war, namely stone tablets.'

'I see,' pondered Arman. 'Then maybe we should be talking to Xemoth.'

'Yes,' screamed the boatman, 'Not me, talk to—'

I pressed the blunt end of my staff firmly against

the man's throat, silencing him again.

'Thank you, Kar,' said Arman, kneeling close and teasing his finger between the staff and the boatman's throat. 'The thing is ... and I only want you to listen. You know this man, Xemoth, and seeing as though we did not follow your advice earlier, we must request it now. There are a lot of boats that sail the Tigris. How can we find this man on any other day?' Arman gave me a slight nod and I withdrew my staff.

'His boat has a white sail, and he flies a large red flag high on the mast. Find him anywhere between Khorsabad and Assur.'

'A white sail and red tell,' Delari laughed. 'He describes half the boats that sail this river.'

'Your problems are not my problem,' the boatman yelled, and he started flipping himself about again on the floor of the boat, trying to break free.

'He does speak the truth though,' said Arman. 'Tahnas never encountered Xemoth's boat in his time at the river but that is the only way he was able to describe it to us. I'm not sure it even exists.'

The boatman stilled himself to listen to Arman.

'I have two more questions for you,' said Arman leaning over the boatman and holding him by the chin. 'Have you seen many of these tablets and why would Sargon even be interested in them?'

'I have seen many. As I told your trader friend, they do not interest me. Xemoth can read them and he told me they contain knowledge greater than counts of grain. Sargon thirsts for knowledge. When he has all the names and all the maps, he will rid this world of savages like you.'

Arman raised himself from his knees and ushered me topside.

'Wait,' said Delari. 'He has more to say.'

The boatman sighed. 'Why did you not wait for Xemoth?' he asked Delari, no longer caring to raise his voice.

'Because I saw through your lies and we have a meeting to attend,' justified Delari. 'Do not concern yourself with our presence. We are not as heartless as the soldiers you were waiting for. I will pay you twenty silver as promised and when the soldiers find you still tied up you can plead for your life with information. Tell them we travel to Agade to kill Sargon in his own palace. Tell them whatever you like.'

'They will kill me no matter what I say.'

'Yet you make your living working for such men.' Delari laughed. 'Forgive me for not feeling pity.'

'What about leaving me one of those one-handed bows?'

'They would kill you if you had one of those.'

'I can hide it.'

'I am sure there are a lot of things you could do or could have done.' Delari signalled that he was done.

'I'll give you silver for the bow,' yelled the boatman. 'Untie me and I'll show you where I stow my precious belongings. Xemoth is not a real man. I lied to ...'

His voice faded as Delari and I climbed onto the deck behind Arman. The river had widened and, as I searched the banks with my eyes, I only sighted two mud brick huts and a collapsed shade shelter. The huts looked unoccupied and the desert on both sides of the river stretched towards the horizon without noticeable rise or fall.

Arman looked ahead to the next gradual bend in the river. 'Fankisi would know the early works. She, like myself, has spent more time away from the village. Only Verian, Seeves and Arcobon would have known exactly what was lost. It scares me to think that almost every work ever scribed is now in our enemy's hands.'

'Salarn and I recovered many broken tablets but no maps,' I informed Arman.

'The boatman mentioned maps in his talk of not being able to read. Our maps show where the Harmins live, mountain passes and places to take shelter when crossing the desert. Sargon's first eastern assault reached Hidalu in the south. Villages south of the city would also feature on the maps now in his possession.'

'He may not have them all yet,' I said. 'If Xemoth still transports such works then maybe they did not all leave Bit-Bunakki with the army. Maybe they are still in use in Borujerd where an army gathers.'

'Maybe the delay is because they were copied first and Xemoth now takes them south to Sargon's treasure room.' Arman glanced back at me, his eyes wide. 'Sargon still has armies in Borujerd and Bit-Bunakki. The threat is close to home and we are far.'

Spittle gathered in my throat and I could not swallow it as quickly as it gathered. There was too much to do and not enough Guardians to make it all happen with the urgency required. I sat down and Arman and Delari decided to do the same.

'Life in Nineveh pleased me more than life in the village,' admitted Arman. 'Nowhere else have I slept so peacefully during the day. I would have been happy to return to my resting spot beneath date palms that overlook the road north until I was too old to even return to the tent at night.'

'Life often summons the most content to duty,' preached Delari as he lay down. 'Rest whenever you can, I say.'

When Arman followed the trader's lead and rested his head back, he was distracted by Uk-Ban standing above him at the mast.

Uk-Ban was fixing his eyes on particular spots on the riverbanks ahead. As the boat passed them by, he turned his head to watch them quickly disappear before focusing his eyes on a new patch of reed.

Arman smiled and closed his eyes. He was asleep a moment later.

***

'Arman,' Senea called out from the stern of the boat. 'We are close.'

Bulrushes lined the western banks, before the patchy dry grass where a group of farmers herded their goats down river with long sticks. Beyond the stretch of grass following the river, high desert ground reached for the horizon. Ahead was the start of the farming land and irrigation channels fenced green crops. A handful of date palms offered inadequate shelter for the number of farmers exposed to the sun in their gruelling work. Closer to the city, an escarpment formed a natural protective wall against raids from the north. The city of Assur was still no more than a haze of hot stone in the distance but already we could make out the reflective gold statue of the God Amarutu, perched

above the highest ziggurat. It was time to make sufficient plans.

Uk-Ban stayed at the mast as we joined Senea at
the stern of the boat.

'Now that we have left Nineveh, Assur is the only
place we can hope to meet up with Tahnas and Gentuk,' Arman told us. 'I think it is best if Senea and
I ride ahead and we drop anchor upstream from the
port.'

'I agree,' supported Senea. 'Regular traders, not
just soldiers, will recognise this vessel.'

'What makes you certain that Tahnas and Gentuk
will not return via land and ferry across the river closer
to Nineveh?' I questioned. 'Plans do change.'

'Tahnas took plenty of silver for his journey,' began Delari before Arman interrupted.

'We older Guardians make sufficient plans, Kar.
The journey was a search for knowledge and two nights
from now is the arranged meeting time. The meeting
place was always the port of Assur, but it was only
meant to be myself there to greet them. I would have
left sooner if not for the arrival of Uk-Ban. Even if it
requires parting company, one of them will be there to
meet me.'

'They may have already learned what we have of
Xemoth or heard word of your lost Guardians,' added
Delari.

'Either way,' continued Arman, 'The port of Assur
is where we meet to plan the next journey or be it now
journeys.'

I looked at Arman, my face probably whiter than
the sail as I considered all that could go wrong. Even if

we rescued the Pledians and escorted them safely this far west, we still had a river and mountain range to cross. 'I hope they are waiting for you ahead of time.'

'Losing faith, Kar?' questioned Arman.

I smirked. 'I would prefer to be playing in the woods.'

Arman laughed and punched my arm. 'Humour in the face of danger, I like that. I told the men they were wrong about you.'

'Wrong about what?' I asked.

Arman studied my face and then pointed at me and laughed again.

He made me smile.

'I think we are close enough,' advised Senea.

We were approaching the first major irrigation inlet and Arman agreed. Senea coursed the boat towards the western bank and Delari lowered the anchor to further slow our stop. The vessel slid effortlessly through the reeds and banked itself in the mud.

The Guardians wasted no time. Arman lifted the boarding plank and let it rest on solid ground. Senea checked his stores were secure and led his mare from the boat, followed by Arman and his mare.

'I will make first contact with the craftsman, Frif, at the northern port,' Arman told Delari before addressing all. 'If need be, one of us will return with word. Hopefully the next time you see us, we will be accompanied by Tahnas and Gentuk.'

'Travel safe, friends.' blessed Delari.

'If something should happen and we part ways in a hurry, I would like to thank you now,' I told Arman.

'It will not happen. I am going with you to Pled.'

I looked at Delari to see if this decision worried him also.

'You and Senea retired early last night,' explained Delari. 'That is why the decision had to be made in your absence. You should always talk to the host before leaving a party.'

Arman flipped himself onto the mount of his mare. 'The fleeing light is faster than the river's flow. I want to know the city before it is dark. Are you ready to ride, Senea?'

Senea stroked his mare's mane.

They trotted away from the river's edge before releasing their horses into a gallop down a path through the fields of millet.

Uk-Ban crossed the boarding plank and stood on foreign soil. He looked back at the boat and watched Delari disappear below deck.

I sat alone at the stern. My eyes kept looking north even though the city of Assur called to me from in front. Uk-Ban also seemed to be paying more attention to a view of the north than the city to our south. Maybe he had seen these lands before or, like me, feared the arrival of Akkadians before Arman returned.

'Do you see me, Kar? I play a game with myself as I think of my brother joining in and throwing mud at me. My face has mud on it from him. You see?' The thought humoured the man from Catal Huyuk and he rubbed mud on his clean tunic.

'Will your brother clean your tunic?' I asked.

Uk-Ban looked down at the muddied hand mark and shook his head. 'You dirtied my clothes,' he yelled. He lifted his tunic and drew a dagger from his hide shorts. As he ran up the boarding plank and turned towards me, I looked past him at my staff and sword stowed on Har Man's mount.

30

The Wait

Scribed by Kar.

I stood by the mast, my palm rested against the course, aged wood that pointed at the gathering clouds. The vessel swayed each time another boat sailed by towards the port and I watched the boats queue, waiting for a chance to load or unload. I was envious of these boatmen who sailed a known path and whose plans did not weigh life against time when a decision had to be made. In one hand, I rotated a silver shekel that was imprinted with the head of Sargon. The king was shown in profile with a bearded chin and a round helmet covering his head. I had never seen a shekel with such detail and I imagined it was crafted in Agade along with a thousand more.

I no longer made plans because they all seemed to end in disappointment. *Sailing an unknown course through life and not trying to predict anything, was that not my father's advice?* Living by the moment, the challenges I faced seemed less weighted. That is why Senea and I had not planned our return. We did not know what we would find in Pledia or even if the silver we carried would be enough to secure a vessel. I had no fear of death, only a fear of doing wrong, and that was hard enough to avoid. I needed to hear some more good advice but the older Guardians seemed too stuck in their ways to acknowledge the profound nature of vision and shared destiny, like I had felt at the Tree. Each of them spoke about the meaning of life differently, like it was unique and unshared. Verian told me that much of what I felt came from my soul—a place between my heart and head. Salarn's words of wisdom left me thinking about all the things I did not know and, if not for the Tree, I may still have been a frightened, young boy playing games in the woods. Elkin's words seemed to make the most sense for they were timeless. 'Walk to the horizon and every horizon after that.' If only it were that simple. Salarn's last words were that I was destined to leave. What if my elder was just telling me what I would do, rather than what I should do? I felt like Salarn did at the Oasis in the Harmin village. I now felt that I should be at home. The Guardians' days were not yet over and maybe I was needed at the tower to ensure this fate. Naten would welcome me and I would gently clutch her soft skin and savour her scent. Lagesh would not welcome my return. He surely imagined more than just the touch of her skin in an embrace.

'You are free now,' said Uk-Ban, as he completed his imaginary tussle with his brother.

'Can I step from the mast?'

'The mast points to the gods who left us. Step from the mast, Kar. Scream abandonment.'

'I can stay,' I replied. I was disturbed but not threatened by his behaviour. Uk-Ban had experienced some form of awakening on the bank of the Tigris River. He had imagined playing with his brother and I saw this as his way of connecting with something he had lost or forgotten. It had changed him, just like I had changed when I released one of Elkin's eleven arrows in the Karun Gorge—Salarn's heaven. I wondered whether someone had since plucked my floating arrow from the water. *Had it made it to new home or was it banked amongst debris and now a part of the gorge?*

Uk-Ban leant close and smiled at me with kind eyes, 'We need only be quiet when on the hunt, my god would say.'

'Who is your god?' I asked, turning and glancing down at the strange man staring up at me. I turned my gaze to the boats of varying size, queuing for a position at the port. 'I disagree, Uk-Ban. Man speaks too much and is only silent when troubled.'

'You are troubled,' assumed Uk-Ban.

'I am. I see trouble ahead.'

Uk-Ban lifted his tunic and sheathed his blade in the belt that held his cloth shorts to his skinny waist. 'I will help?' he said. 'I understand the gods. We are friends.'

I almost laughed. 'You are friends with the gods?'

'Yes,' said Uk-Ban. 'They want me to do something. What that is, they have kept hidden.'

'Do you think they will tell you or will you have to force more men to a mast?'

'Amast?'

The more I spoke with Uk-Ban, the more I realised that he did not understand words I used. I asked the question differently. 'How will you know what you must do?'

'He will tell me one day. I feel him here and that is why I play.'

'He?' I questioned.

'Our god walks among man now. My brother told me I would find him in the west.'

'How did your brother learn this?'

Uk-Ban giggled like a child and looked to his side as if facing his brother, 'You ask us many questions, Kar, and we speak for the first time.'

'I do not mean to offend you, Uk-Ban. It is only that for too long I thought I had all the answers. It seems everything I thought I knew changes with the setting of the sun.'

'Every day we learn something new. Like this river,' explained Uk-Ban, 'it runs that way,' he said, pointing south like this was of great interest.

I knew which way the rivers flowed before I even left the tower and what I also remembered was that, if I asked too many questions, I would miss the answer. 'I am Kar, son of Unbetum and Kinsufa, and my mother, a daughter of Salarn. I travel west to rescue a people that I only know by name. Each day I advance on un-walked soil. Embarking on this journey felt right; however, now that I have travelled this far, I am not so sure.'

Uk-Ban pointed towards Assur and then touched his wrinkled forehead, 'Remember the path you walk in search of the treasure you seek.'

'I feel my path changing with each step, Uk-Ban. Every step troubles me.'

'I understand why you are troubled.' He pointed

at me and strode towards me like he had before, only now his dagger was sheathed and I was bored with his game. 'I already know where my last path will lead me for I have spent a long time planning its course. When it is time, I will return to Catal Huyuk with water from God's Garden. I will lay myself on top of my brother's grave and pour it over my seeping blood.'

'The god you seek, the one who walks among man, does he only have to answer that one question?' I asked.

'He will show me to the Garden where I will find the water I seek. In return, he will ask that I perform one last duty. I will offer myself to his service before returning home.'

'I am not the god you speak of, though I may know of the place you are looking for,' I told Uk-Ban.

'I thought you might,' said Uk-Ban. 'Every step of my journey is destined and I have only faltered once. Your Guardian friends, Arman and Delari, can tell you about my show of anger.'

I wanted to ask Uk-Ban how he knew these things and what it was that allowed him to think this way. Instead of asking another question, I just told him more of myself. 'Salarn, my mother's father, led me to heaven and I will always know how to return.'

'Who is your mother?' asked Uk-Ban.

'Her name is Kinsufa.'

'I do not seek her name,' said Uk-Ban shaking his head. '*Who* is she?'

'She is the most beautiful woman I will ever know. I long for every word spoken from her lips. Even if I am only to hear words of spite, I will find comfort in the sound of her voice. Her presence alone is justification for all the hurt and suffering that prevails in the world we live in.'

Uk-Ban braced himself to Delari's quiet approach.

'She sounds like a goddess,' said Delari. His eyes squinted as they adjusted to the light above deck.

'She is,' I confirmed, stepping around the mast to face him, 'and that is why I know she still lives.'

Delari had only arrived in time for the end of the conversation, after talking further with the boatman and searching through the man's stores. He was anxious about sharing his newly acquired knowledge. He heard Uk-Ban mention his name and, as he delayed his climb to deck, not wanting to interrupt, he heard that Salarn had shown me the path to heaven on Earth. Delari was not usually concerned with matters of a divine nature but listening to Uk-Ban and I converse had made the hair on his arms bristle. 'Do you know what that means?' he asked. He did not wait for a reply. 'You speak of the other side and something you said made a connection. In my time travelling, I have heard many speak of the Garden of the Gods, but I have never heard anyone confirm they knew where it was with such honest assurance. If you were not a Guardian, Kar, I know not what I would do.'

Uk-Ban signalled me to his side with a wriggle of his finger.

I looked at Delari and the trader shrugged.

'You believe your mother is a goddess and that her father led you to heaven on Earth yet you do not think you are a god. Who is your father?' asked Uk-Ban.

'I can answer that,' said Delari. 'Unbetum is the Guardian who will not die.'

Uk-Ban smiled, happy that he had already found the man he was looking for. 'I did not think you would be so young,' he said as he cast his eyes from my head to my feet.

'I am not a god, Uk-Ban,' I stated and grinned at Delari, hoping the trader would support me. 'Maybe like you, I have just taken the time to listen.' I pointed behind Uk-Ban, 'See that silver coin?'

Uk-Ban glanced behind and saw nothing.

I spread my palms and then reached past Uk-Ban and grabbed something.

'What have you got?' asked the man from Catal Huyuk.

'The coin that was behind you.' I spread my palm and revealed the silver shekel.

Delari laughed, 'Sleight-of-hand tricks will not help him, Kar.'

'This is trickery,' said Uk-Ban as he rotated Kar's hands and looked behind for more coins. 'The gods have many children, Kar. I could not name them all and, when the time comes for them to be born man, they are given new names and learn new tricks. Like that god,' said Uk-Ban, pointing excitedly towards the statue of Amarutu standing atop the temple in the distant city. 'If man can shape his likeness, that god must have walked the earth. They are still gods but if they walk as man then they will also be plagued by man's weaknesses and uncertain thoughts.'

I nodded my head. 'I hear what you are saying, Uk-Ban. The man you look for is either Salarn or Sargon. They are the only men I have heard being called gods.'

'Sargon?' objected Delari. 'Please tell me you have not fallen prey to the misguided tales of Akkadians.'

'Whether he be a man or god, Sargon is still my enemy.'

Uk-Ban was happy with my response and spread his arms wide and waited until he had the attention of Delari as well. 'My name is Uk-Ban Shemberat, the only survivor of Catal Huyuk. The gods abandoned us in their search for something greater and my people moved on. The god that man has called Sargon I believe was our last. He was once the essence and honourable lord of labour. The wall of every room in our city was adorned with the horns of bulls, the beasts that fed us. His strength was called on time and time again until a more gainful proposition was entertained. I believe the Bull abandoned his post in heaven to be number one amongst the weaker breed. Know my friends that he is not the god I seek. When he abandoned my people, we abandoned him,' explained Uk-Ban, turning to face Delari. 'The gods have been poisoned by the accomplishment of their disciples on Earth. The mother of all the gods we know is now at our mercy. The strength of heaven now walks the earth and persuades all others to join his blissful existence. Even Anu, the Father God, has abandoned the mother of his children and now watches from the stars in hope that he will not make the same mistake again when he travels forth to the next world or returns to rebuild ours.'

'What mistake did he make?' asked Delari, his voice sharp and his brow creased.

Uk-Ban pointed his finger southwest towards the statue of Amarutu. 'Letting gods walk the earth after they created man. They liked what they saw and stayed too long. If I can get water from God's Garden and resurrect my people, then uncorrupted hope still remains.'

Delari clapped his hands together louder than necessary. 'You know everything, Uk-Ban, last survivor of Catal Huyuk. You say your people were abandoned by the gods but did not the same gods let you survive?'

Uk-ban ignored Delari and turned to face me. 'Kar, you say you are not a god. I am a stranger, yet you place faith in me. You listen to me even though what I am saying may come across as foolish. You do not dispel my views because you try to understand first. Is this not how a god would listen. A god knows everything yet when they hear a man speak nonsense they sympathise with his weakness and are drawn to his plight.'

'The gods do not stop to listen,' said Delari as he paced the deck.

'Why not?' I asked Delari. 'Do they enjoy our pain?'

'Maybe for the same reason they chose to flood the world,' answered Delari. 'They wait for Sargon to gather the people and then they will wipe cities from our maps like blood from a plate. That is why I do not care for their ways and, like the Guardians, prefer the life between named places. I normally avoid conversations such as this because they always end the same way. Some people believe in gods and some do not. And then there are people like me who believe they exist but decide not to concern themselves with matters out of their control.' Delari grunted as he pushed past Uk-Ban to reach the boat's stern.

Uk-Ban looked at me and I also decided that it was best to leave the rest of our conversation until another day. I sat down with my back rested against the mast.

'I would like to meet the man called Samor,' he said, standing over me and blocking the sun.

'I am sure you will meet,' I answered. 'Samor of the Harmin Village knows the place I mentioned and will help you find the man or god you are looking for.' Two of the barges that were still docked when we left Nineveh passed by and I feared that our seized boat would be recognised or Xemoth's vessel would pass by before Senea and Arman returned. Whilst the barges flew the Akkadian red tell, there were no soldiers aboard.

Uk-Ban patted me on the shoulder and smiled. 'I did not think I would find an answer so soon,' he said before crossing the boarding plank and returning to the riverbank. He pointed at a group of farmers and started walking their way before I called him back.

As he walked in a circle scuffing the ground with his feet, I reflected on my own path. It was easy to question oneself once on the road. I kept learning new things and questioned what changed my mind. Was it abandonment if Uk-Ban kept living and never returned to the collapsed mountains that he used to call home?

Uk-Ban looked back at the boat as Delari ventured below deck again. He decided he too would explore beneath and see what had caught the trader's fascination.

***

Delari placed a stone tablet next to me and then sat down a few paces away, on the boat's bow.

I examined the inscriptions and its coloured finish. 'I have seen this tablet before with my own eyes. Pardensai carved it and Verian kept it freshly painted and on display. I learned my way west from this very map.'

'If we were thieves then there would be a lot of interesting items we could acquire. Claiming a Guardian treasure without offer I am sure you agree is justified.'

'What else does he have?' I asked, excited to see more.

'Swords, silver, beautiful furs and a box filled with bridles. I could smell the leather and cranked it open.'

'See what I found,' announced Uk-Ban, poking his head above deck.

Delari laughed at Uk-Ban's find, 'Yes, many a fishing spool too.'

Uk-Ban dropped a line without bait and jiggled it in anticipation.

'Where do you go from here, Delari?' I asked.

'Arman has decided to travel with you, so I will join the others. East to the tower, I imagine. Depending on their plans I might halt at the Harmin Village and return west again.'

'I never meant to separate you from Arman. I know you are good friends.'

Delari slid closer and rested his hand on my shoulder. 'Good friends understand why sometimes they must part.' He moved his hand to my arm and looked me in the eye. 'I will see him again and no god will have any say in that eventuality. You hear me, Kar?'

'I hear you. It will be our doing, not the gods'.'

31

Shelter for the Night

Scribed by Gentuk, The Trader's Friend.

Tahnas dismounted on a hot shelf of stone at the base of a low ravine and thanked his stallion for the ride. If we had kept riding, we could have halved our final leg of the journey to Assur to meet Arman before the sun set. With the sun on our backs, it would have been a good opportunity to make up lost time. Here, however, there was a cave for shelter and an opportunity to tend to my wife.

Tahnas waited as I lifted Belline to the ground and then unloaded the horses. He found his wooden gouge and a tightly bound bundle of wood and grass he had carried to start a fire. 'I am going to build a fire inside the cave,' said Tahnas. 'Ubai's men could still be tracking us but we will want its warmth when the sun goes down.'

This was our last night's camp on our return to Assur. We would have already arrived if we had travelled alone. Tahnas had set the pace, with Messim doubling on his mount and his stallion also carrying most of our stores. I followed at a distance, nursing my wife and listening to her groans of pain every step of the way. In Mari, I had dressed her wounds as best I could before our hastened departure. Each time we stopped to rest, I had to tend to them again. After three days on horseback, sharing the pain she voiced unavoidably, I told her that I had to treat them properly.

'No, Gentuk, I can wait. I do not want you to see.'

I kissed her face gently. 'Belline, I have missed you more than a desert without sun and I feel hurt for causing you more pain. It is the only way.' I spread my fur on the sun-heated stone and lifted Belline on top. 'Let Messim take a look while I go fetch salt.'

'Not salt, Gentuk. The pain will kill me.'

'It will hurt less if you are looking at me when it is applied. You will feel better for it in the morning when we ride on.'

Belline did not reply.

Messim sat next to her friend on my fur. 'He is right and you have nothing to be embarrassed about. I saw what Pud was doing when I arrived. He threatened to do it to me once too but I submitted. You are so strong for standing up to him. I might not have mentioned your name to Tahnas if you had not inspired me with your courage.'

***

Inside the cave, Tahnas was still trying to spark a flame. He wore his shoulder fur.

'I have a tunic if you need one.' I shuffled through our stores and found the small pouch of salt and the needle I was looking for. 'My water bladder is almost empty. Can I use some of your water to mix with salt?'

I asked Tahnas.

The dry grass at the end of the gouge began to smoke and Tahnas turned it to flame with a gentle breath. Delicately, he placed it beneath his small fire. 'I can share two mouthfuls. We can battle thirst if the horses can. I have another tunic. I'll change in the morning.'

I placed a pot and the pouch of salt next to him before returning outside.

The sky had changed colour in my absence and now the desert was golden in the reflective light. A fierce red blaze reflected off clouds in the west and stretched east with pink fingers. Beneath the painted sky, rolling dunes and low ravines etched darker shadows across the otherwise unhindered expanse between the cave's entrance and the horizon.

Messim turned to my approach, 'Two of the wounds still weep. She needs to rest.'

'There will be time to rest when we are east of Assur,' I replied, crouching and kissing Belline gently on her trembling lips.

'You fear the path ahead,' said Belline, pulling away. 'I know your many faces and you worry for me.'

'I worry because I feel your pain. You have always trusted me. Trust me now. Let me bathe the wounds with warm, salty water and let me stitch them if I feel it is necessary.'

'I was a fool to think I could escape,' cried Belline to my shaking head. 'You cannot argue. I made a child's decision. If I had only waited till morning.'

'And what of this?' I said, kissing the healed scar on her cheek. 'If you had not tried to escape the first time, we may have never found you.' My eyes filled with tears and I rested my head in Belline's bosom to hide my face. She wrapped her arms around me and stroked my hair.

'Shall I fetch the water,' said Messim.

I lifted my head and wiped my eyes with my sleeve. 'It needs time to heat.'

Messim sat down and loosened her sandles. 'Anywhere I go from here is better. I must thank you for allowing me to join you.'

'You led Tahnas to a lost Guardian, Messim. No amount of silver, strong horses or seasons of service could count fair for that offering.'

'Might I rest then?' she asked.

'Go to Tahnas at the fire. He will care for you. We will wake you before dawn and we will reach Assur before high sun.'

32

A Large Red Flag

Scribed by Arman, The Always Travelling Guardian.

Entry to the port of Assur was difficult by land. High ground surrounding the city and buildings that used the natural defence of the terrain left the triangular port only open to the Tigris. The only other way to enter or leave the port was via a wide lane that began at the heights of the markets, outside the walled inner city. Two-level-high buildings bordered this lane and the alleyways that coursed between the buildings were for the disposal of waste, not paths to anywhere a man wanted to go.

I reminded Senea to stay alert to danger close and afar. He was wary of the soldiers' heavy presence and jealous of the guards in the watchtowers, whose view was sure to even reach as far as our vessel banked up-river. Senea held my reins and waited with the horses as I approached the carpenter's stall at the port. Near-by, a flat boat was being offloaded and a procession of hand-pulled carts moved loads of grain up the lane towards the markets. Trade was also active from the neighbouring vessel that had arrived from the south, loaded with raw materials that seemed destined never to make it to the markets. Leather, cloth and bronze, ready to be fashioned into new items, was exchanged for various produce that merchants offered every step of the walk down the wharf.

***

Senea clutched me by the wrist and steadied himself. 'Was Frif home?'

'Tahnas and Gentuk travelled southwest to Mari,' I said, freeing my arm and inspecting Senea's composure for a moment. 'Frif told them that an army headed that way and they decided to follow.'

'It is getting late. What of the others at the boat?'

'They can look after themselves. Frif has offered us shelter. I think we should find something to eat and then get some rest. What do you think?'

'I think, considering we are at the port, fish would be best.'

I chuckled and cast my arm around Senea's shoulders. 'That is the Senea I remember.'

We tied our horses outside Frif's carpentry stall before searching the port for some fresh fish. We did not have to walk far before finding what we sought. I exchanged a half-shekel for five silver fish, caught that day in the Tigris and each a foot long. It would be enough to feed Frif's family and us.

Outside Frif's stall, a fire was already stacked and Senea had it smoking before the port was shadowed from the setting sun.

'Keep working,' I told Frif, when the woodworker

got to his feet and sought to attend to us.

'At least let my children help?'

Frif was adding the arms to a hand-drawn cart, similar to the ones being used to move grain outside. The last time I was here the carpenter was making tables and, like last time, his family joined him in the task. His eldest, a girl, would drill the wood and his young son would cut it to length, leaving Frif and his wife to assemble the pieces and sell the finished work outside or in the markets if necessary. Behind them were several completed carts signifying the day's work.

'Do they know how to prepare fish?' I asked. Frif's son was just learning to walk when I had last visted. 'I am going to take out the bones and dress the fillets with salt before we cook them.'

'Pakeen is handy with the blade and Lorestia tells me she is too.'

'I can cut fish. I just do not like the smell,' explained Lorestia. Her thick brown hair was shoulder length and hung over her face while she worked.

When she looked up, I leant forwards from the door, astonished by her beauty. Her pale skin was taut on her pointy cheeks and her olive eyes shone like a disgruntled cat. 'Do you eat fish, Lorestia?' I asked.

'When it is cooked white and can be pulled apart with fingers.'

Frif smiled at his wife. 'I tell Ogmanna, it is a good thing our daughter is not opposed to the smell of wood.'

'You are lucky there,' I said, warily glancing back at Lorestia. 'Come then Pakeen, sounds like it is only you and us Guardians who get to finish work early today.'

Pakeen looked at his father again before he lowered his saw. Behind him there was still a pile of planks, marked with charcoal and waiting to be cut.

'You can leave the rest of your work until tomorrow. You worked hard today. Hang your saw.'

'Thank you, Father.'

Once Senea had the fire burning, he felt idle. 'Can I help by cutting some wood?' he asked as he entered the stall. There was no doorway to the stall. The front flap was rolled to the roof during the day and at night it would be lowered, tied and weighted down with bags of sand.

'Rest, Senea. You are providing dinner. That is enough,' insisted Ogmanna.

'I would like to help.'

'I can show him,' offered Lorestia.

Frif gave his approval and his daughter eagerly dropped her drill to show the Guardian what to do.

The task was simple but Senea acted unsure and thanked the young girl for her thorough explanation. Anything apart from the repetition of their daily tasks seemed enjoyable to the children. I sympathised. The monotony of the repeated sawing and drilling reminded me of days re-scribing tablets in the village school.

'Please tell me if I am not cutting them as well as Pakeen and I will try harder.'

'You may not be as precise or work as quickly as my children, Senea, but you can only do your best,' said Frif, smiling at his wife and then winking at the Guardian when Lorestia was not watching.

***

Senea woke late the next morning. Frif and his family were still asleep but the sun had almost fully risen by the time he stepped outside. I had already fetched fresh buckets of water for the horses and four more ready-filled ones awaited the arrival of Tahnas and Gentuk.

'Your confidence in their timely arrival reassures me, Arman.'

'You slept well.'

'Like I was at home.'

'I dreamt of my wife last night. I was feeding her fish through a log wall. I will not bore you with its long story and only convey what I learnt. It was harsh of me to question your journey without plans. Until I started travelling with Delari, I never made plans either and it is only the plans devised by Delari and Tahnas that have me looking further ahead than the morrow. I agree with you now and, seeing as though I am to join your journey, I am sure this will offer you comfort.'

Senea shook his head. 'We need a leader, someone to tell us when we are doing the wrong thing and how stupid we are.'

I shoved him aside and knelt to rebuild a fire. 'Though I will miss Delari's company, I think I'll enjoy travelling with you and Kar. Who knows, by the time we return, Kar might be talking like one of us and no longer find time to play.'

'Without wanting to spoil these dreams, how do our plans stand for today.'

'Nothing has changed on that front, Senea. We have no word to send that would change plans, so let us wait. We will give Tahnas and Gentuk till mid-morning and, if they have still not arrived, I will head back to the boat and remind them of the risks involved in lingering in the company of a seized vessel. Delari is not dependent on my word. If he needs to abandon the boat, he will make the call.'

'If time allows, I might walk up the lane to the markets and purchase some dry food stores?'

I agreed. 'Go now and hurry back.'

He tightened his belt and collected a basket from the side of Frif's stall.

I watched as Senea walked towards the wide lane into the city, soon indistinguishable from the other merchants and traders slowly filling the triangular port.

***

I waited patiently outside Frif's stall for the arrival of Tahnas and Gentuk. Senea had been gone a while but this did not concern me so long as he was back in time for the arrival of the others. That was until I saw a strong-hulled boat arrive flying a large, red flag high on its mast. It had arrived from the south, meaning it had not passed Delari and the others. This raised different concerns. If this was Xemoth, then that meant he had already off-loaded his loot of Guardian tablets and it also signed the owner of the boat we had seized as a liar. The boatman had told Delari that Xemoth was soon to arrive in Nineveh yet this vessel was a day's travel to the south and arriving from a destination beyond Assur. I approached the wharf to sight the owner. If this were Xemoth, I wanted to judge the man's character with my own eyes.

He was tall with a large nose and heavy-lidded eyes. His chin beard was plaited and his shiny skull only held whiskery, short grey hair around his ears. It looked like he had arrived alone but, after stepping onto the wharf, two Akkadian soldiers appeared from below deck, dressing themselves as if they had just woken. I watched him from a distance and mingled with the crowds like a regular dockworker.

Xemoth signaled his guards to wait with the boat before walking the length of the wharf to the port. I waited until he had passed before deciding to follow. Xemoth was a serious looking man and, though he had lost most of his hair and his skin looked as creased as the burning hide of a boar, he was probably the same age as Gentuk, give or take a few seasons. I stood foolishly close to the man when he delayed at the fishmonger's stall at the port.

'Returning for more,' said the fishmonger, singling me out against my will.

Not wanting to arouse suspicion and seeing this as an opportunity to become acquainted with Xemoth, I replied promptly. 'I am riding north en route to Nineveh. Are those smoked fillets still fresh enough to be saved for a meal on the ride?' I asked, hoping to draw the curiosity of Xemoth who was sure to be heading north to the same city mentioned. I could feel the stranger's stare upon me. He sized me up and moved on hastily.

'You would be better with salted fillets, traveller,' said the fishmonger.

'Let me ponder,' I said, noticing that the boatman had already disappeared amongst the crowding morning trade. I made my way through the port and, when I reached the entrance leading to the markets, I stopped and looked back towards Xemoth's boat. It was still docked though I could only spot one of the soldiers. I checked to see that our horses were still tied in front of Frif's carpentry stall before entering the lane in pursuit of the balding boatman.

The crowds were thick, coursing both ways through the steep lane that linked the port to the city markets. The more I tried to side-step my way faster forwards, the more I found myself blocked. I was unable to see more than a few feet in front. New faces passed by and from behind everyone looked the same, carrying baskets and wearing the same-coloured tunic. I was about to give up on ever finding the man when I was bustled from the crowd by two Akkadian soldiers and forced into a shadowed alleyway bordered by two-level-high living quarters. The ground between was lined by the waste tossed from the windows above and had blended into a foul sludge after the recent rain. I toppled backwards and landed in the mess. The soldiers braced themselves after tossing me, only ankle deep in the decay. The stench from this lane made even those passing hurry their step and cup their noses. Xemoth approached and waited until I had attempted to wipe my face clear.

'You have been following me ever since I arrived. Do you want something from me?'

It would not be my best lie that I responded with. 'I saw you arrive from the south. I thought if I befriended you in the markets then I may be able to travel with you north in exchange for service.'

'What service could you offer and how exactly did you intend to befriend me?'

'I planned to tell you not to buy fish at the port as I had it last night and it was dry from the sun and filled with bone. I thought to also offer you a drink at the beer house and tell you about what I heard in Nineveh before I left.'

'What did you hear?' asked Xemoth. He stepped forwards as the two soldiers stepped back.

I thought quickly to assemble a purposeful response. 'A high priest there tells that Assur will fall to a raid from the north. He spoke this news from the city walls like it was word from his god. I tell this in the city and the soldiers care not.'

'That is as foul a lie as the excrement you lie in,' spat Xemoth, making the soldiers either side of him laugh.

'Why would I lie? I only trade on the roads between Khorsabad and Assur. My life, my trade is threatened,' I argued. 'Do you want to know what I think now?'

Xemoth and his fellow aggressors were in the position of power. I lay in the sludge and when I wiped my face it was with hands coated in the same mess. The smell made me retch and I tasted fish from the meal the night before. I smelled rotting fish on my hands. None of the passers-by even spared a glance down the alleyway, turning their noses to its approach, and those who had witnessed me being picked from the crowd had only hurried their step. When Akkadian soldiers were involved, it was best to remove yourself from the scene as fast and as far as possible.

'Entertain us trader. What do you think now?'

I flicked my hand forwards with excitement, slinging sludge onto one of the soldiers in a seemingly unintentional fashion.

The soldier hit with splatters of the foul mess, drew his sword.

'Be patient,' said Xemoth, signalling the soldier to hold back but raising his own discernment as his foot became immersed in fresh excrement and a thousand tiny flies swarmed with the encroachment. 'What do you think?' yelled Xemoth as though it would be the last question he ever asked.

I lifted myself half to my feet and rested my back to the stone base of a building. With my less soiled forearm, I wiped matted hair from my face. Whilst my head was still bent and turned from my aggressors, I studied the length of the alley. Fifty paces from where I sat, or one hundred regretful surges through the sludge, I could see a glint of light announcing the northern end. I faced the Akkadians. 'You!' I yelled, pointing at Xemoth, 'You call me a liar. I call you one. Your guards know not of your secret promise with Sargon.'

There was a delay in the lane behind and one of the guards retreated to tell those lingering to disperse. 'This man is an enemy of Sharru-Kin and anyone who stays will be viewed as one too,' the soldier told the people who delayed in their movement up and down the lane. As soon as the name Sharru-Kin was mentioned, the lingering crowd joined the normal flow of traffic to and from the markets. Only two men remained behind at the entrance to the alleyway. One was an elderly man who required a crutch to walk.

'Did you not hear what I said?' asked the soldier, his hand ready to draw his sword.

'I heard,' said the elderly man. 'This man stands in my path.'

'No, you stand in my path,' said Senea. 'Let me help you.' Senea drew the shoulder of a boy passing by to help support the elderly man as he took the crutch from his hands. Before the soldier knew what was happening, his nose was broken and his throat was crushed by two quick strikes.

I used the distraction to my advantage. When Xemoth turned back to face me the other soldier was nursing a blade in the throat and was dropping to his knees. Xemoth drew a long dagger and I shook my head, signalling that this was not going to be sufficient defence. The old man's crutch, wielded by Senea, collected Xemoth in the back of the head and, still conscious, the boatman collapsed face first into the foul sludge that he had tried so hard to avoid.

Senea returned to the old man in the lane and helped place the crutch under his arm. The old man poked the boy supporting him away and then extended his hand for an offering.

Senea tucked a finger behind his belt and found a half-shekel. 'That is all I have.'

'All I have,' yelled the man hysterically. 'They come again. Praise Anu. They come again.' He waved his free arm about and divided the crowds as he hobbled away. For a moment, he drew all's attention to himself and away from the happenings in the alleyway.

Senea stepped into the alleyway and away from the new commotion.

'Is he leaving?' I asked, kneeling on Xemoth's back and holding his face aloft by a fisted grip of his plaited beard.

'Yes,' replied Senea, 'do what you have to do. Do it quickly.'

Xemoth pleaded for his life in between face-first plungings into the mess that I knelt in. Senea used this opportunity to remove the clothes from one of the soldiers and make sure both were dead before he buried them deeper in excrement. He heaped it on with a shovel he found nearby and held his breath to the slurping sound that unleashed a stench only comparable to a rotting corpse at the point when the belly expands and pops.

'I will give you more silver or weapons than you could imagine,' begged Xemoth.

'I asked what you transport by boat.'

'Food, weapons, people, whatever I can.'

I sunk his head again and held him down for a long while. When I felt the man struggling for a breath, I raised him only high enough so that his mouth would taste the waste as he gagged for a breath of life. Only content once Xemoth had received a mouthful, I asked my question differently. 'What was on your last load?'

'Many things,' answered Xemoth, pointlessly retching and spitting to remove the taste from his mouth. 'Most items are wrapped and I do not even know what they are.'

I waited as Xemoth expelled his guts repetitively. 'I am told you can read and you have seen the clay and stone tablets from the east.'

Xemoth struggled with many thoughts and possible lies before answering. 'I saw them. I transported them long ago and even stole a few. I still have those and will give them to you without ask of offer.'

'What do they say? The ones you stole.'

'They are maps. More valuable than any words and unseen by Sargon.'

'I am not sorry I made you eat that mess. I got a taste myself and wanted to share the experience.' I shoved Xemoth's face into the sludge once more and then stood like a wet dog ready to shake myself dry. 'How was your morning, Senea?'

'I have stores for my father and Tahnas if they have not already parted in your absence.'

'My fault again, is it?' I asked as I wiped myself clean and dressed in the salvaged Akkadian's uniform.

Xemoth was void of any substance to expel but continued to heave. 'You will be safe if you can make it to my boat,' he said, hoping for his life to be spared. He crawled towards us.

'He could assist,' said Senea. 'Are you heading for Nineveh?'

'Yes, you should travel with me and escape this city,' said Xemoth as he got to his feet at the edge of the muck.

My sword would have lopped off his hand at the wrist. The dull blade that I had acquired from the Akkadian guard only broke bone and severed skin. A thin dagger fell from Xemoth's hand as he raised it defensively and a thick splatter of blood was pumped from his throat when I slashed the sword up under his chin. I stepped back as he collapsed in the sludge.

'We still have a problem,' said Senea. 'You do not look like an Akkadian.'

'I am tired of playing dress up,' I complained,

wriggling my arms and legs to find comfort in my new costume. 'Why does it always have to be me?'

Senea frowned. 'Hide your tunic that hangs below your leg armour and put on a helmet. That is all I can suggest.'

'Less rings, try this necklace, paint your eyes. This never happened in the Guardian days.'

'These are still the Guardian days, Arman,' said Senea. He walked out into the flow of people heading between the port and the markets and disappeared amongst the crowd.

***

Senea returned ahead of me to Frif's stall to collect our furs and horses. He bundled two neat packs and led our horses towards the centre of the port. There were no stalls here and the crowds were thick. I joined him, dressed like an Akkadian soldier, and dropped my leather sandals near his feet. My sandals and my abandoned tunic—now coated with indescribable muck and lying in the rarely frequented alleyway—were the only items I owned that were made by my late wife. I prized them above my sword that had saved my own and other's lives on so many occasions. It had hurt me to watch Uk-Ban squeeze his un-bathed feet into the leather accustomed to my personal contours and, like now, it was a sacrifice to part from them. I did not want to head west with nothing else remaining of my former life with my wife. She was sure to be with child after our last night together. In the new west, such memories would strengthen my conviction.

Senea bent and picked up my worn sandals and added them to one of the bundles. He kept his distance from me. This was wise because I was trying to act like an Akkadian soldier.

Through the laneway joining the markets to the port, Tahnas and Gentuk led their horses. I saw Belline again. The other woman's face was unfamiliar. I turned excitedly towards Senea but he had strayed from my company. Flies were gathering at my armpit and drawing unnecessary attention my way. I lifted my arm and loosened the strap on my breastplate. A fish head fell loose. When I regained sight of Tahnas and Gentuk, they were at Frif's stall; Tahnas handed his reins to Gentuk and entered alone. Gentuk continued towards the river, immersing himself in the bustling, late morning crowd. Most of those moving to and from the wharf were dockworkers or boatmen. Traders, like the fishmonger, and builders, like Frif, had their stalls positioned on the southern side of the port's triangle that pointed like a trap to the only lane in or out of the city. Behind the traders' and builders' stalls, long high-walled graneries completed the other sides of the river's enclosed port.

Senea had not noticed their arrival. I grunted louder and signalled Senea with my eyes. He looked my way and turned in time to see Tahnas leave Frif's stall.

33

The Meeting

Scribed by Arman, The Always Travelling Guardian.

‘Arman! The boat.’

I stood at a small distance to Senea, acting like I was on guard duty in my latest costume. The uniform I wore, or possibly my stench, made people avoid me and I accepted this, hoping the guards posted in the stone watchtowers would also perceive me as one of their own. I faced the wharf, confused at first by Senea's softly spoken words. He had noticed something else as I watched the Guardians, Tahnas and Gentuk, arrive with Belline and a stranger. Beyond the crowds of the port and the wooden wharf that secured many a shipping vessel, I focused my eyes on a boat approaching from upstream. Delari controlled the sail and it looked like Uk-Ban was plucking planks from the deck at the steer end next to Kar at the rudder.

‘Mother,’ cried out Senea. He abandoned me and pushed his way through the dockworkers when he saw Belline stooped over on the back of his father's mare.

‘Something tells me we will be leaving this city in

a hurry,' I whispered to my mare.

It did not recognise my face in a helmet or the strange scents of the armour I wore. My own mare turned its brown nose, snorting with agitation and blowing bubbles through its nostrils. This drew the attention of Tahnas. His hand moved to his sword hilt and I quickly announced myself. 'Hold your strike.'

Tahnas recognised my voice and looked twice at my face before accepting it was me. 'What have we walked into, Arman?'

'Keep your distance. There are two soldiers near the granary already watching me and looking for an excuse to engage.'

'I assume you also encountered trouble or you would not be wearing a soldier's uniform.'

'We met some Akkadians this morn. Senea and I killed two soldiers and the owner of the vessel flying the large red flag. The young Guardians arrived in Nineveh two nights ago,' I explained, seemingly talking to myself as a group of fishermen joined a queue between us, waiting to draw water from the well. 'I am travelling with them to Pled.'

Tahnas shook his head. 'Pled is lost. The Akkadian army was already in Mari when we left four days ago. We found Belline. We all need to return home.'

'That may be enough to convince them. Get to the boat. I will have to follow at a distance.'

'The boat?' Tahnas faced the wharf.

Behind Xemoth's boat, Kar and Delari arrived with pace from upriver. The seized boat shook the wharf and almost bounced back into the river's flow, catching hold of Xemoth's vessel by its bow and knocking the armour-clad guards who stood watch from their feet. Wedged behind the other vessel, there was hardly a need to tie the boat.

'Bandits,' bellowed Delari as he jumped onto a nearby mooring post, flailing his arms about in a desperate search for attention. 'A hoard approaches from the north. Flee to the city.'

Delari's voice echoed through the crowded port and, after a moment of timeless silence, the inhabitants scattered like startled deer. The laneway was not wide enough to accommodate their retreat and the boats too few to support the weight of those who ran towards the river to escape.

Behind Delari, Kar bounded across the deck of our seized vessel towards Xemoth's boat. He stood on the tightly bundled reed edge and leapt onto Xemoth's. The leather covering his staff's bladed end was already folded down.

The guards on Xemoth's boat followed the young Guardian behind a raised cabin on the deck and I did not see them again.

Tahnas stepped to my side. 'Is this part of your plan?'

'We planned to meet them upstream. They are here for a reason.'

'For whatever reason that may be, Delari wants us to board the boat. He would know that talk of bandits would not make Guardians turn away.'

'He does not know that I'm dressed as a soldier. I can't follow with two horses.'

'Let me ...' and he said no more when I turned towards the approach of the two guards who had been watching me since my arrival in the port. Tahnas weaved between abandoned carts, some fully loaded, and took the reins of his stallion from Senea.

The citizens of Assur had almost vacated the port. Those not pushing towards the wharf or crouched beneath the watchtowers were slowly disappearing up the lane towards the city centre. Dressed as an Assurian or Akkadian, if there was a difference in their costume, I could not be seen trying to help the Guardians escape. Instead, I led two restless mares by their reins back to the well in the middle of the port's triangle.

'Senea,' cried out Belline, 'stay with me.'

His mother had returned to him and now he was walking away. He was walking my way. I held Senea's mare and my own. Despite his mother's objection, Senea kept walking away from the wharf until he was on his own in the almost vacated port.

'Are these your horses?' I called out to him, as he approached. 'They are ours now. Move to the city.' Four soldiers now surrounded me and I welcomed their arrival and pointed to Senea. 'Come and claim them if you like,' I yelled and the soldiers walked towards him with their swords drawn, signalling this would not be allowed.

Senea turned to their advance and ran to join the back of the crowd shuffling onto the wharf. Escape through the city and by river was blocked, and above us stood the archers in their high watchtowers.

Tahnas was wearing a clean long-sleeved tunic. He removed it and handed it to the woman riding his stallion. Clothed in only his leather skirt and sandals, Tahnas's foreboding appearance, heightened by his raised sword, cleared a narrow path through the Assurians packed onto the wharf tighter than penned goats.

Senea was separated from Tahnas and the others. He looked back at me and then up at the watchtowers. Soon the sun would be behind the towers and the archers' view would be to their advantage.

34

Port of Tribulation

Scribed by Kar.

The thick hull of Xemoth's vessel seemed unbreachable. It floated a caravan's load with ease. Above deck, six horses were tied, three either side of a square cabin. Below deck, there was room to stand between the crates of weapons, armour and varied artifacts. I found a bronze spear amongst his cargo and drove it downwards into the tightly bound reeds that formed the bottom of the vessel until the tip found a gap. With my feet pressed against the extension of the mast below deck, I forced my weight against the spear. It did not move. I pulled the spear from the hull. Cool water trickled in and touched my toes. I drove the spear downwards again. There was a loud crack, like a branch had fallen in the woods, and water pooled around my sandles. I pushed my weight against the spear again and crept my feet up the mast until I was suspended with my feet higher than my shoulders. My short sword dangled in its sheath from my belt. I pushed my legs straight. The spear shifted and my feet slipped off the mast. I landed in water reaching my ankles.

I collected two Guardian clay tablets that I'd set aside and stepped up a short ladder to the deck. Like the stone tablet inscribed by our late elder, Pardensai, these tablets were painted and detailed the locations of cities, rivers and mountains that separated the East from the West. The cracked and faded green paint that signified the woods east of the Zagros Mountains drew my eyes. A man on the deck leant close. His head blocked the light of high sun. I held the tablets to my chest and pushed my way through strangers that had gathered in my time below deck. Both Xemoth's and the seized vessel were now filled with dockworkers and fishermen, alike in their white tunics and coveralls. With my staff slung between my shoulders and the tablets gripped firmly, I jumped towards the edge of the boat I had arrived on. My short sword slapped my thigh as I landed and my staff almost sent me backwards when it caught the edge between my legs. I slid from the edge onto the crowded deck.

Uk-Ban was seated near the mast, his fingers bloodied from his feverish plucking of planks. I knelt next to Uk-Ban and handed him the tablets. 'Take them east with you.'

'We must leave this place together and go to the Garden.'

'You should return to the tower with the others. Tell your story to Salarn and my father, Unbetum. Tell Samor in the Harmin Village if you pass his way,' I said. 'Xemoth's boat will sink. There are more tablets in his cargo. It had to be done.'

Uk-Ban stood to inspect the neighbouring boat and I squeezed my way towards the wharf side of the vessel. I sighted Tahnas parting the masses and leading two women on horseback towards Delari who waited for them with his hand held high. Beyond the wharf, I saw the mares belonging to Senea and Arman, surrounded by soldiers. I drew my stare back to Tahnas as the strong man arrived to meet Delari. Making my way closer to them along the edge of the boat, I overheard Tahnas say, 'He is dressed as a soldier.'

At first glance, I did not recognise the woman seated on Tahnas's stallion, led by Gentuk. When I looked again, her face was unmistakeable. The scars on both her cheeks only made her appearance more real. Belline was my mother's closest friend and she still lived.

I looked past the well to the back of the port where there was a laneway bordered by watchtowers. Looking into the sun, I could count five archers in each tower. There was a deep rumble, the sound before an approaching storm, and for a moment I thought the city that climbed the slope towards the highest temple was collapsing towards the river. Those who had escaped into the lane, spilled back into the port faster than they had retreated. Following them out of the lane were the Akkadians we had seen approaching from the north. The lane amplified the clap of a hundred hooves as the battalion's armoured steeds descended to the port.

We had seen the Akkadians riding south to Assur from upriver and knew that we had to sail before they reached us but we did not have to sail fast into the Port of Assur and Delari did not have to make his announcement from the mooring post. Our plan changed in a moment when we saw the large red flag on Xemoth's boat rippling in the wind. I steered the boat towards the wharf, not thinking of an escape. My impetuous decision had left Arman stranded.

The soldiers already present before the arrival of the battalion were grouped near the well in the centre of the port. Arman was among them, dressed in the same uniform and holding the reins to his mare and Senea's.

Still carrying the clay tablets, Uk-Ban found me amongst the scared folk seeking refuge on the deck of the boat and straining it to tipping point. 'Kar,' he called out.

I leapt onto the wharf when a gap emerged between the frightened Assurians locked to dock.

Hearing my name, the other Guardians and Delari looked about and their gaze followed Uk-Ban's pointed finger towards the port.

'Did he not see us?' yelled Delari.

For a brief moment, Tahnas's eyes met mine.

'He saw you all,' answered Uk-Ban.

Tahnas handed the reins of his mare to Delari and climbed onto one of the mooring posts. 'People of Assur,' he yelled, only able to draw the ears of those closest for he was not the only person raising his voice. Everyone was calling out, fearing for their lives and struggling to stay in contact with those they knew. 'They were not bandits. They were soldiers arriving. The city is safe.'

Only a few heard his words. The message passed slowly from ear to ear and was not sufficient to clear the fear or turn the people around. Being amongst the last to vacate the port, it was a struggle for the Guardians to make it this far, and now the boat they needed to escape on was already occupied by dockworkers, fishermen and others caught in the fray.

The battalion of soldiers flanked the port's triangle and the guards in the watchtowers had their bows raised. Several officers, adorned in bronze breastplates and helmets, grouped with Arman and the soldiers of Assur who were the first to arrive in the centre of the port. The Akkadian battalion had established their presence, and with Tahnas's word of false alarm spreading, the commotion on the strained wharf stilled. The people waited anxiously now in fear of the soldiers' next move. Only I left the packed wharf and walked towards the soldiers manning the port.

I had retied the leather sheath to the bladed end of my staff and walked slowly, like I needed it for balance. Around me, dust still settled from the stampede of the battalion into the port. The officers who had arrived from the north were consulting the soldiers of Assur, including Arman.

'It rammed our wharf,' said an Assurian soldier, pointing towards our seized vessel. 'The man with the exposed chest stands above the man who insighted the fear.'

The Akkadians needed the people of Assur to still themselves and retreat to the city before the wharf itself surrendered to the weight of such an assembly. Several Akkadian officers stayed with the soldiers of Assur as one advanced alone to re-establish order.

I stood in his path dressed in the bland coverall I had recently acquired. My hair was still tied back low on my neck and I hoped I looked less like a bandit. 'They are my horses,' I told the mounted Akkadian.

'Fetch them boy and keep moving away from the

port.'

Walking wide of him, I approached the Assurian soldiers gathered in the centre of the port around the well.

Establishing trust with the people was not going to be easy for the Akkadian officer. Instigating fear and making people submissive to their rule was their true and often-demonstrated strength. I stopped behind the mounted Akkadian officer at a small distance to our horses and the Assurian soldiers assembled near the well. From the lane that provided the only other escape from the port, more soldiers arrived and they were ordered to hold their position.

The senior officer stayed mounted on his steed as he addressed those filling the wharf and the docked vessels. 'People of Assur, my name is Derahmus, first liege officer to Sargon and commander of the north-eastern frontier.' His voice travelled far. 'It is my duty to protect the people of Assur and all cities to your north. That boat,' he yelled, pointing across a sea of faces to the one Uk-Ban still shared with strangers, 'was stolen from the port of Nineveh and we are here to salvage its load and rescue the boatman. No one but those responsible for the crime have anything to fear. I request that you return to your homes and clear the wharf before our advance.'

The seized boat rocked from side to side as the people turned hastily, looking to name someone as the owner or perpetrator. The sway of the boat and the resulting meeting of bodies made many fall from the sides, and the ensuing chaos as occupants rescued friends from drowning only added to the commotion.

Tahnas and the other Guardians were still cornered on the wharf near the boat's bow and they too wanted to regain control of the vessel. 'Move towards the port,' shouted Tahnas. I could hear him from the port but those occupying the boats held the positions they had fought to attain.

The wharf was too crowded to accept their weight should they disembark. Those closest the port had to clear the way first and then they might make a desperate dash to safety. The people of Assur stood braced like crouched chickens. In the stillness, I noticed the movement of one man. Senea was making his way closer to the boat by swinging under mooring ropes. He was grappling a path between the wharf and the swaying vessels that would crush a man should he fall between. The wharf creeked beneath the weight of the people and I thought of the snapping sound that preceded water breaching the hull of Xemoth's boat.

Dehramus looked over my head to the watchtowers. A strange holler of foreign words had him turn back to the wharf.

I don't think anyone knew what Uk-Ban said but the manner in which he held the clay tablet aloft conveyed significance.

'*Yei mih aiy, yih mih aiy*,' bellowed Uk-Ban. The cracked edges of the tablet and its inscriptions still coloured with paint displayed a world far beyond their elevated city gates and the river portals. 'This is what they come for,' announced Uk-Ban. 'I am the one they want. Return to your city and let me face them alone.'

The crowd at the start of the wharf began to shuffle into the port and the people on the deck of our seized vessel created a circle around Uk-Ban. It was equally a brave and crazed move by the man from Catal

Huyuk. A man lunged at him with a blade and was held back by three other men.

Tahnas looked my way from his position on a mooring post and, closer, I saw Derahmus, the mounted first liege officer, give the command. His raised hand dropped to his side.

From the watchtowers, arrows were released. Most of these arrows splattered into the river beyond the docked boats. One flew a perfect course to Uk-Ban and, if not for the clay tablet, it would have split his chest. Deflecting off the clay, the arrow fell into the water near to Senea.

Chaos broke out in anticipation of more arrows being loosed.

Derahmus urged the people forwards and, as room was created, those closest to Uk-Ban leapt from our seized vessel and filled the space provided on the wharf.

Senea was the first to find his way to Uk-Ban's side and he stabbed a man in the arm when he saw the man attempting to slay Uk-Ban with a fishing spear. When another man leapt from behind, also wielding a blade, Senea stuck his blade into the assailant's shoulder and shoved him into the gap between the boat and the wharf. The vessel rocked against the wharf before he hit the water and crushed the man's head. Blood spurted from his split skull faster than I had seen a man empty his bladder at the drinking hut in Bit-Bunakki.

The people began to leave the wharf and, upon seeing that they were allowed unhindered entry to the port, began to move faster.

Arman approached and offered me reins. 'Take your horses towards the market, young man,' he ordered, still pretending he was a soldier. 'Lead the people away from the wharf. I will follow to ensure you do not linger.'

The officers agreed with Arman's instructions.

'Make sure he does keep moving. And you others need only stand back,' commanded one of the officers from Derahmus's battalion. 'Move to the flanks of the port before you frighten the people's advance.'

The soldiers of Assur followed the officer's orders, apart from one. Something about Arman made the Assurian suspicious. He approached the officers and prompted them to take a closer look at Arman's face. Gesturing at his own face and helmet, and then pointing at Arman, it seemed he was concerned with more than just the length of Arman's beard.

'It's only us now, Kar. I had to turn Senea away,' explained Arman as he walked me towards the lane.

'I found two Guardian tablets on Xemoth's boat,' I informed Arman. 'It transports weapons and maybe more tablets, so I made sure it will sink.' We were on our own ahead of the people disembarking from the wharf and, whilst we had left the immediate presence of the officers, we walked towards a gauntlet of Assurian soldiers at the entrance to the lane.

'Soldier,' one of the officers called out from behind. 'What is your name and rank?'

Arman kept walking, hoping the officer was talking to someone else.

'He may just want to commend you,' I suggested, without turning or stopping.

'Wishful thinking, Kar,' said Arman. He glanced back and saw that one of the soldiers of Assur was still with the officers. They were not following but he needed to respond.

He had been made out as an infiltrator, though their pause made me question how convinced they were. Our knowledge of the army's ranks was limited but we had learnt many Akkadian names and we also knew that everyday more soldiers were recruited. Each time a city-state was claimed by the Akkadians, new men were enlisted and Sargon's army grew in size. Sargon was fighting wars on all corners of the earth, against peoples he did not know, with the help of soldiers who only knew their king by name and fanciful story. Even an officer in Assur could be forgiven for believing he was one of them.

'I am Isvah of Eshnunna. I have no rank as I am yet to fight.'

I stopped and waited for Arman. The clearing of the wharf was finally in the Akkadian's favour and the officer would not want to be responsible for halting its progress. 'Do you know this soldier?' he said, pointing at the Assurian responsible for the delay.

'He looks like all the other Assurians to me. I only arrived this morn from the south,' replied Arman, slowly walking back towards them. 'I travel with Xemoth, escorting a shipment of weapons to Nineveh,' added Arman, quickly finding use for the information I had supplied.

'On your way then soldier,' said the officer, convinced by his story.

Arman signalled me to keep going and followed me towards the next stronghold.

'I would know you if you travelled with Xemoth,'

yelled the Assurian soldier standing amongst the mounted Akkadian officers.

'Let your comrades in waiting challenge him,' ordered one of the mounted officers. 'Find your place on the flank, soldier, before you upset our progress.'

'I do not like this, Arman,' I told him. 'You smell like meat in a boar trap and your beard is twice the length of any other soldier's. We need to delay until the people from the wharf can mask our movement. Fifty or more Assurians who do not know you await us at the lane entrance.'

'Next to others our difference will be sighted. This is the best chance we have. They want us to pass unhindered so that the others do the same.'

I stopped short of the soldiers waiting at the lane and looked back. 'They will not let us pass.'

Arman turned and saw that the soldiers were now dividing those who left the wharf into queues. The Akkadians were not just clearing the wharf. They seemed set on bringing justice to those responsible for seizing the vessel in Nineveh.

'You might be right, Kar. I find myself short of other options. We could mount the mares and rush them.'

'Let them come to us. Maintain your deception as long as you can and let us distract the soldiers whilst the others escape.'

'Your father would never forgive me for agreeing with such a stance. Of all the times to make a stand maybe this is the day.' As a latter thought, Arman then asked, 'Are you familiar with the Wrath of the Gods routine?'

'Yes,' I said, my eyes widening. 'I scribed that tablet at least three times in the school.'

'Prove it then,' challenged Arman.

I let go of the reins and waited for Assurian soldiers to advance from the laneway. It was not long before the order was given and eight soldiers set forth to enquire upon my delay.

'It is a campfire tale,' informed Arman, referring to the Wrath of the Gods routine previously mentioned. 'Gentuk devised the plan but he has never tried it. One night, a quiet night by the fire in the village circle, we were discussing our encounters with barbarians and a question was posed. How could one Guardian enable escape from an entire horde without loss of life?' Gentuk explained that the only way was to convince them you were not men.'

'Everything happens for a reason, Arman. Even a long tale has purpose. Hearing such stories from Verian at the end of the day made every scribing lesson worthwhile.' I hastened my step forwards in front of the horses and Arman to explain my delay to the Assurian soldiers advancing from the lane.

'He has been ordered to keep advancing,' Arman told them.

'I cannot continue without the rest of my family,' I complained. 'We are on a pilgrimage to Zidonia and the unrest at the port has separated us.'

'Everyone is to make their way to the markets,' said one of the Assurian soldiers. 'We offer you safe passage and only ask that you leave your weapons behind."

I'm sure Arman wanted to tell me that this was

a good offer but instead he just sighed and shook his head, knowing that a Guardian would always choose to go another way rather than part with their weapon.

'My staff and sword have been blessed by a high priest in Nineveh. Allow me time to secure them to my steed as I do not want to pass without them,' I told the soldier who had responded.

'It is not a matter for negotiation.'

A soldier advanced on me and, judging me by size, did not feel the need to draw his sword. He took hold of my staff and punched me in the face. I held onto my staff as I fell to the ground with blood spilling from my nose.

'You fool,' raged Arman, forced now to assume his role in the routine. 'Do you not know who this boy is?'

Those watching from where they were ordered to queue saw the soldier's actions and, as Arman and I were the first to leave the port, they were once more set on retreating. The queue of people in the port shuffled and I saw at least ten men leave the gathering and sprint back to the wharf. Blood continued to drain from my nose as I stood and looked at the mounted Akkadian officers.

Derahmus ordered his horsemen to seal off any retreat to the wharf and leave those remaining stranded. He then called two mounted officers to his side. 'One of you is to ride north and the other to the south. Each of you is to take four soldiers and board any vessel heading this way. Make them dump their loads if necessary. I will not allow those who have seized the vessel to escape. Make your way back to Assur and intercept any boat that leaves the port.'

The Akkadian officer who had allowed Arman to escort me towards the lane had watched our progress, and he was disappointed by the welcome given. He signalled his comrades to maintain their positions and rode towards the laneway to rectify the problem before it further impeded progress.

Arman was wrestling with the other soldier when the officer arrived. Upon seeing the officer advance, the other assembled soldiers took backwards steps and stood to attention.

'Release each other, soldiers,' demanded the mounted Akkadian officer.

Arman released his hold and, when the opposing soldier saw it fit to land another punch, Arman retaliated. He caught the soldier's fist and pulled him close for an almighty head butt. Both men wore copper helmets and the impact sounded like the clash of rival bulls. The Assurian soldier walked in a daze and was allowed to collapse without the saving support of one of his idle comrades. The Assurian people who saw the confrontation unfold applauded the result and Arman could not hold back his smile.

'Are you trying to cause upset, Isvah?' asked the officer, referring to Arman.

Arman gestured towards me, 'The boy feared for his family and that weak-headed soldier would not allow him to carry his toy sword.'

'He has to keep moving. Who is in charge here?' the officer asked the seven Assurian soldiers still standing and separate to their comrades gathered at the entrance to the lane.

The seven Assurians pointed at the soldier lying

unconscious on the ground.

'As such, I am in charge now,' stated the officer. 'Move your stronghold down the lane and only question people once they are out of sight of the port. Here, you are not helping.'

'As ordered,' replied the soldiers in one voice.

'Who is next in charge?'

'I am,' announced one of the seven. 'Dubequan, noble servant of Sargon and liaison with the Guards of Amarutu.'

'Dubequan, see to it that this does not happen again. I want the people to walk up the lane faster than they would descend. Let this boy walk an unhindered path and keep him and your predecessors out of my sight.'

'Yes, my liege,' responded Dubequan.

I nodded my appreciation to the mounted officer but I was offered no further sympathy. The officer could see that I was armed with a sword and staff but had also witnessed how inept I was with drawing either when required. He would be happy no matter how his subordinates dealt with me so long as it did not impede his mission to vacate the port. He rode back to meet his fellow officers, shaking his head.

In the real world, the world Salarn had shown me, I did not need my ears to hear the officer's shared words. The officers' movements were slow and their voices spoke without sound in my head. The one returning to meet his comrades was proud. Another officer was not convinced, his eyes and the turn of his head betraying satisfaction with the returning officer's announced success. He pointed between the watchtowers to the city's temple above the lane. He could not see it through the high sun and sheltered his eyes. Beyond him, Tahnas stood on a mooring post, possibly listening to the real world as well. Next to me, Arman smelt like death's excreta.

Derahmus rode back to his officers near the well in the centre of the port's triangle. He called for the support of twenty riders and they spaced themselves evenly, creating a threatening divide through the centre of the port between the two queues of Assurian citizens. 'I will be waiting at the end of the wharf, tempting the guilty with my blood and keeping watch over the boats,' he announced. 'Though impressed by the aim of the bowmen, I do not trust all arrows to fly true to target. Keep your new weapons close and stay watchful for my raised arm. Be prepared to take shelter if you are close to the wharf.' Dehramus circled his stallion and for a moment I thought he was going to point at me. 'Hernervum,' he shouted, alerting an officer near the well, 'Ride the lane if there is a hold up.' Hernervum's black steed began prancing as if it had received the command.

'Turn boy and keep walking,' yelled Arman. 'Forget your family.'

'I think I see them.'

Arman gripped my arm and turned me towards the lane, 'Keep walking if you want to see them again.'

Salarn had shown me the real world and I carried the strength of a man who had survived eleven penetrating arrows. I would test all I knew and use all I had to escape this city.

35

The Charter of Death

Scribed by Kar.

Arman and I followed the retreating Assurian soldiers up the lane. Behind us, the mounted Akkadians blocked the entrance and took control of the port. The high sun lit the lane, and from the city more Assurian soldiers advanced.

Dubequan, the self-announced noble servant of Sargon, took pleasure in calling all to a halt and ruling what happened next. 'I want the walls of this lane lined by soldiers from this point to the markets. No one leaves any of the doors or walks any pass. We will post ourselves here, ahead of you men, checking again those who are allowed entry to our city. If you disagree with my choice, then I must ask that you restrain yourselves from acting alone. When those held at the port are released, we need them to progress quickly up the lane. I also want twenty soldiers at the entrance to the market to ensure this lane flows one way only and that is away from the port.'

In unison, the soldiers began knocking their swords against their leather armour in acknowledgement of the order. Like ripples after a stone is dropped in a puddle, the soldiers peeled to the walls and tapped the man next to them. The step, followed by a clap of a hand against leather, ran from the soldier by my side and up a lane that looked, by the time the men stepped aside at the top, too narrow for a man to pass though.

Whilst Dubequan spoke, I listened to Arman's quiet conversation with the closest soldier.

'Best to stand aside should the Charter of Death once more wield the idle weapon that has always been by his side.'

'Who, that boy?' the soldier asked, staring at my staff and then my sword.

'I do not know if it is him,' said Arman with a shake in his voice. 'Have you heard the story? I am not going to be a soldier if it means fighting a servant of God.'

'I do not know the story,' said the soldier, tilting his helmet to get a better look at me.

Arman was not allowed a chance to continue the conversation and, as planned, left the soldier to question his concerns alone.

The Wrath of the Gods' routine had not started as scribed. I was meant to have already announced myself as a god and defended myself without drawing a weapon. The routine was pointless if pursued alone. Arman needed me to instigate fear if he was to fulfil his part of the charade properly.

'Let me test what I have explained on these two,' announced Dubequan. 'One is a boy who travels with two horses. He wants to wait for his family and carry his weapons into our peaceful city. The second is a soldier supportive of such demands.'

'This is not what was ordered,' complained Arman. 'Let him pass as the Akkadians demanded.'

I walked freely forwards into the spectacle and dipped my head like I was prepared for judgement.

'Firstly, I ask that you hand over your weapons before entering our city,' requested Dubequan.

'My name on Earth is Kar,' I stated in a loud voice as I slowly unfolded the leather masking the blade on the tip of my staff. 'I have been given many names but I am not the Charter of Death, the one who decides whether you live or die in battle. I killed that demon long ago. This weapon has since been blessed by a high priest and will breathe death on all those who oppose it. I have kept it covered for that reason.'

'That is why I did not force him to leave the port,' Arman tried to explain, seeking refuge behind the closest soldier. 'Let us see this boy out of the city.'

'Charter of Death, you make a mockery of this name,' laughed Dubequan. He saw that his comrades were flighty and sought to remedy that by drawing first blood. 'Hold your demon staff out for me boy,' he requested and waited for the nervous soldier closest to Arman to be ready in case anything went wrong. 'If my sword cannot break your staff then you shall pass and be allowed to take your horses as well.'

I valued my staff almost as much as the tattoo on my shoulder. Like the sword Salarn had forged for me, it was one of a kind. My father might have forged the blade but even he knew that it did not appear by chance at the tree. I held three gifts from Salarn, one being my life. Today, I had all to lose. I drove the butt of my staff against the hardened path of the lane and spread my grasp to accommodate the swing of the soldier's sword. 'If the attempted breaking of my staff will convince you, I will welcome your strike.'

Hernervum, the Akkadian officer posted to the lane, arrived on his black steed. 'It was my suggestion that a superior officer be in charge of the lane. Why is this boy still here?' he questioned Dubequan.

'He is armed and he may even be one of the men you are looking for.'

'The Charter of Death does not draw his blade upon any man undeserving,' announced Arman. He drew the army issued sword he had acquired and laid it to rest on the hardened ground of the lane as he bowed his respects to me. He did not get the reply he was looking for and even I looked in his direction with concern.

'Regather your sword and stand soldier. We are the only charters of death,' proclaimed Hernervum.

Arman stood, reluctantly, pointing at me. 'He told me, though I thought it laughable until now ... He told me that only those who bared arms against him would die today. It was the way he told me. The hairs on my arms stood upright. I thought of not returning to my wife and children because I had tried to kill a boy. A boy.'

Arman's plee weakened the composure of many soldiers close by. They pressed their backs against the building bordering the lane. He was doing well and I had to fulfil my role soon.

Dubequan smirked and raised his sword. 'With your approval, officer?' he requested.

Hernervum puzzled over Arman's story and for a moment the officer looked concerned. Eventually he turned from Arman and nodded his approval.

Dubequan swung hard but he did not aim merely to break the staff. His blade was angled at my fingers. I released my grip to save my hand and lost control of my staff. It rattled across the ground as I jumped backwards.

'He is still armed,' alerted Arman.

'Finish him before the crowds arrive,' ordered Hernervum, trotting his restless steed.

Dubequan stabbed at my chest but I was quick on my feet and stepped clear of the blade's reach. I drew my small sword and made a stand. My body contorted to accommodate the fine line between death and parry and I followed its course with my blade. I then walked away, withdrawing it from an upward drive into Dubequan's chin with fluid motion, whipping its entanglements free. Gore splattered against the wall and over the guards who stood still with their backs pressed against the stone. They would have seen Dubequan's helmet jump as if my sword had popped through the top of his skull. It was Dubequan who jumped defensively and created this appearance. His chinstrap guided my blade towards the back of his skull.

Hernervum ordered the nervous Assurian soldiers near Arman to advance and, when they hesitated, I sheathed my sword and reclaimed my staff.

Witnessing Arman surrender his blade and their lead soldier die despite me, a boy, only being armed with a short sword, made the soldiers hesitant to obey orders.

'Kill him,' ordered the mounted officer, redirecting his command to the soldiers standing on the other side of the lane, their backs also held to the wall.

'I have heard stories of such a day, my liege. I think we should just let him pass,' suggested Arman.

'Maybe Sargon should decide whether I pass,' I said.

'I speak for Sargon,' bellowed Hernervum.

'And I speak for the gods who speak to Sargon,' I replied, in my loudest voice. I displayed my palm as I walked towards the closest Assurian.

The soldier raised his sword and I stepped casually past it and reached behind him and tapped his helmet. I stepped back rotating a silver coin between my fingers and placed it in his hand. Pointing at Hernervum, I yelled, 'Tell all what has happened.'

'It is a silver shekel showing the face of Sharru-Kin,' declared the soldier. 'The boy pulled it from my helmet and I did not have a shekel.'

Down the lane, I noticed more soldiers removing their helmets for the chance of a hidden reward.

Hernervum's steed reared back and he shouted, 'Assurian soldiers are a disgrace to Sargon's name. Fooled you are by tricks played in drinking houses.'

'I will fight him,' called out a soldier from far down the lane. He broke rank and walked forwards into the gauntlet of soldiers lining the lane towards the port.

'At least one of you has courage,' yelled Hernervum.

'I apologise, my liege,' whined Arman, keeping to his act. 'The boy whispered strange words on our walk back from the port and I fear that the Wrath of the Gods is at play.'

'The Wrath of Gods?' laughed Hernervum. 'You are a fool and will be dealt with as a traitor after I am finished with this boy.'

'You call him a boy because I did,' Arman told Hernervum. 'Those present know what I have preached. My ignored warning will be heard by our king.'

'Stand back,' Hernervum ordered Arman. 'Have him stand back,' he ordered the soldiers near to Arman.

Two soldiers approached Arman and they grabbed his arms and pulled him to the side of the lane. He did not resist.

I knew that cunning swordplay and sleight-of-hand was not going to be enough. I had told Uk-Ban that I was not a god but now I wished I were one in this situation. A god would not use only what was in his hands. A god would move the earth or sky in his favour. I said a quiet prayer to my gods. 'Enki, the pattern maker, I stumbled into your gorge a lost child. Hear now that I want to guide others your way.'

Hernervum heard people entering the lane behind and was embarrassed to have not fulfilled such a simple duty. We were holding the advance of all the others and only one soldier was brave enough to step from the wall and face me. The officer drew a side bow, like the one Delari had showed the boatman, and started to fasten a wooden bolt as he waited for the only brave soldier to arrive.

My prayer continued and my voice grew louder. 'Mother Ki, I have felt your warm embrace and want it to grow ever stronger and touch more people. I fear your death more than my own.'

Hernervum was not experienced with his new weapon and he rode his steed to block my path as he fumbled the bolt he was trying to lock into place.

The soldier approaching hastened his step down the lane.

I turned my prayer to the sky and looked beyond the officer's head to the clouds slowly building towards a storm behind the temple atop the massive ziggurat in the city's centre. 'Enlil, as the God of air, breathe life into these soldiers who hold me against my will.' The sun passed behind a cloud and for a moment the lane was cast in shadow. 'Isvah, claim what is yours,' I bellowed.

Arman stumbled on his feet like he had been unsettled by an invisible presence. He removed his helmet and reached forwards. I handed him a throwing blade and Arman rotated it in his fingers, quickly taking aim at the officer.

'Lower your aim, soldier,' requested Hernervum, who was interrupted a moment short of raising his side bow.

Arman stared back at him with blank expression.

Light returned as the cloud passed and, as I waited patiently for one lone soldier to approach, a deep rumble of thunder reverberated off the walls of the lane.

'It is true,' a soldier with his back to the wall nearby I heard say.

'Keep your backs to stone and you will not be harmed,' I advised. 'I will give your city light again.'

The soldiers closest heeded my advice.

Hernervum was still not convinced that the work of any god was at play. He had, however, seen the way Arman twirled the blade and thus was not prepared to doubt his aim. His hope was rekindled when the soldier that had wrestled with Arman earlier gained consciousness.

The Assurian soldier wobbled on his feet as he drew his dagger. His stare and dagger were aimed at Arman.

'Isvah,' I warned.

Arman struck sideward, his blade cutting the advancing soldier's throat.

Hernervum raised his side bow and was not allowed the time to release the bolt. The throwing blade sailed from Arman's hand and met with the officer's unprotected face. The sound of bone cracking made those close by squirm and Arman dropped to his knees before flipping himself on his back and convulsing his body like fish pulled from the water.

The soldiers standing closest maintained their distance, as far as the walls would allow. Hernervum's steed trotted in a circle and blood squirted from the Akkadian rider's face. When they saw one of the Guardian mares step close and nuzzle their estranged comrade, they grew more convinced that something strange was at work. Arman's convulsions eased with its touch until he lay still.

'This is gods' play,' stammered one of the soldiers and he drew his sword and placed it at his feet.

Those standing either side of me drew their swords and dropped them. The soldiers manning the pass towards the city looked upon the spectacle of the trotting black horse ridden by the lifeless Akkadian. Only one soldier remained confident and, with his sword already drawn, he paced towards me. Otoug, the Akkadian who Salarn assassinated in the Desert City, was considered the tallest Akkadian soldier. He was my imaginary foe when I trained alone. I now faced what had to be the tallest Assurian. The soldier's steps were sure. He was clad in armour. I wiped my sweaty palms across my forehead and gripped my staff with fresher hands.

The Assurian citizens permitted to return to the city had begun to enter the lane and those leading the procession had stopped at a distance in view of the disturbance ahead. Once more the people of Assur were trapped, their movement hindered in both directions.

36

Into Ersetu

Scribed by Arman, The Always Travelling Guardian.

I lay on the ground, looking up at my mare's large brown face. She had recognised me, despite my stench and strange uniform. This was pleasing. Regardless how many soldiers were convinced by our display, we would surely meet more resistance before we left this confining lane. We had to escape the city and, without horses, we could not avoid capture and persecution—death. I rolled my head to the side and feigned fright by holding my eyes wide as I looked at the Assurian soldiers who had dropped their swords. They beckoned me towards them. I needed to stay on the ground until I had a new plan. Like the night I lay in the trampled burnt grass outside the fort east of the Zagros Mountains, I had to consider every turn of my head, lest I be sighted as an imposter. I slowly raised a hand to my mare and when she leant close, I shielded my face with my arms. With my mare still standing over me, I glanced up and down the lane. The soldiers standing close would hopefully think I was frightened of the horse. They might have thought me a fool. There was no laughter.

Between the people of Assur at the port end of the lane and the Assurian guards filling the upward course of the lane to the city, Kar stood before a soldier twice his size. He looked taller than my mare and wore a helmet often reserved for senior officers or kings. It was similar to the helmet worn by Derahmus, the leader of the mounted battalion who had stormed into the port. Unlike the other soldiers, this massive Assurian's helmet protected his nose and curved downwards from his eyes, protecting the rest of his face and his neck. Only his mouth, accentuated by a short chin beard was exposed. His bronze long sword was almost the length of Kar's staff yet seemed to weigh as much as a dagger in his giant hands.

'My Assurian friends tell me that you are the Charter of Death,' said the soldier, his voice deeper than mine but not coursed by age or illness.

'No, they heard wrong. I killed that demon,' said Kar.

'That only gives me hope because he kept trying to kill me and could not do it,' boasted the soldier.

Kar huffed. 'That knowledge should worry you. Anything you thought you knew has changed.'

'What I learnt is still the same. Forget whom you call yourself. I have fought you before and this time I know my adversary.'

The huge Assurian knocked the hilt of his sword against his leather breastplate and my mare startled. She trotted up the lane, before turning. Beyond her smooth brown legs I saw a place I never wanted to tread again. It was more than a gap between two of the many stone-based homes that bordered the lane. Between these two buildings was a place so foul of taste and smell that I, having been exposed to it, might never taste food again.

'Raise your weapon to my sword.'

I did not know whether the large soldier smiled with false courage or anticipated victory. Only his eyes could reveal his true confidence and they were cast in the shadow of his helmet's visor. His balanced stance showed he was ready to strike or retreat and, should he lose hold of his sword, his arms looked strong enough to twist Kar's head from his shoulders. The young Guardian had never used the staff against anyone else in combat but his confidence signalled otherwise. If it was his weapon of choice, an extension of his arm that gave him added strength and the reach of a giant, it might be enough to even the fight. I thought Kar's playtime had ended in the woods; however, this experience seemed to excite the young Guardian. He looked down at me and smiled like he did when we camped in the woods opposite Verian's Pass. There was no crease of concern between his deep green eyes. His thin arms looked as tensed as bows ready to release arrows. The blade on his staff was unblemished. It was bright even without the sun's face upon it.

I waved my arms about as I leapt to my feet. A soldier stepped from the wall and pulled me clear of the fight arena. I acted confused and defensive at the same time, beating his arms away and then welcoming them. It was the soldier that I had warned earlier and he calmed me and told me that I was right about the boy.

'What boy?' I asked.

The soldier held me still and pointed at the confrontation, 'He is not a boy. He is the Charter of Death. Witness.'

Without a commanding officer, the soldiers, except those closest, stepped from the walls and watched with concerned amazement. Assurian spectators blocked the port end of the lane and, nearby, those dwelling in the two-storey homes bordering the lane opened their wooden windows to watch the duel from above. The people of Assur were held by fear and equally weighted interest. Those first in line at the port end of the lane would have realised that the same boy who had been knocked to the ground as they queued now had every soldier, bar the one he was about to fight, standing to attention. The people did not need to hear me mention that the Wrath of the Gods was at play. Kar, with my help, a sleight-of-hand trick and timely weather changes, had now confirmed the routine. As word of one boy fighting the rest was shared, the people waited in anticipation, ready to bow in appreciation and coupled amazement should he prove successful in the duel. The people of Assur wanted him to be successful and began chanting, 'One boy, our fight. One boy, our fight.'

The Assurian soldiers responded by rapping the flats of their swords against their leather armour. Those separate from the walls edged their way closer down the lane.

Kar twirled his staff above his head, roped it around his waist and then stopped it next to his side, signalling with a nod that he was ready. The moment Kar drew his staff to rest, the soldier attacked. Kar lifted the blunt end of his staff from the ground and slapped the soldier's strike aside. The soldier followed Kar's sidestep and attacked again. Kar twisted the staff and pushed the soldier's sword wide with force. The soldier stumbled backwards and then charged forwards even more aggressively. Kar jumped clear of the sweeping blade and then swung his staff low, collecting the soldier's leather-guarded legs. Kar then thrust his staff forwards, blade first, and the soldier parried it as he rolled to the side. The young Guardian then swung it full loop hoping to connect on the other side. Again, the massive soldier was too quick. He blocked the attack and felt the staff's strength. Stepping backwards, the soldier blocked three more quick strikes from the staff. The staff had longer reach when Kar gripped it at one end and the soldier's attempt to split the weapon in two had failed. It was no ordinary staff and the disciples of Sargon were surely growing more convinced that they were beholden to the incited Wrath of the Gods.

'Why do you not tell me your real name? And do you not at least have to know my name?' asked the soldier, stealing time to rest.

'My name is Kar. You can call me a foe no more and end this duel.'

'I call you a forgotten friend,' said the soldier as Kar twisted his staff one way, and then the other in a confusing manner.

As the soldier stepped to the side, the blunt end of Kar's staff met with his hand and he lost hold of his sword. The staff twirled again and rattled the Assurian's helmet, knocking him to the ground. Leant backwards, faced by the bladed end of Kar's staff, the soldier raised his hands as a sign of defeat.

'Remove your helmet.'

The soldier obliged, tossing it aside with such thrust that it connected with the wall and cracked the clay brick surface above the stone foundations. He was exposed, yet Kar seemed more focused on the broken clay on the wall. Kar stared at the wall and the fallen soldier did too, when his life was not ended. I wished to prompt Kar but I could not think how. The tall Assurian's face was familiar. I feared Kar might force his blade upon the man before he was recognised.

Kar turned back to face him. 'I knew you in time,' he said. 'I did not want to kill you when we duelled in the village circle and my stance has not changed. You shall join me in my pilgrimage to The Great Sea.' Kar offered his hand to his friend who had become a soldier and helped him to stand. In view of the people of Assur that were watching from one end of the lane and the windows above, and the Assurian soldiers who barred our retreat on the upward course to the city, Kar drew the sword Salarn had crafted for him alone and offered it to the soldier. Only Kar and I knew that the defeated Assurian soldier was Tuley, Garforn's son, and Kar's friend when he was a boy. He was the big boy who had taught Kar how to move without sound.

Tuley stood before Kar and received the sword. 'I have so many questions,' he said.

'Take mount, soldier of Assur, and Isvah of Eshnunna, find your mount as well.' Kar took the time to address the six soldiers who had surrendered their weapons. He approached each individually and delicately touched them between their eyes. He then tamed the restless dark steed carrying a limp body. The horse reared as he pulled the officer loose. Kar regathered the reins and held them taut until the horse had calmed itself. He handed the reins of the steed to me and stepped ahead of his gestured followers towards the barred entry to the inner city.

Tuley and I did not take mount. I summoned Tuley and handed him the reins to the armoured Akkadian steed. The Guardian mares carried necessary stores and I ensured they were bound tight. If the soldiers standing closest were not preoccupied, I might not have been given an opportunity to delve into Senea's pouch of silver. The soldiers who received Kar's touch felt their faces and rejoiced in view of heightened senses and, by their words, an indescribable feeling of joy that consumed them. None of the soldiers understood what had happened when Kar touched them. He had touched them all the same way and they now felt the charter of life, not death, giving strength to their movement. They called the people of Assur forwards behind us.

'Kar,' I said to his back. He faced the steep climb to the inner city, filled by the entirety of the Assurian army. 'That is not our escape.'

He looked at me with one of his eyes squinted.

'We did something great today but unless you are prepared to do it all again, we cannot continue on this path.' Assurians released from the port ascended the lane. Soldiers barring our retreat, descended. 'We will not be afforded safe pass through this city. Its homes and walls trap us and the entire city is perched on mountain steeps.'

Tuley stilled the Akkadian steed next to me and sheathed his long sword.

'We must go another way.' I faced one side of the lane.

'Where does that lead?' asked Kar.

'It is best if we don't know.'

'I trust you, Arman. I blame myself for–'

'Hold your blame. Bless me as you did the first soldier.' I knelt behind Kar, holding the reins to my mare and Senea's. Next to me, Tuley showed his new sword to soldiers who approached him. He warned others back with an arm the size of my leg.

Kar turned and touched me between my eyes with an extended finger.

'Ride the gap,' I told him. 'I'll follow you into the caverns of Ersetu.'

He looked down the alley that stretched for fifty filthy paces before light announced an end.

'Keep moving. I'll see you on the other side.'

'The other side of the pass, not in the next life,' said Kar. He took the reins to Senea's mare and led her towards the narrow gap between the buildings. He had only taken a few steps when an Assurian soldier took issue with his path.

'See what he has done,' I shouted from where I still knelt in the centre of the lane. I loosened the straps to my leather breastplate and a silver shekel fell.

The soldier challenging Kar's progress was distracted.

I released the reins to my mare and bent to pull the breastplate over my head. Silver was scattered on the ground at my feet.

From all sides of the lane, Assurian soldiers rushed to claim a loosed shekel. Some of the silver landed flat and other shekels rolled on their sides across the hardened dirt.

I led my mare away from the soldiers scuffling on the ground and through gathering Assurians to the alley. Kar had already entered on Senea's mare. The foul sludge, a blend of waste tossed from the windows above, was never meant to be disturbed. It reached the mare's knees and Kar sat high on his mount as she stepped slowly. I leapt onto my mount and fastened my reins in one hand, straightening my mare's head to the course. Glancing over my shoulder, I saw Tuley leading the Akkadian steed and forcing his way between disjointed assemblies of soldiers. Fights had ensued following the scurry for silver and a group of soldiers, further up the lane, were searching their helmets and armour in the hope of discovering more shekels. When Tuley looked my way, I raised my arm and lowered it in the direction of the alley. I encouraged my mare to take her first step with a flick of the loose end of the reins. She trotted into the sludge and I flicked the loose end of the reins again, before she turned. Like Kar, I sat high on my mount, my thighs and knees holding my weight forwards. Her hooves plunged with slurping sounds into the slurry of human waste, releasing vile stenches. My mare's eyes bulged. Her whole body resisted her next step. I bent my wrist, further tightening her reins.

'The boy is leaving,' yelled an Assurian soldier at the entrance to the narrow alley. His shout had the shrill of a woman's voice. As he turned to gather more attention, he was lifted from his feet from behind. Tuley threw him face first into the sludge. The tall Guardian attempted to mount and the Akkadian steed wheeled, knocking him back into the lane. He pulled the reins taut as it reared. An ordinary man would have been lifted from his feet by the flighty black stallion. Tuley led it back to the alley and tried again to mount. The Akkadian steed bucked. Its hind legs thumped an Assurian soldier in his breastplate and another in the face. Before the steed raised its head, Tuley mounted. He kicked its flank and it bounded into the alley before rearing. Had Tuley fought the steed's resistance, he might have pulled it down with him into the abandoned excrement of Assurian's guts. He chose to fall alone. Letting go of the reins, he fell backwards, his back and then legs slapping the surface of the muck. Tuley stood and, as the black steed weighted itself on its haunches, he swung his arm and slapped its hind. The steed lifted its front feet and bounded deeper into the alley.

Hastened by the commotion behind, my mare raised its front legs from the grip of the sludge and took another step. 'Beautiful girl,' I said to my mare. I sat as high as I could and leant my weight over her front legs, urging her to continue.

'Keep to the western side,' said Kar. He was nearing the end of the lane and I could see that his mare, Senea's mare, had encountered sludge as deep as her belly. She slipped into a pool of slop that reached her flanks and Kar flicked his reins. She bounded out, resuming a fast trot when she reached solid ground to one side of the alley at the northern end.

My mare stepped slowly, the plunging and immersion of each hoof unsettling a new surprise—rotting fish heads, animal bones and entrails alive with the wriggle of white worms.

'Hurry your old mare, Arman,' yelled Tuley.

My mare plucked another hoof from the muck and reached to plunge it again. 'She is faring well, Tuley. Don't fall behind.'

Tuley slapped the steed's hind. 'Have you never ridden through mud? Spoilt beast.' His slap sent the steed cantering through the slop like it was water.

My mare lunged, her front legs finding ground, hind legs kicking below the surface, never lifting me. I slid into the excrement and waded towards the dry surface ahead.

The Akkadian steed found sure footing and strode into the deeper pool of waste.

Tuley was swimming to keep up. Only his arms and head breached the suface. Behind him, at the entrance to the alley from the lane, many Assurians gathered to watch. No one appeared to be following. Many were laughing. The Assurian with the shrill voice, the one Tuley had thrown into the mess, had removed some of his uniform and was bent over, his mouth projecting a stream of vomit.

I stood on higher ground against the western wall of the alley and pulled my mare's reins towards me.

Her legs were thrusting and kicking before a hoof found grip and she staggered onto firmer ground. I stepped backwards, guiding her close to the wall. The sludge was only hoof deep on the high side. A step away from the wall, solid ground ended like it does at a river's bank. 'Slowly girl,' I told my mare. She blew her nose and some of the gathered filth hit my lips. I spluttered but resisted lifting my arm to wipe my face. We had almost made it through. I glanced behind. Where the alley ended, there was a narrow rocky flat before a steep edge. I had seen this escarpment when I approached the city from the north with Senea. The city climbed a desert rise towards the clouds and the buildings completed the sheer edge. I stepped into the light of the western sun and guided my mare out of the alley and uphill, away from the fall. Over time, the clog of waste that filled the alley had seeped around the building on the lower side and over the steep edge. It stained the cliffs like weeping blood.

'I will help Tuley,' said Kar as he strode down the narrow edge between the buildings and the top of the escarpment. He had tied Senea's mare to a length of wood extending from the clay wall of a home further up the rise. There were few other places to secure a horse.

We were at the height of a pine above the farming land and I could see the bends and turns of the Tigris as far as the horizon. 'Tuley has lost control of the steed,' I told Kar as he bounded past me. 'Fend it from the fall.'

Kar looked at me and over the edge before he entered the alley.

I loosened my hold on my mare's reins and stroked her nose. Her eyes were still bulging from the ordeal. I lay the reins on her shoulder and stepped to the side, so that she could see Senea's mare. She looked at the other mare. I tapped her side and encouraged her up the slope. When she began her walk, I returned to the alley.

The Akkadian steed was deep in the mess that filled all bar the higher side of the alley at our end. Tuley was plunging closer, ten paces behind. He kept pausing to expel his guts. It was hard to not stop because the sickness grew in your mouth and nose before it reported to every limb of your body.

Kar eased a foot into the foul brew and reached for the reins. The steed threw its head as it sunk deeper and Kar clutched the leather. It stared at Kar as he leant back, trying to pull it free.

I reached over Kar's shoulder and gripped the reins behind his hands. 'I have him.' Kar was trying to pull the steed up a riverbank. I could see this foul river's slow flow and knew it best to not fight it. I walked towards the lower wall and led the steed deeper into the mess. 'This stallion is a fighter, Kar. If I can get him out, make sure you are between him and the mares. The Akkadian steed hurled its head back and I slid closer to the deep pool that coursed around the stone footings of the last building in the alley. 'Tuley. I need you to encourage it from behind.'

Tuley had just found solid ground against the wall on the high side. 'Yarr,' he yelled, his voice echoing down the alley towards the Assurians gathered at the far end.

I stepped closer to the edge of the escarpment, where sludge was creeping down the cliff from the alley. A few pointed rocks breached an otherwise uninterrupted fall. This was the point of the slow but sure emptying of gathered waste. The steed scrambled his hooves beneath the surface and sunk deeper. I turned him to a straight path out of the alley. When his hooves hit the wall of the building on the eastern side of the alley, the steed took fright. He kicked hard and bounded out of the sludge and onto the precipice. My mud-coated sandals slid as I stepped uphill and heaved the reins high over my shoulder. Beneath my elbow was the edge and the steed pranced itself when hardened sand collapsed to the weight of its hind hoof. I lent my weight back and the steed's next bound propelled him towards me. The black steed knocked me from its uphill path and its hind leg kicked me near my groin as I fell beneath.

Kar blocked its escape with a twirl of his staff. It reared, its front hooves beating the air in front of his face. The young Guardian stood his ground.

Tuley crawled out of the alley and after looking up the slope, released everything he had left inside of him.

I wretched each time he expelled himself. There was nothing left in me.

Kar held his staff to one side of the restless Akkadian steed and then brought his hand to its snout. He touched its nose and it jolted. When he wiped mess from its legs, it calmed.

'I am pleased they were feeding you,' I said to Tuley.

He spat until his mouth was free of sticky entanglements.

I rolled onto my side and scraped thick layers of the alley's sludge from the soles of my sandals, using the stone corner of the building. It hurt to raise my leg. There was a distinct print of a horse hoof on my tunic beneath my belt and I was certain I would find the same print on my skin.

Tuley stood and offered me his hand. 'Are you ready to ride again?'

I exhaled and raised my arm. He held all my weight in my rise and released me slowly, checking if I could stand unaided. I nodded.

Kar had managed to calm the Akkadian steed. He signalled Tuley and I to slip past.

We hugged the wall until we were on the high side of Kar and the Akkadian steed. My mare wheeled to Tuley's approach and I asked him to stand back as I re-gathered her reins. 'She's a good horse, just frightened she is.' I led her past Senea's mare, still tethered, and up the narrow pass. I did not know where this path would lead us. It seemed to end at the inner city wall that stretched to the cliff's edge, one hundred steep steps away. Foul sludge leaked across our path five more times before this higher point.

'What brought you to Assur?' asked Tuley, leading Senea's mare uphill behind me.

'Our search for Guardians taken west.' I did not tell Tuley that we held no hope for him. 'Tahnas found Belline. He arrived at the port before the Akkadian battalion.' I looked down the next alley and loosened my hold of the reins as I leapt across the sludge escap-ing its neck. My mare bounded over and followed me up the rise. The sun was creeping behind the battle-ments atop the wall.

'Was she ... the same?' asked Tuley.

I paused at the corner of the next alley. 'We all change, Tuley. Belline looked like a survivor in need of some recovery time at the tower.'

'The tower?'

'See this.' I pointed down the alley.

Tuley loosened his hold of his reins and stepped up to the mess spilling from the alley to see what I had noticed. 'The soldiers still man the lane yet they saw us escape.' He looked at me, his mouth open as if he were about to say more.

'The citizens of Assur have been allowed to return.'

'We rode that foul alley for no reason.'

'Remember Verian's Pass.' said Kar as he approached. 'Keep moving if you have not found an escape.'

I stepped over the leaking sludge and continued up the rise.

Tuley followed my lead. 'What of Verian's Pass, Kar?' he asked.

'The Assurians were ordered to man the walls to the lane,' said Kar. 'Let's hope they maintain their position as we move on.'

I wished to be following Kar, as my leg that had been bitten by the stallion's hoof was stiffening with each step. We passed another waste-filled alley. Like the others, its horrid brew drained across our path and over the cliff. The inner city wall loomed above us and it was not until I reached its footings that I saw our only remaining passage. Until this point, our path up the slope was the width of a horse. It ended at the inner city wall. There was only room for a nimble goat to continue west between the wall and the cliff face. The final alley, between the city wall and the last building on the rise, led back to the lane we had escaped from. I stepped back behind the last building, before I was spotted, and tilted my head to view the top of the city wall. It appeared to be unmanned.

'I can guess where we go from here,' said Tuley with a smirk. He stilled Senea's mare and gazed north over the farming land far below. 'I've never seen beauty like this. The crops grow as straight as wooden tables.' His mouth was held ajar when he looked at me. He tilted his head and turned to face the buildings that bordered the top of the escarpment. 'If I lived in one of these homes, I would remove bricks to create a window.' He counted with his fingers on one hand the number of windows that faced north.

He was amusing to watch. From his Akkadian chin beard to his sandals, he was coated with human waste yet, like an experienced Guardian, he had found strange time to ponder. I loaded a bronze bolt in my side bow and gently touched the lever to ensure it was tense. My last throwing blade was tucked behind my belt.

'See how few windows there are, Kar,' said Tuley, pointing them out. 'Our village was like this. You look out of a hut and you only see the next hut or the village wall.'

'Walls are a weakness,' said Kar. He stopped behind Tuley and slid a hand up the reins to the steed's mouth. He stroked its neck. It was agitated but did not pull away.

'This last passage follows the city wall to the entrance to the markets at the top of the lane,' I told them.

Tuley nodded and bit his lip.

'And it is guarded by many, Tuley, as it seems you are aware.'

Tuley raised his arms by his side and shrugged. His father, Garforn, would have mocked ignorance this way. It was a simple ploy. Tuley doubted my plan but he waited for me to play it out before he asserted his disagreement.

I was certain our progress would have been halted if we continued up the lane to the city and it seemed I had only delayed such an encounter. 'Would we have made it to the end of the lane if we did not divert from our course?' I asked. 'Guardians don't ask what could have been. Here we are. Where from here?'

Tuley pointed one of his long fingers in the direction of the last alley. 'Is it like the others?'

'It is dry. A small gutter of waste gathers against this wall along its length,' I said, tapping the building next to me.

He watched me. His eyes followed my hand back to my throwing blade at my belt and across my waist to the side bow I held in my other hand. 'I should follow you and Kar on the Akkadian steed. Allow them to think I have tracked you all the way.'

I stepped towards Tuley and took the reins to Senea's mare.

Kar held the Akkadian steed as Tuley approached. 'Let him see you, Tuley,' said Kar. 'Let him know you are taking control.'

Tuley gripped the reins above Kar's hand and placed his other hand on the steed's neck. 'Hold him, Kar.' Tuley reached above and untied the leather armour secured to the stallion's chest. His fingers struggled to find the knot and he drew Kar's thin sword from his belt to cut the leather ties. The steed's breastplate began to slip and Tuley pulled it free, releasing the waste that had gathered. He stepped around Kar and threw the soaked leather over the cliff. 'Stanf,' he shouted on his return. The steed braced its legs and Tuley took the reins. 'Ride fast and point upwards at the city wall if you need me to move to the front.'

Kar strapped his staff to his back and leapt onto Senea's mare.

I gathered all my strength and stepped high enough to crawl onto my mare's mount. My hoof branded leg made it difficult for me to sit upright. 'Let me ride first, Kar. What remains of my Akkadian costume might still convince them I am an ally.'

We entered the alley and rode to the high side, next to the city wall. It was a steep slope to the gutter on the opposite side and only on the high side could the horses find even footing. The soldiers did not notice our canter until we were almost upon them. My side bow was held behind my mare's thick neck. I glanced over my shoulder and, behind Kar, I saw Tuley riding the black steed with Kar's thin bronze sword held high. I did not change my mare's gait until I was upon the hapless soldiers. They stepped clear of my path as I trotted my mare into the lane. Assurian citizens queuing at the arched entrance rushed inside and two gate guards stepped into the lane, armed with bronze tipped spears. I looked back at my path into the lane and saw that the soldiers had diverted all attention this way. My teeth clenched. All Kar had to do was ride out behind me.

The soldiers stepped into the alley.

The gate guards inspected me and I directed them back to the gate. I circled my mare amongst Assurian citizens moving up the lane. Beyond the arched entrance to the market square stood four more soldiers. We were almost free. Kar and Tuley should have followed me out. I trotted my mare back to the alley I had escaped from. I could see over the soldiers' heads.

Three soldiers moved along the city wall, blocking Kar from riding the high ground. Senea's mare had balked. Her hind legs were tilted on the steep decline to the gutter.

Kar drew his staff and pointed it upright at the wall's battlements.

Tuley drove a heel into the stallion's flank and it cantered past Kar on the high ground.

The soldiers, who had entered the alley, braced themselves against the wall as the steed rushed past them. There was not room enough for them all. The first two soldiers to meet the stallion's stride, managed to emerge on the other side. The next soldier met the steed front on. He was bunted from the wall and trampled in his fall.

Tuley held himself upright in his mount as the stallion reared before the final row of soldiers blocking his escape.

Kar bounded his mare back to high ground and charged at the two soldiers still standing against the wall. They leapt from his path and Kar rotated his staff behind his back. Like a whip, his staff's blade lifted their helmets and lashed their faces as he rode by.

The Assurian soldiers backed into the lane to avoid the raised hooves of Tuley's stallion and Kar's determined approach.

I kicked one of the soldiers in the back of his helmeted head and the pain that coursed through my hip almost saw me fall from my mount.

Tuley also struggled to maintain his mount. He

fended the strike of two soldiers with Kar's thin sword, whilst turning the steed from a fall into the gutter of waste as it stepped into the lane.

Kar entered the lane with pace and released his reins to wield his staff with both hands.

An Assurian gate guard, armed with a bronze tipped spear, had positioned himself ahead of Kar in the centre of the lane and looked ready to take down the horse and rider.

Kar swung his staff to block the spear aimed at the mare's chest and in the same movement, the rotation of his staff smashed the guard's helmet from behind.

The guard staggered but did not fall.

Kar trotted Senea's mare back to the centre of the lane and lifted his staff above the dazed Assurian's head. He struck the guard on his shoulder, near his neck, with the blunt end of his staff.

Tuley rode his stallion over the guard's collapsing body and circled it before a new line of defence. Four soldiers and a gate guard blocked the arched entrance to the inner city.

I followed Kar's trot towards the gate and Tuley steadied the steed behind us. He would have seen that the might of Assuria, the people who fed and protected the city with trade from the river, were below us in the lane. The market square that Senea and I had crossed when entering the city was abandoned. In the vacated square, the hide coverings of empty stalls flapped in the breeze. The entrance to the ziggurat that climbed from this highest point in the city seemed unguarded beyond this final row of Assurians.

'Drop your weapon, boy,' said the soldier standing

in line with the path through the square towards the ramped entrance to the ziggurat. 'Whatever deception you worked on the others has lost its power. The God, Amarutu, sees all.'

'Point one out to me, Kar,' I begged, slowly sweeping the aim of my loaded side bow across the forlorn faces of the armoured guards.

Kar stared at the commanding soldier standing in his path and jiggled his staff in one hand. 'You are in our way,' he told him.

'Fight me. I want you to,' the soldier requested, boasting courage not shared by his comrades. They stood back.

'If that be your will.'

The soldier was watching the bladed end of the young Guardian's weapon. With a quick tilt, Kar sharply tapped the handle of the soldier's sword with the blunt end of his staff. The soldier's own sword was driven upwards between his skull and helmet. Blood spilled down his neck as he collapsed and the other soldiers quickly cleared a path before anyone else was needlessly killed.

I kept my side bow aimed on our retreat to ensure they did not follow.

Tuley rode the Akkadian steed ahead of us in our westward exit from the city.

Kar wanted to join him until I gave him cause to hold back. 'Tuley is breaking shackles,' I told Kar. 'Let him be alone with those he faces before us.' I pointed west and from our height we faced dark clouds forming an early end to the day.

We passed a headless soldier when we entered the

lane on the western side of the Ziggurat of Amarutu. Further down the steep lane, we sighted the displaced head in a water trough. I could only imagine the now headless Assurian's last thought as a massive man as black as his steed, bar his face, approached.

37

Wrath of the Gods

Scribed by Gentuk, The Trader's Friend.

I would later hear that my campfire tale, the Wrath of the Gods routine, had severely disrupted the Akkadian officers' plans. Those trapped on the wharf could see that their fellow citizens were also detained and, when select mounted soldiers attempted to split their force in numbers, the people dared not let them pass. Instead, they conglomerated at the far end of the wharf, impeding progress. The mounted Akkadians leading the progression onto the wharf soon saw the drawing of innocents' blood as pointless. If they had continued, the river would have run red. An Akkadian amongst the mounted assault of the wharf returned to their commander and explained their failure. I knew what the first liege officer's next call would be. 'Give me the word,' I yelled without raising my head too far above the deck of our seized vessel.

'Whenever sufficient armour is ready, so are we,' replied Tahnas, admiring the protection I had placed on the three horses already aboard.

'I will count to three, Tahnas.' I signalled Delari

and the elderly man called Uk-Ban to be ready. 'One, two, three.'

Tahnas led his stallion aboard first and was followed by Senea leading my mare.

Uk-Ban and I quickly dressed the horses with armour made from split planks from the deck. Xemoth's sinking vessel had freed our boat's hold to the wharf and only the rope I had secured with a slipknot held the vessel to dock. I pulled it free and hoisted the sail as I swung to the other side of the deck. Delari made use of the additional porthole, made possible by the planks Uk-Ban had pried free, and appeared at the steer without needing to cross the deck. He pushed the rudder towards the port and angled the boat into the river.

The Akkadian officer, bidding for control of the port, proceeded with his next course of action. The speed of our departure must have put him under immense pressure. Xemoth's boat was sinking rapidly and the people who had lingered on the wharf had halted his order to release arrows until this crucial moment. He ordered his mounted soldiers back from the wharf and signalled the guards in the watchtowers to release their arrows—with five fingers splayed on each hand he waved forwards three times. So desperate was he for a result that he followed the descending arrows towards the furthest reaches of the wharf, forcing those who remained in his way to jump into the water or meet his swinging sword.

Right up until the last moment, Tahnas and Senea dressed the horses with hide, fur and even planks of wood that I had tied together with Uk-Ban's assistance. When the first rain of arrows connected with the boat,

Tahnas, Senea and I took shelter behind our now armoured horses. We looked at each other and waited for the pattering sound and streaking sight of arrows to cease. At the steer of the boat, Uk-Ban popped his head up next to Delari and smiled at us taking shelter. He tossed another piece of ready-made armour across the deck towards us and we watched as it fell short. Delari had covered himself with a similar assembly of linked plank armour and also a fur. Three arrows stemmed from this fur. One burned for a moment and then turned black. He stayed at the rudder.

We were almost out of the watchtowers' reach, but desperate high-flying arrows were still connecting with the hull. Arrows dressed in flame met with the sail and thankfully we had wet it enough to avoid it being burnt. Tahnas rolled out from the cover of the horses and lifted the armour made available to cover the hide of his stallion.

Now that our course had faced the boat eastward across river, the horses' hinds were exposed. Tahnas detected movement in the corner of his eye as he placed the strung planks and immediately took shelter. The angle of the descent and the hardness of the wood saved Tahnas's stallion, only to have Tahnas bear the brunt of the deflected bronze bolt as it followed him to the deck.

The Akkadian commander bellowed blasphemous words from the wharf. Next to him, Akkadians stripped themselves of armour and ventured onto Xemoth's sinking vessel to salvage what they could of its cargo.

Senea and I still sheltered behind the horses. We saw the bolt deflect off Tahnas's shoulder and disappear into the water. 'Reach out for me, Tahnas,' I beckoned, fearing the officer may release another bolt.

Tahnas gave no response

'Pull him to shelter,' screamed Delari.

'Do not touch me,' mumbled Tahnas, as I leant towards him.

'It is all right,' declared Uk-Ban. 'The Akkadian only had one bolt.' Uk-Ban waved victoriously at Derahmus, the commander of the battalion, and his soldiers, made useless by the expanse of water now separating us.

Tahnas rolled his head to the side, unable to look up at me. 'He got me. I can't feel my arm. Let me rest until it is time to ride.'

'Keep us mid-stream, Delari. I will play the sails,' I said, returning to duty and ignoring my friend upon request. As I lifted the sail to full height and angled it due south, I questioned myself. Those who suffered the most seemed to be turning me away. I stared up at the sail and concentrated on the wind, pretending my wife and Tahnas were returning in good health.

Senea was not appointed a duty and, in a calm voice, asked, 'Tahnas, tell me what to do.'

'Go talk to your mother.'

Senea was hesitant to leave him. He eventually obeyed.

I watched the strong warrior bang one of his fists on the deck. Tahnas would not bang the other for a while. The bronze bolt had deflected off wood before deflecting off bone and soaring onwards into the river. Tahnas might have dropped just in time. Although the bronze bolt had sculptured a path that exposed bone, no bone appeared broken.

Uk-Ban expressed how proud he was to be travelling with us. I did not know at this time that he had crafted the bronze bolt that had dropped my friend. I disliked his early triumph as I came to terms with the hurt and death caused in the rescue of my wife.

'Guardians you are, and Kar was right in giving me reason to stay aboard. My destiny has never felt so certain. I will meet Salarn or find Samor in my travels and Tahnas, a man who put his life before his horse, will be what I, Uk-Ban of Catal Huyuk, first share with my new gods.'

Delari placed his hand on his chest and then extended the same hand towards me.

I returned his gesture. He still looked the same age as when I had first met him when Arman was a boy. He was at the steer of the boat and I looked ahead and behind from the mast as we sailed deeper into Akkadian territory. The walls of Assur climbed an escarpment towards a darkened sky. Weighted clouds battled the sun. Ahead and to the east, the river and desert was cast in a ripened blood glow.

We passed Akkadian soldiers sent south, boarding a vessel on the western shore outside of Assur, and sailed by on the far side of the river. One of the soldiers drew a weapon similar to his commander's, a side-bow, and released a bolt. His aim was not lifted high enough and the bolt penetrated the water, a boat's length short. I watched a scout disembark to return to Assur with word of our passing, causing the pursuing vessel from this dock further delay.

The winds of a growing storm were on our side and, in view of Tahnas's injury, I advised Delari that it was best to stay water-bound as long as possible. We entered the mouth of the Lower Zab and began sailing east against the river's flow. Down two Guardians and accompanied by two new friends, we were returning home with a rescued Guardian. The fate of Arman and Kar might never be mine to know. I would repeat it all again to see Belline safely home. I would have jumped in front of a bolt if I knew that it would mean Belline saw Lagesh again.

38

The Strength of Seven

Scribed by Kar.

We rode west towards The Great Sea on our quest to rescue the Pledians. The storm rolled in the opposite direction, blackening the skies above Assur. I was still clothed by the coverall I had found on the boat and Arman and Tuley remained dressed in armour. We encountered many Akkadian scouts on the first leg of our journey west and the soldiers' uniform, or possibly our stench, convinced each potential adversary we were allies or otherwise, better left alone.

'I feel out of place riding with you men,' admitted Tuley. 'I do not know how you could ever see me as a Guardian again after what I have done.'

I smiled at Tuley. 'I am the one who feels out of place, riding with two soldiers.'

Tuley raised his lip and it looked like he was trying to smile.

'Your father would be proud of you, Tuley,' said Arman, 'Like I am.'

'I only knew it was you when you called me a forgotten friend,' I explained. 'You fight like a Guardian, you are tattooed as one and now you fulfil such a role in Senea's stead.'

'Not all of that is true,' explained Tuley. 'I aimed to kill you, Kar.' He lifted his sleeve to show that his tattoo had been cut from his shoulder. It had left a deep scar and in its place was the mark of an Akkadian soldier—a circle inside a four-pointed star. The colourless mark was burnt into his flesh.

'They tried to do the same to my father. Salarn found the man responsible and corrected the change by stabbing him in the heart.'

'This will be remedied a different way,' said Arman. He directed our course across the flat ground between twisted pillars of hardened sand that stood like slowly collapsing gravestones. Some of the pillars were five times the height of a man and we rode in their shadows long before passing them and encountering the next. 'You missed out on many Guardian teachings, Tuley. Kar was lucky enough to meet up with Salarn and, as you can tell by your own experience, he has lived up to his namesake. He is a warrior of the East. You, however, may be the greatest weapon we have against the West. Whilst you may not have heard the confidential plans of officers, words exchanged in your camps could still influence many decisions we make from this point forward.'

'You want to know of Sargon's plans?'

'Spill your mind as if begging forgiveness. Forget for a moment that we bless you with understanding and rightful pass already.'

Side-by-side we rode late into the night before finding a suitable place to camp. Amongst a rare circle of date palms, we camped without food or fire. The light of the moon and stars stayed with us.

Arman removed his armour and the rest of his clothes. 'Rub every part of you in the sand. Clean your blades and clothes.'

The rub of sand helped in removing remnants of the waste-filled alley from leather and bronze. My coverall had been splattered with the same mess and it seeped into the cloth like blood. The rub of sand did not remove the stain or stench of the alley from our clothes. I gently scrubbed my legs, fearing they might be stained also if I rubbed too hard.

The thick trunks of the palms offered us a small amount of shelter and a place to secure our horses. Arman suggested that we enter Mari dressed as civilians. He also thought it best to stay in possession of the armour in case it was of benefit later in the journey. There was not much other talk that night before we fell asleep, only to wake countless times during the night to the cold touch of every sweeping wind.

***

The advancing soldiers had left Mari by the time we arrived. Arman met with an old friend at the port on the eastern bank of the Euphrates. He offered us safe haven in the city until we were ready to move on.

'Keep your silver. I have lived in debt to you since we first met,' said the elderly farmer. He had only just returned from the fields when Arman approached him. His tunic was clean and he carried neither hoe nor shovel. His beard was combed straight and his skin was not soiled like the men he walked in with.

'Take it for your family then. Saving your life

made mine better. Verian praised me for my diplomacy that day long ago and I received a hero's welcome when I returned home to the Guardian village. Thanks must go to Garforn's recount of the day.'

'I am glad to hear that, for my life has also been blessed. The counter whom I robbed did as you instructed. I repaid the debt with free labour. We became friends. I am now the counter and spend my days recording what is gathered and exchanged. I have not picked up a farming tool since and I am considered an educated man. Representatives of the King beseech me each day for reports on the harvest and trade. I repay my debt to you by being honest with my workers.'

'Then all debts are settled. In view of your honest nature, may I trust that we are left alone tonight and that all talk of our arrival is also kept silent?'

'The granary is off limits without my permission. Wash your foul scent before you encroach. I'll empty the troughs myself in the morn. No one will bother you,' the counter assured Arman. 'It is good to see you well but you smell like death's door.'

'I'm sure I do. Can I ask you one last request?'

'Anything.'

Arman walked ahead with his friend towards the flat barges ferrying people and animals across the river. Unlike Assur, the ports of Mari were not walled and the ground was flat. Between the white-stone city wall and the west bank of the Euphrates were farmers' huts, merchant stalls and a granary. A wide hardened dirt road led from the wharf to the city gate, between small, mud-brick buildings.

***

Later that night, Arman revealed how he planned to remedy Tuley of the loss of his tattoo.

'Until now the mark of the Guardian has only ever been applied by one of two men. The sons of our founder can no longer continue the tradition. Council is not required to decide who is best to fulfil the role. Unbetum is the one. He will be our new elder, I am certain. He taught me the true significance of our tattoos. Even the older Guardians, Arcobon and Lan, learned from him. Our fathers' strength is carried with us on our coloured shoulders and, Tuley, you need your father's strength for this journey. For that reason, I think it is best to tattoo you now rather than wait until we are back at the tower. Do you agree, Kar?'

'I agree, Arman. My father would see us as fools for doing anything other than what you suggest.'

'And my father's strength should not be abandoned any longer,' supported Tuley. 'He deserves to live on through my deeds. I will accept any tattoo, Arman, so long as it reminds me again of whom I once was. Everything was taken from me when the Akkadians killed my father and sacked the village. I did not need to be shackled when they cut my tattoo and branded me. I am ashamed to say that I surrendered to a new life.'

The Guardian who had been made a soldier stripped to his loincloth and stilled himself to vacant thought as Arman prepared to slice a new tattoo on his scarred shoulder. Arman's sharpest blade rested on a hot stone near the fire while he bathed Tuley's shoulder in warm salty water. The counter had supplied Arman with the paint he needed, paint used normally to adorn walls and clay statues. Arman requested that Tuley close his eyes and I walked respectfully to the far side of the fire.

'The mark of Akkadia that has been branded in place of your true calling shall remain. This new tattoo will give you the courage Garforn had when he put his life before all others.' Tuley squirmed as Arman sliced his shoulder in different directions and pushed paint into the fresh wounds. 'Many died that day in the village and some may say it was inevitable, no matter what was done. When your father, Garforn, made a stand with the village walls in sight, he made every other Guardian proud to stand in defiance. Arcobon also made a stand that day in view of such courage. I deepen your scar to fill you with the bravery of both men. When you ride tomorrow, it will not only be Kar and I by your side but your father and Arcobon as well. It will be three Guardians with the strength of seven, counting our tattoos, that head to Pled.'

Tuley had attempted a smile many times since we encountered him in Assur. I knew the width of his real smile. Again, I had to look closely to see his latest attempt turn his lip as he opened his eyes wide and then shut them in the same instant.

39

Passage

Scribed by Unbetum, The Guardian Who Will Not Die. The Tree.

The Guardians were turning in for the night and Fankisi once more sought to help Salarn down from his throne. He seemed unable to walk unaided and so she only helped him to the rug on the floor. Lagesh was the only one who shared the floor with Salarn and was suprised every morning when he woke to find Salarn seated once more in his throne. When Fankisi approached Salarn that evening, he was asleep with a curious smile relaxing his face. She touched him gently and checked he was still breathing by holding her ear to his mouth. She did not like waking him.

'I am going to read by torchlight, Fankisi. I will keep an eye on him,' said Lagesh.

'What are you reading?' asked Lan. The old Guardian's return to the tower had coincided with Jamine's inability to walk the steps alone. He held his wife's hand as he bent to inspect the tablet.

'Pardensai's tale of the journey south,' said Lagesh.

Fankisi approached. 'Does it mention Parbi?'

'The one I read last night did. "I follow the voice for it is buoyant and boundless." You know everything happens for a reason, Fankisi. I cannot wait for Parbi to speak properly. He seems to know things I do not already.'

'I want him to stay young forever,' said Fankisi. 'Do you have the tablet you speak of with you?'

Lagesh put down the one he was about to read and shuffled through the stack he had accumulated from the shelves in Salarn's study.

'I am sure it will be the same as the one I read in the village school. I do like reading it.'

I continued extinguishing the torches on the ground floor, leaving one burning in the brace near to Lagesh and keeping one in hand for our walk up the stairs.

Lagesh handed a tablet to Fankisi. 'Sleep well. I expect to see Salarn seated in his throne again when I wake.'

Fankisi looked at Salarn lying on the fur. She stepped to his side and adjusted his blanket.

I guided Lan and Jamine up the stairs and lit a candle for Fankisi before I extinguished my torch.

***

Late that same night, I woke to the light of a burning torch. Salarn stood at the door to the room on the top floor, his face downcast and pale. Upon seeing me wake, he returned down the stairs slowly with a heavy limp. I closed the door quietly behind and followed Salarn's light down the stairs, reaching his side outside the next room. 'What has happened, Salarn?'

A contorted grin strained his face. Salarn tried to say something but his mumbled words made no sense. He continued slowly down the stairs and led me between the columns on the far side of the tower before coming to a stop facing the wall. Salarn tapped his chest and then tapped mine. He handed me the torch and walked away. I held the torch closer to the wall and made out the painting Salarn must have completed whilst we slept. Salarn was skillful with the brush and blade in his day, although this painting was a message more than a work of art. I could tell that Salarn had tried to paint faces on the figures before giving up and concentrating on what was most important. The men depicted in his painting were facing one another and the ground between was an even line. One of the men in the painting was handing the other a sword. I knew it to be a sword because this was one of the things Salarn had paid meticulous attention to. The sword had a thin blade with a strong hilt.

'What is it?' asked Lagesh, startling me with his approach from the darkness.

'Salarn painted it,' I answered, looking behind to sight my elder, Salarn.

'He has drawn Kar,' said Lagesh, pointing to the arrows stemming from the shoulder of the one depicted handing over his sword.

I drew the light away from the wall and walked past the table, towards the throne. Salarn was not seated there. 'Did you see him?' I asked Lagesh.

'Salarn? No.'

I ran to the tower door and found it ajar.

Lagesh stepped to the side of the door and gathered his bow and quiver of arrows. 'Why would he go outside at night?'

I did not have an answer. For many nights now, I had been watching the skies alone from the roof of the tower and knew that for the next few days the dark moon would reign. It was not the time for any man to begin a journey unless they knew the path well.

Lagesh stepped outside the door behind me with his bow raised. 'I can hear someone at the stables.'

I directed him to lower his aim.

'Should we not go to him?'

'Stand your ground, Lagesh, and forget your weapon.'

Lan appeared through the door and was followed a moment later by Fankisi.

'What is happening?' inquired Lan.

'A Guardian begins his last ride,' I said, looking endlessly into the night.

'Who?' Fankisi questioned, tilting her head to make out our faces in the light of the torch.

Lan held her back as she tried to run towards the stables.

'Say your farewells from a distance, Fankisi. Let him be alone,' I advised. I held the torch aloft, lighting all our faces and allowing us a clearer view of the horse and rider leaving the stables.

'Farewell, Salarn,' Fankisi called out, 'I pray for you. I pray for us all.'

Lan patted her comfortingly and pulled her close when she tensed as if she were about to rush from his side.

We watched Salarn's mare carry him beyond the

raised torchlight and away into the woods.

'Talk to us, Unbetum,' requested Lan, 'I did not think the day would ever come.'

'Salarn knows that it is his time, just as we know it is our time to be strong. Our future is uncertain but by foreseeing it as blessed we will work the course of life in that direction. There is a way to learn of our elder's final journey. I will visit the tree at first light and complete his story. Do not ask me to say more for I have also dreaded this day.' I lowered the torch and led the others back inside to view Salarn's painting.

Fankisi wanted to travel with me to the tree. I explained why I had to visit alone. 'The tree will not speak to me if it's crowded.' It was a lie. My understanding of the Tree's intentions never divulged such thought. What I did know is that Salarn had been preparing me for this day and the Guardian days that followed. The Guardians needed to know where Salarn went and I needed to know what to do next. I handed the torch to Lan and he set about lighting the torches surrounding the throne and the giant's fur.

When Fankisi saw Salarn's blanket, she rocked her head back and groaned. She then ran to it and fell to her knees, lifting the blanket and holding it to her face as she sobbed.

All in the tower would soon be awake. I looked up and saw Jamine hobbling down the steps.

Lan lent his weight against Salarn's stone throne. He pulled on the long strands of hair that only grew around his ears and on the back of his skull.

I looked his way from the door.

Lan straightened himself and gave me a slight nod.

***

Beneath the leafless branches of the tree, I sat with a clay tablet in my lap. Everything was still a shape without colour. I thought of my last conversation with Salarn on the roof of the tower. He had reminded me that when a god dies on Earth, their strength is shared with all. Then he asked me if I could administer this end. I thought I had questioned Salarn about the meaning of life but, in reflection, his response questioned my role. Would I change the world if I could?

The tree moved, not enough to see but enough to feel as I sat on one of its thick roots that tapered into the ground, south towards the tower. I pushed myself to my feet and stepped backwards. From the grass between the woods and the trees, I noticed something that I had not seen on my first visit. The tree only had four raised roots. One tapered into the ground in the direction of the tower to the south. I walked towards the raised root that entered the ground to the west.

'I see you now,' I said to the tree as I looked up through its maze of curled branches, still painted black in contrast to the glow of dawn. When I sat on the root that tapered into the ground west of the tree, I felt heavy. It was like the weight of a horse pressed my scribing blade into the tablet. I lifted the blade from the tablet and looked at the woods. The woods formed a wall. There was not enough light to see gaps between the trunks. I knew the gaps were there. I had ridden through them to reach the tree. I trained my eyes to the wall of the woods that stood beyond the clearing of green grass, also black. I closed my eyes and gasped at a sudden sight. I had seen Salarn and heard his mare's step on stone. My eyes were wide again staring at the black wall of the woods. I closed my eyes, hoping to see more. Everything was dark. I listened to the birds and tiny winged animals fluttering about in the woods. I slowed my breath. Salarn was west of me, probably entering or riding the mountain pass. I had only seen a glimpse of his journey. The clay tablet in my lap felt heavier than ten stacked on top of each other and I thought of my scribing blade, the length of a finger, weighing like a horse and digging into the clay when I tried to adjust its stroke. *Do not predict life or it will grow more haphazard by the moment.* I'd forgotten my most important governing principle. Do not try to control life. I placed the clay tablet in the grass and leant back on the root that tapered into the ground to the west of the tree's trunk. My scribing hand fell to the earth with the weight of gold. I exhaled and when I took my next breath, I was on a horse. A breath later, I was above the horse and rider.

The two bandits who kept dutiful watch over the northern pass heard Salarn's approach. The soft light of dawn showed he was riding alone and carried little. Hidden in its element, Salarn's winged companion flew up to the men hiding in the crevice and squawked at them. They climbed down the cliff and approached Salarn, cautiously surrounding his mare. One of them lunged forwards ...

I sat upright, gasping for breath. My mare snorted. I could see her shape in the grass. She held her head high and looked to be facing me. I was beneath the tree again, still sitting on a raised root. Above me there was movement. The branches moved gently in a breeze. One branch appeared to grow a new limb. It extended slowly to one side, pointed at its tip. I remained still. Faster than a blink, the limb curled back and disappeared. I huffed as I leapt to my feet, pacing backwards into the grass. I looked at the branch from a distance and saw more movement. It was not the tree moving. Stepping along one of the higher branches was Salarn's winged friend.

'I saw you far from here,' I said to Karun, the black bird.

It spread its wings and soared past me before flapping vigorously to ascend above the woods to my west. If what I had seen was a dream, it was the most real I'd ever experienced. I had seen the bandits' faces and I had seen them approach Salarn. Had I witnessed his end, I questioned myself. I returned to the same spot beneath the tree. In front of me, the trunks of trees and branches were beginning to find their own shape in the black wall of the woods. I sat down and purposefully rested my arm on the raised root. My mind did not travel with the Gods' speed to Salarn's destination. I closed my eyes. The pine trees creaked and groaned as they fought for their place in the woods. My body tightened in the chill of air before the sun. I nestled in against the trunk of the tree. It shed the warmth of a fire. 'It's always warm,' Kar had told me when he first brought me to the tree. I had remained unconvinced until now. For too many nights, I had watched the skies from the height of the tower's roof. At the base of this tree is where I needed to be. I fell asleep, I think.

Elkin was setting a trap on the western foothills when he spotted Salarn riding past. He looked south towards the entrance to a cave and then above as if he could see me floating in the sky. Salarn's mare carried on west into the open desert and Elkin knelt and said a silent prayer.

I woke from my dream, if it was a dream. The grass was green and the pines hung and poked their branches into the clearing, their trunks knowing not to encroach. I rolled my head and saw the white branches of the tree that curled low before reaching for the sky. My mare did not snort but, I knew again, I was not alone. 'Lagesh, step out where I can see you,' I said.

'Did you hear me?' he asked as he stepped from the woods into the clearing. His reluctant-to-open eye seemed more focused on the tree as he looked at me.

I thought of the four directions of the tree's raised roots. 'I could tell you some of the story now or the whole story later.'

'I can wait. Lan sent me with food and water. I did not abandon my post.'

I stood and stumbled when I tried to walk towards Lagesh. A weight was upon me again. 'Can you carry your stores closer?' I asked.

'I received a vision when Kar showed me the tree,' said Lagesh. 'I don't want for that to change. I'll leave the food and water here if you will allow.'

'Share my gratitude with Lan and those at the tower. I will return when I have heard all the tree needs to share with me.'

Lagesh nodded his head to me and bowed to the tree as he walked backwards into the woods.

I turned and looked up at the tree. My head lowered and my body completed a proper bow. I felt warm and no longer weighed down. My horse whinnied and I heard the hooves of Lagesh's horse crunching pine needles as it trotted away. I walked out to my mare and stroked her neck. She followed me through the knee-high grass to where Lagesh had placed a wrapped bundle. Inside the bundle I found flatbread, salted boar meat and a bladder of water. I sat where the bundle was placed and took a bite of the flatbread. I found it hard to swallow my dry mouthful. Salarn was in the desert. It was not the time to eat. Guardians ate when they found rest. I wrapped the cloth around the food and bladder of water and carried it with me closer to the tree. Beneath a thick limb of the tree, where the grass thinned close to its trunk, I placed the bundle. I stepped over the raised root that tapered south into the ground and approached the one that sat high before disappearing towards the west. The warmth of the tree was there as soon as I sat. I looked west and could only see the trees beyond the clearing. My view ended at the woods but the tree I sat at was Mother Ki and when I forgot myself there was no limit to my vision.

I sat silent. Ki, the tree, was also quiet and still. Around us the pines bent and swayed to a wind that did not touch us. I breathed deep and a moment later I leapt from water. My senses awake where my body was not present.

Samor, Chief of the Harmins, was washing his face at the oasis when he was drawn to Salarn's approach. He dried his face and watched from the far side as the mare came to a stop and Salarn slipped from her mount to drink. Samor's slow approach signed that he understood why our elder was travelling alone.

'Kardeen is cooking your favourite meal as we speak. Let me help by guiding your mare to our stable.'

The mare bent a leg and knelt to aid Salarn's climb

onto the saddle. She followed Samor to the stable. It was a quiet entrance between the many huts without any people.

Kardeen sat up and watched Samor help Salarn inside the hut. The Guardian's eyes were closed but not clenched. It was as if he did not have the strength to see anymore. Samor signalled that he should be offered the tail when the lizard was cooked and Kardeen agreed. All were silent until Boroe arrived.

'Salarn is here,' he rejoiced upon seeing the mare in the stable. Boroe entered the hut and was immediately signalled to be silent. 'Why is he alone?' asked the young Harmin.

'He is riding to heaven, my son.'

Boroe observed the others' silence and they treasured their last meal with Salarn. Only when Samor handed him a bowl containing meat stripped from the cooked lizard's tail did Salarn open his eyes. He looked at the three men and tried to say something. His softly mumbled words were not understood.

Salarn left the hut at dawn and left without a farewell.

Boroe woke before the other Harmins and saw that Salarn had already left. He woke his father and Kardeen lurched to life nearby upon hearing their voices. Boroe ran ahead to the stable and realised that the mare was gone. 'I did not hear him leave,' said Boroe, returning to meet the others standing in front of the hut.

'This way,' instructed Samor. He ran past the stable, leading the others between crumbled buildings toward a high rolling dune.

Kardeen slowed to a crawl halfway through the climb and Boroe returned to his side and helped pull him to the top.

'Watch him ride away, Harmins. We are the last people he will ever see.'

Salarn's mare trotted through the night to the Karun Gorge. The Guardian elder woke and leant forwards in his mount to whisper his last commands. Kneeling, she allowed him to climb off unaided. She nudged his face softly with her snout and steadied her bent leg for a long while, should her master decide to climb back on. Salarn's legs were void of strength and he stumbled, clutching hold of a rock before he collapsed on his face. His mouth was dry and he looked about through bloodshot eyes. He was ready. There was no need to taste the water once more or settle his thirst. Such sensations were not needed where he was going. Salarn managed a fleeting glance back at his mare. She was grazing and this assured him that he had not ridden her dry. He was thankful and inspired by those who had helped him without request. Filled with hope for a better future and eager to shatter silence with a new mouth, Salarn gathered the last of his strength and stepped to the edge.

Water spilled with the weight of stampeding horses into the gorge beneath and there, Salarn surrendered. His head dropped first and then the rest of his body followed. The wall of water governed his descent and, head first, he plunged into the basin below. A thousand possible futures graced my mind's eye as his limp body bobbed to the surface and was battered against rocks on its course downstream.

40

A Call East

Cairo, Egypt 1850.

The moon cast its full face over Cairo and the river valley to my east. I removed my pocket watch and angled it towards the light. It was almost eight. In the thirty-two hours since my meeting with Lateef and Babu in the old library, I had only slept for about six hours. I was tired, yet tingly and awake with excitement. My fingers trembled as I shut my pocket watch and faced east again. The view from my window was calling me out. I could not disclose to Victor what I had discovered in the book but I thought, if I phrased it right, I could tell him more of my planned movements on the morrow. He was staying in the same guesthouse and, whilst I had never admitted it before, Victor knew me more than I knew myself. I was only focused whilst my mind was occupied. The repetitive drilling of a hole, the over talk about ancient beliefs and the reading of a narrative that relayed biblical text tested me. It was all a test.

I extinguished the candles, slipped on my shoes and gathered my coat and the keys to the room. As I turned to inspect my room before leaving, I noticed moonlight stretching through the open window in reach of the bed. It was safe to leave the shutters open as I was on the third floor and the night was still. The setting, however, reminded me of a scene from the book. I pictured Fankisi sleeping soundly, dreaming of her husband and unawares of a devious guard's impending visit. The book was stowed beneath a folded sheet with a pillow on top. It was safe, I hoped. I stepped outside into the corridor and locked my door behind, turning the knob twice to check it was secure.

***

My host, Hu, was excited to see me and begged to offer me an evening meal. I resisted his offer and a secondary offer to escort me to Victor's room on the second floor. 'Stay seated,' I kept telling him as he tried to accommodate my needs.

'A fresh towel, warm water?'

'I am happy,' I told him, spreading my palms and then signalling him again to relax. 'Thank you, Hu.'

'Hu ... Hu,' I heard his wife call out from the next room.

I signalled him to attend to his wife. He stayed standing and smiling at me as I returned to the stairs.

***

On the second floor, I knocked on the first door and waited, listening for movement inside. I heard nothing. At both ends of the corridor, candles burned inside wall-mounted glasses. From the second room, in the middle of the corridor, I heard chatter and noted the thinness of the walls. It was another reason to be careful in sharing words with Victor. I rubbed my face and felt the prickle of two-day stubble. My appearance was most likely behind Hu's numerous offers of service. The Egyptian hospitality rivalled that received in the finest hotels back in London. Nevertheless, the quality of the accommodation was not as finessed. Our chosen guesthouse was modest. We got what we paid for with only two water closets on the ground floor and a shared privy in the shadowed lane. I decided to knock once more. It was a gentle knock, hopefully not enough to rouse Victor if he was in deep sleep.

He reefed the door open, 'Knock, knock, ginger.'

'Damn it,' I startled.

'Do you remember the game?'

'I do. Did you think someone would be playing it with you.'

'Got to be on your toes, Fred. Come in, I was just fixing myself a cognac and I have some bread and dips.'

'Wonderful,' I replied. His room smelt of mint and garlic.

Victor walked ahead to a drawing cabinet and poured me a glass from a half empty bottle. 'It's a Hennessey pale.' With his own glass in hand, and wearing a singlet and knee length trousers, he walked to his window and welcomed the fresh air. His jacket and shirt were laid out on his bed and he still donned his new hat.

'How was your day?'

'This morning, I visited the foreign office and then I ventured across town to ...' Victor turned from the window and smiled at me. 'Honestly, Fred, do you care? Forget the pleasantries. Your day and tomorrow are all that matters to me.'

I sipped the cognac and appreciated its taste.

'Have some bread,' offered Victor. 'I have already eaten.' He shifted a chair close to the window and then sat down on the corner of the bed.

'I am contemplating a mission east,' I said as I perused Victor's assortment of dips and flat breads.

'I'm listening.'

'I have a verbal confidentiality agreement with Babu.' I turned to face him. 'Do you plan to accompany me to the meeting?'

Victor lifted his Coke and placed it by his side on the bed. His long hair was flattened around his skull and he sprung it to life by tossing it with splayed fingers. 'The unearthing of artifacts in Nineveh is ongoing. It is my next assignment if nothing better is on offer.'

'So, should there be something else, something risky, you might join me?'

'Of course, Fred.' He leapt to his feet and then paused in his advance as I took my first bite of dip-coated bread. 'I'm with you not because I think you're onto something. I can't beat Layard any other way. Every claim at his site will gain his name. You must have something better. Do you have something better?'

'I do, potentially. First I must see what the others think.'

'Chance they say no?' questioned Victor.

'Lateef would have asked for your time, not mine, if he had thought you would oblige. And if you favoured their desired dig in Nineveh, then he and Babu would have been over the moon. I do not favour a dig in Nineveh. As you say, it has been claimed. I believe their first quest should be to find a new site.'

'An unknown site,' paraphrased Victor, 'very interesting, Fred. Tell you what, you get me in on this meet with Lateef and his pal, Babu, and I'll make sure I only join Layard if we are both on the payroll.'

'Agreed.'

***

I woke with the light on Friday morning and hurried downstairs to use the privy. Hu met me on my return and offered me a fresh towel and a basin of water. This time, I accepted his offer. My advice on a dig site might not be to Babu's liking and I believed my appearance would have some sway in his decision.

Victor, smarting his Coke, and I, feeling better after a shave and quick wash, walked the dusty streets of Cairo towards the old library. We found Lateef seated on the sandstone stairs leading up to the grand entrance.

He roused to my approach, not noticing Victor in my company, 'I am not angry that Layard found Gilgamesh's tablets. Your colleague will discover that all he has is an introduction. We have the epic.'

'You preach what I must keep silent,' I responded, signalling to Victor.

Lateef slapped his head. 'I cannot keep quiet now that I know it is real.'

Victor extended his hand in greeting. 'I will help you own your discovery.'

'Mister Ascott,' said Lateef, quickly composing himself and shaking Victor's hand vigorously. 'I thought you'd left our city.'

'He likes to surprise people,' I told Lateef. 'He can even attend meetings without invitation.'

'You are most welcome this day,' said Lateef to Victor before leading us up the stairs. 'Babu hoped you would arrive early, Fred.'

As we entered the library, a bell tolled and announced noon.

***

'Dressed I am for an important occasion,' said Babu as he crossed the drawing room floor, walking stiffly in a tailored white suit, a ruffled shirt and a red tie.

'Pleasure to meet you, Sir,' said Victor, stepping past me to shake hands with the librarian first.

'The pleasure is mine, Sir,' complemented Babu as he extended his hand. 'Lateef and Fred both confirmed that you had left. Your surprise presence is most welcome, be it still a surprise.'

'Pretend I am not here, or on the contrary, take advantage of my intrusion. As I explained to Fred on our walk here, I am with him all the way, all the way on the archaeologist's wager. I could win with discovery or lose with years of my life wasted. I have no idea what is at stake if we choose not to side with Layard.'

'I have a good feeling about this wager,' Babu told us. 'I have dressed for an important occasion and I have prepared also for a long lunch. I do not, however, want this to be a vain attempt at coaxing your support of our proposed dig. I want to hear appraisal of the work read before we are seated. Tell me, Fred, what does the work mean to you? Do you believe there is more to find in Nineveh?'

'Without a doubt, there is more to be found in Nineveh,' I answered. 'In view of reading the work ...' I paused and looked at the table. Babu had laid out maps of the lands branching from Egypt to the Zagros Mountains. I unbuckled my shoulder purse and removed my diary and the text loaned to me. I opened my diary where it was parted with a ribbon. 'My ink map, that you see before you, is more valuable than your extensive display,' I told Babu.

He frowned but nodded respectfully.

'Every dot and line on the page of my diary is based on the text you shared with me.'

Victor leaned close and then looked up at me and across the table at Babu.

'Do tell,' Lateef encouraged me. 'I thought you might favour somewhere else after reading it complete.'

'I have not read it all,' I admitted. 'After only reading two parts, I would like to propose a different destination.'

'You stopped reading for a reason,' inquired Babu, looking very uncomfortable in his attire.

'I did question the validity of the work on the first night. Then I just read it for what it was. I eventually restrained myself from not continuously asking for whom the tale was intended or for what purpose. I added to my map as I read.' I pointed to my ink lines and indicated how some parts matched with the detailed maps of the Zagros Mountains on Babu's table.

'Why did you stop reading?' questioned Babu.

'Only because our meeting was today.'

'I see,' said Babu, loosening his tie.

'Babu, I'm not sure you understand me. My map complements yours. I show you my map only to convince you that I need time to read the final part.'

Victor cleared his throat in an exaggerated fashion and waited until he had all's attention. 'We know where Nineveh is, so what is that mark below, Fred?'

I lifted my diary from the table and handed it to Babu. 'The triangle represents a city's port. We can track the changing course of the river and unearth Assur.'

'Is it beneath a city?' asked Babu.

'Is it?' asked Victor.

'Don't ask me before looking for yourself. Assur is mentioned in the text as a major city. To its north there is an escarpment and by boat it takes a full day's travel via river from Nineveh. The city is elevated by a natural rise. Assur, a name unknown outside of the text, is my proposed dig site.'

I considered that Babu would be left speechless. His delayed silence was unapproachable.

'Fred, might we have a word.' Victor cornered me and whispered to my ear. 'Well done.'

I looked beyond his embrace. Lateef was placing my drawings with real maps. 'Don't try too hard, Lateef.'

'Why?' he replied.

I looked for Babu. 'Babu is in charge, right?'

'Yes.'

'Where is he now?' I asked.

Victor opened the door to Babu's private study and jumped backwards with his hands raised.

From the other entry to the drawing room, two

men entered wearing dark frock coats and began bundling the maps.

'The diary is mine,' I declared. They took it anyway.

Lateef grabbed the book and held it behind his back.

Babu pushed past Victor, followed by two Egyptian police officers. They wore white bush jackets and trousers and one had his sidearm drawn. 'Relax gentlemen, they will take our maps to the authorities and thus lodge our claim without fee. Let us eat well as we plan our departure.'

I looked to Victor.

'I'm already packed,' he told me.

Acknowledgements

As I reflect on the journey to completing my second novel, I am once more reminded that I did not travel alone. It is an epic undertaking to write an epic novel and I feel it nostalgic and timely to note that my life and the lives of those who assisted me in this novel's creation have changed over the years between its conception and publication.

Special thanks to Margaret Monroe, now Margaret Kerlin. The historical accuracy and deeper development of characters in this ancient Akkadian world are in no small part owed to your constructive appraisal of the first draft, more than a decade ago. Your appreciation of the work continues to inspire me to delve further into the unknown.

Cathy, I'd like to confirm that there is no intended connection between the title and your maiden name. Sub-consciously, your prior surname might have indeed inspired my hypothesis that the strength of heaven, the bull, found rebirth. Thank you, Cathy de Vos, for your return to edit the extended version of Book 2 in the trilogy.

Thank you, Sue, for proofreading my novel. I'm

grateful for the time you have so willingly dedicated. Your praise is encouraging and your technical feedback was crucial in getting my novel to this point. I enjoy sharing my writing with you.

Book 2, with its introduction of multiple character perspectives, was always going to be a massive endeavour but it was not until all of these characters took on a life of their own that I realised the immensity of the world being created. With me, like a second guardian to the development of these characters, was Peta. Your enduring support, Peta, cannot be expressed in words. I dedicate this novel, the heart of the epic, to you.

I extend my thanks once more to Rebecca McCallion, The Writer's Edge, for her manuscript appraisals, edits and proofreads. Rebecca, your thought-provoking advice is invaluable and I'm most appreciative of your willingness to halt further reading and offer me time when narrative complications arise.

Special thanks to Daniel Greenup for his cover design and the creation of an authentic map. You never cease to amaze me, Daniel.

To the reader, thank you for joining me on this journey. Without you, my novels are just words on a page. Only through your reading can characters and their world come alive.

About the Author

J.P. Manning is a senior English and history teacher on Queensland's Capricorn Coast. Manning's writing expertise and historical knowledge allow him to weave fact and fiction together to take readers on an unforgettable journey into a forgotten age. Enter the Bull's Burrow is his second novel in his Guardians of the East trilogy. His debut novel, Eleven Arrows, was published in 2020.

www.ingramcontent.com/pod-product-compliance
Lightning Source LLC
Chambersburg PA
CBHW020000120726
47903CB00004B/1075